Thomas E. Lightburn served for twenty-two years in the medical branch of the Royal Navy, reaching the rank of chief petty officer. He left the service in 1974 and obtained a Bachelor of Education Degree (Hons), at Liverpool University. After sixteen years teaching at Liscard Primary School, Wallasey, he volunteered for early retirement. He then began writing for the *Wirral Journal* during which time he interviewed the late Ian Fraser, VC, ex-Lieutenant RN, and wrote an account of how he and his crew in a midget submarine, crippled the Japanese cruiser, *Takao*, in Singapore. Thomas is a widower and lives in Wallasey, pursuing his favourite hobbies of soccer, naval and military history and the theatre.

Also by Thomas E. Lightburn

The Gates of Stonehouse
ISBN 978 184386 203

Uncommon Valour
ISBN 978 184386 203

The Shield and the Shark
ISBN 978 184386 301 2

The Dark Edge of The Sea
ISBN 978 184886 400 4

The Ship That Would Not Die
ISBN 978 184386 463 9

The Summer of '39
ISBN 978 184386 5612

A Noble Chance
ISBN 978 184386 647 3

Beyond The Call of Duty
ISBN 978 184386 714 2

The Russian Run
ISBN 978 184386 840 8

Deadly Inferno
ISBN 978 184386 736 4

Mission into Danger
ISBN 978 184386 994 8

The Hidden Enemy
ISBN 978 178465 132 9

Triumph Over Fear
ISBN 978 178465 5327

All published by Vanguard Press

Operation Iceberg

Thomas E. Lightburn

Vanguard Press
VANGUARD PAPERBACK

© Copyright 2023
Thomas E. Lightburn

The right of Thomas E. Lightburn to be identified as author of
this work has been asserted by him in accordance with the
Copyright, Designs and Patents Act 1988.

All Rights Reserved

No reproduction, copy or transmission of this publication
may be made without written permission.
No paragraph of this publication may be reproduced,
copied or transmitted save with the written permission of the publisher,
or in accordance with the provisions
of the Copyright Act 1956 (as amended).

Any person who commits any unauthorised act in relation to
this publication may be liable to criminal
prosecution and civil claims for damages.

A CIP catalogue record for this title is
available from the British Library.

ISBN 978 1 80016 758 2

This is a work of fiction. Names, characters, businesses, places, events and incidents are either the product of the author's imagination or used in a fictitious manner. Any resemblance to actual persons, living or dead, or actual events is purely coincidental.

Vanguard Press is an imprint of
Pegasus Elliot Mackenzie Publishers Ltd.
www.pegasuspublishers.com

First Published in 2023

Vanguard Press
Sheraton House Castle Park
Cambridge England

Printed & Bound in Great Britain

CHAPTER ONE

On a bitterly cold Monday morning on 9th January 1939, Gunter, Heinrich and Adelheid Schmied, had finished breakfast. It was a little after eight thirty. The wireless was switched on, and they were sitting in the lounge listening to the sharp, cutting voice of Adolf Hitler extolling the virtues of Germany's occupation of Austria. As Hitler finished his speech, the telephone rang.

'I wonder who that could be ringing so early in the day, dear,' he said to his wife. Gunter's voice was quiet, clear and refined, typical of a well-educated German.

'I'll go, Papa,' said Heinrich, standing up. 'It might be my friend, Otto.'

'Better let your father go,' Adelheid said, motioning Heinrich to sit down. 'It'll probably be someone from work.'

Gunter went into the lobby and lifted the receiver. A few minutes later, he returned to the lounge.

'Well, who was it?' asked Adelheid.

'It was the *Abwehr*,' Gunter replied. 'I have to report to Admiral Canaris at ten o'clock.

Suddenly a feeling of tension filled the air.

'I shouldn't look so worried, dear,' Adelheid said. 'He probably needs a new suit.'

Admiral Canaris was head of the *Abwehr*, the equivalent to Britain's Secret Service. It was a tall, non-descript, red-bricked, four-storey building situated on 76/78 Tirpitzufer, a wide thoroughfare close to where Heinrich and his family lived. To the public, the *Abwehr* was something of a mystery. Some thought it once belonged to a shipping firm that had gone bankrupt; others considered it a secret gambling den, or even a brothel. Blinds were drawn across the windows and entrance was gained by pressing a series of numbers on the side of a stout oak door. Everyone, including female secretaries, wore civilian clothes.

Gunter was a master tailor, working for *Manheimers* in central Berlin. Gunter had visited the *Abwehr* before to measure Canaris and top-ranking officers for uniforms and suits. Therefore, he was sworn to secrecy as to what went on inside the building.

Gunter left his apartment at 9.40 and took the lift to the ground floor. As he went outside, an icy northerly wind attacked his face, making his eyes water. Everything was covered in a thick blanket of sparkling white snow, and a leaded sky promised more. In his right hand he carried a silver-topped cane. The other held a small, brown, leather briefcase. A Cossack-style, fur-lined hat kept his head warm, as did a yellow woollen muffler, and the black leather gloves kept his hands warm. Under a fleece-lined overcoat, Gunter wore his best grey suit made of English worsted wool, a white shirt and his old regiment tie with a black swastika on a maroon background.

Feeling his shiny leather boots crunch into the snow, Gunter made his way down Benalerstraser and arrived outside the *Abwehr* at ten fifteen. Doing his best not to slip on the icy surface, he carefully walked up four wide stone steps and inserted the code. The door opened, and after stamping his feet free of snow he entered the building. Inside, the atmosphere was cold, damp and gloomy. He hurried up a winding staircase and along a dimly lit corridor and stopped outside a plain oak door. After removing the muffler and brushing his coat and hat free of snowflakes, he knocked on the door and went inside into a small reception office. An elderly, pale-faced woman with short, wire-wool hair was sitting behind a desk, typing.

As Gunter entered, she looked up from her typewriter. 'You must be Herr Schmied,' she said, while giving Gunter a weak smile.

'Yes,' Gunter said, nervously shuffling his feet.

'Just knock and go in, she said, nodding towards a door next to a green filing cabinet.

Gunter remembered Canaris as a tall, thick-set man, with well-groomed fair hair, a prominent nose and a firm jaw. However, it was Canaris's steely-grey, heavy-lidded eyes that seemed to stare right through him that Gunter remembered most.

Canaris was Hitler's mystery man. After a distinguished career in Germany's navy during the First World War, he became head of the *Abwehr* in 1938 and soon extended his spy ring from 150 men to 1000. Canaris was married to Erika, and although they had two daughters, the marriage was an unhappy one. Consequently, Canaris lived alone in a small apartment on the outskirts of Berlin and was rarely seen in public and was devoted to Hitler. It was Canaris who suggested that the Star of David was worn to identify the Jews.

'Thank you,' Gunter quietly replied, and opened the door.

Admiral Wilhelm Canaris was sitting behind a large mahogany desk, on which a red telephone lay surrounded with an assortment of documents, one of which lay open in front to him. A large, ornately framed, coloured painting of Hitler hung on a wall behind the desk. Black curtains were drawn across a window overlooking Benalerstraser. This was a wide boulevard, close to where Gunter lived. The leather-bound books, lining three of the walls, armchairs and ornate chandelier always reminded Gunther of his old headmaster's study. Gunter immediately recognised the dark-blue, pinstriped suit he had made for Canaris a year ago. His pristine white shirt, silver tie, well-groomed grey hair and clear-cut features made him look more like a solicitor than one of the most powerful men in Germany.

'*Heil* Hitler,' cried Gunther, standing rigidly to attention and shooting out his right arm.

'Ah, my favourite tailor. *Heil* Hitler,' Canaris replied, raising the palm of his right hand. 'Do sit down,' he added, indicating one of two black, leather armchairs. As he spoke, the admiral's steely-grey eyes Gunter remembered, creased into a tepid smile. 'How is your English, Gunter?' Canaris asked, sitting forward and proffering his hand.

'Like my son, Heinrich, I speak it fluently,' Gunter replied, feeling Canarias's firm handshake.

'And your wife?'

'A little,' Gunter replied, feeling himself tense up.

'Very good!' Canaris exclaimed. 'So let us speak in English, because I have something very important for you and your family to do for the Fatherland, and practising the language will do you good.'

'Anything for Germany,' he replied enthusiastically.

'I see by your record,' Canaris said, tapping the document with a finger, 'that you have been to England.'

'Yes,' Gunter replied. 'As you know, I'm a master tailor. Two years ago, I visited London for a week, attending a tailors' convention. I stayed with some colleagues in an apartment in a place called Balham.'

'And what was your impression of the English?'

'I thought they were very courteous and helpful.'

'Excellent,' snapped Canaris, sitting back and folding his arms. 'It is precisely because of your background that you have been chosen for this assignment. In three weeks' time, you and your family are going to live in London. At seven a.m. on Monday 30th, you'll be taken to Tempelhof and flown to London. When you arrive there, you'll be taken by car to your new home. But more of that later. '

A look of surprise came onto Gunther's face. 'London, Excellency, what on earth for?'

'To perform a special duty for the Fatherland,' Canaris replied. 'You and your family, especially your son, are to collect any information that would be of assistance to the Third Reich.' He paused momentarily, then with a look of concern etched in his eyes, went one. 'When war breaks out, it could be dangerous. Do you think you and your family will be up to it?'

Having regained his composure, Gunter replied, 'Yes, Excellency, I'm sure we can.'

'Good man,' said Canaris, smiling. 'Now, everything I'm going to tell you is top secret and will be in a document that I'll give you before you leave. Understand?'

'Yes, Excellency,' Gunter answered.

'Before I continue, would you care for some coffee?'

'Thank you, Excellency,' Gunter answered, now feeling relaxed. 'That would be fine.'

Canaris leant forward and pressed a button on his intercom.

'Two cups of your splendid Brazilian coffee, please, Eva,' he said in German.

'Very good, Excellency,' Eva replied.

Canaris sat back in his chair, and giving Gunther a look of satisfaction, said, 'I'm sure you have heard the wonderful news that Austria is now under the control of the Fatherland?'

'Yes, Excellency,' Gunter replied. 'I read in the paper that our glorious army was welcomed with much cheering and flowers.'

'As you have no doubt learnt from the Fuhrer's speeches, he is determined to make Germany great again,' Canaris answered, with a look of defiance. 'Hitler has already broken the Washington Naval Treaty preventing Germany from building a strong navy, but I know for a fact that submarines have already been built, some of which are already at sea. 'And,' he added with a sly smile, 'the Fuhrer has designs on Czechoslovakia, and who knows, maybe France…'

'But surely France's Maginot Line would prevent this?' Gunter replied.

'Ah, my friend,' said Canaris, touching his nose with a finger, 'there are many ways of skinning a cat.'

'If we did invade France, this would mean war with Britain, as they have a treaty with the French,' Gunter said, sitting forward in his chair.

'You are quite right, Mr Smith,' replied Canaris. 'In my opinion, war with Britain is inevitable. And that, of course, is why every piece of information, from whatever the source, is important.'

As Canaris finished speaking, a knock came at the door and the secretary entered carrying a silver tray containing two cups of coffee. Immediately the aromatic aroma of coffee filled the air.

'I've put a little brandy in them, Your Excellency,' she said, handing each of them a cup and saucer.

'Thank you, Eva,' Canaris replied, 'and please, see that we are not disturbed.'

Canaris took a sip of coffee, licked his lips and went on. 'In London we have rented a fully furnished terraced house for you and your family. It's in Waterloo, close to the station. A position has been arranged for you with Bernard and Roberts, a fashionable tailor's in Jermyn Street, whose specialty is making uniforms for officers. Here, you may overhear an officer mention something that might be important to Germany. As Heinrich is good at mathematics, he will be employed as a junior clerk at Barclays bank in the Strand. You will both be given a telephone number to report anything of interest, no matter how trivial it may sound. Your code name is "Tiger". A man named Mr Joseph will answer. You will identify yourself then pass the information on to him. Is that clear?'

'Yes, Excellency. Quite clear,' Gunter nervously replied.

'Needless to say, Bernard and Roberts will not be aware of the real reason for your presence, so be careful. Adelheid will remain as an ordinary housewife, listening to gossip about sons and relatives in the armed forces, reporting anything important to you. Now, about Heinrich. How old is he?'

'Heinrich will be twenty next week,' Gunther replied, picking up his cup and taking a good sip of coffee.

'Splendid. Now listen carefully. I have a special task for him,' Canaris replied. 'As you know, Britain has the largest and strongest navy in the world, and as such, carefully guards its secrets. A month or so after arriving in London, you are to order Heinrich to join the Royal Navy as a wireless operator and explain why. As a wireless operator, he will be privy to classified signals. In doing so, he will obtain vital information regarding ship's movements, especially convoys.' Canaris paused, opened a drawer and took out a leather case the size of a shaving kit. 'This contains a transmitter, a collapsible aerial and earphones. Heinrich must transmit on eighty-five megacycles and report his ship's movements to the German ambassador in Buenos Aires, whose code name is "Jackal". Heinrichs code name will be "Lion". The ambassador will then pass any information directly to me. And when we go to war, details of convoys will especially be important. Do you think Heinrich will be able to do that?'

'Yes, Excellency,' Gunter firmly replied. 'Heinrich is a good German and is very clever. I'm sure he'll be more than capable of doing whatever is required of him. '

'Now listen carefully,' stressed Canaris. 'You and your family are to pose as Austrian Jews, born and bred in Vienna. To the British authorities, the reason for your leaving Germany is because Jews, as you know, are being rounded up and sent into custody. Your Christian name will remain the same, but your surnames will be changed to Smith. Your wife's Christian name will be Adelaide, and your son's name will be Henry. You will each be given identity cards. Is that clear?'

'Yes, Excellency,' Gunther replied.

'All these instructions, plus details of money that will be placed in your local Barclays Bank, will be contained in the letter you will be given before you leave,' said Canaris, sitting back in his chair and folding his arms. 'Commit them to memory then destroy them. However, there is something else I have to tell you. The mission I am sending you and your family on is very dangerous. When war breaks out and you are caught, as spies, you will be shot.'

Canarias's words sent a shock wave running through Gunter. This was something he hadn't expected.

'However, it's vital that you must not be discovered.'

Canaris opened a side drawer in his desk and took out a buff-coloured envelope and two small wooden boxes, each with a golden swastika on its lid. 'In here,' he said, taping the envelope, 'are your orders, documents and travelling instructions, and each of these,' he added, picking up a box, 'contains a capsule of cyanide.'

Gunther knew very well what cyanide was used for, and he felt a shiver of fear run down his spine.

Using a tiny, silver key, Canaris opened the boxes. From each one he carefully took out small, yellow capsules and showed them to Gunter. 'One for you and your wife, the other for Heinrich. When you arrive in London, keep them unlocked, because if you are caught, you'll have to use them in a hurry. Just one bite and it'll be over in seconds.'

Staring at the capsules, Gunther felt the blood drain from his face. 'You mean…'

'Yes, you must sacrifice yourselves,' Canaris replied, with a steely glint in his eyes. 'But remember,' he added, replacing the capsules in each box, 'this is purely a precautionary measure. I'm sure it won't come to that.'

'My God, Excellency, I hope you're right,' Gunther replied. He opened his briefcase, and with trembling fingers accepted the keys and placed the boxes inside.

Canaris stood up and proffered his hand, saying, 'Good luck, Mr Smith, and rest assured, the Fatherland will reward you and your family well for your work.'

'That's if we're still alive,' Gunther muttered to himself, as he shook Canaris's clammy hand.

Later that evening while Heinrich was in bed, Gunther told Adelhied about their mission. Adelhied's immediate reaction was one of pride. However, it was only when he mentioned the cyanide capsules that Gunther saw fear in his wife's eyes.

'But don't worry, *Liebling*,' Gunther said, giving Adelhied's hand a reassuring squeeze. 'I have Canarsie's word that it'll never come to that.'

CHAPTER TWO

An acute sense of destiny surged through Wireless Operator Henry Smith as he walked down Brad Street, a short, narrow road of red-bricked terraced houses close to Waterloo Station. The time was two p.m. on Wednesday 26th July.

Smith was tall and broad-shouldered, with straight, well-groomed, fair hair, a fresh complexion and intelligent, dark-blue eyes. At school, the only two subjects he had excelled at were mathematics and geography, both of which he always came top of his class. He left school at sixteen and obtained a junior post at the local bank. Two months after arriving in London, his father told him he had received instructions from Admiral Canaris, ordering him to join the Royal Navy and request to be a wireless operator.

'But why a wireless operator, Papa?' enquired Heinrich.

For the next half an hour Gunther explained why this was important.

The next morning, bubbling with excitement, Smith went to the RN Recruiting Office on the Strand. He told a grey-haired chief petty officer that he wanted to join up and be a wireless operator.

'I'll make a note on your request, son,' replied the chief.

After passing a basic maths and English test, a doctor examined him and found him medically fit. Two weeks later, he received a one-way travel warrant to Portsmouth.

After six weeks "square bashing" at Victoria Barracks, Portsmouth, he was sent to the navy's communication training base in HMS *Mercury,* a shore base in Petersfield, Hampshire. Smith found the training easier than he anticipated. His expertise at Morse code and speed of transmission enabled him to come top of his class. On completion of the eight-week course, he was drafted to HMS *Dolphin,* the navy's main submarine base in Gosport. His use of the Wavemeter G56, the navy's latest wireless transmitter, was exceptional. Shortly after Smiths eighteenth birthday on Saturday 22nd July, his divisional officer, Lieutenant Hadley, sent for him.

'I've received a request from the draftee in barracks for my best wireless operator to be sent to HMS *Endeavour*. Would you like to volunteer?' Hadley asked, folding his arms and sitting back in his desk.

My God, thought Smith. *This is the chance I've been waiting for. A ship, and a chance to do something worthwhile for Germany.*

'Yes, sir, I would,' came Smith's eager reply. 'When do I leave?'

'*Endeavour* is in Devonport alongside number five wharf,' Hadley replied. 'You are to take four days leave, then join her on Tuesday 25th. Pack your gear and it'll be forwarded to the ship. In the meantime, take only what you'll need on leave. I'll inform the chief in the regulating office to prepare your travel warrant and draft chit. Now, off you go, and good luck.'

Shortly after seven a.m. the next morning, Smith, carrying a canvas holdall and wearing his number one uniform, left *Dolphin*. He took the Gosport ferry across to Portsmouth and caught the eight thirty train to Waterloo. After a journey lasting almost three hours, Smith hurried from the station. Ten minutes later, walking down Brad Street, two elderly women standing on the opposite side of the street gave him a friendly wave.

'Better lock up our daughters, Bessie,' one of them said. 'The navy's here. Welcome home, Henry,' she added with a smile.

Smith gave them a sheepish grin and waved back. This would be the first time his parents would see him in his bell-bottoms. Even though it was the uniform of a potential enemy, a sensation of pride ran though him as he arrived outside number 10. Like the rest of the terraced houses, it was built of red bricks. For a few seconds he stood and looked around. Since he left two months ago, a few things had changed. Then, the front door had been painted a dull brown; now it was bright green. Instead of matching yellow curtains covering the two top windows, net curtains had taken their place. The only thing that hadn't changed was the small, brass doorbell. His hand trembled slightly as he pressed the bell and heard its familiar ring.

The door opened and a small, portly woman with a round, fleshy face and bright, brown eyes, greeted him. 'Heinrich der Liebling,' she said, kissing Smith warmly on the cheek. 'Your Vater, he is home. Come,' she added, giving him a hug, 'he vill be very pleased to see you.'

Her English was spoken with a distinct guttural Germanic inflexion. Smith's father was a master tailor, working for a firm in Saville Row.

'Thank you, Mutter,' Smith replied, dropping his holdall on the step. 'It is good to be home,' he added, returning her kiss.

'How smart you look, unt I see the navy has taught you how to flirt,' his mother replied, giving him a friendly dig in the side.

She was about to take his hand and lead him inside, when Smith's father, a tall, straight-backed man with thinning, grey hair, appeared behind Smith's mother. She immediately moved aside, allowing Smith and his father to warmly shake hands and embrace.

'Welcome home, Heinrich,' said his father. 'It's good to see you, and how well your uniform fits your look.' Lowering his voice, he added, 'Even if it belongs to the wrong navy.' As he spoke, his rheumy, grey eyes creased into a warm smile.

'And it's good to see you looking so good, Papa,' Smith replied.

'Come,' said Smith's father, as he picked up his son's holdall. 'You must be tired after your journey.'

Smith followed his parents along a narrow corridor leading to the kitchen filled with familiar mouth-watering smells of his mother's baking. They turned left and entered the front room. A few paintings of the Lancashire countryside hung on the walls papered in pale green, and from a high, white ceiling hung a large, yellow lampshade. A well-polished oak sideboard adorned with photographs of Smith as a young boy, lay snugly against a side wall. In a corner, a wireless lay on a small, shiny oak table. A dark-green carpet covered the floor, and a half-moon-shaped white rug nestled in front of a fire grate surrounded by white tiles. Above, on a marble mantelpiece, framed family photographs lay either side of an ornate clock encased in brown oak. Above the mantelpiece hung a mirror that enhanced the reflection of the sun's rays streaming through the window.

'Remove your mackintosh and sit down, Heinrich, while I take your things to your room,' said Smith's father. His voice suddenly became quiet and conspiratorial. 'Your letter sounded very exciting. Going to a ship on a special mission, and the information you can obtain is just what the Fatherland needs.'

'And tea I will make, then you can have one of my freshly baked scones,' his mother added, taking hold of Smith's cap and tenderly brushing her hand over its round surface.

Smith sat down on one of the two black leather armchairs resting either side of a matching settee. Ten minutes later, he and his parents were enjoying warm scones and drinking tea.

After taking a sip of tea, Smith's mother gave him an anxious look, then, speaking German, asked, 'How long have we got you for, dear?'

'Not long, I'm sad to say,' Smith replied. 'I have to join the ship in Plymouth on Tuesday morning, so I'll have to catch the midnight train on Monday, from Paddington.'

'Please,' interrupted Smith's father, raising a hand. 'Let us speak English at all times. As the poster says, "Walls have ears". Now, Heinrich,' he went on, 'tell us more about this ship and where it's going. Then I'll let you know how you can help our glorious Third Reich.'

Gunter Schmidt met Adelheid in Berlin at a friend's house when he was on leave from the army in 1915. Gunter was twenty-five. Before the war, he had been a minor official in Weimar Republic's government. Adelheid was twenty and was secretary to a manager of a shipping firm.

Gunter was a sergeant, but due to his organisation skills he quickly rose to the rank of *hauptmann* (captain). In 1916, while was serving in the trenches, he was badly gassed. After a brief spell in hospital, Gunter was discharged from the army. In 1918, he and Adelheid were married and rented a fully furnished top-floor apartment on Altonaer Strattse, a leafy road overlooking the Tiergarten. A year later, Heinrich was born.

After the war, the Germans, especially former officers, considered the war was the result of a widespread Jewish conspiracy. The reparations imposed upon them by the Versailles Treaty were considered unduly harsh.

Food was scarce. Unemployment was rife and beggars roamed the streets. This allowed the rise of communism and extreme right-wing politics. Clashes between the two parties were commonplace.

In 1921, Hitler became the leader of the National German Workers (Nazi) Party. Using the Jews as the reason for the poor state of the land, Hitler promised reform and prosperity. Hitler's message appealed to former officers who joined the Nazi Party. Among them was ex-*Hauptmann* Gunter Schmidt.

Adelheid shared her husband's views and attended the various meetings chaired by Hitler or one of his acolytes.

At *kindergarten* (primary school), Heinrich showed a natural aptitude for mathematics and foreign languages, especially English. Later, at *grundschule* (elementary school), he came top of his class and obtained the coveted *Allgermeine Hochschulreife* (the equivalent of the English School Certificate).

In 1934, at the age of sixteen, instead of going to university, Heinrich left school to follow his father's profession: making uniforms for Hitler, Canaris and members of the *Abwehr*. Using his perfect English, Heinrich was able to converse with visitors from Great Britain wishing to purchase one of his father's expertly tailored suits. Heinrich joined the Hitler Youth and soon became indoctrinated in Hitler's dream of a Fatherland devoid of Jews. Like so many Germans, he fell under the hypnotic spell of Hitler, who, using his persuasive style of oratory, blamed the leaders of the Weimar Republic and Jewry for Germany's downfall. Heinrich's handsome, Germanic features attracted the opposite sex. However, other than a quick fumble at parties, Heinrich never felt comfortable in the company of girls, and his dedication to the Fuhrer's cause left him little time for such distractions.

As he grew older, Heinrich felt indifferent to the treatment of the Jews and paid little or no attention to such incidents as *Kristallnacht*, when, in 1933, windows of Jewish houses and businesses were smashed.

One evening in March 1936, his father took Heinrich to hear Hitler address one of the meetings. Heinrich became mesmerised by Hitler's dynamic oratory and always remembered seeing Hitler thumping the podium and hearing him screech, "Remember, during negotiating the Versailles Treaty, no member of the army were allowed in the Hall of Mirrors. They took no part in the meetings and were kept out while the politicians surrendered our proud birth right to the enemy."

A month later, to the delight of his father, Heinrich joined the Nazi Party. This allowed him to wear the party button with its red Swastika on a white background on the lapels of his suits and jackets.

CHAPTER THREE

'But why on earth would the admiral of the fleet want to see me, sir?' Lieutenant Commander Robert Miller was standing in front of Commander Daniel De Pass, the commanding officer of Miller's ship, HMS *Cossack,* a Tribal class destroyer.

Miller was twenty-nine and stood a little over six feet. His dark-brown, wavy hair parted neatly on the left was a shade lighter than his heavily tanned, clear-cut, handsome features.

In contrast to Miller's deep-blue, intelligent eyes, De Pass' eyes were strikingly clear blue. He was sat behind a wide, highly polished mahogany desk cluttered with official papers, and folders. Next to a heavy-looking, brass ashtray rested a framed photograph of a small, attractive woman with short, dark hair, holding the hands of two young boys. Behind the desk, on the bulkhead painted pale green, was a framed, coloured photograph of King George V1 and Queen Elizabeth.

The deck was covered in a dark-blue carpet inlaid with tiny, silver anchors. Strips of neon attached to the low-slung deckhead provided clear lighting. A well-stocked wine cabinet rested next to a door which led into a small galley. Nearby stood a green, metal filing cabinet, two black leather armchairs and an elegant coffee table. Like everything else, it was screwed to the deck.

The time was nine a.m. The date was Saturday 15th July 1939. *Cossack* had returned from the Mediterranean a week ago and was berthed alongside Fountain Lake Jetty in Portsmouth Dockyard.

'How on earth do I know?' De Pass replied impatiently. His voice was sharp and commanding. 'All it said in the signal was that you were to report to Admiral Sir Roger Backhouse in Whitehall, room twenty, the day after tomorrow at one thirty. And,' he added sternly, 'don't be late. I served under Backhouse when he was a captain, and he's a stickler for punctuality.'

With a puzzled expression on his face, Miller looked at De Pass and asked, 'Any idea what it's about, sir?'

'Your guess is as good as mine, old boy,' De Pass replied, shrugging his shoulders slightly. 'But it must be damn well important. After all, it's not every day a lowly lieutenant commander is summoned to see an admiral.'

'Quite, sir,' muttered Miller, then, with a bewildered sigh, slowly turned away and left.

On the morning of Monday 17th, shortly after "colours", Miller left *Cossack* where a tilly — a blue van with RN painted white on both sides, used exclusively by the navy — took him to Portsmouth Harbour Station. The sky was an eye-catching blue, and an early morning sun promised another warm day. Wearing his best doeskin uniform, Miller bought a copy of *The Times* then caught the nine thirty train.

During the three-hour journey to Waterloo, Miller had plenty to think about. If it was a disciplinary matter he was being sent for, surely it could have been dealt with on board his ship. Whatever it was, it had to be something very important. His wristwatch showed he only had twenty minutes before his meeting. Remembering Commander De Pass' warning, he quickly detrained, and feeling his heart rate increase, hurried across the crowded concourse to the arched exit and hailed one of several taxis parked outside.

'Where to, Guvnor?' asked the driver, as Miller opened the passenger door and climbed inside.

'Whitehall, Admiralty building, and hurry, please,' Miller replied, glancing anxiously at his wristwatch.

'Important meeting, eh,' the driver enquired, as he switched on the ignition.

'Yes, indeed,' Miller answered.

At first, the afternoon traffic along Southampton Row and Kingsway was relatively light. However, Miller's nerves were on edge, as halfway down the Strand, the taxi became stuck in a convoy of traffic. In what felt like an eternity, the taxi reached the end of the Strand then turned left into Whitehall. The taxi stopped opposite a row of red-brick buildings, one of which contained the Admiralty. The time was 12.55.

Miller paid the driver, and dodging traffic, hurried across the road to the Admiralty building. With dark-blue slated turrets, this section of the road looked more like a medieval fortress than the place that housed one of the most important offices in the armed forces.

Miller quickly made his way through a small archway and showed his paybook to a tall, keen-eyed policeman standing outside a stout oak door.

'Room twenty, sir,' said the policeman. 'First floor, along the corridor, second door on your left.'

Taking the steps of a curved staircase like an Olympic hurdler, he arrived on the first floor. The sign on the door, painted in neat, gold letters read, "Admiral of the Fleet". Feeling his heart doing a cadence in his chest, he knocked and went inside. The room was small but well equipped. In one corner, next to a door, was a green, metal filing cabinet. Close by, under a small window, was a sink above which was a mirror. Then came a table on which lay an electric kettle, cups and saucers, and a half-full bottle of milk. A pretty, dark-haired third officer Wren was sat behind a desk. In front of her was an old Imperial typewriter and an open file. As Miller entered the room, she looked up.

'You must be Lieutenant Commander Miller,' she said, giving him an approving smile. 'Please go straight in; you're expected.'

'Thank you,' Miller replied, taking off his cap.

The time was exactly one p.m. He took a deep breath, straightened his tie, knocked and opened the door.

The atmosphere was pleasantly warm, and the seasoned smell of rich tobacco contrasted sharply with that of mansion polish. Next to a cocktail cabinet was a large globe of the world, resting on a set of claw-like wooden hands. The walls were lined with leather-bound books along with framed photographs and paintings of warships, old and new. A wide bay window overlooked Horse Guard's Parade. A small, delicate-looking glass chandelier hanging from a white, stuccoed ceiling gave the finishing touch to a room that looked more like that in a gentlemen's club, rather than one belonging to the most powerful officer in the Royal Navy.

The first person Miller saw was Rear Admiral of the Fleet, Sir

Roger Backhurst, a tall, square-jawed man with dark, piercing eyes and thinning grey hair, whom he recognised from his pictures in newsreels and newspapers. He was sitting behind a wide, mahogany desk. In front of him a document lay open.

On his right, sitting on an armchair, was Admiral Sir Dudley Pound, a small, stocky, fair-haired man with intelligent blue eyes and a heavily lined, pale complexion. Miller had met him briefly a year ago during a ship's inspection.

On Pound's right sat two civilians. One of them had a Ryan-like, grey-haired halo around a shiny, bald head. His face was pale and lined, and a pair of rimless glasses rested precariously on the bridge of his slightly hooked nose. The ill-fitting, grey pin-striped suit he wore was badly in need of pressing, and his gaudy pink shirt and a red and white polka dot tie made him appear somewhat eccentric. He was smoking a well-used meerschaum pipe. In front of him, resting on an elegant coffee table, lay a small wooden box.

The other man had thick, white hair, a tobacco-stained moustache and was dressed in a conservative dark-grey suit, cream-coloured shirt and a Marron University tie.

'Ah, Lieutenant Commander Miller,' said Rear Admiral Backhurst, standing up and proffering his hand. 'Do take a seat, and don't look so worried. We're not going to bite you,' he added, indicating to an armchair facing his desk. 'And smoke if you want to.'

'No, I don't,' Miller replied.

'Coffee?'

'Yes, thank you, sir,' Miller replied, as they shook hands.

Backhurst sat down and pressed a small red button on his desk. Seconds later, the Wren opened the door.

'I take it you gentlemen would like coffee, also,' said the admiral, glancing at Dudley Pound and the two civilians.

'Na fer for me, thank you,' replied the man in the pink shirt. He spoke with a sharp Scottish accent while lighting a cigarette.

'Four coffees, please, Pamela,' said Backhurst.

As soon as the Wren left, Backhurst looked inquisitively at Miller and said, 'Now, I expect you're anxious to know why I've sent for you?'

'Yes, indeed, sir,' Miller answered, nervously licking his lips.

'Now, before I go any further,' Backhurst replied cautiously, 'I must stress that anything that is discussed in this room is top secret and must not, under any circumstances, be repeated. Is that firmly understood?'

The admiral's words sent a feeling of alarm running through Miller. 'Yes, sir, perfectly,' he replied.

'Good,' replied Backhurst. 'The officer next to me is Admiral Sir Dudley Pound. The gentleman smoking a cigarette is Doctor Charles Wright, Director of Scientific to the Admiralty. Next to him is Angus Mackenzie, Professor of Geology at Cambridge University.'

'Pleased to meet you, gentlemen,' Miller said, shaking their hands while feeling somewhat puzzled by the presence of such eminent academies.

'Now, let's see,' said Backhurst, glancing at the document on his desk. 'You're twenty-nine. Sadly, seven years ago your wife was killed in a car accident while you were at sea. You had no children nor have you any brothers and sisters. When on leave, you live with your parents — Harold, who is a retired Master Mariner, and Maud — in Wallasey. You have a First in Geography, obtained at Liverpool University. Before joining the service, you were employed by the firm of Charles Salvestan and Company of Leith and served as Navigating Officer on board the S. S. *William Scoresby.*' Backhurst paused momentarily, then added, 'Am I right, so far?'

The mention of Dorothy's accident sent a pang of guilt running through him. How well he remembered her pleading with him to give up the sea, settle down and have a family. But what could he do if he came ashore? Sit behind a desk and count paper clips? Like many young men living on Merseyside, he was attracted to the sea. He joined the Merchant Navy as a junior officer and did several trips at sea.

After telling Dorothy he was going away on yet another voyage, he vividly recalled her throwing a cup of tea at him and angrily yelling, "You bastard. You love those ships more than me?"

And perhaps she was right. He did love the sea more than anything. While he was away, she got drunk and crashed the box Ford into a tree and was killed. Her memory continued to haunt him. Maybe if he had come ashore and settled down, she would be alive today.

'Yes, sir,' Miller replied. 'The *Scoresby* was built for service in the Antarctica and was loaned to the British Royal Research Company for geological and survey work in the southern hemisphere.'

'And did this include visits to South Georgia?'

'Yes, sir. As I recall, we went there several times,' Miller replied.

'So you became quite familiar with South Georgia and the whims of the Southern Ocean?'

Miller suddenly felt decidedly uncomfortable. 'Yes, sir, but that was five years ago,' he quietly replied.

'Well, now,' Backhurst said, staring at Miller with his keen, pale-blue eyes. 'I'm sending you back there again.'

'Good lord, sir, what on earth for?' Miller exclaimed, sitting forward in his chair.

At that moment the door opened, and the Wren Officer came through carrying a tray containing four steaming hot cups of coffee.

CHAPTER FOUR

'Relax, dear boy, and let me explain why,' Backhurst replied, as the Wren handed each person a cup of coffee. 'Thank you, Pamela. Hold all phone calls and make sure we're not disturbed.'

'Very good, sir,' she answered, then flashing Miller an inviting smile, turned and left the room.

'As I'm sure you know, the situation in Europe is pretty grim,' Backhurst said, after taking a sip of coffee. Now that Hitler has occupied Czechoslovakia and Austria, the Wehrmacht are doing so-called maneuverers on the Polish borders. Despite Chamberlain's guarantee of support for France and Poland, we can expect war between ourselves and Germany at any time.'

'Yes, I'm well aware of that, sir,' Miller replied, slightly irritated, 'but, with respect, what has this got to do with me being sent into southern waters?'

'I think I'd better let Doctor Wright explain,' Backhurst said, nodding at the white-haired gentleman with his tobacco-stained moustache.

'Thank you, admiral,' said the doctor. His accent, clear and concise, reminded Miller of a BBC announcer. 'Without sounding too technical, I'll come straight to the point,' he added, giving Miller a confident smile. 'In my opinion, one of the most important factors that we'll need if war breaks out will be RADAR, which, as you probably know, is an acronym for "Radio Detection and Ranging" and is invaluable for identifying aircraft. As yet, our warships, including your own, only have SONAR, which can only be used for sound navigation, ranging detecting submarines, but I'm sure you know all that.'

'Yes, I do, sir, Miller said, watching the doctor take a good swig of coffee.

'Quite so,' the doctor replied, dabbing his mouth with a

handkerchief. 'Now, inside every radar set is an electron. At present, the wavelengths produced by the electron are too long to be really effective.' He stopped talking and finished his coffee. 'What we need,' he added, placing the cup and saucer on the table, 'is an electron tube with the shortest wavelength.'

'But don't the Germans have radar, sir?' asked Miller.

'Yes, they do,' the doctor replied cagily, 'but we don't know how effective they are.'

'According to the prime minister, radar stations are being set up around our coastline,' Miller said, after draining his cup. 'Surely this will give us enough warning of enemy aircraft?'

'Ah, yes,' the doctor replied, lighting a cigarette, 'and that is one of the reasons we urgently require something that will shorten the electron's wavelength. Now, perhaps Professor Mackenzie can enlighten you more,' he added, turning his head to one side and exhaling a cloud of blue tobacco smoke.

The gentleman in the pink shirt gave Miller a quick smile, and holding his pipe, bent forward and tapped the top of the wooden box. 'Part of my work at Cambridge deals with Minerology. And the contents in this box is the main reason for your mission.' He spoke with a refined, mellifluous Scottish accent.

Millers' eyes immediately became focussed on the box. It was small, with a lid held fast by a tiny, silver lock.

'Three years ago,' continued the professor, 'a man named Hector Weir, who had been one of my students, gained a First in Minerology. However, in 1937, work was scarce, so he and his wife, Cora, and Angus, his eleven-year-old son, immigrated to the Falkland Islands. They were granted land around the capital, Stanley, and became one of the many sheep farmers, producing wool for export.' He paused momentarily and took a few puffs on his pipe.

In an instant, a cloud of blue smoke arose, accompanied by the coughing of the two admirals, Doctor Wright and Miller.'

'Och, I'm sorry about that, gentlemen,' said the professor, using a hand to waft away the smoke. 'Now, where was I?' he added, placing his smouldering pipe in a brass ashtray.

'You were telling us about a Mr Hector Weir rearing sheep in the Falkland Islands, sir,' Miller replied, who was becoming slightly agitated at the professor's prevaricating.

'Och, yes, Weir,' pondered the professor. 'Bright, young man. Retained his interest in geology. He owned a small but sturdy fishing boat with an outboard motor. He and his son would visit various islands, collecting fossils and anything else of interest. During one such trip in November a year ago, a storm blew them off course. Now, South Georgia is nine hundred and sixty miles from Stanley. And as you can imagine, the journey was hazardous, to say the least. They finally arrived at Bird Island, on the northern tip of South Georgia. Before arriving there, they managed to send out a distress signal. Of course, it was too weak to reach Stanley. Luckily, it was picked up at Grytviken, a Norwegian whaling station fifty miles on the western coast of the island. The Norwegians sent a boat for them, who contacted Stanley to say they were safe. They remained at Grytviken for a week. Fortunately, a deep-sea tug arrived from Punta Arenas in Chile with stores for the whaling station. Four days later, the tug took the fishing boat in tow and took Duncan and Peter back to Stanley. During their time at Grytviken, Duncan and Peter explored the island, looking for fossils. A mile away from the whaling station, near the foot of a mountain on the northern coast, he found this.'

The professor unclipped the lid of the box, and as if handling a newborn baby, took out a small bundle wrapped in green velvet. He laid it on the table and carefully unwrapped it, revealing a small lump of shiny, blue-grey stone.

'What yer see before yer is a rare mineral called "grapholite". Duncan didn't know what it was, so, to cut a long story short, he sent it to me. After discovering its valuable properties, I dispatched it by special currier to Doctor Wright.'

'Thank you, professor,' said Miller, sitting back in his chair and folding his arms, 'but I'm still none the wiser as to why I'm here.'

'Patience, dear boy,' said Brockhurst, raising a hand. 'I'm sure Doctor Wright will enlighten you.'

The doctor cleared his throat and fixed his perceptive, pale-blue eyes on Miller. 'As Professor Mackenzie pointed out, grapholite is rare, and as far as we know, is only found on a few small islands in the southern hemisphere. One of these is South Georgia. I will not bore you with complicated chemical formulae. Sufficient to say, it contains vital properties that could, if used in the production of electrons, shorten its wavelength. And if we do that, it'll put us well ahead of anything the Germans have. It'll enable those radar stations that are being built round our coast to detect earlier attacks by enemy aircraft. It'll also improve the range on warships.' He paused and lit a cigarette, then added, 'However, there are three types of grapholite: alpha, beta and gamma. Alpha was the type Duncan found, and dare I say it, will help us to shorten the war when it comes. The other two are worthless. However, to achieve this, we will need a sample of alpha grapholite.'

'And you are being sent to South Georgia to find this alpha grapholite and bring it back to us,' interrupted Admiral Pounds. The mission will be called "Operation Iceberg". Very appropriate, don't you think?

'Quite so, sir!' exclaimed Miller, furrowing his brow. 'But when, may I ask, will this take place?'

'I'm coming to that,' Admiral Pound replied impatiently. 'A year ago, the government bought a passenger ship, the MS *Flynderborg,* from Marshal Shipyard, Denmark, and renamed it HMS *Endeavour.* She was built to take tourists sightseeing to the Arctic. Her two Wain Diesel engines can do up to twenty knots. *Endeavour* will embark one hundred and twenty officers and men, all of whom have been passed medically and dentally fit. *Endeavour* has been refitted with mess decks and a sonar dome under her bow. Her air conditioning and oil-fired central heating has been retained. A six-inch, long-angled, breech-loading gun has been concealed in a large box-like area used previously as recreation area. It is now called the gun hangar. It's an extension of the after section of the superstructure and can be accessed through the quarterdeck. A section of each bulkhead has been fitted with metal shutters. Each can be electronically raised and lowered by pressing a button on the side of each shutter. This allows the gun to be trained in any direction. Six shells have been installed in a steel rack. Your first lieutenant has the key. As we are not yet at war, this armament is only to be used in self-defence. Understood?'

'Yes, sir,' Miller replied.

'And finally,' said the admiral, 'the ship's bows are in the process of being re-enforced with an extra four inches of a stronger type of steel plating, ideal for cutting through the thickest ice.'

'With respect, sir,' Miller replied, slowly shaking his head, 'although South Georgia is some 6,000 miles from the Antarctic Circle, the Southern Ocean, with its icebergs and its mountainous seas, is the most inhospitable part of the world, especially during the height of winter.'

'I quite understand your concerns,' Admiral Pound replied, 'but there it is. Now, *Endeavour* is in number two dry dock in Devonport Dockyard and is expected to complete her refit in another week. Considering that the few officers who have had knowledge of this area are retired, you are to be promoted to commander and have a crew of a hundred and twenty-six officers and ratings. Lieutenant Commander Pollard is your first lieutenant. His mother is from Stockholm, and he speaks fluent Swedish and German. He's also just competed communication course at *Royal Alfred.*' The admiral paused momentarily, then asked, 'Are there questions?'

Considering Miller had been lieutenant commander for only a year, the news of his promotion came as a pleasant surprise. *But* pondered Miller, *I wonder if the wily old fox knows more than he's telling me?*

'Just a few, sir,' Miller replied, pensively stroking his chin. 'As it'll be necessary to dig the grapholite out of the rocks, we'll need picks, shovels, hammers and chisels, and of course, warm clothing.'

'All that will be provided and sent to your ship,' said the admiral, 'as well as snowshoes?'

'I shouldn't bother with those, sir,' Miller replied, 'They'd only get in the way, especially if we have to climb over rocks.' For a few seconds Miller paused, then, with a look of concern, continued, 'If war breaks out while we're away, sir, would there be any danger of a U-boat attack?'

With a slight air of caution in his voice, the admiral replied,

'They do possess XB U-boats with an endurance of over 6,000 miles, but I doubt if you need to worry about them, as they are used for minelaying and can only fire torpedoes from aft. Besides, they won't know your position, and as the Southern Atlantic is so vast, it would be like looking for a needle in a haystack.'

'Thank you, sir, that's very reassuring,' Miller replied, 'but with respect, I've been to South Georgia during winter. The ice can be so thick, it's virtuously impassable. Remember what happened to Shackleton?'

'Yes, indeed,' the admiral replied, 'but that occurred when his ship, *Endurance*, got trapped in the Weddell Sea ice pack, much further south than where you'll be going.'

'Nevertheless, sir,' Miller replied cagily. 'I have grave reservations. Why can't this wait until October when the Antarctic winter ends and conditions improve?'

The admiral slowly shook his head. 'Sorry, old boy. Speed is of the essence, as war could break out anytime.'

'Very well, sir,' sighed Miller, 'when do I join *Endeavour*?'

'You are to take seven days leave then join *Endeavour* on Monday 17th July. There will be no official commissioning ceremony. *Endeavour* will sail on Friday 28th for a two-day engine and boiler trial, and providing there are no problems, you leave Plymouth on Monday 31st. Your first port of call will be Rio de Janeiro, where you take on fuel, give a few days leave and be contacted by Sir Geoffrey Knox-Johnson, the British ambassador. On your way there, you are to complete your work-up. You will then proceed to Punta Arenas to take on extra fuel and then sail for Stanley, where you will embark Mr Weir. After collecting the grapholite, you are to return to Stanley, land Mr Weir, then make haste to Rio, refuel again, then sail for home.' The admiral paused, picked up a glass of water, took a good sip, then continued. 'You may inform the officers about the true reason for the mission. You can tell the ship's company that the reason for the journey is to collect data on the weather and ice-flow. It is only when you arrive in Stanley that you are to let them know the ship is going to South Georgia and why. Is that clear?'

'Yes, sir, but just how much of this grapholite will we need?'

Miller asked.

'Actually, not a great deal,' said Doctor Wright, leaning forward and stubbing out his cigarette in a large, brass ashtray. 'A quarter of an underweight should be enough, because having found the formula, we can then produce our own.'

'And when will my promotion begin, sir?'

'Straight away,' the admiral replied. 'And all I've told you will be contained in a letter marked "secret and confidential", that'll be sent to you before you sail.' Proffering his hand, he smiled and said, 'Good luck and congratulations.'

'Thank you, sir,' Miller answered, shaking the admiral's clammy hand, thinking that dodging icebergs would be more important than the three golds rings he would wear on each sleeve. 'One last thing,' said Admiral Pound, raising a hand. 'At a time and place, as yet unspecified, you'll be embarking a mineralogist, who will work with Mr Weir to ensure you collect the correct specimens.'

'I only hope he doesn't suffer from seasickness, sir,' Miller replied with a wide grin.

CHAPTER FIVE

'Good meeting, sir?' he asked, as Miller stepped onto the quarterdeck and saluted.

Miller slowly shook his head and replied, 'I'm not quite sure. Is the captain still on board?'

'Yes, he's left a message for you to report to him as soon as you returned,' Jackson answered. 'He sounded rather anxious. I hope you didn't upset dear, old Admiral Backhurst.'

'Perhaps I should have,' Miller replied, with a sly grin.

The captain's cabin was on a passageway directly under the bridge. Miller arrived and knocked on the door. The captain's gruff voice told him to enter.

'Ah, pilot, come in and sit down,' said De Pass, indicating an armchair. 'The admiral has informed me what is happening, so let me congratulate you on your promotion. No doubt it came as a bit of a surprise?'

'Yes, it did, sir,' Miller replied. 'That and several other things.'

On the evening of Tuesday 18, July, Miller, together with *Cossacks* officers, had a farewell celebration. The next morning, after "colours", wearing a dark-blue cap and blazer, white shirt, naval tie and grey slacks, he said a final goodbye to them. In doing so, he couldn't help but feel a pang of regret, having got to know each one so well during the past year. Their good wishes along with many of the ship's company rang in his ears as he walked over the brow. Carrying a green "Pussers" suitcase and Burberry, he climbed into a tilly. (The term "Pusser" is naval parlance for anything belonging to the RN.)

At Portsmouth Harbour Station, Miller bought a copy of *The Times* and caught the eight-thirty train to Waterloo, arriving three hours later. A taxi took him across north London to Euston. Before boarding the 11.15 to Liverpool, he telephoned his parents. Miller hadn't been home for over six months. Needless to say, they were overjoyed to hear he was coming home on leave.

During the five-hour journey to Lime Street, Miller remembered the many precarious hours spent on *William Scoresby's* enclosed bridge, feeling her shake violently as the huge waves of the Southern Ocean crashed over her bows. The experience never failed to put the fear of God into him. Nevertheless, in some perverse way he found himself looking forward to it again.

Outside Lime Street station, Liverpool basked under a sun surrounded by puffy, white, altocumulus clouds. Miller caught a taxi to the pier head in time to board the MV *Royal Daffodil* that would take him across the *Mersey* to Wallasey.

As the ferry boat berthed port side alongside Princess' landing stage, muscular arms of the deckhands received heavy hemp lines from shore staff and expertly secured them around bollards. This was quickly followed by the sharp tingling of chains allowing the two wooden gangways to be lowered; one for passengers leaving and the other for those embarking.

The time was a little after three o'clock. A feeling of *déjà vu* swept through him as he recalled how often he had done this journey during his years at Liverpool University. He joined the crowd of afternoon shoppers and boarded the *Royal Daffodil* ferryboat. He walked across the deck to the starboard side, placed his suitcase on the deck, leant against the wooden guardrail and gazed nostalgically across the grey-green waters of the Mersey to Wallasey.

A warm wind blew downriver, caressing his face. Away to his left, almost out of sight, stretched the dockland, including Gladstone Dock, which, during the Second World War, would become the base of Captain 'Jonnie' Walker's famous 36th Escort Group. On the opposite side of the river, looking like giant praying mantises, cranes from Cammell Lairds shipyard dominated the sky over Birkenhead. Ferry boats from New Brighton and Birkenhead sailed leisurely across the river. Tugs lay at anchor waiting to assist cargo ships into docks. Passenger liners belonging to Cunard and P and O lay further down Princess' landing stage. Dredgers, carrying silt from upriver, mingled with bulky barges, while perched on top of Liverpool's famous Liver buildings, Cormorants peered imperiously over the river and city.

The journey across the Mersey evoked more memories. Leaning against the ferryboat's wooden guard rail, Miller looked across the river to Wallasey's ferry terminus with its modern clock tower and felt a schoolboy thrill running through him. This feeling was increased as he saw a wide, yellow ribbon of sand stretching along Wallasey's shoreline to New Brighton's pier. He could just see the top of Riverview, the thatched cottage where he was born, nestling snugly at the bottom of Caithness Drive. He couldn't fail to see the massive, red-brick tower buildings dominating the skyline along with a section of the Figure 8 roller coaster and the arch of the Ferris wheel, all of which were part of New Brighton's popular fairground.

Suddenly the excitement of seeing places he knew so well turned to sadness, as it was in the tower's spacious ballroom where he had met Dorothy. The *William Scoresby* had been in Hull dockyard having repairs, and he was on a weeks' leave. He was twenty, and he wore a grey suit, white shirt and maroon tie. It was a Saturday night. The ballroom was crowded. A mixture of perfume, tobacco smoke and music filled the air. Hanging from an elegantly arched ceiling, two large, silver balls slowly revolved, bathing everyone and everything in glittering specks of light. The orchestra was playing a waltz, the only dance he was confident doing. For a few seconds he stood still, before plucking up enough courage to approach her.

She was nineteen and stood a little over five feet. He vividly recalled how beautiful she looked in a long-sleeved, ankle-length, red dress, standing talking to a taller girl dressed in pink. Her brown hair was cut short. He remembered how her dark-brown eyes, set in a pear- shaped face, creased into a smile when he asked her to dance. He also remembered how embarrassed he felt when he trod on the tip of one of her high-heeled shoes, stumbled awkwardly and nearly fell over. She accepted his awkwardness with an understanding smile, and said, "Not to worry, no bones broken."

While they moved around the floor, he introduced himself, and she did likewise. When the dance ended, he nervously asked her if she would like a drink, and much to his surprise, she accepted. While she sipped her beer shandy, she told him she worked in Boots Chemist in Liscard, Wallasey's main shopping centre, and she lived with her parents. When he said he was an officer in the merchant navy, he remembered how impressed she seemed.

When the dance finished, they left, caught the number 1 bus and got off near St Nicholas's Church. He took her hand and escorted her to a large house in Manor Road. Over the next two weeks they met every night. A year later they were married, and they rented a top-floor flat in Warren Drive, overlooking the river.

The dull *thud* of the ferry boat bouncing against Wallasey's landing stage interrupted his reverie. He picked up his suitcase and stood well back as a burly deckhand slid open the wooden barrier. This was quickly followed by a bone-shaking clatter as the gangway was lowered onto the deck. Miller joined the crowd and hurried up the sloping slipway. After paying his two-penny fare at a turnstile, he managed to catch a number 1 bus. He handed the conductor a three-penny piece and received a small, green ticket. Then, hugging his suitcase, he took a seat on the lower deck.

The time was a little after four o'clock. The journey along King Street and Sea Bank Road took ten minutes. He left the bus opposite the top of Caithness Drive. No matter how often be had been away, the thrill of coming home was always the same. As he hurried down the sloping drive that led onto the promenade, he recognised Harold's three-year-old dark-red Austin 7. It was parked at the end of the drive, opposite a wrought iron gate that led into the back entrance of the cottage. The tall, laburnum tree in the back garden was in full bloom and had sprinkled the grass with a carpet of bright-green petals. The squeaking of the gate must have alerted his parents, because as he walked down the four stone steps leading onto a flagged patio, the back kitchen door opened and his mother and father appeared.

'Darling Robert, welcome home,' cried Maud, throwing her arms around him.

Maud was fifty-seven, two years younger than Harold, and

stood a little over five feet. They had met at a dinner party in 1906 and were married a year later. Maud's shoulder-length, fair hair was tied in a bun. Her pale face was round and chubby, and as she spoke, tears welled up in her pale-blue eyes. The white apron she wore over a short-sleeved, red dress emphasised her matronly figure.

As she kissed him warmly on the cheek, the nostalgic smell of her lavender perfume, and face powder, evoked memories of his youth and childhood.

'It's good to be home, Mum,' Miller replied, taking off his cap. 'You look as young and beautiful as ever,' he added, feeling his throat contract while giving her a loving hug.

'Hey, don't forget me,' said Harold, reaching out for his son.

Miller disengaged himself from Maud, and they shook hands. 'How are you, Dad?' he said, holding Harold's six-foot, burly frame at arm's-length. 'You're looking very fit.'

The healthy-looking tan, along with the grey sideboards and dark-brown, wavy hair, added to his father's already distinguished, clear-cut features.

'That's due to plenty of brisk walks along the prom,' Harrold replied, 'plus the fact that your mother and I have given up smoking several months ago, haven't we, dear?'

'Yes, and jolly difficult it was too,' Maud answered dutifully.

'But I think you've lost a little weight since we last saw you,' said Harold.

'We'll soon change that, won't we dear?' said Maud, putting her arms around them. 'It so happens that I've got Bob's favourite steak and kidney pie in the oven.'

'I thought I recognised the smell,' Miller replied, using a finger to tenderly remove a tear from running down Maud's cheek.

'Come on, Bob,' Harold said, picking up Miller's suitcase. 'Let's get you settled in, then we can all have a good chin-wag.'

'And while you're doing that, I'll put the kettle on,' added Maud, taking hold of Miller's arm and escorting him into the kitchen.

Nothing much had changed since he was here almost a year ago. The net curtains, covering the small window, looked the same, as were the glossy-white-painted walls. The familiar stout, wooden table and chairs stood in the middle of the concrete floor which was covered by a well-worn, brown carpet. Above a section of cupboards containing crockery and shiny brass pots and pans, were shelves lined with jars of homemade jams, potted plums and apricots. The brass taps over a deep, marble sink gleamed. However, a new gas cooker and refrigerator gave a touch of modernity to the otherwise Victorian surroundings.

They left the kitchen and walked into a corridor leading to the cottage's front door. Miller knew the door opened onto a narrow, gravelled pathway that bisected a garden, which, at this time of the year, was a riot of colour. At the end of the pathway, a wrought iron gate, red with rust, opened onto the promenade.

Maud remained in the kitchen while Harold and Miller stopped at the bottom of a short staircase.

'I'm sure you know where your room is, Bob,' Harold said, handing Miller his suitcase. 'Gin and tonics in ten minutes.'

'Thanks, Dad,' Miller replied, looking at framed photographs of passenger ships and cargo vessels, lining the staircase wall.

Miller's old room was at the top of the landing, next to the bathroom. When he opened the door, he felt he was stepping back in time. With a pang of nostalgia, he noticed his cricket bat and rugby boots, now devoid of mud, in one corner. The dark-green carpet hadn't changed, nor had the pale, brown wallpaper and the coloured paintings of Cheshire's flat but attractive countryside. The low-slung, cream-coloured ceiling and pink lampshade were the same. Even his small bed, with its glossy, yellow eiderdown, bedside table and lamp hadn't changed. In one corner, next to the wardrobe and small chest of drawers, was a slightly scratched mahogany table. It was here where he had sat for many hours under the glare of angle-poise lamp, studying for his degree. However, the outstanding feature of the room was the wide, bay window overlooking the promenade. From here it commanded a breathtaking view of Merseyside's dockland and river, a scene that never failed to ignite his senses.

In winter, the wild north-westerly winds sent angry, green waves exploding onto the promenade. With a smile, he recalled seeing schoolboys dodging the waves as they attempted to avoid being drenched. The summer and autumn months brought crowds to the beach, enjoying family picnics and building sandcastles. The fairground was constantly full of locals, and visitors from all over the country, and in the evening they could enjoy a variety show at either the Floral Pavilion or Tivoli theatres.

Today the promenade was crowded with people enjoying the balmy evening sunshine. The tide was on the flood. For a few minutes he watched, as the rippling waves of the incoming tide sneaked onto the yellow sand. In less than an hour the water would be lapping against the promenade wall. How often he had stood and seen large liners, cargo vessels and grey-coloured warships come and go, wondering where they had been. Little did he realise that one day he would find out.

CHAPTER SIX

Miller took off his Burberry and hung it along with his cap behind the door. After unpacking his suitcase, he went to the bathroom, had a quick wash, combed his hair then hurried downstairs into the lounge. Yellow curtains were drawn across a bay window, allowing the evening sunlight to filter though. A dark-green carpet covered the floor, and a small but elegant glass chandelier hung from a white, stuccoed ceiling. In one corner, next to a Chippendale coffee table, stood a well-stocked wine cabinet. On a wall opposite, framed photographs decorated the top of a highly polished mahogany table. On the marble mantelpiece, a photograph of a youthful-looking Miller rested next to a pale-pink Ormolu clock. A curved metal fireguard lay on a tiled hearth in front of an unlit log fire. Hanging over the mantelpiece, an ornately framed, coloured painting of the Queen Mary added a nautical touch to a tastefully furnished room.

Harrold and Maud were sitting on a black Chesterfield settee. In front of them, resting on a round, glass-topped coffee table, were three long-stemmed Waterford crystal glasses, a small bucket of ice cubes, a large bottle of Gordon's gin, and bottles of tonic water.

'Now, sit down, my boy. Help yourself to a G and T,' Harold said enthusiastically.

'Just what I need, Dad,' Miller replied, sitting down in an armchair and mixing himself a drink.

Harold did the same for Maud and himself.

'To our dearest Robert,' said Harold, raising his glass. 'Here's to calm sailing and a safe return home.'

'Hear, hear,' chimed in Maud, as they clinked glasses and toasted Miller.

After finishing their drinks, Maud refilled each glass. It was then Miller sensed that Harold was about to ask the question every serviceman on leave dreaded. Miller was right.

'I know you don't want me to ask, Bob,' Harold said, 'but when do you have to be back?'

'Next Tuesday,' Miller quietly replied, 'and incidentally, I've been promoted. I'm now a commander and have been given command of a...' He paused momentarily, then went on. 'Frigate. At present, she's in Devonport, undergoing a refit.'

'A commander no less!' exclaimed Harold. 'Isn't that wonderful, Maud, and his own ship to boot. Heartiest congratulations, my boy,' he added, slapping Miller on the back.

'Marvellous, darling,' Maud said, standing up and kissing Miller warmly on the cheek. 'Had you mentioned it earlier, I'm sure your father would have opened a bottle of champagne, wouldn't you, dear?'

'Indeed, I would,' Harold, replied, beaming with pride. 'But we'll certainly have one at dinner.'

Shortly afterwards, they moved to the kitchen and enjoyed Maud's tasty steak and kidney pie, washed down with a bottle of Bollinger. During the meal they discussed the possibilities of war.

'I read in *The Times* that we're to be issued with gas masks,' Maud remarked, as she sipped her champagne.

'Well, dear,' Harold replied, 'the Boche used gas in the last war, so it's better to be safe than sorry. What do you think, Bob?'

'I quite agree with you, Dad,' Miller answered, topping up his father's glass. 'The gas left thousands blind after the war.'

'I read also that air raid sirens are being practiced in Paris,' said Maud, 'and people are being asked to cover their windows with black curtains to blot out the light in case of an air attack.'

'If war does break out, I fear it'll take a lot more than gas masks, air raid sirens and blackout curtains to stop the Germans,' Harold said, furrowing his brow. 'Look what happened to Guernica two years ago during that terrible Civil war in Spain. The German bombers flattened the town, and over one and a half thousand people were killed or injured. So I think that makes it all the more important to be prepared.'

'Well, since then, thank goodness, several new warships have been completed,' Miller said, dabbing his mouth with a serviette.

'Is your ship one of them, Bob?' asked Harold.

'Err... no, Dad,' Miller answered, trying not to sound evasive. 'She's a few years old.'

'And where will you be going, dear?' Maud asked, as Miller was about to top up her glass.

For the first time all evening, Miller felt uncomfortable. 'Actually, we're going on a trip to the Antarctic to monitor the ice-flow and study the weather,' Miller replied.

'Ah, so that's why you've been promoted,' remarked Harold. 'You must be the only officer in the Royal Navy that's familiar with that part of the word.'

'You're probably right, Dad,' Miller replied, taking a sip of his coffee.

'But it does seem a waste of a ship and manpower,' Harold replied, shaking his head slightly. 'Especially with the country facing its biggest crisis since 1914. I mean to say, if war breaks out, we'll need every ship we have.'

Doing his best to change the subject, Miller picked up his empty glass, and smiling weakly, said, 'I say, Mum, is there any more champagne left? All this talk about the Antarctic is making me thirsty.'

However, the dubious look in Harold's eyes as Maud refilled Miller's glass showed that his father still had his doubts about his son's explanation for his forthcoming voyage to the Antarctic.

After dinner they sat in the lounge, enjoying coffee and brandy. At nine o'clock they listened intently to the BBC, as Alvar Lidell's distinctive voice reported more bombing of cities in China, by the Japanese.

'The Japanese fought on our side during the war, didn't they, Harold?' asked Maud.

'Yes, they did, dear,' Harold replied, nodding slightly, 'but according to *The Times,* they're desperately short of raw materials, and that's the reason they invaded China, so who knows whose side they'll be on if there's another war. What do you think, Bob?'

'Well,' Miller replied thoughtfully, 'we have lots of interests in the Far East, so whatever the Japs do, we must be on our guard.'

The next six days seemed to pass extraordinarily quickly.

Miller had dinner with a few old university friends, saw *Gone With The Wind* at the Capitol Cinema and visited his old headmaster at the Grammar School. He proudly presented Maud with a fluffy doll won at the fairground's shooting gallery. Later, Miller and his parents enjoyed strolling along the promenade eating fish and chips wrapped in an old newspaper. On Sunday morning, Harold drove Miller to Rake Lane Cemetery where he placed red roses on Dorothy's grave.

Monday evening's dinner was a subdued affair. Miller's parents knew that the next day their son had to catch the ten o'clock train from Liverpool to Plymouth. Consequently, the atmosphere was strained and the conversation slightly muted.

'My last ship before I retired was the P and O liner *Reno Del Mar,*' said Harold, doing his best to raise everyone's spirits. 'Most of the stewards and cooks were women and had never been to sea, so the doctor was kept busy dishing out seasick tablets. I'm sure your MO won't have that trouble, eh, my boy?'

'No, thank goodness,' Miller replied, taking a good sip of champagne.

After dinner, Harold suggested a walk along the promenade. 'It's a little overcast, so I suggest you take your Burberry. '

'Good idea, Dad,' Miller replied. 'It'll help Mother's lovely steak and kidney pie to go down.' However, he sensed his father wanted to speak to him alone.

'You two go ahead. I have a few things to do,' Maud replied, giving Miller a kiss on the cheek.

Ten minutes later they left the cottage and walked along the promenade towards New Brighton. Under an old raincoat, Harold wore a Paisley sweater, baggy, brown corduroy trousers and a pair of thick-soled, walking shoes. Miller's service Burberry, worn under his dark-blue blazer, and grey slacks made him feel slightly overdressed. Darkness had fallen, and a warm, balmy breeze blew downriver, caressing their faces. The tide, lapping gently against the sea wall, was in full flood. Lights from ships, the docks and Liverpool's Liver Buildings lit up the skyline. The nerve-jangling rattle of the Figure 8 rollercoaster, and the variety of sounds coming from the fairground, showed that even though it was ten o'clock, people were enjoying all the fun of the fair. Couples, strolling arm in arm, diplomatically ignored an occasional boy and girl sitting on a seat, oblivious to the world, passionately kissing, while high above in an inky-black, cloudless sky, a full moon shone down, turning the river into a carpet of glittering diamonds. After passing the Tivoli Theatre and New Brighton Pier, they sat down on a bench.

'I've never told you this before, but in 1917,' began Harold, sitting back and staring across the river, 'I was first mate on a liner ferrying troops across the Atlantic from America to England.' His voice was subdued, and Miller noticed a faraway look in Harold's eyes as if he were in another place. 'The weather was fine, just like tonight. We were in a large convoy of tankers and cargo ships. Royal Naval frigates and sloops provided protection against U-boats. Suddenly there was a god almighty explosion as a tanker was torpedoed. Seconds later the sky lit up as the tanker erupted into a huge swirling ball of fire.'

For a few seconds he paused. It was clear to Miller that the troubled expression on his father's face showed that he was having difficulty reliving an event he would rather not remember.

'I'll never forget seeing men jumping into a sea into water, their clothes ablaze. Then, all of a sudden, the tanker capsized and sank. There were only a few survivors, including myself and the captain. It was a sight I'll always remember.'

Miller had never heard his father speak so emotionally, and he felt a lump in his throat

'Good lord, Dad, it must have been terrible on those convoys,' Miller replied, placing an arm around Harold's shoulder. 'I'm not surprised you haven't told me before. Now, I suggest we find a pub and have a pint of Threlfalls. And don't worry, if war does break out while I'm away, I'll be safe as houses in the Antarctic.'

They arrived back at the cottage a little after ten thirty.

'I can tell you enjoyed yourselves,' Maud remarked, smelling beer as they entered the lounge. 'It's lucky I've made some coffee.'

For the next ten minutes they sat quietly in the lounge, sipping their coffee.

Finally, Maud, her voice shaking slightly, managed to ask

Miller, 'What time will you be leaving tomorrow, dear?'

'It's a seven-hour journey to Plymouth, and the train leaves Lime Street at nine thirty,' Miller quietly replied, 'so I'd better catch the ferry from New Brighton about eight.'

'I've ironed your shirts, dear, and packed some ham and chicken sandwiches,' Maud replied, doing her best to fight back tears. 'And I'll add a flask of tea in the morning.'

'And I'll give you a call at six,' said Harold. 'That'll give you a chance to have a good breakfast.'

'Right, then,' Miller replied uneasily. 'I'll see you both in the morning.'

After giving Maud a quick kiss on the cheek, he smiled weakly at Harrold then hurried upstairs to his room.

Conversation at breakfast was muted. Miller knew from past experience that saying goodbye to his parents was never easy. After toying with his eggs and bacon, he quickly downed his cup of tea, and avoiding the downcast look in his parents' face, stood up. Other than a freshly laundered white shirt, he wore the same clothes he had worn when he came home.

'Your case and Burberry are in the lobby, son,' Harold said, as he and Maud slowly stood up.

'And I've packed a woolly scarf, dear,' Maud said, doing her best not to cry.

'Right, then,' Miller replied, glancing at his wristwatch. 'I'd better be on my way

Shortly after seven thirty, Harold drove Miller through New Brighton and stopped at the bottom of Victoria Road, opposite the entrance to the pier. Maud had insisted she come along and sat quietly at the back of the car.

Miller climbed out and helped Maud to step onto the pavement.

'It's just after seven thirty, so you've plenty of time. The ferry boat is just coming in,' Harold said, trying to break the tension in the air. 'And it looks like being a lovely day again,' he added, glancing up at the cloudless, blue sky, 'so you won't need your Burberry.'

He opened the boot and took out Miller's suitcase. This was

the worst moment of all. How Miller wished he could just pick up his suitcase and hurry away.

Knowing from personal experience what his son was feeling, Harold said, 'Better give your mother a kiss and be off with you, son.'

'Oh, Bob, dear,' cried Maud, throwing her arms around Miller and kissing him warmly on the cheek. 'Please take care of yourself and remember to write.'

Feeling his throat tighten, Miller simply nodded.

'God be with you and your crew, Bob,' said Harold, as they firmly shook hands. 'And come back to us safe and sound.'

Miller quickly picked up his Burberry and suitcase, joined a small queue of people at the turnstile, then paid his 3p fare. Without looking back, he hurried along the landing stage onto the *Royal Daffodil*. As the ferry pulled away, Miller leant against the wooden guard rail and saw the tiny figures of Maud and Harold, waving. With a heavy heart, he waved back, wondering when, or if, he would see them again.

CHAPTER SEVEN

A little before nine thirty, Miller boarded the Cornish Express and found an empty first-class compartment. Three hours later, after a quick stop at Crewe, the train arrived at Bristol. Rumbling into the West Country, Miller opened his suitcase and enjoyed Maud's coffee and sandwiches, wondering what the future had in store. What would *Endeavour* be like? How would she handle during a rough sea? Then there was the ship's company. As commanding officer, he would be responsible for everyone and everything on board, especially if war broke out. He looked on it as a great challenge, not only to his seamanship, but to his leadership.

After leaving Exeter, the train hugged the beautiful Cornish coastline. Suddenly, away to his left, the panoramic view of the English Channel burst into view. The sea, sparkling under the sun, looked calm and peaceful.

A little after four o'clock, billowing clouds of steam, the train slowly shunted into Plymouth's North Road Station. Miller put on his Burberry and cap, picked up his suitcase and alighted onto the platform. He followed the small crowd down a flight of steps and along a tunnel leading to the concourse. After showing his travel warrant to an inspector, he left the station and hailed one of several taxis parked nearby. A warm, westerly wind attacked his face and sent clouds scudding across an otherwise clear, blue sky.

'Where to, my 'andsome?' asked the driver, poking his grey-haired head outside his window.

'Devonport Barracks, please,' Miller replied, climbing inside the taxi, placing his suitcase on the back seat then climbing in.

'You must be an officer,' said the driver. 'I can tell cos I were in the Andrew meself, and ratings didn't wear civvies.'

'Quite so,' Miller replied curtly, not wishing to pursue the conversation.

The drive down Union Street, with its numerous bars and dance halls, brought back memories of when he was a young midshipman on board a minesweeper. As they drove into Devonport, Miller could see a host of warships ranging from bulky aircraft carriers, majestic battle ships, cruisers and destroyers lying alongside wharfs or anchored in the River Tamar.

'My God,' he muttered to himself, 'there must be half of the home fleet out there.'

Driving along Keyham Road, Miller could see the grey-stone buildings of the Royal Naval Barracks poking over the brisk wall on the left-hand side of the road. The taxi stopped outside the barrack's main gate. The time was four thirty. Miller paid the driver, collected his suitcase and Burberry, opened the door and climbed outside. After showing his paybook to a stern-faced petty officer, he went into the guard room, a small, low-slung building with a large window. Here, Miller was met by a tall, fresh-faced officer.

'Can I help you, sir?' he asked.

Commander Miller, joining *Endeavour*,' Miller replied. 'I believe she's in number two dry dock.'

The term "Andrew" is derived from the name of a press gang officer in Nelson's time.

'One moment, sir,' replied the officer, who turned away and examined a list of ships pinned to a notice board. '*Endeavour* has been moved and is now alongside number five wharf. If you care to wait inside,' he said, indicating a wooden seat at the back of the room, 'I'll get a tilly to take you to her.'

A few minutes later the tilly arrived. The driver, a tall, two-badge matelot, climbed out and slid open the passenger door, allowing Miller to put his suitcase on the seat then sit next to it.

'*Endeavour*, I believe, sir,' said the matelot, starting the engine.

'Yes,' Miller answered. 'Number five wharf.'

'A mate of mine, Leading Signalman Knocker White, is due to join her in a few days. At the moment, most of the ship's company are in Jagos. He told me he volunteered: some sort of special job, so he said.' (Jagos is a nickname for RN Barrack's Devonport.)

'Indeed,' came Miller's noncommittal reply.

They drove down a sloping road, past several large, grey-stone buildings, St Nicholas's Church and a covered drill hall. Further along, Miller noticed four gun emplacements in the middle of a parade ground.

The driver gave a throaty laugh and said, 'A welcoming committee in case Hitler's bombers decide to pay us a visit, sir.'

The wharf was a hive of activity. Lofty cranes were loading stores onto the flight deck of an aircraft carrier. Similar scenes were being carried out on another warship.

'That carrier's the *Courageous*,' said the driver. 'In front of her is the *Hood*. Looks like they're storing ship before sailing. Your ship is tied aft of them.'

Miller was too surprised to speak. The ship he could see looked nothing like what he imagined. Her hull was painted a vivid red which contrasted sharply to her white superstructure and squat-shaped, yellow funnel. The name, *Endeavour*, painted in white, stood out on her on her round stern.

The driver stopped near the foot of a metal gangway situated midway along the upper deck. It was then that Miller saw the ship's pennant number, A17, painted white on the side of her hull. Further along a splayed mast, formed by two sections, rose from either side of the well deck, ending in the crow's nest. A Jacobs' ladder was secured on the starboard side of the upper deck.

'The lads call her *The Red Lady*, remarked the driver, as he applied the brake.

'I'm not surprised,' Miller muttered to himself, as he slid the door open and climbed outside onto the cobbled wharf.

He was now able to take a closer look at the ship that would be his home for the foreseeable future. Thick, hemp ropes stretching from the quarterdeck, mid-ships and fo'c'sle were secured around bollards on the wharf. The square portholes bore evidence of her civilian antecedents.

Further aft came what looked like a large, grey hangar. Miller knew this contained the low-angled, six-inch gun and steel shutters that could be electronically raised and lowered. A covered passageway swept from the port side of her deck to the fo'c'sle.

On either side of her bow a red anchor was secured inside a slightly rusting hawser.

A Jacobs ladder is a portable gangway that can be lowered down the side of the ship.

Two large sea boats were secured on board on davits. A wry smile played around Miller's lips; only the white ensign hanging from a jackstay on the quarterdeck showed she belonged to the Royal Navy.

A section of the ship's wooden gunwales amidships had been removed to allow a metal gangway to be placed on board. Miller looked up and saw a tall, broad-shouldered lieutenant commander standing at the top of the brow. Next to him stood a two-badge petty officer and a leading seaman holding a silver bosun's call. Miller was about to step onto the gangway when a leading steward hurried down to meet him. He looked about twenty-two and was well-built with a pale, fleshy face.

'Allow me to take your suitcase, sir,' he said in a thick, Geordie accent. As he spoke, the corners of his dark-blue eyes broke into a welcoming smile.

'Thank you,' said Miller, handing then suitcase to him. 'And what is your name?'

'Blake, sir,' he replied. 'A few days ago your trunk arrived. It's in your cabin.'

Miller gave Blake a quick nod then followed him up the gangway. As Miller stepped onto the wooden deck, the shrill sound of the bosun's call filled the air.

This was quickly followed by the pipe, 'Attention on the upper deck. Face aft.'

Miller took off his cap and stood to attention while everyone saluted.

The "Carry on," pipe finished, then the tall officer stepped forward, and proffering his hand, said, 'Lieutenant Commander Pollard, sir. First Lieutenant, welcome on board.'

He spoke with a distinct West Country "burr", and in doing so, the corners of his pale-blue eyes set in his lightly tanned, clear-cut features, crinkled into a warm smile. Richard Pollard was twenty-seven, six feet tall and married to Delia, a staff nurse working in

Freedom Fields hospital, Plymouth. After obtaining a first class honours degree in foreign languages at Exeter University, he joined the navy. *Endeavour* was his fourth ship, the others being a minesweeper, a frigate and two destroyers.

'Thank you, Number One,' Miller replied, noting Pollard's firm handshake. 'Please stand everyone at ease.'

'If you follow me, sir, I'll show you to your cabin. It's directly below the bridge on the foredeck, next to the wardroom. All the ship's company have arrived. The cabins and mess decks are fitted with air conditioning units,' he added, as they bent their heads and entered the ship's citadel. 'This is a recent innovation, because most of HM ships have yet to have them,' he said, as they walked up three flights of stairs, along a passageway and stopped outside a cabin marked "Commanding Officer" in gold lettering.

'As you know, Number One,' Miller said to Pollard, 'we sail on Thursday for a two-day trial, then, all being well, we leave Plymouth on Monday.'

'Yes, sir, the officers have been put in the picture, and the harbour engineer will join us and oversee the workup,' Pollard answered.

Miller's cabin was surprisingly big and smelt of Mansion polish. The bulkheads were painted cream, and a blue carpet covered the floor. A strip of neon attached to the deckhead provided a clear, all-round light. A wardrobe rested next to an oak chest of drawers overlooked by one of the ship's ubiquitous, square-shaped portholes. Close by was a well-polished mahogany desk on which rested a leather-rimmed, pink blotting pad. A high-backed wooden chair, complete with cushion, was tucked under the desk. A similar chair lay nearby. Attached to the bulkhead in front of the desk was a telephone and voice pipe. Next to these was a metal plate showing a list of telephone numbers. Close by was a shiny, brass, angle-poised lamp. Above the desk were two shelves containing files, folders and an assortment of official documents, all of which were secured by a wooden crossbar. An open door led into a sleeping area. This consisted of a made-up bunk resting on a well-polished series of cupboards and shelves. Then came a tall mirror and a wardrobe, all of which were firmly screwed into the deck covered with brown linoleum. A side door opened into a small bathroom tiled in white.

'Blake has unpacked your trunk and suitcase and stowed them in the sports store, sir,' said Pollard. 'I hope you can find everything.'

Noticing Blake had placed a framed photograph of Harold and Maud Miller on a corner of his desk, he smiled and replied, 'Thank you, Number One, I'm sure I shall,' then added, 'I'd like to meet all the officers in the wardroom before dinner. Shall we say, six p.m.?'

'Very good, sir,' Pollard replied.

'Incidentally, Number One, I believe you speak Swedish,' Miller said, taking off his cap and hanging it on one of two hooks on the door.

'Yes, sir,' Pollard replied. 'Also German.'

'I'm very impressed,' Miller answered, raising his eyebrows. 'Please carry on.'

No sooner had Pollard left than Miller opened the wardrobe and saw two uniforms, both with the three gold rings on the sleeves. One uniform was made of serge, his everyday working rig. The other one was made of soft doeskin. This would be the uniform he would use for official occasions. He took it out and placed it onto the bunk. He picked up one of the sleeves, and like a lover caressing his sweetheart, he ran his fingers over the slightly rough edges of the three gold rings. He took down his cap from a shelf and gently touched the gold leafing clustered around the rim, silently praying he could prove worthy of such unexpected honours.

After a bath and shave, Miller put on his doeskin then examined himself in the long wardrobe mirror. His new uniform fitted his six-foot-plus frame perfectly. And once again, he felt a sense of pride, staring at the three gold rings on each sleeve.

A sharp knock on the door distracted him.

'Come,' he said, turning away and quickly sitting at his desk.

Leading Steward Blake came in. 'Excuse me,' he said, slightly nervously, 'but I hope I stowed your gear properly.'

'Yes, thank you,' Miller replied, 'especially for putting a new blade in my razor; the old one was a bit blunt. Incidentally, what did you do before you joined up? '

'I was a waiter at the Savoy in London, sir,' Blake quietly replied.

'My favourite hotel,' Miller replied with a smile. 'Now, please carry on. I'm sure you've plenty to do.'

'Will you be taking your dinner here, sir, or in the wardroom?'

'In the wardroom, and thank you,' Miller answered, as he stood up.

'Just press that buzzer on your desk if you need anything, sir — day or night,' Blake replied.

'Right,' Miller said, then with a grin, added, 'I hope I won't trouble you too much.'

Five minutes after Blake left, Lieutenant Commander Pollard knocked and was told to enter.

'Officers are in the wardroom, sir,' Pollard said, 'all accept the doctor. Unfortunately, one of our wireless operators was suddenly taken ill with appendicitis. The doctor has taken him to the naval hospital.'

'Poor chap,' Miller said. 'I expect he'll be away for some time. We'll need a relief for him.'

'I've already been in touch with barracks, sir,' Pollard replied. 'A replacement will be joining us before we sail.'

CHAPTER EIGHT

The first thing Miller noticed as he entered the wardroom was a magnificent, silver candelabrum standing majestically in the middle of a long, highly polished mahogany table; electric lighting from the cream-coloured deckhead made it glitter like a Roman candle. High-backed, padded chairs rested snugly opposite each sitting set out with silver cutlery, Wedgewood plates and long-stemmed Waterford wine glasses. A quick glance around showed bulkheads panelled in oak, on which hung framed photographs of famous warships — past and present. There were no portholes. Punkah louvres from boxed-in shafts lining the bulkhead provided excellent ventilation. The deck was covered with blue carpeting embossed with tiny, silver anchors. At the end of the room, a white-coated steward stood behind a small but well-stocked bar, behind which hung a large, framed, coloured photograph of King George V1 and Queen Elizabeth.

Some officers sat on leather armchairs. Others stood around smoking cigarettes. A slight air of apprehension permeated the air as the conversation centred upon their new commanding officer.

'Before he joined up,' said a tall, fair-haired officer, 'I heard he was a navigating officer with some company supplying stores to the Japanese whaling station in South Georgia.'

'Well, at least he'll be familiar with the southern ocean,' added another officer.

'I wonder if that's anything to do with this being his first command,' pondered a small, round-faced officer, stroking his clean-shaven chin.

'Well, we'll soon find out,' chimed in another officer, carefully stubbing his cigarette out in shiny, brass ashtray.

As Miller entered, each officer stopped whatever they were doing. Those who were sat down immediately stood up.

Miller suddenly felt nervous. Standing in front of him were the faces of officers he would, in the coming months, recognise better than his own.

'Please, gentlemen,' Miller said, 'stand easy, and if you must, do carry on smoking.'

Miller's veiled criticism of smoking was heeded as the officers stubbed out their cigarettes.

As Miller finished speaking, a tall, three-badge PO Steward wearing a short, pristine, white jacket, handed him a cup of coffee. 'Thought you'd like this afore you carried on speaking, sur,' he said in a thick, West Country accent.

'Thank you, PO,' Miller replied, accepting the cup and saucer. 'And what is your name?'

'Feneck, sur,' he answered, giving Miller a toothy grin. 'I've left an urn of coffee, and cups on the bar, in case anyone gets thirsty.'

'Good idea,' said Miller. 'Now I want you to leave the wardroom, then go to your mess and return in an hour. Understood?'

'Yes, sur,' Feneck firmly replied.

'Right, carry on,' Miller said, before taking a sip of his coffee.

As soon as Feneck left the room, Miller looked around and said, 'If anyone wants coffee, do help yourselves.'

Several officers did so then waited anxiously for Miller to speak. Miller finished his coffee and placed his cup and saucer on a nearby table. Placing both hands behind his back, he looked around, and with a stern expression, said, 'What I have to tell you is top secret, and for the time being, must remain within the confines of this room.' He paused for a few seconds, allowing his words to sink in. 'Our mission, code-named "Operation Ice Berg", is to go to South Georgia which is nearly eight thousands miles away, and collect samples of grapholite, a mineral vital for the use in electronics, should war break out. As you know, gentlemen, we leave on Thursday for a two-day workup. Providing all goes well, we sail on Monday for Rio de Janeiro, where we will embark a scientist. We then make for Punta Arenas, after which we sail for Stanley in the Falkland Islands. Here we take on board Mr Duncan

Weir, a civilian who has been to South Georgia and knows where to find this grapholite.' Miller went on to tell them about the six-inch gun. 'Just for protection, you understand. Any questions so far?' he asked, noting the surprised expressions on many of their faces.

A dark-haired officer with bright, pale-blue eyes, raised his hand. 'Err… I have one, sir.'

'Yes, and you are…? Miller tentatively replied.

'Lieutenant Morgan, sir, navigating officer.'

'And your question, Pilot?'

'Charts for the Southern Ocean and the Antarctic, sir,' Morgan replied. 'I don't have any.'

With a wry smile playing around his mouth, Miller calmly answered, 'Don't look so worried. They'll be arriving tomorrow.'

'Lieutenant Rogers, sir — supply officer. So that's why fur-lined coats and gloves arrived yesterday. I believe it can get a bit chilly in that part of the world.' His voice, spoken with slightly posh accent, reminded Miller of a BBC announcer.

'Yes, you could say that,' Miller replied, with a wry smile. 'Between minus nine and fifteen degrees Centigrade. So I hope we've been sent plenty of long johns.'

This remark was greeted with a few outbursts of laughter that immediately reduced the tension that was palpable.

'Where will be taking on fuel on the way home, sir?' asked a tall, red-headed, slightly overweight officer, sipping a coffee. 'Lieutenant Duncan — engineer.' The sharp *burr* in his voice was straight from the Scottish Highlands.

'All being well,' Miller answered cautiously, 'at Punta Arenas.'

Duncan gave Miller a quick searching look, then said, 'Och, how d'yer mean, sir, by "all being well"?

'Because, in my experience, the weather and contrary winds in that area can make berthing difficult,' Miller replied cagily.

'And from what we've heard about you, sir,' MacDonald replied with a wry smile, 'you should know about that.'

Miller didn't reply. Instead he looked at the tall, well-built officer with light-brown hair and intelligent, grey eyes.

'Lieutenant Young, Gunnery Officer, sir,' he said, then added, 'You may like to know that the six-inch shells arrived three days ago and are stowed in the gin hangar.'

'Thank you, Guns, I'm aware of that, but here's hoping we won't have to use them,' Miller replied, with an air of stoicism.

A slightly built officer with deep-set, grey eyes half raised a hand. 'Lieutenant Willis, sir, wireless officer, sir,' he said, smiling. 'As you know, I have lost one of my WO's.'

'Yes,' replied Miller,' 'Number One has told me. A relief should arrive before we sail.'

A thick-set officer with pale-green eyes and weather-beaten features raised a hand. 'Lieutenant Ward, sir, deck officer, sir.' 'How much of this grapholite will we need?'

'Good question,' replied Miller. 'I'm told about a hundred weight.' He shot an inquisitive glance at Pollard and asked, 'Has it arrived?'

'Yes, sir,' Pollard replied. 'It's made of oak, and as instructed in the signal I received, I've stowed it in the hold.'

Next to Ward stood a small, dark-haired young man with penetrating, blue eyes. 'Lieutenant Jenkins, sir, deck officer, sir,' he said in a rich, Yorkshire accent. 'How long do you think we'll be away? You see, I've just received a letter from my wife telling me she's expecting.'

'I'm not sure, Jenkins,' Miller replied, smiling, 'but I don't think it'll take nine months. And by the way, congratulations.'

'Thank you, sir,' Jenkins replied.

A medium-sized officer with a pale, round face and well-groomed fair hair half raised a hand.

'Lieutenant Rogers, sir, supply officer. May I ask where the scientist and this civilian will be accommodated when they are embarked, sir?'

'I'm not sure,' Miller replied. 'Do we have a spare cabin for them, Number One?'

'Yes, sir,' Pollard replied. 'We have one next to yours and one next to mine.'

Two midshipman — one tall and gangly; the other one small and stocky — stood nearby, nervously shuffling their feet.

'And who are you?' Miller asked, noticing the apprehensive expressions on their young, slightly suntanned faces.

'I am Midshipman Grant, sir,' the tall one replied. 'And this is Midshipman Travers.'

'We are both deck officers, sir,' Travers added, brushing back a few strands of ginger hair.

'First ship?' Miller asked.

'No, sir,' Grant quickly replied. 'We got our sea legs serving on minesweepers before joining *Endeavour.*'

'I'm glad to hear it,' Miller answered ominously, 'because, where we're going, you'll need them.'

As Miller finished talking, the door opened and in came a tall, dark-haired officer. His slightly crooked nose set in clear-cut features, was a legacy of playing rugby at university.

'Ah, Doc,' someone shouted, 'you've timed it right. The bar's about to be opened. I hope it's well-stocked.'

The remark evicted a small burst of laughter. Besides being responsible for the medical wellbeing of the crew, the doctor was also the wardroom wine caterer.

Miller turned, and proffering his hand, said, 'Pleased to meet you, Doc, I'm Commander Miller. How's your patient?'

'Surgeon Lieutenant Ryan, sir,' the doctor replied. 'Wireless Operator Green was admitted to the naval hospital at Stonehouse this morning and is now in surgery.'

'Thank you, Doc,' Miller replied, as they shook hands. 'Keep me informed about his progress. Now,' he added, smiling while looking around, 'if there's no more questions, mine's a Horse's Neck.'

CHAPTER NINE

After lunch, Miller addressed the ship's company over the tannoy and told them where the ship was bound and the reasons for doing so, ending with, 'At this time of year, the climate in Stanley can be below zero, so you'll be issued with fur-lined clothing. If you wish to grow a beard, remember to put in a request. That is all.'

In the seaman's mess, Able Seaman Brown turned to his oppo, Able Seaman Lewis, and said, 'Blimey, Joe, if we all grow a beard, we'll look like Father Christmases.'

'Not you, Buster,' Lewis replied, grinning like a Cheshire cat. 'You're so fuckin' ugly, I can't understand how any girl would look at you, let alone marry you and give you two kids'

At two thirty, Miller changed into white overalls, and along with Pollard, did a tour of the ship. They started on the bridge. The first thing that caught his eye was a sturdy, hard-backed chair resting on the raised wooded platform. Without thinking, he ran a finger over the cold, wooden seat, expertly carved to fit a backside. It was here he would, in all kinds of weather, spend many days and nights.

As if reading Miller's thoughts, Pollard said, 'Don't worry, sir, I'll make sure Blake provides you with a comfortable cushion.'

'Thank you, Number One,' Miller replied with a grin. 'But I expect I'll need more than one before we return home.'

He then turned his attention to his surroundings. Six windows, complete with windscreen wipers, proved a clear, all-round view of the fo'c'sle and welldeck, and he noticed three vessels covered in black tarpaulin.

'The big one's the captain's launch. The other two are lifeboats,' said Pollard. 'That small crane you see secured to the deck is used to hydraulically lower them over the side.'

Directly in front of the chair was the conning intercom and

pelorus, an instrument used for taking compass bearings. Facing these was a wide, well-polished dashboard containing sets of dials, intercoms, a voice pipe and the ship's tannoy. Nearby were telephones connecting to the engine and boiler rooms. To his left was the binnacle and telegraph repeater.

'Well, Number One,' Miller remarked, glancing around as they left the bridge, 'it certainly is big enough.'

A flight of stairs led to the wardroom flat and two cabins: one belonging to Miller; the other was empty. Then came the sickbay. On the deck below, a passageway led to the senior ratings mess, Chief Coxswain's office, and the NAFFI shop, its shutters closed until "stand easy". Next came the rum and victualling stores. Making their way aft, they passed the officers cabins, a small mail office of Able Seaman Chalky White, the ships "Posty" and the Pay Office.

A long passageway and a hatchway led into the gun hangar.

The six-inch gun was mounted on a round, steel base in the middle of the deck. The breech was open and the muzzle pointed aft.

'That small lever by the side of the gun sight chair can be used to swivel the gun,' Pollard said.

'What about the recoil?'

'That's controlled by small, steel rockers under the mounting, sir,' Pollard replied.

'Here's hoping we don't have to use it,' Miller replied.

They turned and made their way forward. On the starboard was the seaman's mess. The stokers' mess was opposite. They continued down two decks into the engine and boiler rooms. After a brief word with Lieutenant Duncan, they left. Next to the boiler room was the ship's laundry. This was a small, well-equipped room run by ratings whose complexions suggested they had spent too much time below decks.

'What's your name?' Miller asked the tallest one.

'Able Seaman Cox, sir.' He spoke in a rich, Devonian accent

'And you are?' Miller said, looking at the smaller one.

'Able Seaman O'Hara, sir,' he replied, with a distinct Irish brogue.

'Have either of you had any experience in a laundry before joining up?'

'To be sure, sir,' O'Hara quickly replied. 'I worked in Belfast Steam Laundry afore I joined, sir.'

'And you?' he said, staring at Cox.

'Me mam taught me how to iron and press trousers and to starch me old man's collars, sir,' Cox replied, with more than a hint of pride.

'Well, make sure you don't put too much starch in mine,' Miller replied with a grin. 'Carry on,' and was only too glad to leave the laundry's humid atmosphere.

A narrow, dark stairway led to the hold. Pollard switched on an electric light, revealing a small area cluttered with wooden boxes, tools of varying kinds and an assortment of tinned foodstuffs.

'That oak chest you see lying against the bulkhead next to the stack of hemp rope, sir,' said Pollard, 'is one we're taking to South Georgia to collect the grapholite. As you can see, it's secured with a padlock, and those leather handles on each side should make it easy to carry.'

'And I'm the only one who has the key, Number One?'

'Yes, sir,' Pollard replied. 'It's in the bottom right-hand drawer of your desk.'

Another corridor led them up to the sonar compartment — a small, well-lit, air-conditioned room under the ship's bow. A dark-haired, two-badge leading seaman wearing earphones was sat in front of table. Facing him was a flat-faced, pale-green element in a spherical housing. Underneath was a set of dials and switches. Above this was a bridge control panel and intercom. Upon seeing Miller and Pollard, the operator quickly removed his earphones and stood up, revealing a six-foot, heavily set frame.

'This is Leading Seaman Hardman, sir,' Pollard said, noticing dark smudges under Hardman's pale-blue eyes. 'He is one of the two operators we have on board. The other is Leading Seaman Harris. At sea, they work twelve-hour shifts.'

'Don't you find it a bit claustrophobic down here?' Miller asked Hardman.

'Not really, sir,' Hardman replied. 'You get used to it, like.'

'And what were you doing when we arrived?' Miller enquired.

'I was just seeing if everything was in working order,' Hardman replied.

'And is it?'

'Yes, sir,' Hardman answered confidently.

'Good, carry on,' said Miller, as he and Pollard turned and left.

The tour ended in the bilge with its maze of pipes suspended from a low deckhead. By this time, their once pristine white overalls were streaked with dirt and oil.

'How about finishing with a climb up the mast to the crow's nest sir?' Pollard said jokingly, who, like Miller, was panting like a racehorse.

'No, thank you, Number One,' gasped Miller, wiping beads of sweat from his brow with a handkerchief. 'That's enough exercise for one day. I suggest we return to the wardroom where you can buy me a large Horse's Neck.'

CHAPTER TEN

Shortly after morning "colours" on Monday, 24th July, Commander Miller stood on the quarterdeck of HMS *Endeavour*. Watching sailors busily offloading boxes of stores being carried on board, he felt a tingle of excitement run down his spine. In seven days the crew would set off on a journey that would take them almost halfway around the world and encounter the most inhospitable climate in the world.

'When do think storing will be finished, Number One?' he asked Lieutenant Commander Pollard who was standing next to him.

'The supply officer told me this is the last lot, sir,' Pollard replied.

'Good,' Miller said firmly. 'We've already taken on fuel, so we should be ready to sail for our workup tomorrow.'

'Providing the wardroom's wines and spirits arrive later today,' Pollard replied jokingly.

Activity was prevalent in every department throughout the ship. In the engine and boiler room, Chief Engineer Paddy O'Malley and Chief ERA Jack Jones stood on the shiny, metal plating, checking oil pressure gauges and fuel tanks. At the same time, a group of stokers, sweating profusely, were keeping a wary eye on temperature dials and piston readings.

Paddy O'Malley was over six feet with tired, brown eyes, whose sparse, dark hair was almost hidden by streaks of white. The stokers thought he was weaned on diesel.

By comparison, Jones was small and stocky built with a halo of grey hair, which, along with his round, florid features and rheumy pale-blue eyes, made him look like an elderly monk. Both he and Paddy had served almost twenty-two years and were due for a pension.

Under the eagle eye of portly Chief Cook Sandy Powel, he watched as Leading Cook Tug Wilson and his staff of four cooks prepared a steak dinner for the ship's company. While down below in the stockroom, Stores Petty Officer Bill Holden ensured the large jars of neat rum were safely secured.

Meanwhile, in the wardroom, PO Feneck was putting the finishing touches to the small, silver candelabra, while his stewards, using the best cutlery, were busy laying the table for lunch.

Just before midday, Leading Sick Berth Attendant John Hailey arrived on board carrying a large cardboard box full of medical stores. Hailey was a little under six feet with a fair complexion and deep-set, dark-brown eyes. Before joining the navy he was a staff nurse in Doncaster General Hospital. After his initial training in the Royal Naval Hospital at Haslar and because of his medical background, he was awarded his hook.

The sickbay consisted of two rooms next to each other. One room contained a well-equipped consulting room. A leather examination couch rested snugly against the starboard bulkhead. Above this was a solitary, square porthole. Then came a desk, an old Imperial typewriter, two chairs and a tall medicine chest. In one corner was a stainless steel sink. Above this, a small mirror was screwed into the bulkhead. Close by, resting on a table, lay a stainless steel steriliser. Next to these was a small, well-lit anteroom used for examining glass slides under a microscope, and urine testing. The room next to the sock bay consisted of three bunks lying athwart ships. Two were for patients, and the other one provided a billet for Hailey, as he was on call twenty-four hours a day. A side door led into a bathroom painted in pale-green.

'Looks like Haslar has sent everything you ordered, sir,' Hailey said to Surgeon Lieutenant Ryan, opening the box and placing each item on the top of the examination couch. 'Including the two dozen tubes of that sun cream as well as twelve dozen boxes of condoms.

'I only hope the condoms are used,' replied the doctor, 'because according to recent medical reports, Rio is rife with VD.' Almost as an afterthought, he added, 'Don't forget to make sure all the first-aid boxes, especially the one in the main galley, are well stocked. '

'Already done, sir,' Hailey replied, 'and I've put emergency medical stores, plus instruments, in a wardroom cupboard, in case we have to use it as an emergency OT.'

Knowing the ship would be away from land for long periods, the doctor muttered, 'I'm haven't done my FRCS, so I hope it won't be necessary to use them.'

By midday, storing was completed, "Up Spirits" was piped, and with the exception of the duty watch, all hands went to dinner. On any small ship in the navy, rumours of all kinds abound, especially on one such as *Endeavour* with its tightly knit officers and crew.

'You know, Shady, there's summat odd about this ship,' Able Seaman Brown said to Able Seaman Lane.

They were the seaman's mess. Each rating was standing in line, while Leading Seaman Waters dipped his Bakelite cup into an aluminium "fanny" and poured out the daily issue of rum into each ratings cup, glass tumbler or mug. Unlike the senior ratings, whose rum was issued near, junior ratings was diluted to two of water to one of rum.

'What makes you think that, then?' Lane replied, offering his glass tumbler for Waters to fill it.

'One of the wardroom stewards told me he overheard the captain telling the "Jimmy" (First Lieutenant) to make sure nobody was to go into the hold without his permission,' Waters replied. 'Now, I ask you: who the fuck would want to go down there anyway?'

'Don't ask me,' grinned Lane, watching to make sure Waters hadn't kept his thumb inside the rim of the cup, as he doled out the rum. This trick, if not noticed, ensured there would be some rum (euphemistically called "The Kings") left over for general consumption.

'Apparently it's a bloody great oak chest and it's got a fuckin' big padlock on it, and no bugger knows what it's for or what's in it,' chimed in Able Seaman O'Hanlon. 'I 'eard it from one if the wardroom stewards.'

'And we 'avent taken on board picks and shovels for checkin' the weather,' added Able Seaman Lewis.

'Not to mention a couple of bloody big 'ammers and chisels,' said Able Seaman Thompson. 'Have you 'eard anything, Dutch?'

'Search me,' Dutch replied, casually shrugging his shoulders. 'Maybe we're gunna dig fer hidden treasure.'

In the senior ratings mess, suspicions concerning the box were also rife.

PO Sam Martin sipped his rum and said, 'You know, Len,' he said to Chief G I Len Mills, 'I can't help wondering why we have that bloody chest in the hold. It don't seem to be serving any useful purpose, and the bloody thing's locked and only the captain has the key. Odd, isn't it?'

'Maybe it contains the old man's personal supply of gin,' Mills replied, in a thick Devonian accent.

'I agree with Sam,' said Chief Bosun's Mate Bill Conyon. 'It does seem a bit funny, like.'

CHAPTER ELEVEN

Shortly before four p.m. on Tuesday 25th July, OOD, Lieutenant Ward, Petty Officer Collins and QM Brown stood on the quarterdeck and watched as WO Smith struggled up the gangway. He wore a Burberry, and a hammock was slung over his right shoulder. In his left hand he carried a "pussers" green suitcase. Inside the suitcase, the transmitter and box containing the cyanide capsule were safely stowed under his number two uniform and clothing. While on leave, he had taken the transmitter to the backyard and familiarised himself with the equipment. He unzipped the leather bag and was surprised to see how compact everything was. The earphones were smaller than those he was used to and were tucked neatly into a side pocket, alongside a coiled-up aerial. He noticed that various dials, transmitter keys and switches were florescent. He removed the small aerial and plugged it into a tiny side socket and switched on the transmitter. He plugged in the key pad then tuned in to eighty-five mega cycle wave band. He considered sending a test message to Berlin but quickly changed his mind realising it might be intercepted by the Secret Service in London. Confident he could transmit, even in the dark, he carefully repacked everything and returned indoors.

'Wireless Operator Smith, sir,' he said, stepping over the brow. He dropped his hammock and suitcase on the deck and gave Lieutenant Ward a smart, parade ground salute.

'Welcome on board, Smith. Stand easy,' replied Lieutenant Ward, returning Smith's salute. 'The QM will show you to your mess,' he added, nodding at Brown.

'This way, matey,' Brown said, taking hold of Smith's hammock. 'You're in the seaman's mess, same mess as me.'

Smith picked up his suitcase and followed him. A few minutes later they arrived in the mess and were immediately greeted by

Able Seaman O'Hanlon.

'Don't tell us yer relief 'as arrived, Dinga,' he said, grinning at Leading Wireless Operator Bell, who was sat at the mess table, writing a letter.

'Shit in it, Scouse,' replied Bell, 'and give my opposite number a mug of tea; that's if there's any left in the fanny.' Turning to Smith, Bell held out his hand, and after introducing himself, said, 'You can sling your mick next to mine, and your locker's the one over there. The key's in the lock. When you've stowed your gear, I'll take you to see Lieutenant Willis. He's the wireless officer and our divisional officer.'

'Any idea when we're sailing?' Smith asked Bell.

'Tomorrow, for two days sea trials,' Bell replied, adding, 'Then, hopefully, we'll sail on Monday.'

'Where to?' Smith enquired, accepting a mug of tea from O'Hanlon.

'Rio de Janeiro, Stanley in the Falklands, then South Georgia, wherever that is,' Bell replied, 'to monitor the ice flow and weather.'

'But,' interrupted O'Hanlon, 'we think there's more to it than meets the eye. We've taken on shovels, picks and a bloody great chest, and you don't need them to check the weather.'

As he spoke, the pipe, "Duty watch, fall in on the quarterdeck" came over the tannoy.

Twenty minutes later, Smith and Bell were standing outside Lieutenant Willi's door. Bell knocked and was told to enter.

Lieutenant Willis was sitting at his desk, writing a letter. He looked up as they came in.

'This is Wireless Operator Smith, sir,' Bell said. 'He's just joined us.'

'Welcome on board, Smith,' said Lieutenant Willis, a dark-haired officer with intelligent, grey eyes. He stood up and firmly shook Smith's hand.

'I take it you're familiar with our transmitter?'

'Yes, sir, I am,' Smith replied confidently.

'Good. Have you shown Smith where the wireless office is?' he asked Bell.

'No, sir,' Bell replied.

'Then do so at once. Now carry on,' Wills said dismissively.

The wireless office was three decks below the bridge.

'It's a lot smaller than I imagined,' Smith remarked, glancing at the paucity of space surrounding the swivel chair and mass of dials and switches.

'We do twelve-hour shifts,' Bell replied. 'So there's only one of us on watch at a time.'

'Fine by me,' Smith answered, realising that would give him plenty of time off-duty to go ashore and send messages to Buenos Aires without fear of interruption.

That evening, Smith decided to write home. Except for Leading Seaman Knight and Leading Seaman Waters, who were playing uckers, the mess was empty. Smith opened his locker and stowed his kit away. He found his writing pad and fountain pen, sat down at the end of the table and wrote in English:

"Dear Mother and Father,

As we sail tomorrow, I thought I would write and tell you what has happened so far. We sail this coming Monday. Our first port of call will be Rio d Janeiro. Then onto Stanley in the Falklands, after which we sail for some island called South Georgia, not far from the Antarctic Circle. We have been told that the reason for such a long journey is to monitor the ice low, the winds and weather. However, instead of scientific equipment, we have taken on board shovels and picks, as well as a chest that is kept locked away. This has made myself and the crew suspect that something is not quite as it seems. You may not hear from me for some time, as we will be at sea. But I will write whenever I can.

Your beloved son, Henry."

He placed the letter in an envelope, sealed it, licked on a penny stamp and left the mess.

As he did so, he heard Knight shout, 'They're you are, Pincher, me old gash bucket. You owe me a week's tot!'

'In yer dreams,' Martin replied. 'Now give me a ciggy and let's start again.'

Satisfied that his parents would be relieved to hear from him, Smith found the post box and returned to the mess in time to hear "Stand easy," being piped.

CHAPTER TWELVE

At precisely seven a.m. on Wednesday 26th Lieutenant Commander Pollard knocked sharply on Miller's door and was told to enter.

'Ship ready for sea, sir,' Pollard said, removing his cap, 'and a Mr Jefferson, the dockyard engineer, is on board.'

'What's the weather like?'

'Cloudy, with a cold northerly breeze,' Pollard replied.

Miller was sitting at his desk, sipping a cup of coffee. He looked up and said, 'Thank you, Number One. My compliments to Mr Jefferson. Tell him I'll be up straight away.'

During the night, Miller had difficulty sleeping. He was only too aware that, in the morning, he would take *Endeavour* to sea for the first time. He also knew that all eyes of those on the bridge would be on him. Like Miller, they would be wondering how well he would handle what was, in essence, a civilian ship, so different from a destroyer or a frigate.

'Morning, everyone,' Miler said cheerfully, as he arrived on the bridge. 'And you must be Mr Jefferson, the engineer. Welcome on board,' he added, smiling at a tall man, forty-odd, wearing pristine, white overalls. His round, pale face was heavily lined and grey sideboards peaked from under a black flat cap.

'*Chief* engineer,' Jefferson emphasised, as they shook hands. 'And I'd be glad if someone could take me to see your engineer.' His Cornish accent, spoken with conviction, was sharp and distinct.

'Of course,' 'Miller replied. 'My first lieutenant will show you to the engine room.'

'This way, sir,' Pollard said, indicating a hand.

'Thank you,' Mr Jefferson answered coldly, and followed Pollard as they left the bridge.

'I think we're going to have trouble with that one, Pilot,' Miller remarked to Lieutenant Morgan, realising that, for the next two days, the dockyard engineer would, technically, be in charge of his ship.

'Well, if we do,' Morgan replied with a grin, 'I'm sure Jock and Paddy will deal with him, sir.'

At one p.m., Mr Jefferson came up from the engine room and ordered Miller to increase speed from its fifteen knots to twenty knots. 'Just to test the engines. As I'm sure you know, the ship's manual states that it would be dangerous to the engines if this was increased.'

'Of course,' Miller replied caustically. 'I'm well aware of that.'

'Good,' Jefferson replied pompously. 'Now if you'll excuse me, I'll return to the engine room.'

No sooner had Jefferson left the bridge than Miller contacted O'Malley.

'Before you say anything, Chief, tell the engineer officer that increasing speed was Mr Jefferson's idea.'

By the time twenty knots was reached, the ship's bulkheads were vibrating as she dipped in and out of the choppy sea. On the bridge, Miller and the others felt the deck shake.

Shortly after two p.m., Jefferson contacted Miller. 'Everything seems in order down here, so I'm reducing speed to fifteen knots,' he said. 'So you can return to Plymouth whenever you want.'

'Thank you, Miller. Nice of you to tell me,' he muttered under his breath, while quietly replacing his voice pipe.

At sea the following morning, after "stand easy", Miller decided to increase the speed from fourteen to twenty two knots.

'Is this wise, sir?' asked Pollard. 'You heard yesterday that Jefferson said going over fifteen could be dangerous.'

'Then let's find out,' Miller replied, unhooking the engine room intercom.

Chief O'Malley answered.

'Captain here, Chief. In five minutes, I want you to increase speed to twenty knots. And don't worry, I'll take full responsibility for any damage to your precious engines. Understood?'

'To be sure, I do, sir,' O'Malley replied. 'But Mr Jefferson, the person standing next to me won't like it.'

How right he was.

A few minutes later, Mr Jefferson, his face red with anger, arrived on the bridge, followed by Lieutenant Duncan and Chief O'Malley.

'I insist you reduce speed immediately,' Jefferson shouted, looking daggers at Miller. 'Your engineer officer and I agree that if you don't, the piston rings on the propeller shafts on these Wain Diesel engines could burst.'

'What do you think, Chief?' Miller asked O'Malley.

'Well,' O'Malley replied, pensively stroking his chin, 'the ship's manual is only a guide, and I've been an engineer for twenty years and have worked on these types of engines before, so in my opinion, going slightly over the speed limit should be safe.'

'I don't agree with you, Chief,' Mr Jefferson retorted, glaring angrily at O'Malley.

'If anything happened to the piston rings, how long would it take to repair them? Miller asked Mr Jefferson

'I'd say about a week, as the whole system would have to be stripped,' Jefferson replied.

'Do you agree, Jock?' Miller asked Lieutenant Duncan.

'Aye, but I'm only guessing, mind,' Duncan replied cagily.

'And you, Chief?'

'Hard to say, sir, but a week's probably right,' O'Malley replied.

'Well, gentlemen,' Miller began, 'as you know, time is a very important factor. And having heard your opinions, my decision is to proceed as I ordered.'

Jefferson and Duncan were about to speak, when Miller raised up a hand. 'Gentlemen,' he said gravely. 'If war breaks out and we meet a German warship in the middle of the Southern Ocean, we'll need all the speed we can get. So it's better to break down now where the problem can be safely fixed. Now, please carry on. I'm sure you've got plenty to do.'

As soon as they left the bridge, Miller unhooked the tannoy and told the ship's company what was about to happen. 'Don't be alarmed if you hear the bulkheads creaking and groaning; just hold onto anything you can.'

In the wheelhouse, QM Brown was standing by the telegraph

repeater. He gave Chief Coxswain Moore a worried look and said, 'It's a wonder he didn't tell us to wear life jackets, eh, chief?'

'Pipe down and keep yer eyes peeled on the telegraph,' Moore replied impatiently.

As the ship gained speed, everyone on the bridge felt the deck vibrate, and they held onto whatever they could. In the engine room, all ears listened anxiously for any untoward noises coming from within the pipes, while watching as the speed dial climbed agonisingly towards the red mark signifying danger.

Twenty minutes later Miller contacted the engine room. 'How is everything, Chief?' he asked MacDonald.

'Mr Jefferson looks as pale as a ghost, and as you can probably hear, it sounds as if there's a bloody earthquake,' O'Malley replied, using a piece of cotton waste to mop sweat from his face. 'The marker's almost on the red, so if yer dunna mind me saying so, sir, don't push yer luck.'

'Point taken,' Miller calmly replied. 'Now, kindly tell Mr Jefferson I intend to reduce speed in five minutes. That should bring the colour back in his cheeks,' he added jokingly.

In the engine room, O'Malley gave Mr Fergusson an all-knowing look and said, 'Now then, I told you there was nothing wrong with the pistons.'

Shortly after nine a.m., *Endeavour* entered Plymouth Sound. Half an hour later the ship was secured alongside number four wharf, facing seaward.

Mr Jefferson went onto the bridge to see Miller. 'I'll have to report my warnings to you in my report to the admiralty,' Jefferson said, as he and Miller timidly shook hands.

'Of course, I fully understand,' Miller replied. 'But as you witnessed, the trials went off perfectly,' he added with a wry smile.

CHAPTER THIRTEEN

At precisely seven thirty on Monday, 31st July, the pipe, "Hands fall in for leaving harbour," echoed around the ship. By eight a.m. the last heaving line was hauled on board. Seconds later, the engines came alive; the bubbling noise of the ship's wash quickly followed, allowing the ship to slowly move away from the wharf. High above in a grey sky, a veiled sun hid behind a broad canvas of cirrostratus clouds.

On the bridge, Pollard turned to Miller, and with smile, said, 'Next stop, Rio, eh, sir?' Like the captain and those on duty, he wore a woollen sweater under his duffel coat.

'Yes, and I hope the weather is a damn sight better than here,' Miller answered briefly, as a gust of bitterly cold westerly wind attacked his face.

A few seconds later, PO Signalman Watts came onto the bridge, holding a signal pad. 'Message from C-in-C, sir. It reads: "In Rio, you will embark Professor L. Penlowe. Godspeed and Good Luck."

'Mmm… a professor, no less,' muttered Miller, raising his eyebrows. 'Reply and say, "Thank you, sir; will make him most welcome."

As *Endeavour* approached two destroyers tied up further down the wharf, Miller went out onto the port wing.

He nodded to QM Able Seaman Brown who immediately piped, "Attention on the upper deck. Face then port."

The pipe was accompanied by Miller returning the salutes of the officers on the bridges of the two destroyers.

By 10 a.m., the verdant fields of Cornwall, Drake's Island and the grassy slopes of Plymouth Hoe had faded away as *Endeavour* entered the choppy waters of the English Channel.

'Remember, Number One,' Miller said to Pollard, 'for every

fifteen degrees of longitude west, the clocks must go back an hour. Better put it on the notice board.' Miller paused, and after pensively stroking his chin, went on. 'And when we practise action stations, check to see everyone knows where to go, and ensure lifejackets are worn. If war does break out I want us to be fully prepared for anything.'

Pollard gave Miller a searching look and said, 'Such as, sir?'

'Who knows, Number One,' Miller replied, shrugging his shoulders. 'I've been informed that the German pocket battleship, *Graf Spee,* is somewhere at sea.'

'Heaven forbid we meet her,' Pollard replied, then turned away to study one of several ships coming up and down the busy seaway.

That evening an atmosphere of excitement ran through the ship. Rio de Janeiro was the next stop, then down south into places that nobody on board, except the captain, had visited. Even the hardened senior ratings, many of whom had never served on the South Atlantic Station, couldn't hide their eagerness to visit the exotic sights they had only seen on the cinema or in travel magazines.

'I wonder what the food is like,' said Chief Cook Harry Jacobs to PO Feneck.

'A damn sight better than yours, I bet,' Harry jokingly replied.

'And served by gorgeous dark-haired beauties with big tits,' added Bill Conyon.

'From what I've seen on the pictures, those South American judies are essence,' Able Seaman O'Hanlon said to Able Seaman Williams.

It was just after six p.m. Supper in the seaman's mess was over. Several ratings were playing uckers, reading dog-eared copies of *Nature* and *Lilliput* or writing letters that wouldn't be posted until the ship reached Rio.

'I bet they love it,' Williams replied, before taking a sip of tea from a chipped enamel mug. 'It's the heat: it drives 'em crazy.'

'How the fuck d'you know that?' asked O'Hanlon.

'It was very hot when me and the missus went to Brighton last year,' Williams answered surly. 'That's why we've now got twins.'

'I hear the girls sunbathe naked on the beach,' chimed in Able Seaman White. 'No cozzies, nowt.'

'I wish you lot would shit in it,' cried Able Seaman Night from insides the confines of his hammock. 'I've got the middle, and listening to yous has given me a hard on and I can't sleep.'

'Then 'ava a wank and shut up,' chimed in Able Seaman Lewis.

During the next day, LSBA Hailey organised a first-aid party. This consisted of PO Feneck, Stores Assistant Jack Jones, Cook Greenwood and Cook Murray. Using Neil Robertson stretchers, volunteers were moved around the ship to the sickbay. Under the watchful eyes of Pollard and Chief Bosuns Mate, Bill Conyon, damage control and fire drill exercises were carried out.

At the same time, gunnery drill was practised. This proved vital and was carried out as follows: Chief GI Mills would unlock steel brackets housing the shells. The breech was opened by Able Seaman Jerry Jacobs. Able Seaman Donaldson lifted up a shell, placed it inside the breech and closed it. At the same time Chief GI Mills would press the appropriate button to raise the metal shutter. On the gun direction platform, Lieutenant Young was able to determine the range and fall of shot. He would telephone this to Chief G I Len Mills, who would then pass the information to gunlayer, Leading Seaman Morris, sitting on a metal stool, his eyes clamped against a round, spidery gunsight. Lieutenant Young's order to fire was telephoned to Chie Mill. The order was given to Morris who squeezed the curved trigger situated by the side of the gunsight. Able Seaman Donaldson, using asbestos gloves, would open the breech. The shell casing would then be ejected, and if necessary, another shell inserted. Jacobs then closed the breech. If a degree alteration was required, the process would be repeated.

'Not quick enough, chief,' Lieutenant Young reported by telephone to Mills. 'It took over four minutes between loading and firing the gun. And remind the guns crew that we only have six shells.'

'Aye, aye sir,' Mills replied, glaring disapprovingly at the gun's crew. 'I don't know what they taught 'em at Whale Island, but if this 'ad been Jutland, the Boche would 'ave blown us out of the water afore we got our first salvo away.'

'Practise twice a day until things improve,' snapped Lieutenant Young. 'And I suggest a shell is kept in the breech. It'll save time in case we have to move quickly.'

Mills gave Young a searching look, then said, 'You sound as if yer expecting trouble, sur.'

'Well, you never know, Chief,' Young replied warily. 'If war does break out, we'll have to be on our toes.'

'Proper job, to sur,' Mills replied with a grin.

'What good will a paltry six-inch shell do if we meet a Jerry battleship, Chief? Day asked Able Seaman Jacobs. 'They have twelve and fourteen inch guns.'

Mills placed both hands on his hips and gave a loud laugh. 'Stop worryin' my 'andsome. If that 'appens, you'll no nowt about it. Now go and get me a mug of tea.'

Meanwhile, on the bridge, Miller was in deep conversation with Pollard.

'Action stations was a shambles, Number One,' Miller said, shaking his head. 'Each section was slow reporting that they were closed up, and I saw two ratings on the well deck without life jackets. It simply has to improve. I want it practised every day without warning. That should keep them on their toes,' he added with a sly grin.

'Very good, sir,' Pollard replied. 'And as we'll be at sea for long periods, may I suggest inter-mess quizzes, and fishing.'

'Splendid idea,' Miller replied, momentarily regretting he hadn't thought of it. 'And don't forget to put regular bulletins from the BBC Overseas Service on the notice board. I'm sure they'll be anxious to hear about the situation in Europe.'

'I agree, sir,' Pollard replied. 'According to the latest report, Nazi troops have occupied part of Danzig.'

'Yes, I heard it,' said Miller, furrowing his brow. 'It doesn't look good. As you know, we have promised to safeguard Poland against invasion.'

After leaving Lands' End, the ship was immediately hit by the heavy rollers of the Atlantic Ocean. Low-lying cumulonimbus hid a pallid sun. As the ship dipped precariously in and out of the sea, sheets of rain began battering against the thick glass bridge windows.

'Port ten, Number One,' Miller ordered, sitting on his chair, listening to the sound of the rubber wipers squelching to and fro. He glanced forlornly at Pollard and said, 'Better pipe — all hands keep clear of the upper deck.'

Pollard, grasping hold of the binnacle, grinned at Miller and said, 'At least this weather will help the crew to find their sea legs, sir.'

'Just as well,' Miller replied, clutching the sides of his chair, 'as it'll get a damn site rougher when we reach Cape Horn.'

By the morning of Tuesday August 1st, *Endeavour* entered the deep waters off the north-west coast of Africa, some three hundred miles beyond the Canary Islands. Much to the relief of the ship's company, the weather had changed overnight and tropical whites became the rig of the day. The sea was calm and the sky an eye-smarting blue. The next day, balmy trade winds, together with rays from the early morning sun, bathed everything in gentle warmth.

'You know, PO,' Able Seaman Brown said to Able Seaman Watson, 'toffs would pay a lot to go on a trip like this.'

Brown and Watson were among several ratings stretched on towels on the quarterdeck. All of them were stripped to the waist, soaking up the balmy rays of the afternoon sun.

'Aye, but I bet they have to pay through their noses for it,' Watson replied. 'And get the best-looking girls.'

'Which reminds me,' Brown went on, 'the doc says Frenchies will be available in the sickbay.

Throughout the next four days, the north-east trade winds caressed the faces of those men working on the upper deck.

Endeavour crossed the Tropic of Cancer and continued on a south-westerly course.

Shortly after one p.m. on Tuesday, 8th August, Miller was on the bridge, sitting on his chair, flipping through the signal log.

Pollard turned to him and said, 'Excuse me, sir, but I thought I'd remind you that in two days, we cross the equator.'

'Thank you, Number One,' Miller replied, closing the log and smiling. 'But I was well aware of that, because two days later we arrive in Rio. Furthermore,' he added, 'the Pay Bob tells me the currency in Brazil is the real, and the exchange rate is ten reals to the pound. Better put that on Dailey Orders. And as we'll be in Rio for two days, I intend to give the crew shore leave. And put on the main notice board, "Crossing the Equator Ceremony will take place on the well deck on Thursday." That'll give Chief Bosun and Chief GI plenty of time to get prepared. I believe it'll be the first time you've crossed the equator, Number One?'

'Yes, sir,' Pollard replied.

Miller threw back his head and laughed, then said, 'Just wait till King Neptune and his press gang gets their hands on you, old boy.'

Throughout the next day, Chief Bosun's mate, Bill Conyon, and CGI Len Mills, along with a work party, prepared everything on the well deck for the ceremony. A large, red, rubber dinghy was filled with sea water. A solid-oak, high-backed chair, borrowed from the wardroom, rested close to a wooden plank leading into the dinghy.

At one forty-five on Thursday, 10th, six, heavy-set ratings mustered on the well deck. Each one wore black eye patches, courtesy of LSBA Hailey, and an assortment of colourful, piratical bandanas. With their faces streaked with black boot polish, and wooden truncheons tucked menacingly into the waists of baggy football shorts, they looked as if they were off to a fancy dress party. Two ratings, one of which held a wooden "razor," arrived carrying a large aluminium "fanny" full of soapy water.

Behind them came Chief Bosun's mate, Bill Conyon. He wore a tatty, string white vest and oversize, blue bathing trunks. In one hand he carried a six-foot wooden trident painted silver. On his mop of thick, grey hair, rested a crown made of wire wool. Beaming like a Cheshire cat, he eased himself onto his "throne". With his bulging stomach and false white beard, he looked the epitome of King Neptune.

Next to him stood his lieutenant, CGI Mills. His six-foot-plus frame was stripped to the waist. He wore a red towel around his ample waist with a pair of smiling mermaids tattooed either side of his hairy chest, obtained years ago in Hong Kong.

With a wide grin, Mills looked up at the bridge and gave a thumbs up to Miller.

A minute later, Miller's distinctive voice came over the tannoy. "D'yer hear there? This is the captain speaking. All landlubbers who haven't visited King Neptune are to report to the well deck. Refusal to do so will be met with the full force of the press gang."

In the seamen's mess, Able Seaman Peter Cronin was about to climb into to his hammock. He had shared the morning watch with Able Seaman Lane and had a "make and mend." 'If they come for me,' he said, 'tell 'em I'm sick.'

As he finished speaking, the mess door opened and in came PO Thompson. He wore a pair of oversize, red football shorts and brown sandals. His face and upper body were daubed with black shoe polish. Behind him came four of Neptune's henchmen, similarly dressed.

'Arrh, my 'andsomes,' Thompson said in a mock West Country accent. 'I hears there's a young lad who hasn't visited King Neptune.'

'You can all fuck off,' yelled Cronin. 'I've been on watch all morning, and I'm gunna get me 'ead down.'

Wearing a sly grin, Thompson said, 'You don't say.' Then, glancing behind, cried, 'Grab 'im, me hearties!'

Seconds later, struggling and yelling every obscenity he knew, South was dragged out of the mess, along the corridor and through a hatchway onto a well deck, overlooked by many of the ship's company.

'Ah,' growled King Neptune, 'another shirker, eh? Anything to say fer yerself afore I pass sentence?'

'Get stuffed,' yelled Cronin, doing his best to wriggle free from his captors.

'Tick him off the list, Scribes,' King Neptune said to Leading Writer Jenkins. 'And send him to Davy Jones's locker.'

He gave Len Mills a thumbs down. After a quick splash of foam around Cronin's face, he was shaved and tipped into the water.

Others, including LSBA Hailey whose cries of, "But I can't

swim and I'm an only child", were ignored by the press gang. A few minutes later, Smith was dragged from the wireless office and met a similar fate.

With the exception of Surgeon Lieutenant Ryan, and Midshipman Grant who was on duty, the rest of the officers had 'crossed the line' in previous warships. Ryan feigned pressure of work and beat a hasty retreat to his cabin. LSBA Hailey accepted his fate with good humour. The loudest cheer of the afternoon was reserved for Lieutenant Commander Pollard. Pleading mock innocence, he was escorted by Mills and his cohorts to the quarterdeck. With King Neptune grinning mischievously, Pollard was shaved and received an early bath. Later, everyone who had met King Neptune, would be given a "Crossing the Line" certificate.

CHAPTER FOURTEEN

Shortly after seven a.m. on Saturday, 12th August, Able Seaman Lewis, in the crow's nest, lowered his binoculars and cried, 'Land! Land roughly twenty ten miles off the starboard bow.'

Straight away, Miller and everyone on the bridge turned, and using their binoculars, focussed on a dark, thin line stretching on the horizon away to their right.

'What's our position, Pilot?' Miller said, without lowering his binoculars.

'Latitude — twenty-two degrees west; longitude — thirty degrees, sir,' Lieutenant Morgan replied confidently, 'which puts us off the coast of Rio de Janeiro.'

'Alter course ten degree to starboard. Steer green one three zero,' snapped Miller.

Below in the wheelhouse, Chief Coxswain Moore repeated the order.

Seconds later the ship heeled slightly to the right.

'What a lovely day for a visit to Rio,' Pollard remarked, shielding his eyes from the glare of the sun. In a whispery voice, he added, '"The clouds were pure and white as flocks of newly shorn."'

'Wordsworth?' Miller asked, lowering his binoculars and giving Pollard an inquisitive glance.

'No, sir,' Pollard quietly replied. 'Keats.'

'My goodness!' Miller exclaimed, raising a hand in mock benediction. 'Is there no end to this man's talents?'

'I'm sure you'll be interested to know, sir,' Morgan remarked. 'During the night we sailed through the Doldrums, and the barometer has risen from fifty-five degrees to sixty-six degrees Fahrenheit.'

'I'm not surprised,' Miller replied, using a handkerchief to wipe away perspiration from his face. 'Thank goodness for the air conditioning.'

By eleven a.m., Rio de Janeiro, surrounded by several rocky islands, could be seen tucked neatly around a wide, horseshoe-shaped harbour. Silhouetted against the stark, blue sky, a range of jagged, black mountains rose like giant sentinels behind the city. The roofs of terracotta houses, glistening in the morning sunlight, lay in tiers behind the rows of multi-coloured hotels and buildings that stretched alongside a wide white ribbon of beach. Away to the north, perched on the summit of the massive Corcovado — "Hunchback" in Portuguese — Mountain, stood the majestic figure of Christ the Redeemer. Both his hands were outstretched, blessing everything and everyone below. Looking incongruously out of place amongst such picturesque settings, the dark, cone shape of Sugar Loaf Mountain, lying on the northern end of a peninsula, rose majestically in the air.

'Wow!' exclaimed Jumper Collins, the starboard lookout. 'That must be the Copacabana beach. It looks just like in that film, *Flying Down to Rio* with Ginger Rogers and Fred Astaire. I saw it with my missus before we sailed.'

'Looks like a great run ashore,' added QM Brown, grinning mischievously.

Ignoring their remarks, Lieutenant Morgan said to Miller, 'According to my chart, sir, we are approaching Guanabara Bay.'

'So I see, Pilot,' Miller replied, noticing several liners and merchant ships tied up alongside wharfs and jetties. 'Send a signal to the harbour master. Say: "Request medical clearance and berthing instructions."'

A few minutes later, WO Smith arrived on the bridge holding a signal. 'Message from the harbour master, sir. It reads: "Welcome to Rio de Janeiro. pilot will come on board twelve p.m. and direct you to number six wharf, southern end of the harbour. Professor Penlove will come on board. Medical officer will accompany to issue Pratique. (Pratique is a certificate stating the ship is free from disease.)

'Better inform the MO to expect a visitor,' Miller said to Pollard. 'And tell Blake to make sure the spare cabin is ready.'

'Very good, sir,' Pollard replied, and left the bridge.

'Wonderful, sir!' exclaimed Lieutenant Morgan. 'According to my chart, number six wharf is about a hundred yards at the northern end of the Copacabana beach, within easy reach of the city.'

'That'll please the crew,' Miller answered, then glancing at Smith, added, 'Reply: "Thank you, a pleasure to be here."' He then unhooked the wheelhouse intercom. 'Slow ahead. Steady as she goes.'

'Aye, aye, sir,' Moore replied. 'Steady as she goes, sir.'

Minutes later, WO Smith came onto the bridge holding a signal pad. 'Message from British Ambassador, sir. "To Commanding Officer, HMS *Endeavour*, from British Ambassador. Please come to dinner, seven p.m. Dress informal. Transport will meet. Sir Geoffrey Knox."'

'Reply, "Many thanks. Look forward to meeting you."'

By eleven thirty, *Endeavour* was roughly two miles away from the harbour entrance.

'Looks like a motorboat approaching from starboard, sir,' Pollard reported.

'Thank you, Number One. Stop engines, then lower the Jacobs ladder starboard side.

Twenty minutes later, Miller left the bridge, and along with Surgeon Lieutenant Ryan, waited as a sailor hooked the motorboat onto the base of the Jacob's ladder.

"Attention on the upper deck; face the starboard," echoed over the tannoy.

'I say, sir,' Pollard said to Miller. 'I wonder who that gorgeous woman in the blue dress and ridiculous white hat is.'

'Heaven only knows, Number One,' Miller replied, watching as one of the motorboat's crew grasped her hand as she carefully stepped onto the wooden grating. 'But I do believe she's coming on board.'

Holding onto a black shoulder bag, she looked up at Miller, and smiling, took a firm grip of the rope guard rail with her right hand and began to carefully walk up the Jacob's ladder. Behind her came the pilot, a small, swarthy man wearing white gloves and dressed in a dark-blue uniform. He was followed by a tall, dark-skinned man wearing a single-breasted, grey, pin-striped suit, white shirt, maroon tie, and he carried a brown, leather briefcase.

Miller guessed the woman to be in her mid-thirties. She was about five feet six and wore smart, flat-soled, dark-blue shoes. Strands of auburn hair hung loosely from under a white, wide-brimmed hat. As she stepped on board, a gust of wind blew against her dress, showing the outline of her legs and well-endowed figure. All eyes became transfixed.

'A woman on board is bad luck,' muttered a rating standing to attention.

'I don't fuckin' care,' drooled a rating next him, 'as long as she does a turn.'

'Pipe down, there,' snarled Chief Gunnery Instructor Len Mills, 'or I'll 'ave yer guts fer garters.'

Stepping onto the open section on the starboard guard rail, the woman proffered her hand to Miller, and flashing a set of even white teeth, said, 'Professor Linda Penlowe. Would you be kind enough to ask one of your men to fetch my case?' Her accent, spoken in a mellifluent, West Country accent, was pleasantly clear.

'Of course,' Miller replied, noticing how beautiful her emerald-green eyes were. 'Do as the professor asks,' he said to QM Brown, who, with a surprised look on his face, hurried down the gangway.

After hauling out a large, black, leather suitcase from the motorboat's stern, he carried it up and placed it on the deck near the professor.

'Thank you,' said the professor, giving Brown a grateful smile. 'That was very good of you.'

'A pleasure, miss,' Brown replied, blushing slightly.

Miller gave a nervous cough and shook her hand which was surprisingly soft. Part of her pear-shaped, heavily tanned face and slightly upturned nose were barely visible under the shade of her hat.

'Forgive me for staring, professor,' Miller replied, 'but I was expecting...'

'A man, perhaps?' she said, raising her eyebrows.

'Err... yes,' said Miller, feeling somewhat embarrassed.

'No problem,' replied the professor, removing her hat and shaking down a mass of shoulder-length, fair hair. 'Being a woman,' she added, noticing how strikingly handsome Miller's sunburned features looked, 'in what is essentially a man's world, has never bothered me. And from what I have seen during my brief stay in Rio, women are employed in all kinds of work. Is that not so, gentlemen?' she remarked, turning around and addressing the two men standing behind her.

'This is true, Professor, especially if they speak English, which is good for the tourist trade,' said the man in the blue uniform. 'I, myself, speak good English. I am Jose Luciano, the harbour pilot, and this gentleman is Doctor Cavilio, the port medical officer. It has been a long time since we were honoured by a visit by one of His Majesty's ships.'

'It is an honour to be here. Welcome on board, gentlemen,' Miller replied.

The pilot delicately moved his gloves and shook Miller's hand.

'This is Lieutenant Commander Pollard, my second-in-command.'

'And I am Surgeon Lieutenant Ryan, the ship's doctor.'

After they shook hands, Miller looked at Pollard and said, 'Show the professor to her cabin and have Brown carry her luggage. And Doc,' he added, glancing at Ryan, 'take Doctor Cavilio to the sickbay, while Number One and myself take the pilot to the bridge.'

'Very good, sir,' Pollard replied. 'This way, miss,' he indicated with a hand, 'and be careful not to bang your head as we go through the hatchway.'

As she turned to leave, she flashed a warm smile at Miller and said, 'Thank you, captain; I'm sure we'll get along nicely,' then followed Pollard.

'The ship's medical records are in the sickbay, sir,' Ryan said to Doctor Cavilio. 'Please follow me.'

'*Obrigado, Senhor,*' Cavilio replied, taking out a bright-pink handkerchief and wiping lines of sweat from his round, fleshy face. 'My Ingleesh, it ees not so good, but I understand and can read,' he added, giving Ryan a tobacco-stained, toothy grin.

Ryan led them down a flight of stairs along a passageway to the sickbay. As he opened the door, LSBA Hailey, looking slightly nervous, stood up from behind the desk on which rested an open ledger.

'This is my assistant,' Ryan said to Cavilio.

'*Obrigado, Senhor,*' said Cavilio, as he shook Hailey's hand.

'He has a list of all the ship's company's medical history. I take it you have them ready, Hailey?'

'Yes, sir,' Hailey replied, picking up the ledger. 'It contains up-to-date lists of the ship's company's medical history. As you can see, sir, it's all in order and has been signed by the captain.'

'*Umbrigado*,' Cavilio replied, placing his briefcase on the desk. He accepted the ledger and began running a podgy finger down each list. As he did so, he glanced up and looked inquisitively at Ryan, then said, 'My wife, she likes your Ingeeglish gin. I am told you have theese on board, yes?'

You crafty bastard, Ryan thought. '*No gin, no pratique.*' He gave Cavilio an understanding look and replied, 'Indeed we do. I'm sure something can be arranged before we dock.'

'*Obrigado, Senhor,*' Cavilio replied, and unclipping his briefcase, he handed Ryan a small, white paper. 'And 'ere eese pratique,' he said, giving Ryan another of his tobacco-stained smiles.

'And now,' Ryan replied, 'I suggest we adjourn to the wardroom, as I expect you'll need a large gin, as we'll be getting under way soon.'

From the bridge, Jose Luciano navigated the ship safely into the harbour. Twenty minutes later, *Endeavour* was tied up alongside a wharf close to a busy dockyard. Special sea duty men had been dismissed and a metal gangway lowered in place. Miller and Ryan stood on the brow next to Cavilio, whose briefcase now displayed a large bulge. Miller thanked both officials and shook their hands.

When Ryan returned to the sickbay, Hailey gave Ryan a searching look and asked, 'What would you have done, sir, if he had refused to grant us pratique?'

'Simple, really,' Ryan replied. 'I'd have offered him two bottles of gin instead of one.'

CHAPTER FIFTEEN

'Would you believe it, Number One!' Miller exclaimed. He had just finished reading a signal WO Smith had given him. 'It's from the port harbour master. There's been a cock-up, and our mail has been forwarded to Stanley.'

Miller and Pollard were standing on the quarterdeck. The time was eleven thirty. "Up spirits. Cooks to the galley" had just been piped.

'That won't go down well with the crew,' Pollard replied. 'It's been over a week since we left Plymouth, and naturally, we're all anxious to hear from home.'

'Yes, indeed,' Miller replied. 'Perhaps you'd announce it, and details of leave. Meanwhile, I think I'll go and see if the professor is settling in.'

With a mischievous smile playing around his lips, Pollard replied, 'Lucky you, sir, but what *exactly* is she here for? I must admit, she *is* rather good-looking, but if she walks around the ship in that dress she wore coming on board, she'll cause a mutiny.'

'I've been told she's here to work with Mr Weir,' Miller replied.

'Then may I suggest you watch out for her eyes,' Pollard replied, with an impish grin. 'They're as green as ivy, and I suspect, just as dangerous.'

'Be careful, Number One,' Miller said reproachfully, 'or you'll end up a first lieutenant of a Thames barge.'

'Point taken, sir,' Pollard replied, 'but what about shore leave for the ship's company, sir?'

'The usual routine. And remember,' Miller went in, 'VD is prevalent in Rio, so ask the doctor to make sure condoms are available. After all, we don't want to leave Rio with half the crew suffering from gonorrhoea.'

'Or worse,' Pollard replied warily. 'Incidentally, sir, Rio de Janeiro means "River of January", as it was discovered by Portuguese sailors on January 1st, 1502.'

'Yet again, a hive of information, Number One,' Miller replied, grinning before leaving through an open hatchway into the citadel.

He made his way up three sets of stairs leading to the wardroom flat. For a few seconds, he stood outside the professor's cabin. After nervously clearing his throat, he knocked and was told to enter. The professor was standing near her bunk, unpacking her suitcase. She had removed her hat, allowing her shoulder-length, auburn hair to tumble freely.

'Sorry to interrupt you, Professor,' said Miller, noticing the distinct but appealing smell of perfume hovering in the air, 'but I thought I'd see if everything is all right.'

'Bathroom on-suite and plenty of room, thank you, captain,' she replied, folding a thick, yellow sweater and placing it among several other items of clothing. 'And Blake has been more than helpful.'

'Good,' Miller replied firmly. 'Incidentally,' he added, somewhat hesitatingly, 'what were you doing before you came here? And I take it that you know the purpose of the mission?'

The professor stopped what she was doing and looked at Miller. 'Two months ago, I was seconded from Cambridge University to San Paulo University to take part in an expedition to see if iron ore could be found in the Sierra du Mar mountains. Three days ago, I received an urgent message from the dean, asking me to fly immediately to Rio and report to Sir Geoffrey Knox-Johnson, the British ambassador.' She paused momentarily, and using a hand, brushed back a few strands of hair from her eyes. 'I did as requested, and for the past two days I've been staying with the ambassador, who told me why I was here and impressed upon me the importance of the mission. Very exciting stuff, eh, Commander?'

'I suppose that's one way of putting it,' Miller replied sanguinely.

'There, now,' said the professor, placing her hands on her hips and staring at Miller.

By God, Miller thought. Pollard was right; those eyes could, under certain circumstances, reduce a man to rubble.

'I hope that satisfies you. If so, I'd like to finish unpacking.'

'Yes, of course, and thank you,' Miller replied. 'However, I was told there are three grades of grapholite: alpha, beta and gamma, and alpha was the one we're after.'

'Yes, that's correct,' said the professor, picking up a pair of red, silk pyjamas. 'And the only way to differentiate between them is by doing a special test. And that is what I'm here to do. After that, I shall leave the ship when we stop at Rio on the return journey from South Georgia.'

'I see,' Miller replied, pursing his lips. And is the test complicated?'

'Not really,' the professor replied, placing the pyjamas neatly on top of the set of black, lacy underwear. 'I place a drop of a special chemical onto each specimen. Grade A, the type you are looking for should turn bright green, as opposed to B and C, who don't change colour.

'I see, Professor,' Miller answered warily. 'Your test ensures that we collect the correct grapholite.'

'*Exactly,* Captain,' the professor replied, impatiently.

'Thank you, Professor,' Miller said. 'I must say, I'm very impressed. Without your expertise, the mission could fail.'

'Oh, I'm sure your government would have found another mineralogist equally capable,' she replied, with a weak smile.

'You are far too modest,' Miller said. 'Now, the time is four p.m.,' he added, glancing at his wristwatch. 'Dinner in the wardroom is at seven thirty. I'm sorry to say I won't be joining you, as I have an appointment with the British ambassador, but I'm sure my first lieutenant will look after you. By the way,' he added, 'dress for dinner is informal.'

'I'm glad it is, although I have brought a few things with me for special occasions,' she replied.

'Forgive me for mentioning it,' Miller said, 'but as you'll be using ladders and stairs to get around the ship, may I suggest you wear something appropriate.'

'You mean something like this,' she replied, lifting out a set of dark-brown, zip-up overalls. She noticed how handsome he looked, especially when embarrassed.

'Ahem,' he replied, feeling his face redden. 'They'll be most appropriate.'

'You see, Captain,' she said, smiling coyly,' I have been on ships before, and I'm aware that sailors have, shall we say, "roving eyes". And as we're discussing formalities,' she added, placing the overalls on her bunk, 'I suggest you stop calling me 'Professor'. As I told you when we were introduced, my name is Linda. Now, can I finish unpacking?'

The nervousness Miller had felt, suddenly left him. 'Of course,' he answered. 'And I'll pass your request to the officers,' he added, with a shy grin.

As Miller left the professor's cabin, Pollard's voice came over the tannoy. 'First lieutenant speaking. I regret to tell you that our mail has been sent to Stanley in error. Leave in Rio is as follows, to all except those on duty: five p.m. till six a.m. then twelve p.m. till six a.m. Rig of the day, number seven. White bellbottoms, white front and shoes and round cap for matelots. White shirt, trousers, peak cap and shoes for other ranks.'

'Just my fuckin' luck, Smithy,' LWO Bell moaned. Bell and several other ratings were in the seaman's mess, sipping mugs of tea and enjoying one of the chefs' sticky buns. 'No mail from me missus, and I'll be on duty while you'll be shaggin' yer lugs off.'

'Never Mind, Dinga,' said Smith. 'I'll stand in for you and go ashore tomorrow, as it'll be almost dark when you leave the ship, and I want to go and see what the view is like from that statue of Christ.'

'Fuck me,' Able Seaman O'Hanlon yelled. 'All that talent ashore, and he wants to climb up a friggin' mountain and look at the view. He must be either queer or off his rocker.'

'Fine by me, oppo,' Dinga replied, giving Smith a friendly nudge in the ribs. 'I'll think of you when I'm fuckin' my brains off.'

Ignoring Bell's spurious remark, Smith was too preoccupied with wondering how he could send a message to Canaris, informing him of the ship's movements, as it was too dangerous to transmit on board, and small though his transmitter was, it was too bulky to hide in his uniform. With an air of frustration, he realised he would have to wait until they reached Stanley. By that time the weather would be cold, and he would be able to conceal his transmitter under his thick clothing.

Shortly after seven p.m., the wardroom door opened and Professor Penlove entered. Those officers who were sitting in chairs immediately rose to their feet. The rest stood in silence. Word, that a woman was on board, had reached them, and they expected to see some stout, straight-faced, grey-haired academic. Instead, they were confronted by a very attractive woman with shoulder-length fair hair, wearing a knee-length, pleated, black skirt. The small, silver Saint Christopher hanging between her open-necked white blouse set against the paleness of her neck, gave the onlookers the impression of someone, who, despite being aware of her femininity, was also at ease in her new surroundings.

'Good evening, gentlemen,' she said, smiling warmly. 'My name is Professor Penlowe, but in case your captain hasn't already asked you to do so, please call me Linda. I'm a mineralogist, and I'm here to help you as much as possible.'

Her agreeable attitude and engaging smile immediately put everyone at ease. Therefore, over dinner, the atmosphere became relaxed, talkative and informal.

As Miller was absent, Linda sat next to Pollard at the head of a long mahogany table.

Lieutenant Morgan, sitting opposite her, looked across, and blushing slightly, asked, 'May I ask what made you become a mineralogist, Linda?'

'Well, you see,' she replied, after taking a sip of port, 'I was born and bred in Porthleven. That's a small fishing village on the southern coast of Cornwall.' As she spoke, everyone stopped talking and listened intently. 'From an early age, I would explore the rocky coast and collect shells and stones. One of the rocks I found had the imprint of a fish. I showed it to my teacher, who, to my amazement, told me it was over a thousand years old. From then my interest in rocks increased, and later I studied minerology at Exeter University. Much later, I did my PhD at Cambridge, and,' she added, with a disarming smile, 'here I am.'

'I see you're not married,' Lieutenant Morgan remarked, noticing she wasn't wearing a wedding ring.

'I was once,' she quietly replied, 'but,' she went on, avoiding Morgan's eye, 'not any more.'

'Then there's hope for all of us,' Morgan jokingly remarked.

'You never know,' Linda replied, smiling. 'Now, would someone replenish my glass. Your red wine is excellent.'

After wishing everyone goodnight, Linda excused herself, and as Pollard escorted Linda to her cabin, Engineer Officer Duncan looked around at his fellow officers and said, 'Och, now, that's what I call a bonnie lassie.'

'I agree, Jock,' said Lieutenant Rogers, somewhat salaciously, 'and I bet the captain thinks so also.'

CHAPTER SIXTEEN

Next morning, Smith sat eating his breakfast, listening to his mess mates relating licentious stories about their run ashore.

'Everywhere we went, every bar was full of girls,' said Able Seaman Brown, chewing a piece of bacon. 'We couldn't go wrong. Isn't that right, Joe?'

'Too fuckin' true, oppo,' replied Able Seaman Lewis. 'One of them gave me the best bunk-up I ever had.'

'As long as that's all she gave you,' added Shady Lane, slurping his tea. 'I hope you used a jonnie.'

'Rubbish,' Lewis replied. 'Using them is like washing yer feet with yer socks on.'

'I saw you in a bar, and you disappeared with a gorgeous party with big tits,' said Lane, 'and I bet you forgot to use one.'

'I did use one, but the fuckin' thing burst,' Lewis replied.

'No wonder you looks knackered,' chimed in Able Seaman Collins. 'He didn't get back on board until after five this morning.'

'You mean, just before you,' Able Seaman Lane said, with a lecherous grin.

'Fuck off,' replied Collins, flicking a piece of soggy bread at Lane.

'I expect you'll be going ashore this afternoon, eh, Smudge?' asked Bell.

'Yes,' Smith replied, using a piece of bread to wipe his plate. 'Sounds great, by the way, Dinga. There's nothing to report; all was quiet in the wireless office yesterday.'

Shortly after one p.m., Smith, along with ten ratings, were fallen on the quarterdeck. The afternoon sun, set in a deep, clear, blue sky, bathed everything in an all-embracing warmth, complimented by a cool, southerly breeze.

'Remember,' snapped, duty Perry Officer Sandy Powel, 'the

ship I under sailing orders, and leave expires at 0630.'

After going ashore, Smith stood on the wharf, admiring how the Atlantic's dark-green waters changed to a pale, shimmering green, as it broke along the edge of the snow-white sands of Copacabana Beach. He approached one of the several taxis parked nearby.

'Do you understand English?' he asked a small, balding taxi driver with a swarthy, wrinkled face

The driver flashed a row of uneven, tobacco-stained teeth and said, 'Yes, senour, I speak *leetle* English.'

'How much to the top of the Christ statue?'

'Ten cruzie, I take you to car park,' replied the driver. 'Eeer, a train will take you to top.'

'OK, let's go,' Smith replied, and climbed into the back seat of a battered old Ford that had seen better days.

They drove through the dockyard, and after passing a large bay crowded with colourful fishing vessels, they emerged onto a busy dual carriageway separated by a narrow, concrete central reservation. One carriageway ran south along the harbour's coastline, and the other took traffic in the opposite direction. Flat-roofed, white-stoned houses were nestled behind rows of colourful hotel, bars and cafes. However, it was the Copacabana Beach, with its dazzling, white beach stretching in a wide arc around the bay, that held Smith's attention.

'The beach is — 'ow you say — beautiful, is it not, senour?' the driver said, glancing over his shoulder. 'We call it, "the smile that greets tourists." But right now, not many people on the beach. Siesta. People sleep.'

'And later on?' asked Smith.

The driver threw back his head, laughed heartily and said, 'Many cars and lots of tourists. Everyone eat, drink and make love.'

They drove down the southern section of the carriageway. After stopping at several pedestrian crossings guarded by large *Stop* and *Go* traffic lights, the driver turned up a steep, narrow road.

A few minutes later they arrived at a wide, gravel-covered car park full of expensive looking Roadsters and Cadillacs. At one end of the car park, tourists, laughing and joking, boarded one of the funicular's three compartments. Smith noticed that the dual railway track went straight, before turning and disappearing up the blind side of a mountain.

Smith opened a pocket in his money belt and paid the driver. Feeling lines of sweat running down his back, he made his way to a large, wooden kiosk. Inside an opening, a grey-haired woman sat taking money and handing tickets to a group of tourists. Nearby, a sign painted in red and written in Portuguese, Spanish and English, stated: "Twenty cruzie to see the statue of Christ the Redeemer." Smith bought a ticket and joined a small line of tourists making their way to the train. Smith followed them and climbed into a long compartment lined on either side by wooden benches. Smith sat down next to a woman wearing a gaudy, pink dress and a white, floppy hat. Next to her sat a small, overweight man in a red and yellow polka dot shirt, white Bermuda shorts and leather sandals. Under a white Stetson, his round, flabby face was badly sunburned.

'I take it you're from the British ship that docked this morning?' the woman asked, using a hand to make sure her hat was on properly.

'Yes, I am,' Smith replied, realising his uniform had attracted not only her attention, but also others in the queue.

'Well, I sure hope you folk don't go to war with Germany,' she said in a distinct, southern drawl. 'Because Roosevelt has given us his promise not to get involved like we did in the last war. Isn't that right, Homer?' she added, glancing sternly at her partner who had taken off his Stetson.

'Sure is, Martha,' Homer replied, using a large, white handkerchief to wipe beads of sweat from his near-bald head. 'I say, let the "Limey's" fight their own goddam war.'

'No need to swear, dear,' she replied curtly. 'Now sit back and don't you dare smoke one of your horrible cigars.'

Homer shrugged his shoulders and stared boringly out of a window badly in need of cleaning.

The view of the city was blocked as the funicular slowly moved upwards. Halfway through a thick forest of tall trees, a funicular rumbled past them on its way down. Fifteen minutes later the train slowly rattled to halt alongside a wide, wooden platform.

Several yards away, two flights of concrete steps led the tourists up to a round, stone balcony. Crowds of visitors were already there. Some leant on the balustrade uttering prayers and crossing themselves. Others, straining their necks, stared up in wonder at the gigantic statue of Christ the Redeemer.

'Holy smoke, Homer,' Martha gasped, shielding her eyes from the sun. 'It certainly is mighty big.'

'Sure is, honey,' Homer replied, who was also looking at the statue. 'It must be at least two hundred feet high.'

The statue stands 98ft (30metres). Each arm span is 92ft (28 metres) and was completed in 1931.

After admiring the colossal statue, Smith walked to the balcony and immediately caught his breath. As far as he could see, the sparkling, blue ocean and cloudless sky merged with the horizon. At the foot of the forest stretched rows of colourful hotels, casinos and shops. To this was added the rippling waters of the sea paying homage to the edge of the wide, dazzling, yellow beach.

'Good heavens,' muttered Smith, 'everything looks so small. It's like a scene from Lilliputian land in the film *Gulliver's Travels*.'

However, his view of what he thought was a millionaire's paradise, changed dramatically. On the other side of the city lay stretches of small, wooden shacks and poorly built houses. Sanitation appeared to be insect-ridden cesspools. Children dressed in filthy rags played among bins overflowing with garbage. Old women, bent with fatigue, collected firewood, while old men sat in groups, smoking tobacco from long, white pipes.

'*Mein gott*,' Smith muttered to himself, shocked and disgusted at the stark contrast to the luxury living, and terrible poverty. He looked gravely up at Christ the Redeemer and wondered why he could permit such a thing to happen.

Smith turned around, and after walking down the steps, bought a cold beer from a stall. After finishing his drink, he disposed of the can in a waste basket then joined several other visitors and boarded the funicular. Upon arriving in the car park, he caught a taxi to Copacabana Beach.

By this time it was five p.m. Siesta was over, and the beach was crowded with people in bathing costumes, relaxing under the shade of an assortment of colourful sun umbrellas. The sun was comfortably warm, and the pulsating beat of the samba filled the air like a national anthem. Smith bought an ice-cold can of lemonade from a stall. Taking good gulps of his drink, he stood and watched heavily bronzed boys in skimpy shorts, and dark-skinned girls wearing tight-fitting swimming costumes, kicking up mounds of sand while playing soccer and volleyball.

After disposing of his empty can, he took off his shoes and socks, tied the laces and hung them around his neck. He walked down a slipway onto the beach and immediately felt the heat of the sand warming the soles of his stockinged feet. He found a shaded area at the foot of the sea wall and lay down. He rested his head on his cap, closed his eyes, and with the balmy sea breeze caressing his face, he fell asleep.

CHAPTER SEVENTEEN

Smith couldn't remember how long he had slept, but when he woke up, he was surprised to see a girl sitting in the sand, staring at him. A small, brown bag hung loosely from her shoulder, and the short-sleeved, button-down, green, floral dress she wore was tucked neatly under her bare legs. He blinked a few times then stared into her crystal-blue eyes, wondering who she was.

'I was hoping you would wake up,' she said, smiling while flicking a few strands of her short, light-brown hair from her eyes. Her English, spoken with a slight Latin inflection, was soft and precise. 'I was passing and noticed your uniform and how peaceful you looked.' She didn't mention how taken she was by his tousled mop of fair hair and handsome, clear-cut, lightly tanned features. 'Are you from the British ship that arrived this morning?'

'Err, yes,' Smith replied, nervously running his tongue along his dry lips.

'My name is Katrina,' she said, 'and what is yours?'

'Henry,' he answered, noticing how the paleness of her brown face and arms contrasted sharply with those of the girls on the beach. 'You speak English very well,' he continued, sitting upright and brushing sand from his arms. 'Do you live in Rio?'

'Yes, I was born here, but my mother is from Los Angeles in America. She married a man from Rio, and they moved here twenty years ago. It was she who taught me English.'

With a minimum of effort, she stood up, revealing a five-foot-plus shapely frame. In doing so, Smith noticed her ample breasts jostled tantalisingly under her dress.

After brushing sand from her arms and legs, she glanced at her small, silver wristwatch, then said, 'The time is six o'clock, and it'll be dark soon. Are you hungry?'

Realising he hadn't eaten since midday, Smith replied, 'Yes, come to think of it, I am.'

'There is a small restaurant near the Grand Hotel where I work, that sells the best Feijoada in Rio.'

Smith gave a quick laugh and said, 'Sounds very exotic. What's in it?'

'Black bean stew with vegetables and meat. It's our national dish,' she answered proudly.

'Good, let's go,' Smith replied, hurriedly rubbing sand away from his feet and putting on his shoes and socks. He stood up, and using both hands, dusted sand from his front and his back. After knocking the dent out of his cap, he put it on.

'You look very smart,' she said, smiling, 'Is that the name of your ship on the front of your hat?'

'Yes, HMS *Endeavour,*' Smith replied, and with a disarming smile, added, 'And it's called a cap, not a hat.'

'Sorry, sir,' she mockingly replied. 'Now, let's hurry before the restaurant becomes full.'

They left the beach and walked along a pavement, teeming with loud, bustling crowds, cafes, bars, shops and hotels; while all around the ubiquitous beat of the Samba rent the evening air.

'That's where I work,' said Katrina, pointing to a large, five-storey building with a pink façade, set some yards away from the pavement.

Each room had a small balcony facing the seafront. A flagged pathway, flanked on each side with bushes of beautiful red and yellow Bougainvillea, led up to the entrance. A large, neon sign above, embedded in the wall between the second and third floors, proclaimed the name, "Hotel Vista do Mar".

'It looks rather posh. What is it you do?' Smith asked.

'Because I speak good English, and as the hotel is popular with tourists, I was able to get a job as a receptionist,' she replied. 'There are four of us, and this is my day off.'

'Do you live with your parents?'

'Sometimes,' she replied. 'I have a small apartment on the top floor of the hotel that I use when I'm on early call.'

The restaurant was some twenty yards from the hotel. It was almost seven o'clock. Darkness had fallen. The shops, houses and cafes lining the road were lit up. A canvas canopy lay over the highly polished oak restaurant door. Next to this, set in a large glass case, was a menu written in English, Spanish and Portuguese.

Katrina opened the door and was greeted by a small, grey-haired man with a swarthy complexion and dark-brown eyes. He wore a pale-blue, open-necked shirt and a white, stained apron tied around his bulging waistline.

'Ah, *Senhorita* Katrina, how good to see you again,' he said in Portuguese. 'I see you have brought a sailor friend,' he added, giving Smith a toothy smile. 'I am Migel. Do come in, you are more than welcome.'

As they entered the restaurant, the mouth-watering smell of spicy cooking immediately increased Smith's appetite. A pretty, dark-haired girl wearing a white apron over a coloured dress stood talking to a man and a woman sitting at one of the tables. As Migel and his guests entered, the girl turned and gave them a welcoming smile.

With a grin that seemed to be permanently fixed to his fleshy face, Migel showed them to a table covered in a pristine, white tablecloth. In the middle of the table, poking up from inside a curved glass vase, a solitary long-stemmed Bromelia, a flower grown locally, with beautiful red and purple leaves, gave the surroundings a touch of romanticism.

'Two plates of Feijoada, please, Migel, and a bottle of Abbesse.'

A few minutes later, Migel arrived holding a bottle of Abbesse. 'Chilled especially for you,' he said, as he poured the wine out. 'Enjoy,' he added, and hurried away.

'Mmm, delicious,' said Smith, taking a sip then relaxing back in his chair.

Five minutes later, the aromatic smell of spices preceded the arrival of the girl holding a silver tray containing two dishes of food.

'My name eese Maria,' she said, and carefully placed each dish in front of them. Then, with a pleasant smile, she turned and left.

Much to Katrina's relief, Smith found the meat, highly flavoured with spices, very enjoyable.

'Better than the roast we have at home,' Smith said in between mouthfuls.

For a while they didn't speak. Then, Smith, after finishing his wine, gave Katrina a searching look and said, 'I don't mean to sounds personal, but surely a smashing-looking girl like you must have a boyfriend.'

'Yes, his name is Rodrigo,' she replied, averting her eyes, 'but he went away to work on a farm, and that was that.' She nervously dabbed her mouth with a serviette.

'Were you… fond of him?' Smith asked, feeling a slight tinge of jealousy.

'I suppose I was, but what about you?' she asked quickly. 'Aren't sailors supposed to have a girl in every port?'

'Not me.' Smith replied. 'This is my first ship and I've never actually been…' He quickly checked himself, then added, 'Like that.'

'My goodness, I can't believe it,' she said, keeping her voice down. 'You're actually blushing.'

'No, I'm not,' he replied defensively. 'It's the spice in the meal.'

'I think you'd better have some more wine,' Katrina answered, doing her best not to laugh. 'Then we'll go to a bar down the road and listen to a band, and dance. You can dance, can't you?'

He gave her a sheepish smile, shook his head then muttered, 'I'm afraid not.'

'Then,' she replied, shaking her head in disbelief, 'I think we'd better go to my apartment, and I'll teach you the samba.'

The thought of being alone with Katrina in her apartment suddenly made him feel nervous. After all, he had heard several ratings describe, in graphical detail, their erotic encounters. But other than a few clumsy fumbles in the back seat of cars, he had never actually had full sex with a girl.

Katrina paid the bill, and after giving Maria a handsome tip, she thanked Migel and they left the restaurant. Crowds of people thronged the pavements, and high above in a cloudless sky, a full moon and a myriad of twinkling stars bathed everything in a colourful, clear light. They turned left and walked down a side road into the back of the hotel. The stench from of bins overflowing with rubbish didn't seem to affect Katrina but made Smith wince. They walked across the yard, passed a line of fire escapes and stopped outside a wooden door.

'My apartment is on the top floor,' said Katrina, pushing the door open. 'And don't look so worried; I'm not going to eat you,' she added, giving Smith a reassuring smile. 'And there is a lift.'

'Thank goodness for that,' Smith replied nervously.

Inside, the building was dusty and dark. Detecting the nervous inflection in his voice, Katrina took hold of Smith's warm hand and led him to the lift. Using the forefinger on her spare hand, she pressed a small, brass button on the side of the lift door. This immediately produced a series of whirling, clanking noises. Seconds later the lift arrived. Using a handle, she slid the gate open.

'Not much room, is there?' Smith remarked, as Katrina pressed her soft body against him.

'I'm not complaining,' she whispered seductively. She then removed her hand from his, and placing both arms around his neck, drew his face towards her. 'Enough for you to kiss me?' she added, feeling the bulge in Smith's tropical shorts.

Smith tried to move but felt her lips, warm and moist, pressing against his. Then, with a sudden jerk, the lift shuddered to a standstill.

Katrina moved away from him. 'Just as well,' she whispered. 'For a moment I thought you might...' She paused, then with a seductive smile, said, 'You know...'

Smith was too nervous to reply. After leaving the lift, Katrina closed the gate and took hold of Smith's hand. They walked along a narrow, dimly lit corridor and stopped outside a door marked 21 in small, white numerals. Using her spare hand, she flicked open her handbag and brought out a small, silver Yale key. She opened the door, led him inside and switched on the light.

The apartment was small and austere. The low-slung ceiling was painted a dull white, and a pale-green curtain was drawn across a solitary window. A flap of faded, yellow wallpaper hung listlessly from a corner of one of the walls. A threadbare green carpet covered the floor, and lying against a wall was a plain wooden table on which a few vegetables lay on a plate next to a pink enamel mug. A sagging, brown leather armchair rested next to a sideboard containing a brown Bakelite wireless and a framed photograph of a tall, dark-haired man in a white suit and a small, fair-haired woman in long, white dress. An open door led into a small bedroom. Next to this was a small bathroom tiled in pink. Close by, another door lying ajar, led into a congested kitchenette.

'I'm sorry, it's a bit untidy,' Katrina said, hurriedly picking up a towel and bits of underwear and tucking them away under a cushion. 'Before I saw you,' she added, 'I was on my way home to have an early night.'

'Looks OK to me,' Smith replied, taking off his cap. 'You ought to see what my mess deck looks like before rounds.'

'Now,' Katrina said, standing in front of Smith, putting her arms around his neck and pressing herself against him. 'Tell me the truth. I want to know how many girls you have been with. Two, three, or maybe more?'

'I'm, err, not sure,' he muttered nervously, while feeling his face redden.

'I don't believe you,' Katrina replied, noticing lines of sweat trickling down the sides of his face. 'I suspect you've never really made love to girl. Am I right?'

Feeling embarrassed, he averted his gaze and mumbled, 'Well, maybe…'

'Then it's about time you did,' Katrina said, taking his hand and leading him into the bedroom.

CHAPTER EIGHTEEN

Commander Miller left the ship promptly at seven p.m. It was dark, and from a cloudless sky, a bright, yellow moon bathed the city in a warm, clear light. He walked down the gangway and was met by a small dark-haired man wearing a dark-grey suit. He stood holding open the passenger door of a shiny, black Bentley.

'Good evening, sir, my name is Ramon. I welcome you to Rio.'

'Thank you,' Miller replied, and climbed inside. His tropical, white bush jacket, complete with shoulder boards displaying his rank, felt slightly tight under his arms. The matching trousers were a shade too long, and the white leather shoes pinched his toes. The only thing that seemed to fit him correctly was his new cap with its row of silver oak leaves across the peak of the cap.

The drive through the bustling city to the ambassador's residence took ten minutes. They drove past a set of wrought iron gates and up a wide, gravelled path decorated on either side with beds of vivid-red Ceibo, Argentina's national flower. At the end of the pathway, three wide steps led up to a large, colonial-style three-storey building. The lights shining through the windows clearly showed a man and a woman standing a on a patio, behind which was a closed oak door.

The man, who Miller sensed was the ambassador, stood over six feet. His well-groomed, black hair was streaked with grey, and his immaculate, dark-blue, double-breasted suit and a naval tie stood out against his pristine, white shirt. Next to him stood a slightly overweight, dark-haired woman. She wore an ankle-length, pale-blue dress and white, long-sleeved gloves. A double row of sparkling pearls adorned her neck. Miller judged them both to be in their middle fifties.

After stopping the car near the bottom of the steps, Ramon climbed out and opened the passenger door, allowing Miller to ease himself out. Ramon closed the door then walked around the corner of the mansion.

'Good evening, Commander. Ambassador Knox-Johnson,' said the ambassador, proffering his hand as Miller walked up the steps. 'I know how busy you must be, so it's good of you to find the time to come.'

His voice, clear and resonant, reminded Miller of his old college headmaster. While they shook hands, Miller saw the ambassador's dark-brown eyes crease into a welcoming smile. He also noticed how the ambassador's short, black hair, streaked with grey, and deeply tanned, heavily lined face, enhanced his distinguished appearance.

'Thank you for the invitation, sir,' Miller replied, feeling a tiny trickle of warm sweat run down his back.

'Allow me to introduce my wife,' the ambassador said to Miller.

'A pleasure to meet you, Lady Knox-Johnson,' Miller said.

As he felt her tiny, gloved fingers grip his hand, he noticed her dark-blue eyes, set in a heavily made-up, round chubby face, crease into a warm smile.

'The pleasure is mine,' she replied, in a soft, well-modulated voice. Her relaxed manner immediately made him feel relaxed.

'Pay no attention to what she says, Commander,' the ambassador said jokingly. 'She loves a man in uniform, especially sailors.'

'You ought to know, dear,' she said, flashing him a cheeky smile. 'I married one.'

'I take it you were in the Royal Navy, sir?' Miller asked, noticing his tie.

Before the ambassador could reply, his wife chimed in and said, 'Yes. He commanded a destroyer in the last war. Got the DSO, didn't you, Geoffrey?' she added, with a touch of pride.

'Oh, do be quiet,' the ambassador replied impatiently. 'I'm sure the commander isn't interested in old war stories. Come, let's go inside, I'm sure we've lots to discuss.'

As he finished speaking, the door was opened by Ramon.

'Thank you, Ramon. Cocktails in the lounge, and make them

large ones,' said the ambassador.

'Very good, Excellency,' Ramon replied, bowing slightly.

'Splendid man, Ramon,' said the ambassador. 'Mixes the best cocktails in Rio.'

As they walked along a well-lit hallway, the cool air coming from an air conditioner, caressed Miller's face. The lounge was spacious, and as befitting the home of a representative of the British Crown, tastefully furnished. The light from a small but impressive glass chandelier bathed the room in a clear light. For a few seconds Miller stood still and felt his shoes sink into the soft pile of a pale-green carpet. Even though he wasn't an expert of classical furniture, he recognised a set of elegant, hard-backed Victorian chairs, a Sheraton coffee table, and what looked like a Chippendale wine cabinet. A pair of French windows opened onto a well-manicured lawn set in readiness for a game of croquet. Oil paintings of local landmarks hung on two of the walls covered in expensive, dark-red damask. In sharp contrast, but nevertheless easy on the eye, the other walls were designed in pleasant pale-pink and blue stripes.

'Do sit down, Commander,' said the ambassador, indicating to a black leather armchair. Nearby, a small, round, highly polished oak table rested on a multi-coloured Indian rug. Opposite these, a finely meshed metal guard lay in front of an unlit log fire. Lady Knox-Johnson and her husband sat on a black Chesterfield settee. Opposite them was a marble mantelpiece on which framed family photographs rested either side of a shiny, pale-green Ormolu clock. Above these, looking extremely regal, was an elegantly framed painting of King George V in full admiral regalia, and Queen Elizabeth wearing her crown and dressed in a flowing, white gown.

'Is this your first visit to Rio, Commander?' asked Lady Knox-Johnson.

'Yes, indeed, ma'am,' Miller replied, doing his best to relax into the hard material of the settee. 'It looks like a very beautiful city. Unfortunately, we won't be here long enough to take advantage of it.' He paused momentarily, then went on. 'I believe Professor Penlowe stayed with you before she joined the ship.'

'Yes, indeed,' her ladyship replied. 'A charming and very

intelligent young lady. I think my husband was quite taken with her, is that not so, Geoffrey?'

'Yes, my dear,' the ambassador quietly replied. 'Very charming indeed. I informed her about the mission,' he added, glancing warily at Miller.

'She did mention it,' Miller replied.

From his jacket pocket, the ambassador took out a small, silver cigarette case, flicked it open and offered it to Miller.

'No, thanks, sir,' Miller answered, slightly shaking his head. 'I don't smoke.'

Using a small, gold lighter, the ambassador lit his cigarette. Relaxing into his chair, he took a deep puff and slowly exhaled a steady stream of blue smoke.

'Ghastly habit,' her ladyship remarked, frowning, while using a gloved hand to waft the tobacco smoke away.

The door opened and Ramon came in carrying a tray of drinks. 'As you requested, large ones, sir,' he said, placing three, long-stemmed, Waterford crystal glasses on the table.

'Thank you. Dinner in half an hour,' said the ambassador, smiling at Ramon. 'Be good enough to tell the servants.'

'*Si*, Excellency,' Ramon replied, and with a dignified bow, turned and left the room.

'As Ramon and the servants will be in the room, I suggest we leave any discussion about your mission until after dinner,' said the ambassador, taking another puff of his cigarette.

'Secrecy, you know. Can't be too careful, eh, Commander?' added Lady Knox-Johnson, after taking a gentle sip of her cocktail.

'Quite so, ma'am,' Miller replied.

The conversation over dinner, taken in a beautiful, oak-panelled room lined with portraits of stern-faced Portuguese admirals, was mainly about the prospect of war between Germany and Great Britain.

'We should have taken the advice of Churchill and mobilised sooner,' said the ambassador, cutting into a piece of succulent roast beef. 'However, I hear Chamberlain is going to appoint him first lord of the admiralty. That should help you chaps considerably,' he added, giving Miller an approving glance.

'I'm sure he'll insist on building more destroyers,' Miller replied, 'especially for convoy duty,' he added, remembering what his father had said about the last war.

'War, war, war; that's all you men can talk about,' Her Ladyship remarked, as she finished her wine. 'Remember, it's the women who have to stay at home and do the worrying.'

'Yes, dear,' Miller replied, 'but think of the poor soldiers living in fox holes eating tins of bully beef, while the people at home drink beer and fine wines and eat fillet steak.'

'Then why is the government thinking of evacuating children in case there's an air raid?' she replied curtly. 'Not to mention the issuing of ration books and gas masks.'

'A wise thing to do considering the state of things,' the ambassador answered calmly, taking a sip of wine.

'Incidentally, sir, have you met the German ambassador?' Miller asked.

'Yes, I have; Karl Ritter — an obnoxious little man; is that not so, dear?' the ambassador replied, glancing at his wife.

'And so is his wife,' her ladyship replied. 'I'm glad they have their embassy in San Paulo.'

'How far away is that?' Miller asked.

'About four hundred miles south. That's where many of the German immigrants live.

Miller pursed his lips, then asked, 'What do the Portuguese think about the Germans, sir?'

'Rather ambivalent, actually,' the ambassador answered. 'They do trade with Europe but rely on America for tourism, and of course, they watch all the American films. However, I'm sure Ritter has informants in Rio.'

'And the women are crazy over Clark Gable,' Her Ladyship added, with a wicked smile.

'Including you, my dear,' the ambassador said, smiling while gently patting her hand.

Ten minutes later, two elderly, grey-haired servants removed their empty plates and replaced them with small dishes of peaches soaked in wine and covered in delicious ice-cream. This was followed by a glass of port and a cup of coffee.

'I expect you to will have lots to talk about,' said her ladyship, gently dabbing her mouth with a linen serviette. 'So I'll let you adjourn to your study, while I go to my room and answer some letters. Nice to have met you, Commander,' she said, as she stood up and shook Miller's hand. 'And remember,' she added, smiling warmly, 'I'm sure my husband and I would be glad to see you again. Is that not so, Geoffrey?'

'Yes, indeed, my dear,' said the ambassador, as he and Miller stood up.

No sooner had she left than the ambassador looked at Ramon and said, 'Coffee in my study, five minutes.'

Ramon gave him a perfunctory nod then left.

The ambassador's spacious study smelt strongly of tobacco, and mansion polish. Excellent all round lighting was provided by a small, glass chandelier hanging from a high, stucco ceiling. Dominating the room was a large, ornately framed portrait of Joseph 1st, the grey-haired king of Portugal. His small, dark, piercing eyes staring down from over a white marble fireplace, bayonetted anyone who entered the room. Three of the oak-panelled walls were lined with leather-bound books; the remaining wall, embossed in dark green, was hung with paintings of galleons and fading photographs of past presidents. An Axminster carpet, imported from England, covered the floor. In one corner a wine cabinet nestled close to a globe resting on a metal tripod. Close by was a comfortable-looking leather settee and two armchairs. In front of these was an elegant coffee table on which a tobacco-stained meerschaum pipe lay in a shiny brass ashtray. Facing a bay window was a dark, wide, mahogany desk on which rested a leather-bound blotting pad, a wooden ink tray containing an assortment of pens, a red telephone and a metal tray full of official papers.

The ambassador sat down on a settee, and indicating an armchair, said, 'Do sit down, Commander.' He picked up his pipe, and using his lighter, lit the tobacco in the drum. After a few hard puffs, his face almost disappeared into a cloud of billowing blue smoke.

'Now, you know,' he muttered, in between puffs, 'the real

reason why my wife left us alone.'

'Quite so, sir,' Miller diplomatically replied, crossing his legs while feeling the aromatic smell of the tobacco attack his olfactory nerve.

Ramon arrived and placed the coffee on the table.

'Thank you, Ramon,' said the ambassador, easing himself into an armchair. 'And take the rest of the night off.'

'Thank you, sir,' Ramon replied curtly, and left the room.

Miller relaxed into the comfort of the armchair, then asked, 'Have you heard anything from Whitehall, sir?'

'Yes, I have,' Sir Geoffrey replied, reaching forward and resting his pipe on the side of the ashtray. 'Whitehall has reported the incursion of German troops into Poland, and Chamberlain is expected to make another visit to Hitler in an effort to clarify Germany's intentions.'

'What do you, think, sir? Will it do any good?' Miller asked, after taking a good sip of coffee.

'I doubt it,' the ambassador replied, sombrely. 'That bastard seems hell-bent on European dominance.'

'War does seem pretty inevitable, sir,' Miller replied, furrowing his brow.

'I agree, my boy,' the ambassador wearily replied. 'And I think,' he added, picking up his cup and finishing the coffee, 'in my opinion, it could be sooner than we think.'

'And if that happens while my ship is in South Georgia; what then, sir?'

'I am well aware of the importance of your mission,' the ambassador replied, placing his empty cup on its saucer. 'So you must obtain the grapholite and return home as quickly as possible. However,' he added, his tone suddenly quiet and cautious, 'as stated in your orders, on your way home, you'll be putting into Rio to refuel. But,' he added, furrowing his brow, 'there could be a slight problem.'

The ambassador's words sent a sudden feeling of uncertainty running through Miller. He sat forward, and placing both hands on the sides of the armchair, said, 'And what might that be, sir?'

'Now,' replied the ambassador, 'what I have to tell you is of the utmost secrecy. Understand?'

'Perfectly, sir,' Miller replied.

The ambassador picked up his pipe, then said, 'Our sources in Germany have told us Hitler only has only fifty-seven operational U-boats, of which thirty are short-range boats, suitable for the North Sea.' He paused and took a deep puff of his cigar, then continued. 'However, we know the Germans have built eight XB U-boats. These have an endurance of eighteen thousand miles and have a surface speed of twenty miles per hour. Their task, so our spies tell us, is to lay mines, but they do carry two torpedoes that can only be fired from her stern. Luckily, four of these XB's have developed engine defects; two are laying mines somewhere in the Baltic, and two are in Bremerhaven. Also, Donitz has a few destroyers patrolling the western littoral of Africa, searching for cargo vessels coming around the Cape.'

'Excuse me, sir,' interrupted Miller, sitting forward. 'This is all very interesting, but what has it to do with the mission?'

'I'm coming to that,' replied the ambassador, waving his pipe in the air like a baton. 'The destroyers shouldn't pose any danger, but if Admiral Canaris, Hitler's chief of intelligence, gets wind of the real reason for your mission, he could order Doenitz to send one of these long-distance U-boats to intercept you.'

'But sir, the southern ocean is so vast,' Miller stressed, 'that any U-boat would have difficulty finding us.'

'Not if Canaris was told when you were sailing and in which direction,' the ambassador cautiously replied.

'But how on earth could he find out?' Miller replied, alarmed.

'Steady on, old boy,' the ambassador said, raising a hand. 'I'm simply mentioning it to put you on your guard.'

'Thank you, sir,' Miller said, relaxing into his chair. 'For a moment you had me worried.'

'Then,' replied the ambassador, glancing at his wristwatch. 'As it's nearly ten o'clock, I suggest we have a large brandy before you return to your ship.

CHAPTER NINETEEN

At precisely seven a.m. on Monday 14th, Pollard gave a sharp knock on the captain's door and was told to enter. Having had an early breakfast, Miller was fully dressed and standing near his desk.

'Good morning, sir,' Pollard said. 'Ship's ready for sea.'

'Thank you, Number One,' Miller replied, as he stood and picked his cap up off his desk. 'Is there anyone adrift?'

'Two, sir,' Pollard replied. 'Able Seaman Lewis and Wireless Operator Smith. Both were twenty minutes late. They've been seen by the officer of the watch and are on your defaulters.'

'Smith, eh,' muttered Miller. 'A bit unusual for him. He's always struck me as a quiet, conscientious lad.'

'A bit too much to drink, I suppose, sir,' Pollard jokingly replied, as he followed Miller out of the cabin.

Ten minutes later, the pipe sounded: "Hands fall in for leaving harbour at ten a.m. Special sea duty men will be required at nine thirty."

In the seamen's mess, everyone had finished breakfast.

'Where the fuck have you two been?' Waters asked, glaring at Smith and Lewis. 'I hope it was worth it, because the ship's under sailing orders, which means you'll both get a heavier punishment than normal.'

'So what?' muttered Lewis., 'We'll be at sea, so it doesn't matter.'

'It a bloody good job you're not on duty till six p.m.,' O'Hanlon said to Smith. 'You look so knackered you'd probably fall asleep.'

Smith was too tired to make any comment. Instead, he took off his uniform and climbed into his hammock. However, every time he closed his eyes, he felt the warm, softness of Katrina's naked body pressing against his. They were lying on her bed. He remembered her telling him that her doctor had fitted her with a device to prevent her conceiving. He remembered his hands trembling with excitement as, with her help, he took off his uniform. He vividly remembered her sitting astride him, and seeing her firm breasts moving slightly as she guided his enlarged and aching penis inside her burning hot vagina, and the feeling of ecstasy running through him as he climaxed.

'Don't worry, my lovely sailor boy,' she had said, while using a towel to mop away sweat from his chest and face. 'I know this is your first time. But we have all night, and I shall make sure you never forget it.'

With a mixture of tenderness and animal passion, she kept her promise. Throughout the night, she showed him how to make love in various positions, and as the dim shafts of dawn broke through the curtains, he felt as if he had been reborn. He lay in bed cocooned against Katrina's soft, warm body, listening to her steady breathing. He was about to doze off when the heard the sound of a car backfiring. He slowly withdrew an arm from around Katrina and looked at his wristwatch. The time was a quarter to six.

'My God, Katrina,' he muttered, withdrawing his other arm and rolling out of bed. 'I must get back, or else I'll be in the rattle.'

Katrina opened her eyes, yawned, then mumbled, 'What did you say?'

'I've got to get back to the ship, or I'll be in trouble,' he replied.

'No, no,' she whimpered, reaching out to him. 'Please don't go. I'm not on duty till twelve.'

'Sorry, love,' he answered, putting on his uniform. 'You see, I have to go, as the ship is sailing in a few hours.'

'Then let it sail without you,' she pleaded, 'and stay with me.'

'I wish I could,' he replied, breathing heavily, 'but, I promise you, one day I will come back.'

He put his cap on then bent down, and putting his arms around her nakedness, kissed her passionately.

After they broke away, he looked intently into her tear-stained eyes and said, 'You are the most beautiful girl I have ever met, and if it is possible, I really will return.'

Without looking back, he walked into the living room, opened the door, glanced back and left.

Except for a few vagrants and drunks sprawled out on benches, the boulevard was deserted. Dawn had broken, and the great orb of the sun, hovering above the horizon, in a cloudless sky, cast a deep shade of ochre across the dark-blue sea and sandy beach. The quietness of the morning was intermittently broken by the somnolent sound of the white waves rolling gently in from the ocean. Wondering if he would ever see Katrina again, Smith arrived outside the dockyard gates and met Able Seaman Lewis.

'Bugger me!' Lewis exclaimed, staring at Smith's blood-shot eyes. 'I hope it was worth it; you look as if you've been on the nest all night.'

'You don't look so good yourself, Joe,' Smith replied, stifling a yawn. 'What happened to you?'

'Got pissed and fell asleep on a bench,' Lewis answered glumly. 'Some fuckin' run ashore, that was,' he mumbled, as they waked up *Endeavour'* gangway.

Shortly after eleven a.m., *Endeavour* slipped her moorings and slowly moved away from the wharf. On the bridge, Luciano expertly navigated the ship out of the harbour. After passing several large islands, Miller ordered the ship to stop. The Jacob's ladder was lowered. A motor launch came alongside. Miller shook Luciano's hand and thanked him. Luciano climbed down the Jacob's ladder and into the launch. As it roared away, he gave a farewell wave and sat down.

"Hands fall out. Revert to cruising stations. Duty watch muster on the quarterdeck," was piped.

On the bridge, Miller turned to Pollard, who, like everyone else, was watching a Cunard liner sailing majestically towards Rio.

'I bet those rich tourists had more time ashore than we did, Number One,' Miller remarked, with a touch of envy.

'Talking of time, sir,' Pollard replied, 'remember you have defaulters at two p.m.'

In the seamen's mess, the peppery smell of rum, tobacco and rabbit stew hung in the sweaty atmosphere.

'I'll do your duty while you get weighed off,' LRO Bell said to Smith, using a piece of bread to mop gravy from his plate. 'And you'd better have a shave and clean yerself up, or the chief will have a fit.'

'Cheers, Dinga,' Smith replied. 'You can have gulpers tomorrow.' (Gulpers was a good sip of rum.)

At one fifteen, Smith and Lewis, both wearing their Number 7's, reported to Chief GI Mills who was sat in his office, smoking a cigarette. He looked up and checked to see they were properly dressed.

'Right, you two, follow me,' grunted Mills, picking up a clipboard.

A few minutes later, they arrived in a corridor and stopped behind a door leading onto the wardroom flat. Mills, clipboard in his left hand, knocked then opened the door.

Miller was standing behind a tall, wooden plinth with a sloping top. A few yards away stood Lieutenant Willis, Smith's divisional officer, waiting to speak on Lewis's behalf.

'Defaulters ready, sir,' snapped the chief, giving Miller a smart salute.

'Very good, chief, send the first one in,' Miller replied, returning Mill's salute.

Mills opened the door. 'Lewis, you'll be first. *Attention! Quick march. Left right, left right. Attention. Off cap,"* Mills yelled, as Lewis, looking pale and nervous, strode into the room.

Mills closed the door.

Ten minutes later, after being charged, the door opened and Lewis, grinning like a clown, gave Smith a confident wink before disappearing down a staircase.

'Wireless Operator Smith,' snapped Mills.

After giving Smith the same authoritative commands that Lewis had received, Smith marched into the room, stood rigidly to attention and faced Miller.

'Off cap. Wireless Operator Smith, contrary to ship's standing orders and the ship being under sailing orders, was, on Monday the 14th of August, twenty minutes adrift."

'Thank you, Chief,' Miller replied. Looking sternly at Smith, he said, 'You do realise, Smith, because the ship is under sailing orders, this may increase your punishment?'

'Yes, sir,' Smith nervously replied.

'So why were you adrift?'

Smith cleared his throat, then replied, 'I... I got drunk and fell asleep on a bench, sir.'

'Another one. The benches in Rio must be very comfortable, eh, Chief,' Miller remarked, glancing at Mills while doing his best to conceal a smile.

Chief Mills didn't reply. Instead, he nodded slightly and grinned.

'If I may say so,' Miller went on, 'a very poor excuse.' Turning to Lieutenant Willis, he said, 'Anything you wish to say on Smith's behalf?'

Willis saluted, then said, 'Yes, sir. Smith is a quiet, conscientious rating. Since joining the ship, he has performed his duties extremely well. This is the first time he has been in trouble.' Miller looked at Smith's service record open in of him. Then, giving Smith a flinty stare, replied, 'Considering this is your first offence, together with your excellent work record, I shall be lenient. Ten days stoppage of leave and pay. Carry on, Chief.'

'On cap,' yelled Mills. 'Salute. About turn. Quick march.'

Mills saluted Miller, turned and followed Smith onto the wardroom flat.

'If yer ask me, you and Lewis got off lightly,' Mills said to Smith. 'Carry on, and like Lewis, you are to report to me every evening before night rounds.'

Arriving back in the mess, Able Seaman Brown, who was sitting at the table, sipping tea from a chipped mug, said, 'You two could 'ave got off a lot worse.'

'Piece of piss, eh, Smithy,' Lewis muttered, munching on a slice of bread and jam. 'Punta Arenas is our next stop and that's over a thousand miles away, so as we'll be at sea, we couldn't go ashore anyway. Ain't that right, Smithy?'

'I expect so,' Smith replied, hoping that when the ship did arrive at Punta Arenas, he might be able to go ashore, and with luck, contact Buenos Aires.

CHAPTER TWENTY

By five p.m., the misto peak of Sugar Loaf Mountain had faded in the distance, as *Endeavour* left the harbour and cruised into the calm, blue waters of the South Atlantic.

'Starboard ten. Increase to fifteen knots. Revolutions, ten, steer two one zero.'

Chief Coxswain Moore repeated the order. Almost immediately the ship slowly turned to the right and built up speed. 'Steady as she goes, Coxswain. Fall out special sea duty men, Number One.'

'Very good, sir,' Pollard replied. He looked up, and shielding his eyes against the glare of the sun, said, 'Looks like being yet another scorcher, eh, sir?'

'Yes, indeed, Number One,' Miller replied, 'because in a weeks' time we should reach latitude forty degrees, when the weather will change dramatically.'

'How bad will it be, sir?' Pollard asked.

'Waves as high as mountains, blizzards, and cold enough to freeze your balls off,' Miller replied, using a handkerchief to dab beads of sweat from his brow.

'Burr...' Pollard said, feigning a mock shiver. 'Then I'd better get my long johns ready, sir.'

Wearing a sly grin, Miller eased himself off his chair and replied, 'Now that's a thought. Perhaps I should mention that to Professor Penlowe.'

Miller left the bridge, descended a flight of stairs, knocked on the professor's cabin door and was told to enter. The tight, yellow sweater and trousers she was wearing did nothing to disguise her well-developed figure. For a few seconds, Miller stood and stared at her.

'Was there something you wanted, Commander?' she said, smiling coyly, knowing full well what was distracting him.

'Ahem...' Miller replied. 'I just wanted to err... tell you that shortly we will be encountering a change in the climate. It'll get much colder, and we could give you some appropriate clothing.'

'You mean a pair of fur-lined trousers and coats like the Eskimos wear?'

Miller suddenly realised she was teasing him, and felt his face redden. 'Something like that,' he replied.

'Splendid,' Linda said, fully aware of his embarrassment and seeing a reddish hue spread across his clear-cut, attractive features. 'I only hope they don't itch. Incidentally, I've just had a walk around the deck, and I'm happy to say that your crew seem very friendly.'

'I'm not surprised,' Miller answered, pensively stroking his chin. 'If I may say, may I suggest something more... conservative?'

'How gallant of you to say so, Commander,' she replied, nodding her head slightly. 'Now, if you'll excuse me, I must take a shower,' and flashing him an engaging smile, she opened the cabin door.

Feeling the hairs on the back of his neck tingle, Miller left, went into his cabin and sat down.

'Pull yourself together, man,' he muttered angrily to himself, as opened the signal log. 'You've got more important things to worry about than her. After all, she's only a woman.'

However, for some reason, the thought of seeing her every day disturbed him.

During the next day, Miller kept the ship's company occupied by practising everything from "action stations" to "man overboard". This included daily gunnery practice.

Later that day, on the upper deck, ratings were kept amused by watching the schools of dolphins bounding in and out of the sea.

'They always seem to be smiling, don't they, Stokes?' LRO Bell asked Stoker Davis, who, sweating profusely, had come up from the boiler room for a breath of fresh air and a smoke.

'Maybe they know there's definitely gunna be a war, Dinga,'

Davis replied, lighting a cigarette. 'And they're trying to warn us.'

'In that case, give me one of your ciggies,' Bell replied.

On another occasion, an Albatross appeared to have adopted the ship and rode on the thermals generated from the ship's heat.

'Magnificent creatures, eh, sir?' Pollard remarked to Miller, as both officers, shielding their eyes, looked up as it flew close to the funnel. Their wingspan can be up to three metres.'

'And they're not very hygienic,' Miller replied, as, just before peeling away, the Albatross unloaded a stream of white faeces that splattered onto the deck.

'According to my grandfather,' Pollard replied, grinning like a Cheshire cat, 'when one of them shits on you, it's supposed to be a sign of good luck.'

'Perhaps we'll need it, Number One,' Miller quietly replied.

After rum issue that same day, Able Seaman Brown, wearing a clean set of number tens (white fronts, shorts, black stockings and shoes), stood outside the sickbay. His tanned features held a worried expression, and he began to sweat. With his hand shaking, he nervously knocked on the door and was told to enter.

LSBA Hailey was sat at his desk. He looked up and asked, 'And what can I do for you, Buster?'

'Well, Doc,' Brown nervously replied. 'It's me, err... dick.'

'What's wrong with it?' Then with a grin, he added, 'Don't tell me it's dropped off?'

'Might be better if it had,' Brown replied, anxiously shuffling his feet.

'Why is that, then?' Halley asked, noticing how Brown was avoiding his gaze.

Feeling his mouth go dry, Buster meekly replied, 'You see, Doc, it's sore inside when I piss.'

'A burning feeling?' Hailey asked.

Brown nodded and said, 'Sort of.'

'Then you'd better let me take a look,' Hailey replied.

Brown undid his belt and pushed his shorts and underpants down. Hailey slipped on a pair of latex gloves and carefully examined Brown's penis.

'Looks like you may have caught a dose, matey,' Hailey said.

After locking the sickbay door, he went into the heads and returned holding a large wooden box. He unclipped the lid and took out a small spirit lamp, a glass slide and a six-inch piece of thin, brass wire with a tiny loop on the end. Miller removed the top of the lamp, and using a match, lit the wick. He then waved the wire in and out of the flame until the end glowed red.

Brown gave Hailey a startled look and cried, 'What the fuck are you gunna do with that?'

'I'm going use it to put some of the discharge on a slide,' Hailey replied. 'But don't look so worried; I'll make sure the wire's cold.'

'I should bloody well hope so,' Brown replied, 'or else I'll be out of here like a shot.'

'Now, listen carefully,' said Hailey, fixing the slide by passing it quickly through the flame. 'Pull up your gear and go into the heads where you'll find two glass bottles by the sink. I want you to piss in one of them, hold it, then piss in the other one. Got it?'

'I think so,' Brown muttered, fastening his trouser belt.

He went into the heads and returned a few minutes later holding both bottles, each one half full of yellow urine.

'Right,' Hailey said. 'Leave them heads and come back at fourteen hundred to see the MO. And I'm afraid I'll have to stop your tot, because alcohol can irritate the lining of your dick and make things worse.'

'Stop me tot!' Brown exclaimed. 'If I'd known you were gunna do that, I'd wouldn't have come.'

'And then it would have only get worse,' Hailey flatly replied.

'Anyway, what's the piss for, Doc?' Brown asked.

'It'll help to see how bad the infection is,' Hailey replied. 'Now, come back after stand easy to see the MO, who'll take a blood sample.'

'*Blood!*' cried Brown. 'What's that for?'

'It's a precautionary measure to see if you've caught syphilis,' Hailey replied.

'*Syphilis!*' retorted Brown, staring wildly at Hailey. 'How will you know that?'

'When we call in at Rio on the way home, it'll be tested at the local hospital,' Hailey replied. 'Now unlock the door and bugger off,' he added.

As Brown opened the door, he was met by Able Seaman Lewis.

'Don't tell me you've caught the boat up as well, Joe?' Brown said, giving Lewis an inquisitive stare.

'Yeah, I think I have,' Lewis replied solemnly.

'But I thought you said you slept the night on a bench,' Brown said, grinning his head off.

'Well... not all the night,' Lewis timidly replied.

'Before the doc's finished with you,' Brown replied, 'you'd wished you had,' then hurried down the passageway.

A few minutes before two p.m., both ratings stood outside the sickbay. Surgeon Lieutenant Ryan, having been informed about Brown and Lewis, had microscopically examined the glass slides taken earlier and was sitting at his desk.

'Let's have the first one,' Ryan said to Hailey.

Hailey opened the door. 'Able Seaman Brown, sir,' Hailey said, as Buster came in.

'Ah, Brown,' the doctor replied, noticing the contrite expression on Buster's face. 'I'm afraid you have a rather bad case of gonorrhea. So, sit down, and as LSBA Hailey has explained, I'll have to take a drop of blood from you.'

My God, thought Brown as he sat down, placed his arm on a pillow, rolled up a sleeve and turned up his arm on the pillow. *He sounds just like a fuckin' vampire.*

After washing his hands, the doctor cleaned the area at the bend of the arm, using a cotton wool swab soaked in surgical spirits. 'Now, make a fist and clench your hand.'

The doctor picked up a metal 10cc syringe and attached a three-inch steel needle onto the nozzle. Feeling for a good vein, he inserted the needle into the vein and slowly withdrew it. He removed the needle and filled the test tube Hailey was holding, with blood.

'There, now,' said the doctor, placing the needle and syringe into a kidney dish, 'that wasn't too bad. How do you feel?'

With more than a hint of bravado, Brown replied, 'Me, sir, fit as a fiddle.'

Then, with his face turning sickly white, Hailey caught him as he was about to keel over.

'We'd better lay him on an examination couch and raise his legs,' said the doctor. 'Then give him a course of Sulphatriad tablets. I suppose Able Seaman Lewis is waiting outside?'

'Yes, sir,' Hailey replied.' And I believe they're both married with two children.'

'Better tell him to come back in an hour,' the doctor replied, giving Hailey a wicked grin. 'If he sees Brown like that, he'll probably faint as well.'

'Excuse me, sir,' Hailey said, 'if Wasserman blood tests are positive and Brown and Lewis have contracted syphilis, the treatment is injections of Salvarsan, and we haven't any on board.'

'Then we'll have to see if the hospital in Rio can help us out,' the doctor replied, then went on, 'Syphilis used to be treated with mercury, but this was unsuccessful. As a medical student,' he added with a slight grin, 'there was a saying: "A night with Venus and a lifetime with Mercury."'

CHAPTER TWENTY-ONE

During the night, the weather began to change. By five thirty, just as the dawn's grey haze was slowly appearing on the eastern horizon, gusts of wind up to fifty miles began to send gigantic, dark-green waves exploding over the ship's bow.

'In the last hour, the barometer's dropped five degrees, sir,' Midshipman Grant said to OOW Lieutenant Jenkins, with whom he was sharing the morning watch.

Jenkins, like PO Pincher Martin and QM Lane, wore a duffle coat over his tropical whites.

Jenkins was sat in the captain's chair, gripping the sides while watching lines of foamy water fizz along the deck and disappear though the scuppers into the sea.'

'Thank you, Mid,' Jenkins replied wearily. 'Just to think, a few hours ago the sea was like a mill pond.' Rubbing the bristles on his chin, he went on, 'You'd better check our position, as the captain will here shortly.'

'Longitude forty-two degrees, Latitude fifty-five, speed twelve knots, sir,' Grant quickly replied. 'I did it ten minutes ago. That puts us about 500 miles west of Bahia Blanca.'

'Well done,' Jenkins replied. 'Now go and see if you can rustle up a mug of kye.'

Five minutes after Grant left the bridge, Miller arrived.

'Morning, Ray,' he said to Milton, while fixing the loops in his duffle coat.

'Morning, sir,' replied Milton, who immediately vacated the captain's chair and reported the ship's position.

Midshipman Grant arrived carrying two enamel mugs of steaming, hot kye.

'Ah, just what I need, Mid,' Miller said, taking one of the mugs Grant had secretly reserved for himself.

'Thought you might, sir,' Grant said, as he grudgingly handed him the other mug. Then, with the look of a schoolboy who had been given a weeks' detention, he turned away in disgust.

At six thirty, the pipe, '"Eavo, 'eavo, lash up and stow, cooks to the galley," came over the tannoy.

'Looks like we're entering the edge of the Antarctic Basin,' Miller remarked. 'That's the reason for the sudden change in the weather,' he added, switching on the windscreen wipers and watching them swish from side to side. 'Wet weather routine, and rig up lifelines,' he added, shooting Pollard an ominous glance. 'I expect the weather to deteriorate, now that we've reached the Roaring Forties.'

'As you are familiar with this part of the world, sir,' said Pollard, 'when do you think we'll need to issue warm clothing?'

'What's our ETA for Punta Arenas, Pilot?'

'If we increase speed to twelve knots, sir,' Morgan cautiously replied, 'we should arrive there sometime on Friday.'

'It'll soon be close to freezing and we'll need the central heating,' Miller slowly answered. 'So in answer to your question, Number One, I want to leave Punta Arenas as soon as we've taken on fuel. So you'd better warn the supply officer and stores PO to issue warm clothing.'

'Very good, sir,' Pollard replied.

'Should I warn the professor, or will you do it?

'Err, I think I'll do that,' Miller answered quietly.

'Of course, sir,' Miller said, doing his best to suppress a smile.

Miller bent forward and unhooked the ship's tannoy. 'This is the captain speaking. All loose gear is to be stowed away and electric fires turned on whenever necessary, and hands keep clear of the upper deck.'

Just after eleven thirty, Leading Seaman Waters came into the seamen's mess, carefully carrying the rum fanny. Using a hand, he steadied himself against the sudden roll of the ship and lovingly placed it on the mess table.

'Right, you lot!' he shouted. 'Come and get it. And as you two are under stoppage,' he added, grinning at Brown and Lewis, 'you can hold the fanny and make sure it doesn't topple over. And remember what they said in the last war: blobby knob stops demob.'

'Piss off,' grunted Brown, who, like Lewis, had the afternoon watch, and he grabbed his oilskin and stormed out of the mess.

On the bridge, Miller was sat in his chair. He gave a tired yawn then looked at Grant, who, with his sextant resting in the crook of his left arm, was attempting to obtain a midday fix. Able Seaman O'Hanlon stood, balancing himself against the binnacle, holding a pad and pencil in readiness to make a note of Grant's findings.

'I suggest you make an estimate reading as the sun is well behind those clouds,' Miller said to Grant. 'Then find the buffer and check the lashings on both lifeboats. I'll be in my cabin if you need me, Number One,' he added, carefully lowering himself off his chair. 'And keep your eye on the barometer.'

'Very good, sir,' Pollard replied, grasping hold of Miller's chair to avoid falling over.

Miller left the bridge, and steadying himself against the roll of the ship, made his way down a stairway and onto the wardroom flat. He was about to go into his cabin, but decided to see how Linda was coping with the weather. He knocked on her door and heard her voice telling him to enter. Her hair was tied neatly in a bun. She wore brown, zip-up overalls and a pair of flip-flops and was sitting at her desk doing her best to write a letter.

As he came in, she turned around. 'Yes, captain,' she said, fixing him with those eyes he found so disturbing. 'And to what do I owe this visit?'

'I thought I'd see how you were coping with the elements,' Miller replied, feeling his face redden.

'How thoughtful of you,' she replied, placing her fountain pen on her blotting pad. Then, gripping hold of the edge of her desk, she stood up and said, 'As you can see, I've got good sea legs, and I don't suffer from seasickness.'

At that moment, the ship was hit by a huge wave and heeled precariously to port. She gave a short scream, and losing her grip, toppled forward and was caught by Miller. Holding tightly onto one another, they fell against the bulkhead. As the ship righted itself, the strength of his arms, together with the hardness and warmth of his body pressing against her, she felt surprisingly safe. For several seconds neither of them spoke. They stood, pinioned together, looking into one another's eyes.

Finally, Miller, very much aware of the softness of her breasts under her overalls, managed to mutter, 'So much for your sea legs.'

'Perhaps I spoke to soon,' Linda gasped, feeling her heart pounding against her ribs.

'I shouldn't worry,' Miller replied, slowly removing his arms. 'I expect you'll get…'

Another roll of the ship interrupted him, as, once more, she fell against him. The temptation to kiss him was too much to bare, and it showed in their eyes.

'I… I think you'd better leave, Commander,' she murmured, 'before we do something we might regret.'

'Yes,' he managed to say, feeling her body tremble slightly. 'I think you're right,' and moved away.

However, the glazed expression in her eyes showed that she was lying.

As soon as Miller left, Linda threw herself onto her bunk and buried her face in a pillow. 'What on earth are you doing?' she cried, angrily pounding the bedding. 'Falling in love with him would be emotional suicide, especially after Peter…'

Meanwhile, Miller was sitting in his cabin, staring at his desk, deep in thought. 'Better control yourself,' he mumbled to himself.

Falling for her would most certainly detract from the job at hand, and he could not, under any circumstances, allow that to happen. However, thinking of Linda, made it difficult to sleep.

Throughout the next day, the weather continued to deteriorate. During the morning watch on Thursday 17th, the sun disappeared behind a vast bank of black clouds. The ferocity of white-topped waves sent massive waves curling over the bows. A stabbing flash of thunder was quickly followed by sheets of rain, reducing visibility to a mere twenty yards. Then came the wind in wild bursts of fury, that rattled the windows and threatened to loosen the rivets in the steel plating.

Nobody was allowed on the upper deck, for fear of being washed overboard. Everyone off duty took to their hammocks. On the mess decks, crockery was locked away. Cupboards rattled like the bones of a skeleton. In the engine and boiler rooms, stokers clung on to anything at hand, to prevent them sliding on the steel plating. Pandemonium broke in the galley as pots and pans broke away from their supports and clattered around the slippery deck. And in the sickbay, constant clanking of bottles sounded like the delivery of a dozen milkmen doing their rounds.

'*My God, sir,*' Pollard cried, holding onto the compass repeater, as the ship, rearing up like a racehorse, emerged from the dark abyss of another steep trough. 'If this keeps up, we'll need a periscope to see where we're going.'

'Better get used to it, Number One,' Miller shouted, as a jagged fork of lightning erupted across the sky. 'When do we enter the Straits of Magellan, Pilot?'

'Later tonight, sir,' Lieutenant Morgan replied.

'Tell me, sir,' Pollard yelled, in an effort to be heard over the howling wind. 'As you've been here before, why are the straits so hazardous?'

'Because the unpredictable winds and currents make it one of the most difficult routes to navigate,' Miller answered, giving Pollard a warning look.

'No bugger told us that 'afore we sailed,' QM Lewis said to PO Thompson, both of whom overheard Miller speaking to Pollard.

'Well, Joe, my old gash bucket, you know what they say,' Thompson replied, as a sudden gush of wind rattled the windows, 'if you can't stand a joke, you shouldn't 'ave joined.'

Using all his knowledge of the currents, and despite the strong, contrary winds, Miller carefully navigated the ship past Tierra del Fuego, an archipelago of snow-capped mountainous islands lying across the mainland.

At six a.m. on Friday 18th, WO Operator Smith came onto the bridge. The rain had finally stopped. A few miles away, barely visible through the grey haze of dawn, a range of snow-covered mountains formed a formidable backdrop to the sprawling city of Punta Arenas.

'Message from the harbour master in Punta Arenas, sir,' said

Smith. 'It reads: "Berth number two wharf, Madrines dock. Oil tenders to meet."'

'Reply: "Many thanks. Grateful for your help."'

'Any chance of leave, sir?' Smith ventured to ask, hoping he might get ashore and contact Berlin.

'Afraid not,' Miller replied, hunched up in his chair. 'We'll be leaving as soon we've taken on fuel.'

'I see, sir,' Smith said. Feeling disappointed, he returned to the WT office.

A little after seven a.m., Leading Steward Blake came onto the bridge as the ship was coming alongside the wharf. 'Good morning, sir,' he said, handing Miller a mug of steaming, hot coffee.

'Ah, just what I need,' Miller replied, eagerly accepting the mug.

'Breakfast at eight a.m., sir,' Blake replied, before leaving.

'Incidentally, sir,' said Pollard, who was standing nearby. 'Did you know that Punta Arenas began life in 1848 as a penal colony?'

Miller looked askance at Pollard. 'No, I didn't, Number One, but it looks like it hasn't changed.' he said glibly, while peering through the window at the lines of drab, wooden houses stretching inland from the equally drab-looking warehouses lining the dock.

Twenty minutes later an oil tanker came alongside, and refuelling began.

'Now,' said Miller, handing Pollard an empty mug and sliding from his chair, 'I'm going below to have my breakfast. Let me know when fuelling is completed, and if any convicts try to board us,' he added, with a sarcastic glint in his eyes, 'be a good chap and deal with them.'

CHAPTER TWENTY-TWO

With refuelling completed, *Endeavour* slipped her moorings, and making a steady eighteen knots, entered Drake's Passage, a deep, treacherous waterway 600 miles wide, connecting the Atlantic and Pacific Oceans. The fierce westerly winds blowing from Tierra del Fuego continued to batter the ship, and the dark, rolling sea became a mass of raging white horses.

Miller was sitting in his customary chair on the bridge. Like the others on duty, he wore tropical whites. However, anyone on the upper deck had to wear fur-lined jackets and boots.

'What's the temperature outside, Pilot?'

'Minus four degrees Centigrade, sir,' Morgan replied.

'And what's our ETA in Stanley?'

'If we continue at our present speed, and we're not hampered by the strength of the current, we should arrive there in three days, sir,' Morgan replied confidently.

'Thank you, Pilot,' Miller said. 'I'll be in my cabin if you want me.'

With a weary sigh, he heaved himself off his chair, left the bridge and walked down the stairs. He was about to go into his cabin when Linda came out of the wardroom. She wore blue slacks and a red sweater. Behind her, Midshipmen Grant and Travers stood chattering and grinning like two schoolboys. As soon as they saw Miller, they fell silent and stood still.

'We were just leaving, sir,' Grant said, avoiding Miller's steely stare.

'I take it you are the last officers to leave,' Miller asked, giving a quick glance inside the wardroom.

'Yes, sir,' Grant replied, feeling his face redden.

'Then,' Miller firmly replied, 'don't let me keep you.'

As they turned to go, Linda flashed them a warm smile.

'Goodnight, gentlemen, and thank you for a very pleasant evening.' She turned to Miller, and running a hand through her hair, said, 'I know it's a bit late, Commander, but there is something I'd like to discuss with you.'

'Can't it wait until morning?' Miller replied brusquely.

'Well, yes, but it is important,' Linda said, looking expectantly at him.

'All right, then,' Miller answered, opening the door of his cabin. 'You'd better come and tell me what it is that's so important.'

Miller stood back allowing her to enter. He followed her and switched on the lights.

'Now, sit down and tell me what the problem is,' he said, sitting at his desk.

She sat down on the spare chair, and placing her handbag neatly on her lap, replied, 'My worry is this, Commander: if war was to break out while we're in South Georgia, how will you get back safely to England? As I'm sure the Germans will have submarines and warships at sea.'

'A good question,' said Miller, noticing the look of concern etched in her eyes. 'But as in the last war, the U-boats will be in the Atlantic attacking merchant shipping, and remember, the South Atlantic Ocean is vast.' He paused, and giving her a confident smile, went on, 'So you see, the chances of meeting an enemy warship is highly unlikely.'

'That's very reassuring,' Linda replied. 'And I hope you're right.'

'But as you'll be leaving the ship in Rio,' he said, pursing his lips, 'you'll be safe, so why are you so worried about us?'

Linda gave Miller a look that made his heart rate increase. 'Let me answer that by saying I'm becoming rather attached to the ship's crew.' For a few seconds she stopped talking, then, avoiding his eyes, continued, 'Including the officers.'

'I see,' Miller quietly replied. Then, bucking enough courage, he went on, 'Forgive me for being personal, but I see you're not married. Do you... have anyone?'

'Yes, I did,' Linda replied, furrowing her brow and averting his gaze. 'His name was Peter. We met at Cambridge. He died of a heart attack a week before we were due to get married. That was three years ago.' For a few seconds she looked directly into Miller's eyes, then said, 'What about you? I expect you have a wife and family at home.'

'My wife died in a car accident seven years ago,' Miller replied. His voice was quiet and strained. 'I was away at sea. We had no chil…'

A sharp knock on the door interrupted him. 'Come,' he said, feeling his heart pounding against his ribs.

The door opened, and Blake came in holding a tray containing a large mug of coffee, and a sandwich on a small plate.

'Beggin' your pardon, sir,' Blake said, conscious of having disturbed what appeared to be personal conversation. 'The first lieutenant told me you were here, and as you missed dinner, I thought you'd like a sandwich and a drink.'

'That's very thoughtful of you, Blake,' Miller replied, accepting the tray and placing it on his desk. 'Thank you.'

'Can I get you anything, miss?' Blake asked Linda.

'No, thank you,' Linda replied, hastily standing up. 'I was just leaving.'

'Very good, miss,' Blake said. 'Then I'll wish you both goodnight,' he added, then quietly left.

As soon as Blake was gone, Miller stood up and said, 'It seems we both have had our fair share of heartache.'

'Yes, it does. Goodnight, Commander,' she quietly replied, knowing that the emotional bond they now shared would make it hard for her to sleep.

Throughout the next forty-eight hours, the weather continued to deteriorate. The sun, hidden behind the black, low-lying cumulonimbus clouds, became a faint haze. A bitterly cold wind, blowing from the ice cap, together with gigantic walls of the dark-green ocean, rocked the ship like a child's cradle. Then came the snow, slanting down like stair rods, jamming the bridge windscreen wipers and reducing visibility to a mere ten yards. The masts and deck became camouflaged in white. Men off duty took to their hammocks, fully clothed. Meals became a lottery, as plates, mugs and crockery, despite the frantic efforts to save them, slid off the tables like a waterfall.

Then, as if wafted by a magic wand, overnight the weather changed dramatically. The snow stopped falling, leaving the ship covered in a patina of glistening white.

'You know, sir,' Pollard said, pensively stroking his chin. 'It's hard to believe that only a few hours ago the sea was buffeting the ship like hell. Now look at it. It's as calm as a mill pond.'

'I can't say I'm surprised, Number One,' Miller remarked, staring through the bridge window at the icy, blue sky. 'The weather in this area is influenced by large-scale oceanic movements, especially when the warm currents meet the cold Antarctic currents. And that's why it's so unpredictable. But,' he said, glancing warily at Pollard, 'I'm afraid it could all change in the blink of an eyelid.'

During most of the day, all hands not on duty cleared snow away from the upper deck.

'I can't see the point in this,' Able Seaman Lane said to Leading Seaman Waters, as he shovelled a mound of snow over the ship's side. 'The fuckin' snow will be back tomorrow, so this,' he paused, tossing a load over the side, 'is a waste of time.'

'Ah, stop moaning,' Waters gasped. 'What'll yer do if we meet one of those icebergs?'

'Jump into the nearest lifeboat,' Lane replied, standing up and leaning on his shovel. 'Then pray like hell.'

'Do you think the old man will give us leave when we reach Stanley?' Smith asked Lane.

'Buggered if I know, Smudge,' Lane answered, shaking his head. 'Anyway, from what I've read, there's nowt there but sheep and penguins.'

'And Shady would fuck either of them,' interrupted Waters.

At five-thirty on Monday 21st, Able Seaman Lewis, in the crow's nest, reported seeing land ten miles on the starboard beam.

OOW Lieutenant Morgan, and everyone on duty, immediately trained their binoculars away to their right. As they did so, Miller arrived.

'Looks pretty grim to me, eh, sir,' Morgan remarked, focussing on a rugged, cliff-lined coast partially shrouded in grey mist. 'I expect you've been here before, sir?'

'Yes, I have,' Miller replied, 'and it still looks rather grim.'

'According to my chart,' Morgan said, 'the Falkland Islands are an archipelago of small and large islands, and this coastline is part of West Island. Stanley is on the Eastern Island.'

'Thank you, Pilot,' Miller replied. 'I'm sure we're all grateful for your geography lesson. What's the temperature outside?'

'Three degrees Centigrade, sir,' replied Morgan. 'That's thirty degrees Fahrenheit,' he added smugly.

By ten a.m., the ship had passed Jason Island, a cluster of small, uninhabited islands. Three miles to starboard, the ragged outlines of Cape Dolphin and Cape Carysfort formed the backdrop to a windswept stretch of rolling grass covered hills.

'You know, sir,' Morgan said, using his binoculars to scan the terrain,' when Charles Darwin, on board the *Beagle,* arrived here in 1836, he described the Falklands as "a desolate and wretched aspect".'

'And I don't think he was far wrong,' Miller replied. 'But if I were you, old boy,' he added, glancing warily at Morgan, 'I wouldn't mention that to the islanders. The "Malvinas", as the Chilean's call the Falklands, are a mixture of Chileans and immigrants from Europe and Britain. They are a proud lot who live and work hard in a hostile climate.'

At twelve p.m. the ship passed Falkland Sound, a fifty-mile stretch of waterway separating East and West Islands. An hour later, Mount Osbourne, a snow-capped, craggy mountain dominating the rocky tip of East Island, hove into view.

Miller ordered a ten-degree turn to starboard. The ship slowly turned right and cruised past Berkeley Sound, a rocky inlet opposite the sharp promontory off Volunteer Point.

The entrance to Stanley Harbour was marked by two beacons mounted on Port William Hill. The sun was shining, and the water of the harbour sparkled with ripples from a light breeze.

'Hands fall in for entering harbour, please, Number One,' Miller ordered.

Half an hour later, Stanley hove into view. With its large

cluster of snow-capped, wooden houses sloping down from the uplands onto the waterfront, it resembled a small town in Scotland's Outer Hebrides.

For a few minutes, Miller scanned the roads he had walked along an age ago. Away to his right he could just make out the police station, the drill hall and a "cairn". This is a small pyramid of stones put up to mark the spot where Captain Strong of the *Welfare* went ashore in 1790, to claim the Falklands for King George.

'That's a fine-looking church, sir,' Pollard remarked, looking at a red-bricked edifice with a tall, snow-covered, pyramidal tower, situated on a slope close to Ross Road, a wide concrete roadway around the edge of the waterfront.

'Yes, it is, 'Miller replied. 'That's Christ Church Cathedral. It was built in 1892, and it's the southernmost cathedral in the world. And before you ask,' Miller added. 'That ship moored in the harbour opposite the cathedral is the SS *Great Britain*. It was badly damaged in a storm, and it's used by the Falkland Island steamship company as a warehouse. Now,' he said firmly, 'I think it's time I told the ship's company the real reason why we're here.'

CHAPTER TWENTY-THREE

Miller unhooked the ship's tannoy and cleared his throat. 'This is the captain speaking,' he said calmly. 'We have arrived in Stanley, and here's hoping our mail is waiting for collection.' He paused momentarily then continued. 'I'm sure you have been wondering why we've come almost halfway around the world just to monitor the weather. So I thought I'd better tell you the true purpose of our mission. The ship is bound for South Georgia, an archipelago on the fringe of the Antarctic circle.' He went on to tell them about Mr Weir finding grapholite on South Georgia and gave a brief reason for its importance in improving radar. 'Leave will be given to each part of the watch. We depart on Thursday and should reach South Georgia in ten days, providing we're not slowed down by the pack ice. Upon arrival, myself, Professor Penlowe and Mr Weir, along with a working party, will go ashore to the area where the grapholite was found. After collecting some of the rocks containing the grapholite, we'll return to Stanley, disembark Mr Weir and sail north. We will not stop at Punta but continue the long haul to Rio, arriving there, weather permitting, on or about 21st September. We'll refuel, and after a few days leave, sail for England. That is all.'

After replacing the handset, Miller looked at Pollard, and smiling, said, 'That should clear the air a bit, eh, Number One?'

'Yes, sir,' Pollard replied, 'especially that bit about leave and home, but tell me, is their anywhere in Stanley where we can get a decent drink?'

'As I recall, they import their alcohol from Chile,' said Miller. 'There's a small bar along the waterfront, used by the farmers and sheep owners. And another close by is called *The Mucky Duck*, for work hands, and that, I'm afraid, is it.'

'Not exactly the West End, eh, sir,' Pollard replied with a sly grin.

'Well, beggars can't be choosers, Number One,' Miller said.

Smith and LRO Bell had been sat in the wireless office listening intently to Miller's speech, during which time Smith made a mental note of the ship's movements. He also became excited at the prospect of seeing Katrina again.

After Miller had finished, Bell looked at Smith and said, 'If you want, Smithy, you can go ashore first. That'll give me time to write a letter to the missus. All right?'

'Cheers, Dinga,' Smith replied, anxious to inform his contact in Buenos Aires.

Able Seaman Brown, along with several other ratings, were fallen in on the quarterdeck. A promise of snow hung in the low-lying, leaden clouds, and a bitterly cold, polar wind stung their faces and tore at their fleece-lined, knee-length jackets.

'So that's what the fuckin' picks and shovels are for, Joe,' he said to Able Seaman Lewis, standing next to him.

'Aye,' Lewis replied, shuffling his legs to keep warm. 'Just so we can dig holes in rocks like common labourers.'

'I think we should volunteer,' Brown replied. 'At least it'll get us off the ship.'

By one p.m., hands for entering harbour had fallen out. An anchor was dropped, and the ship secured to a buoy 200 yards away from a long, wooden jetty. This was followed by lowering the Jacob's ladder on the port side. Minutes later, a motorboat arrived alongside. Able Seaman White, the ship's "posty", hurried down the Jacob's ladder, where a tall, weather-beaten sailor handed him a large bag of mail.

'Cheers, matey,' White said. 'Pity you can't come on board, or else I'd give yer my tot,' and he hurried back on board.

Meanwhile, Smith came onto the bridge, holding a signal. 'Message from shore, sir,' he said, handing it to Miller. 'It says: "Welcome to Stanley. Mr Weir and I will come aboard at six p.m. Sir William Henniker. Governor, Falkland Islands." Any reply, sir?'

'Yes,' Miller replied. Say: "Thank you. Look forward to seeing you both. Dinner at seven."'

Smith wrote down the reply on a pad then quickly left the bridge.

An hour later, the QM's voice came over the tannoy. 'D'yer hear there? Leave. Leave to the first part of starboard and port watches from four p.m. to eleven p.m. The first liberty boat will leave the ship at four p.m., and every two hours. Cold weather rig to be worn. The last liberty boat will leave the jetty at eleven p.m.' Then came the news everyone had been anxiously waiting for. 'Mail is now ready for collection.'

This was quickly followed by the stampede of footsteps echoing around as ratings left each mess, to Chalky White's office.

These were the first letters the crew had received since the ship had left Plymouth three weeks ago. Regular bulletins about Europe were no substitute for news from home. In each mess, letters were hastily opened, read and re-read.

In the seamen's mess, WO Smith had finished reading a letter from his father, ending with, "Do your duty as ordered. All is well. Mother sends her love."

'From yer girlfriend, Smithy?' enquired Dutch Holland.

'No, my dad,' Smith replied.

'My two are from me missus,' Holland said. 'She wants me to increase her allotment so she can buy a new pair of shoes. Can't understand it,' he added, scratching his head. 'I bought her a pair two years ago.'

In the senior ratings mess, Chief "Chippy" Mick Jenkins, finished reading one of his two letters, then, frowning slightly at Jack Townsend, the portly chief cook, said, 'I don't know about you, but it's too bloody cold to go ashore, so I think I'll stay on board.'

'I think I'll do the same,' Townsend replied, opening a letter he knew was from his wife, 'as I don't suppose there's anywhere in this godforsaken place to get a good meal. What about you, Paddy?' he asked Chief Engineer O'Malley.

'To be sure,' O'Malley replied, 'the Chief ERA and meself will be took busy checking the fuel system that the dockyard engineer in Devonport made such a fuss about.'

'I bet you any money the girls are sex-starved, so we're bound to strike it lucky,' Able Seaman Lane said to Able Seaman O'Hanlon, as he buttoned up his fleece-lined coat.

'Bugger that,' O'Hanlon, replied. 'It's so fuckin' cold that if you take your dick out it'll get frostbite.'

Despite the bitter weather, Lane and a few others were in the mess getting ready to go catch the liberty boat.

WO Smith had just finished fastening his bootlaces. He stood up, and making sure nobody was looking, he quickly opened a drawer in his locker. Like a shoplifter, he quickly slipped the small leather case containing the transmitter, under his jacket, and pushed it firmly into a deep inside pocket. As a second thought, he slipped the box containing the cyanide, into his pocket, praying he wouldn't have to use it.

Shortly after four p.m., Smith and twelve other ratings were fallen on the quarterdeck. Under their fleece-lined, hooded jackets, each one wore their uniform. Low-lying, cumulonimbus clouds disguised a pallid sun, and the fierce southerly wind stung their faces. After a brief warning by OOW Lieutenant Morgan to be on their best behaviour, they walked down the Jacobs ladder into one of the ship's lifeboats. The lifeboat was equipped with an outboard motor manned by Leading Seaman Waters.

'Step lively, you lot,' Waters shouted, as they stepped off the small wooden platform at the base of the ladder, into the boat. 'As I'm freezing my bollocks off.'

'Don't worry, Soapy,' shouted Leading Seaman Knight. 'We'll have a few pints for you.'

Ignoring Knight's facetious remark, Waters shouted to Able Seaman Davis, standing a few feet away, to "Let go for'd line." Seconds later Waters revved up the motor, and Davis, using the end of his hooked landing stick, pushed the lifeboat away from the ladder.

Ten minutes later, the boat arrived alongside the jetty.

As Smith and the others climbed out of the boat, Knight shouted, 'If any of you lot can drag yersells from the bright lights, I'll be back at six thirty.'

Smith, Knight, Lane and O'Hanlon joined several other ratings walking down the jetty. It was now dusk, and ahead of them the lights of the houses on the coast road, reflected in the gloomy, grey harbour waters. Only the cathedral, lying behind the houses on a high rise, was in total darkness.

'Doesn't seem many people around,' Lane remarked, as he saw a solitary man walking a dog up one of numerous sandy lanes leading uphill between the houses.

'I don't blame 'em,' said Knight, cupping his hand around a cigarette and using a match to light up. 'Where the fuck would they go?'

Five minutes later they passed a narrow uphill pathway with a low hedge either side. Close by, the constant wind had begun to peel off the dull-green paint on a square, flat-topped, wooden building. The sound of gramophone music came from inside, and a sign above the door, painted in white, read: "Mucky Duck. Only cash accepted."

Waters opened the door, and they went inside. The room was surprisingly big and well-lit by two electric bulbs hanging from a low-slung, wooden-beamed ceiling. The white-washed walls were bare, and in one corner was a door marked "Lavatory". A small electric fire warmed the musty atmosphere. Wooden benches and a few trestle tables lined each side of a floor covered in dark-brown, beer-stained linoleum.

A small, bald-headed man with a ruddy complexion stood behind a counter, cleaning a glass with an off-white dish towel. The sleeves of his open-necked, red shirt were rolled up, showing a pair of sturdy, hairy arms. His eyes were half closed, and he was listening nostalgically to the melodious voice of Al Jolson singing, "Sonny Boy", which was echoing from a gramophone under the counter. Behind him were three large wooden barrels, complete with small turn keys. Above them was a shelf containing half-empty bottles of whisky with Chilean labels.

As O'Hanlon and the others came in, "Hairy Arms" became alert and looked up.

'By gum,' he said, in a heavy Lancashire accent. 'I wondered how long it would take for you lot to get here, and before you ask, I've got Polar pale ale, or Escudo beer, both imported from Punta Arenas. I'm the manager, and me name's Charlie Woodhouse.'

'What's the strongest, Charlie?' O'Hanlon asked, as he lit a Woodbine.

'Escudo,' Charlie replied. 'I even drink it meself.'

'What d'yer think, lads?' Soapy replied, glancing firstly at Bogey then the other ratings.

'Let's try the Escudo,' someone shouted.

'Great stuff,' Charlie said, carefully filling each glass with a frothy, dark-brown liquid.

In a matter of minutes, everyone, including Smith, was sipping the beer.

In between gulps, Waters licked his lips and said, 'Good tack this, Charlie. Tastes just like Fuller's beer at 'ome. Keep 'em coming.'

As he spoke, the door opened, and in came four middle-aged men. They wore heavy duffle coats, and their faces were partially covered by a hood. Four women, similarly dressed, followed behind.

The tallest of the men threw back his hood, revealing a shock of dark, curly hair and a weather-beaten face half hidden behind a short, greying beard.

'We saw you sail in earlier,' he said. As he spoke, the corners of his pale-blue eyes crinkled into a welcoming smile. 'These people behind me are, like meself, sheep farmers, and these lovely ladies,' he added, grinning, 'are our wives.'

The wives removed their duffle coats, revealing an assortment of coloured woollen dresses. The men did the same. They wore heavy sweaters, and trousers tucked into strong leather boots.

After pleasant introductions, one of the farmers produced a bottle of Scotch whiskey and passed it to Charlie. A few drinks later, the place was filled with tobacco smoke, raucous laughter and talk. Charlie replaced the old record with lively dance music. O'Hanlon and Knight danced with two of the wives. Smith had thrown their duffle coats over chairs and was edging towards the lavatory door.

'What's the matter, Smithy?' O'Hanlon shouted over the shoulder of his dance partner, a small red-headed woman with glasses. 'Got two left feet?'

'Just going for a piss,' Smith replied.

Suddenly everyone cheered, as Knight, doing his best to impersonate Fred Astaire, swung his partner around in a circle. In doing so, he barged into a few other dancers. Smith saw his chance. Like a burglar making a quick getaway, he opened the door and stealthily made his way to a wooden outhouse at the bottom of a grassy path.

For a few seconds he felt his heart thumping against his ribs. He stood still and saw a small hedge running uphill next to the pub. After a quick glance around, he gave the bulge in his pocket a quick touch then climbed over the hedge onto a muddy pathway. He stopped again and listened to the raucous sound of music and laughter echoing from inside the pub. A quick, nervous glance around showed he was alone. With lines of warm perspiration running down the sides of his face, he hurried down the path onto the waterfront road. The dull, sulphur lighting emitting from the lamppost lights would provide perfect cover for the important task that lay ahead of him.

Doing his best to avoid making noise, he walked down the cobbled roadway. A few minutes later he stopped at the bottom of three steps leading up to a wrought iron gate and the railings surrounding the cathedral. Behind the gate, a wide, gravelled path led to a stout, arched entrance, accessed by two steps. Here the path forked left and right around the cathedral.

'Perfect,' Smith muttered.

A quick glance around confirmed his anonymity. Feeling his heart pounding like a hammer, he walked up the steps and slowly opened the gate. He stopped, hoping its rusticated squeak wouldn't give his presence away. Treading softly onto the gravel, he made

his way along the path, then stopped again and held his breath and listened, but the only sounds he heard was music coming from the nearby houses, and the occasional cawing of a bird.

He continued up the path and took the right fork that led behind the cathedral to a graveyard dotted with bushes, a yew tree and tomb stones. Listening to the blood pounding in his head, he found an ideal spot behind a wide, slopping buttress covered in damp moss. He was about to sit down when he heard the gate opening.

This was quickly followed by the sound of footsteps coming up the path. A surge of panic ran through him. As the footsteps became nearer, he caught his breath and felt his heart pounding like an express train. He clutched hold of the transmitter and pressed himself firmly against the inside angle of the buttress. Seconds later, the dark outline of a small, hooded figure wearing what looked like a priest's cassock, passed so close that Smith could see clouds of breath emanating from the person's mouth. Praying he wouldn't have to use it, he nervously groped into his pocket for the cyanide box, but stopped as the footsteps gradually faded way. Seconds later, the jangling of keys and the creaking of a door being opened rent the air. Smith almost fainted with relief and nearly dropped the transmitter.

Smith was about to leave when the baleful, jerky sound of organ music echoed from within the cathedral. He realised that as long as he could hear the organ being played, he was safe. He sat down on the damp grass, and feeling his fingers tremble, he unbuttoned his jacket and took out the small leather case containing the transmitter, earphones and Morse tapper. He pressed a tiny switch and saw the lights on the transmitting and power dials come on. Using the back of his hand, he wiped away a trickle of cold perspiration from his face and put on the earphones. Seconds later he tuned the transmitting dial to eight-five megacycles. Using the forefinger of his right hand, he began tapping out the following message in German: "Lion to Jackal, are you receiving me?" Much to Smith's relief, a second later came the reply: "Jackal to Lion. Receiving you. Go ahead." Before continuing, Smith lifted up one of the earphones and was relieved to hear that the organ music was still being played.

He replaced the earphone and continued: "*Endeavour* at Stanley. Sail for South Georgia on August 24th and arrive there ten days later. Real reason for journey is to collect vital minerals called grapholite, on South Georgia, for the improvement of radar transmission. Should leave South Georgia on either Sept 4th or 5th and return to Stanley on September 11th, then leave for Rio, arriving there roughly 27th. *Endeavour* hull painted red. Pennant number A17. Eagle, out. Heil Hitler."

A minute later came the reply. "Message received. Will pass it on to Berlin. *Heil* Hitler."

Smith took off his earphones, and for a few seconds listened to the organ music. He quickly packed everything away inside the leather case and buttoned up his jacket. Suddenly the music stopped. For a few seconds Smith froze, waiting to hear the door open, but all he heard was the eerie sound of the wind rustling through the bushes.

With his heart thumping violently, he hurried down the path, opened the gate and made his way onto the road. A quick glance at his wristwatch showed the time was eight fifteen. After passing a noisy *Mucky Duck,* he hurried along the jetty just as the eight thirty liberty boat, devoid of passengers, was arriving. He felt his stomach contract and he stopped walking.

'My God,' he murmured. 'I've forgotten to mention in the message that the ship is armed with a six-inch gun, but then…' he added to himself, 'a solitary gun will be no match for a U-boat's torpedoes,' and felt relieved.

'What's the matter, Smudge?' he heard Waters shout, as the boat came alongside the jetty. 'Didn't you like the beer, or summat?'

'No, it's just too fuckin' cold,' Smith replied, and climbed into the boat.

Ten minutes later Smith arrived on board *Endeavour,* saluted the quarterdeck then made his way below.

As he entered his mess, Able Seaman Harding looked up from playing uckers with Yorky Thompson, and said, 'You're back early, Smudge. What's the matter, beer no good?'

'No sheep to shag, more's the like,' added Yorky. 'And that's sippers you owe me, Noddy,' he said, after throwing a six.

Ignoring the ribald comments of a few others, Smith opened his locker, and after glancing furtively around, he quickly placed the leather case and cyanide box under a layer of socks, shorts and white fronts.

At exactly nine a.m. on Saturday 26th August, Canaris arrived in his office. Outside, from a clear, untrammelled, blue sky, an early morning autumn sun shone through the bay windows, bathing the room in warm sunshine. Under a thick black overcoat, Canaris wore black, well-polished shoes, a grey, double-breasted suit, a white shirt, and a tie with a small, red swastika tie pin.

Eva immediately stood up, and holding a piece of paper, said, 'This message came through at one a.m. I think it's the one you've been waiting for, sir,' she said, handing it to Canaris.

'Thank you, Eva,' Canaris replied. After reading the message, his face lit up into a broad smile. 'Wonderful!' he exclaimed. 'Put me through to the Furher, at once,' he added.

Still holding the message, he quickly took off his Homburg and overcoat and handed them to Eva, who hung them up on a hook inside the door, then left. A few minutes after he had sat down, the red telephone on his desk rang.

He immediately picked up the receiver. 'Good morning, Mein Furher. I hope I haven't disturbed you, but I have just received a message from our agent in Buenos Aires.'

'Excellent, what does it say?' Hitler replied, in his usual raspy voice.

Canaris read out the signal's contents, then went on, 'With respect, may I suggest Admiral Donetz sends one of his XB U-boats to intercept *Endeavour?*'

Admiral Karl Donetz was forty-eight. He stood over six feet, with a high forehead and receding brown hair. His intelligent pale-blue eyes set in a slightly, weather-beaten complexion, together with a charismatic personality, commanded instant respect. He was married to Ingeborg Weber who bore him three children. He was supreme commander of the navy and succeeded Hitler as German Head of State in May 1945 until Germany's surrender in May 1945.

'Yes, I will order him to do that,' Hitler replied. 'He is to use his twin guns to cripple her, then send an officer and a boarding party to board the ship. If her captain refuses to tell us where this grapholite is, he is to shoot a sailor every five minutes. That,' he added with guttural laugh, 'should change his mind. After this mineral is found, he is to torpedo then ship.'

'A splendid idea, Mein Fuhrer,' Canaris replied, with an ugly smirk. '*Heil* Hitler,' he added, then replaced the receiver.

CHAPTER TWENTY-FOUR

Two hours after Smith went ashore, the governor's barge came alongside *Endeavour's* port side. Miller gave a quick nod to the QM, whose pipe, "Attention on the upper deck. Face aft," echoed around the ship. Miller, Pollard and OOW Lieutenant Milton stood near the top of the Jacob's ladder, waiting to greet the governor and Mr Weir.

Sir Herbert Henniker, KCMG, was born in Australia in February 1880. After studying history at Oxford, he entered the colonial service. Following several posts in various parts of the empire, he was appointed governor of the Falkland Islands in 1935. It was here, in 1936, that his wife, Helena, died in childbirth.

Sir Herbert was over six feet tall and wore a thick, white woollen muffler that stood out against his black overcoat and trilby. Taking tight hold of the rope guard rails, he carefully walked up the Jacob's ladder. Behind him came Mr Weir carrying a bulky canvas holdall. Weir was a small, stocky man. He wore a thick parka and a fleece-lined hood that partially hid his face and beard.

As Sir Herbert was piped on board, he stood to attention and removed his trilby, displaying a thin layer of greying, fair hair parted nearly on the left. Not being used to naval protocol, Mr Weir stood behind the governor, looking slightly bemused.

Miller stepped forward, saluted them, and proffering his hand, said, 'Welcome on board, Your Excellency. Commander Miller.'

'My pleasure, Commander,' the governor replied, removing a black leather glove, then shaking Miller's hand. 'Damn good to see you; hope you've had a pleasant voyage,' he added, while replacing his hat.

His authoritative voice, spoken in a clipped manner, was sharp and well-modulated. A closer look by Miller, at the governor, showed intelligent, dark-brown eyes set against a tanned, heavily creased face. The small, grey moustache he wore appeared to jerk slightly every time he spoke.

'Yes, we did, thank you, sir,' Miller answered. 'And I take it this gentleman,' he added, turning around, 'is Mr Weir.'

Weir stepped forward, allowing Miller to see a pair of deep-set, keen, pale-blue eyes, and a dark-red beard that covered the lower part of his weather-beaten face.

'Welcome on board, Mr Weir. Hector, I believe it is?' said Miller.

'Aye, that's me name,' Weir replied curtly. He put down his holdall, and without removing his woollen glove, shook Miller's hand. 'But "Jock" will do nicely,' he said, flashing a row of uneven, tobacco-stained teeth.

After introducing Weir and the governor to Pollard, Miller glanced at Lieutenant Milton and said to Weir, 'If you follow this officer, he'll show you to your cabin, then take you to the wardroom. And if Your Excellency would follow me, I'll take you to the wardroom to meet the officers before dinner.'

'And I hope, a large, neat Scotch to warm us both up,' the Governor replied with grin.

'Of course, sir.' Miller replied.

'This way, sir,' Milton said to Mr Weir.

Milton led Weir down two flights of stairs into the officer's flat, then stopped outside a cabin. Using a key, he opened the door.

'Just stow your gear, and I'll take you to the wardroom,' Milton said, and handed Weir the key.

Miller, preceded by the Governor, entered the wardroom. Everyone stopped talking and stood up. Miller immediately noticed how stunning Linda looked, wearing a dark-blue, long-sleeved dress, and an elegant pearl necklace that looked perfect set against her swan-like neck.

'Good evening, gentlemen and *lady*,' said the Governor, smiling courteously at Linda. He introduced himself, then went on. 'I shall be meeting all of you informally, so do relax and carry on smoking.' He turned to Miller, and raising his eyes, glanced appreciatively at the elaborate table setting and the glittering candelabra, then said, 'My word, commander, you do live in style.'

'Only on special occasions such as this,' Miller replied gracefully.

As he finished speaking, Petty Officer Feneck walked up, carrying a small silver tray on which rested a glass of whisky.

'Thank you so much,' said the Governor, accepting the drink. After taking a good sip, he lovingly licked his lips then murmured, 'Mmm... damn fine Scotch; exactly what I needed.'

Just then Lieutenant Milton came in, followed by Mr Weir. Divested of his parka, Weir's untidy, reddish-brown hair and leathery, weather-beaten features, were the hallmarks of someone who had spent a great deal of time exposed to the elements.

'Ah, Mr Weir, do come in and join us,' said Miller, taking Weir by the arm. 'I'm sure PO Feneck will be only too happy to bring you a drink. What'll you have?'

'A wee dram o' whisky will do nicely, thank you,' Weir replied. Noticing the officers wearing their best uniforms, he suddenly felt self-conscious in his black boots, brown, corduroy trousers and open-necked tartan shirt.

Feneck arrived and handed Weir a large whisky. Weir thanked him, and with Feneck watching, he downed his drink in one quick swallow.

'Dinner in ten minutes, sir,' said Feneck, and left the room.

Five minutes later the stewards arrived, and everyone was seated. Sir Henry and Miller sat at the top of the table. To their right, Pollard, Linda and Weir faced one another. The rest of the officers, ignoring seniority, occupied the remaining high-backed chairs. The wine glasses were filled.

Miller remained seated, and raising his glass, said, 'The king.' Linda and Weir were about to stand, but seeing everyone staying seated, quickly sat down. The custom of sitting down while honouring the king dated back to Nelson's time when the deckheads were too low to stand.

After dinner, the port was passed around, and everyone fell silent as the governor stood up.

'Please, do smoke if you want to,' he began.

A few did so, including Mr Weir who produced a well-used, Meerschaum pipe. Within seconds he lit up, and amidst bursts of laughter, almost disappeared under a cloud of bluish-grey tobacco smoke.

'Should you ever need a smoke screen, Commander,' the governor said jokingly, 'I'm sure Mr Weir will come in useful.' After the laughter subsided, the governor cleared his throat, and in a controlled but stern manner, continued. 'Since *Endeavour* left Punta Arenas a week ago, the army and RAF reserves have been called up, and the Royal Navy is now mobilised. Germany has closed the border with Poland and Upper Silesia, and Poland have retaliated by massing troops along her border. In a speech three days ago, Hitler demanded Danzig, the Polish Corridor and the Anglo-French pledge to Poland be rescinded.' The governor paused, picked up a glass and took a sip of water, and with his voice wavering slightly, went on. 'Yesterday, in the Kremlin, Germany and Russia signed a non-aggression pact. With Germany's eastern borders now safe, in my opinion, this will make war in Europe inevitable.'

The governor's remarks were met with stony silence.

Then, Lieutenant Morgan slowly raised a hand and asked the question that was in everybody's mind. 'And when do you think that will be, sir?'

After taking another sip of water, the governor quietly replied, 'I really couldn't say. But rest assured, it'll be damn soon. Any other questions?' he added, noticing the stunned expressions on the faces of his audience.

Taking another puff of his pipe, Weir gave the governor a worried look and said, 'How will that affect us in the islands?'

'I have made arrangements to have the Falkland Defence Force made of volunteers with some sort of military experience,' the governor replied.

'Aye, and what about help from Britain?' Weir asked, using a hand to waft away a cloud of tobacco smoke.

'I'm afraid I can't answer that, Mr Weir,' the governor replied, somewhat reluctantly. 'But I'm sure some assistance will be forthcoming.'

'Excuse me, sir,' ventured Midshipman Grant, timidly raising a hand. 'If war does break out, will *Endeavour* be recalled home before our mission is completed?'

'I very much doubt it, young man,' the governor replied, shaking his head.

'He only asked that, sir, because he has a popsy in Plymouth,' chimed in Midshipman Travers, who was sat next to Grant at the end of the table.

Seconds after the laughter Travers' remark caused died down, the governor looked at everyone and said, 'Now, I'm afraid I must leave you. But before I do, let me say how much I've enjoyed meeting you, and especially dining on the delicious roast beef and Yorkshire pudding. My compliments to the cook — it was an extremely pleasant change after a stable diet of mutton.'

This jocularity produced an immediate ripple of respectful laughter, after which the governor, in a more sombre note, continued. 'You don't need me to remind you that the task before you is very important. As I may not see you again when you stop here on your way back from South Georgia to return Mr Weir into the bosom of his family, let me wish you good luck, Godspeed, and a safe journey home.'

Accompanied by the grating of chairs, everyone stood up as the governor and Miller left the room. They went to Miller's cabin where PO Feneck handed the governor his muffler and hat, then helped him with his overcoat. The governor thanked him and followed Miller down the two sets of stairs, along the passageway, and opened a door leading onto the upper deck. As they did so, a gust of bitterly cold wind attacked their faces.

'Thank you for your hospitality, Commander,' said the governor, as he warmly shook Miller's hand. 'And as we may not meet again, God bless you and your crew, and may your mission prove successful.'

'Thank you, sir,' Miller replied. 'We'll do our best,' and he saluted.

The governor turned up his collar, and with the wind whipping against his overcoat, he carefully walked down the Jacob's ladder and was helped into the barge by the strong hands of a Falkland islander. The engine immediately revved up. The Jacobs ladder was hauled on board and the heaving lines cast off. The time was ten p.m.

As the governor gave a quick, parting wave, "Secure, lights out," cam over the tannoy. Seconds later, the barge left the ship's side and headed towards the jetty.

CHAPTER TWENTY-FIVE

The next morning, Miller, Pollard, Morgan, Weir and Linda were gathered in the wardroom. "Colours" had just finished, and they were grouped around the table, looking at a large map of South Georgia. Each held a cup of coffee, courtesy of PO Feneck.

'Would you kindly show us exactly where you found the grapholite, Jock?' Miller asked, after taking a sip.

'Aye, that I will,' Weir replied confidently. After placing his cup on the table, he bent over the map, and using a forefinger, indicated a spot roughly two miles away from the Norwegian whaling station, Grypviken, and said, 'Here, on the rocks opposite King Edward's Point. I remember seeing Shackleton's gravestone away on a hill to my right, and my son, Angus, telling me he could see some elephant seals on the beach, directly below us.'

'I know where Shackleton's grave is, but are you sure you'll be able to find the same rocks?' Miller asked.

'Och, aye,' Weir replied, patiently stroking his beard. 'I found them below a stretch of ground not far from the whaling station, where Shackleton is buried. But at this time of year, I expect they'll be covered in snow, so it'll be up to your laddies to dig 'em oot.'

'The rocks in this part of the world are a mixture of volcanoclastic sandstone and mudstone,' said Linda, staring intently at the map. 'They are very dense and hard. How did you find the grapholite, Jock?'

Weir took out his pipe, and using a match, lit it. Immediately the aromatic smell of tobacco smoke bellowed into the air. 'Of course, I didna know it was grapholite,' Weir replied. 'It was the colour in the strata in the rock that caught my eye. They were a dark green. I'd never seen rock strata that colour 'afore. I became curious, and as I could na find any reference to it in ma books, I chipped some away and sent a piece to Professor Mackenzie at

Cambridge University.'

'Did you mention this to anyone in the whaling station?' Pollard asked.

'No, I didna,' Weir replied, taking a puff of his pipe. 'And nobody asked me.'

'Thank you, Jock,' said Miller. 'You've been more than helpful, and I'm sure the government won't forget it.'

'Och, I only hope this grapholite helps,' Jock replied. 'Ye see, ma father was in the Black Watch and was killed at Mons in the last lot.'

'Now, this is what I intend to do,' said Miller, staring keenly at everyone. 'As I recall, the whaling station has a long jetty. Therefore, I shall berth there. At this time of year, most of the men, including the manager, will be on leave. So we can't expect help.' He paused and finished his coffee, then continued. 'The party to go ashore will consist of myself, Jock, Linda, Chief GI Mills, two ratings carrying the chest, a rating carrying a pick, another with a shovel, and a rating with a hammer and chisel. One of the ratings should be a leading hand, who'll be in charge of steering the boat as well as helping us. Shackleton's grave is on the top of a steep hill overlooking the eastern side of the harbour and is a fifteen-minute walk from where we will be. Any questions?'

'I take it there will be no shore leave, sir?' Pollard asked.

'No shore leave, Number One,' Miller replied. 'Duncan will keep the engines flashed up, so with any luck, we'll be on our way once we have the grapholite on board. Anything else?'

'What is the weather forecast?' Linda asked.

'That's good question, Linda,' Miller replied, inwardly kicking himself for not mentioning it. 'The pilot tells me it's too early to predict exactly what the weather will be. If, however, the weather suddenly deteriorates, as it's apt to do in these parts, then, I'm afraid, we would have to wait until things improve.'

At that moment, a knock came at the door and PO Feneck came in holding a large, silver coffee pot. 'Anyone care for a re-fill?' he asked, looking around.

'No, thank you, PO,' said Miller, noticing the empty cups on the table. 'I think we've finished here.'

At nine a.m. on Thursday 24th, *Endeavour* up-anchored and left Stanley. Low-lying, ugly, black cumulonimbus clouds partially hid the anaemic sun. A bitterly cold wind blowing from the ice cap, stung faces, making eyes water.

After clearing the harbour, the ship slowly turned right into the open waters of Port William and passed the unlit lighthouse on Cape Pembroke. This, as Miller knew from past experience, was the gateway south into the ice.

By twelve p.m., the sky had darkened. Then came the ominous sound of thunder approaching from the west. Minutes later, large drops of rain splattered against the bridge windows.

'The barometer's falling, sir,' Morgan said to Miller, 'and it looks like a storm is brewing.'

'Thank you, pilot. Pipe, "Hands keep off the upper deck. Wet weather routine."'

Seconds after he finished speaking, a jagged flash of lightning streaked across the sky. Then came a sudden, furious burst of wind. This was followed by lumps of hail rattling against the windows.

Suddenly, visibility became a veiled wall of white.

'You've been in these waters before, sir,' Pollard yelled to Miller, who was stood, holding on to his chair. 'How long do you think this will last?'

'It could finish just as quickly as it began,' Miller shouted. 'I'm afraid we'll just have to wait and see.'

The noise as the elements attacked the bulkheads and upper deck was deafening. In the mess decks, everyone off duty cowered down in their hammocks, hands clasped to their ears.

Throughout the afternoon the ship was battered like a baker pounding dough. Rum issue was postponed. Cooks and stewards, doing a decent impression of being drunk, doled out corned beef and cheese sandwiches.

Just as Miller predicted, by eight p.m. the wind and hail suddenly dropped, leaving the ship glistening like a Christmas tree.

"Rum issue will be in half an hour. Duty watch fall in outside the coxswain's offices," was piped.

'Thank fuck fer that,' cried Leading Seaman Waters, as he climbed out of his hammock.

'And don't forget you owe me sippers, as I beat you at crib before we sailed,' shouted LRO Bell.

'Get knotted,' Waters replied, throwing a boot at Bell, who ducked, allowing it to hit Able Seaman Brown.

Shortly after nine p.m., Miller took a deep, satisfied breath and looked at Pollard. 'What a sight, eh, Number One,' he said, staring outside the windows.

The remnants of the storm clouds had disappeared over the horizon, leaving rays of the sun spreading its orange tentacles across a sheet of glassy, blue sea.

'It certainly is, sir,' Pollard replied. 'Here's hoping it will last.'

However, at nine a.m. on Thursday 29th, Able Seaman Lofty Day, in the crow's nest, reported sighting pack ice roughly fifteen miles dead ahead.

Everyone focussed their binoculars on an extensive stretch of a dazzling wall of white ice, looking incongruously out of place under the vast concavity of a pale-blue sky.

'*Great Scott, sir*!' Pollard cried. 'It looks like an enormous desert of ice.'

'And God knows how thick,' Miller replied, shaking his head. 'It's bound to slow us up.'

'Do you think our bows will be strong enough to cut through it, sir?' asked Pollard, glancing hopefully at Miller.

'Well, Number One,' Miller sighed, his binoculars pinned firmly to his eyes. 'We'll soon find out.' He unhooked the tannoy. 'This is the captain speaking. In a short while we will encounter pack ice. As most of you have never seen it, all ratings off duty should come on the upper deck. That is all.'

In a matter of minutes, ratings, wearing mufflers, duffle coats and fur-lined jackets, crowded onto the upper deck.

'Looks like we've landed on another planet, don't it, Yorky?' Able Seaman Lewis remarked to Able Seaman Thompson.

Both ratings had joined the others leaning against the guardrail, staring in awe as the ship gradually approached the ice pack.

'Aye, that it does,' Thompson replied, feeling a slight brush of bitterly cold wind waft his face. 'Better keep your eyes open for alien snowmen,' he added jokingly.

'Or polar bears,' added Thompson.

'Some bloody hope,' Lewis hastily replied. 'You only find polar bears in the North Pole.'

On the bridge, Miller looked at Morgan and said, 'What's the temperature, Pilot?'

'Minus eight Centigrade, sir,' Morgan answered cautiously.

Miller unhooked the sonar voice pipe. 'How wide is the pack ice?' he asked Leading Seaman Hardman.

'Roughly ten miles, sir,' Hardman replied. 'It looks like a small island.'

Pollard overheard Hardman's reply, looked askance at Miller and said, 'Do you think we could go around it, sir?'

'We could, but it would take at least three days,' Miller replied.

Twenty minutes later, the ship was half a mile away from the edge of the pack ice.

'What's our speed, Number One?' asked Miller.

'Fifteen knots, sir,' Pollard replied.

'Reduce to ten knots,' said Miller, pensively stroking his chin.

'*But sir!*' exclaimed Pollard.' Surely we should increase speed if we're to break through the ice?'

'No, Number one,' Miller replied. 'That's what helped to sink the *Titanic*. She was going too fast when she hit the iceberg.'

Everyone watched anxiously as the ship approached the edge of the vast expanse of ice.

'Good lord, sir,' said Pollard, 'it looks about five thick.'

'Remember, only about a quarter of an iceberg can be seen,' said Miller.

'That's because the ice has nine tenths of the water's density,' Linda chimed in. 'Therefore, most of the iceberg is below the water's surface.'

'Thank you, Professor, that's most interesting,' Miller replied.

No sooner had he spoken than a violent shudder rocked the ship as the bows crunched into the ice. This was followed by what sounded like glass breaking. For a few agonising seconds the ship came to a grinding halt. Suddenly, an eerie cry, reminiscent of a wounded animal, could be heard, as a crack, several yards long, appeared in the ice. Seconds later the ice slowly parted, allowing the ship to move.

'Thank God for that,' sighed Miller, using the back of his hand to wipe away sweat from his brow.

However, he spoke too soon.

Twenty minutes later, with the open sea only four miles away, a dull vibration shook everything as the ship shuddered to a halt.

'It looks like we're stuck, sir!' exclaimed Pollard.

'Yes, it seems so, Number One,' Miller replied, doing is best to sound calm. 'Stop engines.'

'What will you do if we can't cut through it, sir?' Pollard asked cautiously.

Miller took a deep breath, then, staring guardedly at Pollard, said, 'I'm not sure. We could go astern and go around it, but there's no guarantee that we would meet thinner pack ice.

'So, what now, sir?' Pollard asked tentatively.

Miller was suddenly aware that all eyes were on him. He slowly eased himself off his chair and stood staring out of the window. The plight of Shackleton, when his ship, *Endurance,* became slowly crushed by the ice in 1915, flashed through his mind. However, unlike Shackleton, he had wireless contact with the outer world and could ask for help. But given the present weather conditions, how long, he asked himself, would it take help to reach them?

Suddenly he remembered, when he was fourteen, Central Park Lake in Wallasey, had frozen over. He vividly recalled sitting on a wooden sledge and being towed across the lake by his friend, Gordon Laird. He clearly recollected feeling a sudden jolt as the sledge hit a raised section of ice.

'Hold tight, Bob,' Gordon had yelled, as he tugged hard at the tow rope.

He also remembered feeling scared as the sledge rose in the air, as the combined weight of himself and the sledge cracked the ice. For a few minutes he stood, wistfully stroking his chin, wondering if *Endeavour's* twenty-ton weight would be sufficient to do the same. If not, the fate of his ship and the ship's company, would be in the lap of the gods.

CHAPTER TWENTY-SIX

'We seem to have stopped, Commander,' said Linda. 'Is there anything I can do?'

'I'm afraid not,' Miller answered. Turning to Pollard, he said, 'I have an idea, Number One. If it doesn't work...' He paused momentarily, then furrowing his brow, said, 'We could be in for a long winter.'

Miller turned from them and hooked the ship's tannoy. 'This is the captain speaking,' he said, trying his best to sound calm. 'We seem to be up against a very resistant section of the ice. I'm going to restart the engines. Make sure everything is secure, and don't be alarmed if you feel the ship rise slightly. That is all.'

In the wheelhouse, QM Able Seaman Day gave Chief Coxswain Moore a searching look and said, 'What the fuck is he trying to do, Chief?'

'Buggered if I know,' Moore replied, 'but, whatever it is, I hope it works. So keep yer hands firmly on the telegraph.'

'Start engines,' Miller snapped.

Moore repeated the order. Seconds later, the engines sprung to life.

'Slow ahead.'

Everyone held onto anything at hand and waited. In the senior ratings mess, Len Mills looked askance at Stores PO Watts and said, 'Well, me 'andsome, at least we can't capsize.'

Watts gave Mills a withering look and said, 'No, Len, but we can be crushed like sausage.'

In an attempt to defuse the worried expressions on the faces of his mess mates, Petty Officer Martin, grinning weakly, said, 'That reminds me; I wonder if we're on bangers for supper.'

On the bridge, everyone waited, their faces pale and drawn. Still no movement, only an increase in the loud, grating noise, as if the ship was fighting desperately for survival.

'Half ahead,' Miller said, nervously biting his lower lip.

Seconds later, the ship continued to shudder as the engines revved up to ten knots. But to Miller's dismay, the ship remained stationary. He took a deep breath and muttered, 'Right, you bastard, here goes,' and ordered, 'Full Ahead.'

In the engine room, O'Malley, ignoring the limes of sweat trickling down the sides of his face, pushed the engine throttle to "Full".

At first, nothing happened. Then, as if moved by some unknown force, the ship tilted slightly. This was quickly followed by a series of loud, crunching noises. On the bridge, Miller and the others suddenly felt the ship shudder. For a few agonising seconds, the ship remained at a slight angle poised on the ridge of the ice. For what seemed like an eternity, nothing happened. Then, after a series of ear-splitting noises, jagged cracks appeared in the ice. The ship slowly settled down, and to the relief of everyone, began to move slowly.

Miller grasped the professor by the shoulders and cried, 'By God, Linda, we've done it!'

'You mean, you've done it,' Linda replied, looking longingly at Pollard.

In January 2019, an expedition into the Weddell Sea, to find Shackleton's *Endurance*, was led by her captain, Knowledge Bengur, who ordered a similar move when his ship SA *Agulhas* was trapped in the pack ice.

'She's right, sir!' exclaimed Pollard, whose face, like the others on the bridge, was a picture of relief.

Miller didn't reply. He was unaware that everyone was looking at him because he still had hold of Linda's shoulders and was looking deeply into her eyes.

Feeling slightly embarrassed, Pollard gave a diplomatic cough and said, 'Excuse me, sir, what do you want to do now?'

'Oh, slow ahead,' Miller replied, hurriedly removing his hands from Linda's shoulders. 'I don't want to risk damaging the bows.'

'Very good, sir,' Pollard replied, doing his best not to smile.

'Please excuse me, Commander,' said Linda, feeling her

cheeks redden. 'I think I'd better go below.' After casting a quick, embarrassed glance at Miller, she turned and hurried from the bridge.

Watching her leave, Able Seaman Lewis whispered to PO Signalman Dave Watts, 'I wonder if the old man's givin' 'er one.'

'If he isn't,' Watts muttered from the side of his mouth, 'he wants his head examined.'

During the rest of the day, the sharp, crackling noise of the ice breaking up resounded throughout the ship. Finally, by one p.m., *Endeavour* emerged from her icy captors into the open sea.

However, the danger wasn't over. At three p.m., Able Seaman Ward, in the crow's nest, reported seeing icebergs. 'There's three of 'em, roughly five miles on the port bow, sir.'

On the lower deck, everyone had enjoyed their overdue 'tot' and were in the middle of eating lamb stew.

The officers off duty were in the wardroom, enjoying similar fare, when Miller's strident voice came over the tannoy. 'For those who haven't seen an iceberg, now is your chance, as a few have been sighted away to port.'

In the seamen's mess, Brown was sat at the table. He had finished wiping gravy from his lips with an off-white handkerchief. 'I don't know about you lot,' he said, looking at several other ratings, 'but I've always wanted to see what these fuckin' things look like.'

Me too,' chimed in Able Seaman Thompson, who, along with a few other ratings, stood up, grabbed their fur-lined coats and followed Brown out of the mess.

A few minutes later they joined stokers, cooks, stewards and others on the fo'c'sle. About two hundred yards on either side of the ship lay two dazzling, white icebergs surrounded by irregular-shaped chunks of floating ice. The one on the port side looked like a round, squat island. The elements had carved the edges into small mounds, making it look like a huge, wedding cake. The other one was even bigger. The harsh Antarctic winds, had, over time, moulded a series of large, round, uneven crenulations around its splayed body.

'Bloody hell!' exclaimed Able Seaman Lewis. 'So that's what

sunk the *Titanic*!'

'They look like huge mounds of Walls ice cream,' added Able Seaman Holland.

'The *Titanic*'s lookout must 'ave been fuckin' blind,' remarked Stoker Green, blowing into his hands and stamping his feet.

'Pissed, more likely,' added Able Seaman Harding.

'At least the officers won't be short of ice to drink with their gin and tonics,' joked Officer's Steward Williams.

On the bridge, Miller glanced guardedly at Pollard and said, 'Better double the lookouts, especially at night, Number One. Sonar has informed me there are a few more of these beauties ahead of us. What's our speed, Number One?'

'Fifteen knots, sir,' Pollard replied.

'Good, keep it like that,' Miller replied, lowering himself from his chair. 'I'll be in my cabin if you need me,' and stifling a yawn, left the bridge.

The time was ten p.m. Darkness had fallen. From the horizon, the orange rays of the crescent sun changed the calm, dark-blue sea into a carpet of shimmering gold, and the sky to the east was a haze of reds and purples. The effect of the light on the icebergs was startling. They lost their natural whiteness and became a mixture of soft, phosphorescent greens and pinks.

'My God, what a beautiful sight,' said OOW Lieutenant Morgan, who was sitting comfortably in the captain's chair. 'It looks just like a Turner painting.'

He had just finished speaking when the sonar operator, Leading Seaman Hardman, reported sighting the tip of an iceberg two hundred yards directly ahead of the ship.

'Thank you, Hardman,' Morgan replied. He picked up the wheelhouse voice pipe. 'Port ten, full ahead.'

Seconds later, the ship healed sharply to the left, then gathered speed. Lieutenant Morgan and everyone on duty immediately held on to anything to avoid falling over.

Miller arrived just as the ship began to right itself.

'What's the problem, Pilot?' he asked, grasping one of the arms of his chair.

Morgan quickly told him. 'Everything happened so quickly, sir,' he added. 'I didn't have time to inform you.'

'Yes, I see the beast,' Miller cried. 'You did the right thing, Pilot. Reduce speed to ten knots and get back on our southerly course.'

The next two days passed without incident. The sea remained a calm, glassy blue. From a clear, pale, cerulean sky, the sun's rays bathed everything in a deceptive warmth.

On the bridge, Midshipman Grant, shielding his eyes from the glare of the sun, shouted, 'Excuse me, sir, are those birds flying over that iceberg away to port, albatrosses?'

Miller, Pollard and the others, protected their eyes and looked up to their left.

'Indeed, they are, Mid,' Miller replied, 'and it shows we're not too far away from land,' he added, with a satisfied smile.

However, the next day, the weather changed. The bitterly cold southerly wind whipped up the sea into a mass of white horses. A thin film of ice formed on the outside of the bridge windows. Angry, black clouds scudded across the sky. The reading on the bridge barometer showed a dramatic drop from forty to sixty degrees Centigrade.

'I dunno about you,' Perry Officer Thompson remarked to QM Waters, 'but this fuckin' weather reminds me of my missus: one minute all smiles; the next, moody as buggery.'

'I know what yer mean, PO,' Waters replied. 'Mines the same. Maybe if I stopped her allotment, she'd bugger off and leave me.'

'Now, that's an idea,' PO Thompson said, pensively stroking his chin.

Over the next three days, the wind gradually veered to the north. Then, as if my magic, the wind died down, leaving the sea strewn with masses of irregular-shaped lumps of floating ice.

At three thirty p.m., on September 3rd, Able Seaman Lane, in the crow's nest, reported, 'Land, sir; a mountain, roughly fifteen miles away to starboard.'

All heads turned to the right, and using their binoculars, saw glistening, snow-capped peaks high in the sky above a grey band of ectoplasmic mist.

Miller gave a wry smile. 'The tallest mountain, gentlemen,' he said, his binoculars clamped to his eyes, 'is Mount Paget. It's the highest peak of the Allardyce Range of mountains that forms the spine of South Georgia.'

Just as Miller finished speaking, Lieutenant Willis, breathing heavily and looking flushed, arrived holding a signal. 'Excuse me, sir,' he said, handing the signal to Miller. 'This arrived from the admiralty a few minutes ago.'

'*Great Scott!*' Miller exclaimed, after reading it. 'We've declared war against Germany.' He looked up, and after seeing the stunned expressions on everyone's faces, he went on. 'The signal says, "As from eleven thirty a.m. today, Sunday, September 3rd, we are at war with Germany. Commence hostilities. God save the king. Winston Churchill. First Lord of the Admiralty."'

With a worried look on his face, Willis left the bridge. Everyone on the bridge stood in silence, taking in the severity of Miller's words.

Then, Pollard, shaking his head, looked at Miller and said, 'Can't say I'm surprised, sir. Hitler's invasion of Poland was the last straw.'

'Churchill was right, after all,' added Lieutenant Morgan. 'He did warn Parliament that Hitler wasn't to be trusted.'

'That's right, sir,' chimed in Midshipman Grant, 'especially after he signed that pact with Russia last month.'

'You're quite correct, Mid,' said Pollard. 'Now Hitler can concentrate on the rest of Europe.'

'And on Britain,' Lieutenant Morgan added, furrowing his brow.

'What are your orders, sir?' Pollard asked.

'We must prepare for any emergency,' Miller replied sternly. 'Now,' he added, unhooking the tannoy handset, 'I'd better break the news to the ship's company.' He paused, took a deep breath and began, 'This is the captain speaking. I have some grave and important news that will affect everyone.' After reading out the contents of Churchill's message, Miller went on. 'Although we are well away from Europe, nevertheless, we must be on our toes. Action stations, fire drill and gunnery practice will take place without prior warning. If I receive any news from the home front, I'll let you know immediately. That is all.' After replacing the handset, he glanced at Morgan and said, 'What's our position, Pilot?'

'Ten miles north of South Georgia, sir,' Morgan promptly replied.

'Starboard ten, full ahead,' snapped Miller.

His order was immediately repeated by the duty quartermaster in the wheelhouse.

'I'll meet all officers at eight p.m., Number One,' Miller said to Pollard. Then, with a surprised expression on his faced, said, 'You know, Number One. I've just remembered. September the third is my birthday. I'm thirty today.'

'Some birthday present, eh, sir,' Pollard replied, shaking his head and grinning.

CHAPTER TWENTY-SEVEN

Throughout the ship, Miller's announcement of war was met with a mixture of stunned silence, fear and resignation. In the galley, Chief Cook Powel stopped stirring a large metal tub of soup and looked at the other cooks who were busy preparing supper. 'Well, lads,' he said in his gruff, Yorkshire accent, 'at last we know where we stand. Now, let's get on.'

'It's all very well for you, Chief,' said Cook Jones. 'You're not married. What about those of us with a wife and kids? What'll happen to them if we're bombed, as Beaverbrook said we would be?'

'Then we'll just 'ave to bomb the bastards back,' interrupted Cook James. 'Now pipe down and make sure you don't burn the mince.'

The atmosphere in the senior ratings mess was more upbeat.

'Thank goodness Churchill had the sense to call up all naval reservists,' PO Stores Assistant Holden said, while sipping a mug of tea. 'As we're gunna need 'em.'

'Aye, you're right, there, Bill,' added PO Signalman Watts, lighting a cigarette. 'Especially as Churchill has ordered more warships to be built.'

'I expect this'll mean more gunnery practice for your lads, eh Len?' PO Martin said to CGI Mills.

'For bloody sure, my bird,' Len replied. 'Last time it took us only four minutes to load the breech and fire. Lieutenant Young wants it down to at least three minutes. Bloody task master, that's what he is,' he added, while slapping on a thick layer of strawberry jam on a piece of bread.

In the seamen's mess the reaction was sanguine.

'Thank fuck Winne's back,' Brown said, lighting a cigarette. 'He'll take no shit from Hitler.'

'Pity Chamberlain and his cronies didn't pay attention to him a few years ago when the Jerries invaded the Sudetenland,' Moore said. 'He knew then war was coming.'

'Do you think the Jerries will use gas?' Waters asked Moore.

'Who know what that bastard Hitler will do,' Moore answered. 'Thank God everyone at home's been issued with gas masks.'

'Aye, yer right, there, Pony,' added Darby Allen. 'My missus tells me our two-year-old boy has been given one that looks like Mickey Mouse. What do you think, Smudge?' he asked WO Smith, while wiping a few crumbs of bread from his mouth.

When Smith heard Britain had declared war on Germany, he felt like punching the air with delight. In a flash, he imagined Germany invading England; lines of tanks, armed cars and hordes of the Wehrmacht, goose-stepping down the Strand. Hitler would be Chancellor of Great Britain. He and his parents would each be awarded the Iron Cross. Smith would join the SS and become an officer. He would send for Katrina and marry her, with Hitler as best man.

'Great, smashing,' Smith replied, doing his best to sound plausible. 'Maybe it'll mean us getting home quicker,' he added hopefully.

Shortly after dinner, Miller met the officers, Mr Weir and Linda, in the wardroom. 'Please sit down, and smoke if you must,' said Miller, standing in front of them and accepting a cup of coffee from PO Feneck. After taking a sip, he stared gravely around, then, in a calm voice, said, 'I'm sure you know why I have called this meeting, so I'll come straight to the point. While we were in Rio, I was informed that the Germans have U-boats that can travel as far as South America. Therefore, even though we are thousands of miles away from Europe, we must not be complacent. Be prepared to go to action stations at any given time. I will keep you informed of any further developments. Any questions?'

'I have one, sir,' said Lieutenant Morgan. 'If we are attacked by a U-boat, which country in South America could we make for that's neutral?'

Miller finished his coffee, then, with a wry smile playing around his lips, replied, 'Providing we're still afloat, Brazil or

Uruguay would be our best bet. But I sincerely hope it won't come to that.'

'What aboot the grapholite, sir?' Weir asked, taking a good puff of his pipe. 'The "Bosh" must know how important it is, so I expect they'd like to get their hands on it.'

'Good question, Jock,' Miller replied. 'They will no doubt want to board us and search the ship. If that happens, I intend to have it thrown overboard.'

'Then, I suppose, they'll sink us,' Midshipman Grant muttered glumly.

'Surely the Germans would allow us to leave the ship before it was torpedoed, sir?' asked Linda.

Miller suddenly remembered his father telling him that during the last war, his ship had been torpedoed without any warning. Miller pursed his lips and shook his head slightly, then said, 'I wouldn't count on it.'

'Thank you, Commander,' Linda replied tersely. 'That's not very reassuring.'

'I would like to stress,' Miller said, furrowing his brow, 'now that we are at war, it is vital that we achieve our aim and get home as quickly as possible. Therefore, after collecting the grapholite, I'm going to make straight for Rio.' He gave Lieutenant Duncan an expectant look and added, 'Have we enough fuel to avoid stopping at Punta Arenas, Jock?'

'Aye, just aboot, sir,' Duncan replied confidently.

'Thank you,' said Miller. 'Now, if nobody has more questions,' he added, 'please carry on, as I'm sure you've all got plenty to think about,' and he left the room.

That night, Miller slept in fits and starts. His mind became overloaded with worries, ranging from the safety of his parents should Merseyside be bombed, to deciding on the safest course to take after leaving Rio. Should he steer a straight across the Atlantic and risk being spotted by a U-boat, or deviate slightly and make for Gibraltar? And what about Linda? He knew he had fallen in love with her and wondered what fate had in store for them.

Shortly before six a.m., he was woken by the QM's voice calling hands to turn to. Minutes later, Leading Steward Blake knocked on the door and entered carrying a mug of coffee. Upon seeing Blake, Miller slowly pushed himself up and yawned.

'Good morning, sir,' Blake said cheerfully, while handing the mug to Miller.

Miller grunted, 'Thank you.'

Blake, sensing Miller wasn't in the mood for his usual morning banter, quickly left.

Miller was about to take a sip of coffee, when a knock came at the door and Lieutenant Ward came in. 'This came in a few hours ago, sir,' he said, handing Miller a signal. 'I thought it best to wait to call the hands.'

'Then you'd better read it to me,' Miller replied, taking a sip of coffee.

'Yes, sir. It says, "SS *Athenia*, torpedoed and sunk in the Western Approaches, without warning, seven p.m. today, 3rd September. 117 civilians and crew lost. Sir Roger Backhouse. Admiral of the Fleet."'

Miller suddenly felt wide awake and alert. '*Great Scott!*' he exclaimed, spilling coffee onto his blanket. 'The *Athenia* was a passenger ship. I remember seeing her dock in Liverpool. Why on earth would the Germans want to sink her?' With a shake of his head, he handed Ward his mug and climbed out of his bunk.

Miller announced the sinking of the SS *Athenia* to the officers just before everyone sat down for breakfast. For a few seconds, they were too stunned to speak.

Finally, Linda looked at Miller and said, 'Well, that answers the question I asked you last night.'

'That's right, Linda,' Miller replied. 'But remember, our sonar would detect a U-boat, and that would enable me to take evasive action.'

'Nevertheless,' Linda replied. 'In future, I'd better sleep with my lifejacket on instead of a nightie.'

Her risqué remark was met with a ripple of laughter, that not only eased the tension, but made Feneck miss Linda's cup and spill some coffee onto the pristine, white tablecloth.

CHAPTER TWENTY-EIGHT

By nine a.m., *Endeavour* was five miles off the eastern coast of South Georgia. The ugly nimbostratus clouds promised rain, and a bitterly cold southern wind made ripples on an otherwise calm sea. Twenty miles away on the ship's starboard beam, a jagged, snow-covered mountain range was barely visible amongst clouds of dense, grey fog.

'A somewhat foreboding sight, eh, sir,' Pollard remarked to Miller.

'Yes, it is,' replied Miller, 'and it's no better in the summer.'

After consulting his chart, Morgan reported sighting a small, rugged, snow-capped island three five miles on the starboard beam.

'Thank you, Pilot,' said Miller. 'If memory serves me right, that'll be Bird Island. It's a sanctuary for all kinds of wildlife, including albatrosses and cormorants.' Bending slightly to the wheelhouse voice pipe, he ordered a five-degree turn to starboard. Gradually, a series of rocky inlets at the base of the island, hove into view. On some of these, crowds of penguins, ignoring the presence of lumbering seals, flapped their wings then waddled into the water. Miller unhooked the ship's tannoy and said, 'This is the captain speaking. If anyone wants to see penguins, come on the upper deck and look to your right.'

In a matter of minutes, the starboard side of the quarterdeck was crowded with everyone laughing at the penguins waggling about like drunks along the rocky shoreline.

'The penguins you see are Chinstraps,' Miller said over the tannoy. 'The males have orange beaks, the females are pink.'

'They really do look like waiters, don't they, Dutchy?' Able Seaman Brown said to Able Seaman Holland.

'How the fuck would you know, Buster?' replied Holland. 'Since when did they have waiters in pubs?'

'They look bigger than the ones I saw when me and the missus took the kids to London Zoo last year,' said Able Seaman O'Hanlon.

'They were probably Emperor penguins,' chimed in Leading Steward Blake. 'We were told about them at school.'

'I wonder how the males have it away with the females,' Able Seaman Lewis said to Able Seaman Lane.

'With difficulty,' Lane replied. 'Snowballs, yer see,' he added, giving Lewis a friendly dig in the ribs.

Throughout the morning, *Endeavour* continued on her southern journey. Gradually the icy wind became too much for everyone, and they returned to the warmth of their mess decks.

On the bridge, Pollard looked at Miller, who was scanning the coastline with his binoculars, and said, 'I suppose this area is familiar to you from your previous visits, sir.'

'Yes, it is,' Miller replied. 'That rocky inlet you can see is called Right Whale Bay. And if I remember, in a few hours we should pass Prison Island, then Prince Olav Harbour.'

'You know, sir,' Pollard replied, shaking his head, 'with your knowledge of the island, you don't need me.'

'It all seems a long time ago,' Miller said quietly. 'Anyway, Pilot, don't sell yourself short. As you'll probably discover, no amount of experience can cater for the whims of the sea and weather.'

Shortly after two p.m., five miles away to the starboard bow, *Endeavour* passed the snow-covered mountain of Larsen Point. Miller ordered a five-degree turn to starboard, allowing the ship to enter Cumberland Bay. This is a horseshoe-shaped harbour. Flanked on either side were rugged, snow-capped mountains stretching down onto rocky inlets and pebbled beaches.

'Grytviken in sight,' said Morgan, his voice trembling with excitement. 'It's situated at the eastern end of the harbour. But I'm sure you know that, sir.'

'Thank you, Pilot,' Miller replied, using his binoculars to scan the flat-topped wooden houses used by the staff.

Nearby was a large, red-bricked furnace with several tall chimneys. This was the factory where the whale blubber was processed and used for a variety of purposes, from pharmaceutical goods to the foodstuffs. There were large, circular steel vats that he knew was used for storing whale blubber, as well as two bulky, single-funnelled whaling ships tied up on the port side of the long, wooden jetty. Close by were the slipways. From the open sterns of the ships, the dead whales would be dragged ashore, carved up and their blubber sent to the factories and stored in vats. On a hill outside the station, Miller saw the wooden church, painted white, with its tall, black steeple. How well he remembered *Scoresby*'s crew attending services conducted by Jacob Harrison, the ship's commanding officer.

Miller unhooked the ship's tannoy, and with a slight quiver of excitement, said, 'This is the captain speaking. You will be pleased to know that we will shortly arrive in Grytviken, our final destination. After collecting the grapholite, we sail for Rio, then home. Special sea duty men will be needed in ten minutes."

'Thank God for that, sir,' said Pollard, giving a sigh of relief. 'I must confess, there were times that I thought we'd never get here.'

'Me to, Number One,' Miller replied warily, 'especially when we became trapped on that ice shelf.'

By four p.m., *Endeavour* had cruised past King Edward's Cove and berthed alongside the starboard side of the whaling station jetty.

'Would you fancy a draft here, Podge?' Able Seaman Thomas asked Leading Seaman Hardman. Both ratings had finished securing heavy hemp ropes around bollards and were looking around the base.

'Not on your nelly,' Hardman replied, using the back of his hand to wipe sweat from his brow. 'It's too fuckin' isolated for my liking, and those mountains surrounding the place give me the jitters.'

'I know what yer mean, mate,' Thomas said. 'Give me a run ashore down Union Street, any day.'

'I don't know about that,' interrupted Able Seaman Lewis. 'Some of those seals I've seen look better than the parties in the "Paramount". (The "Paramount" was a dingy dance hall in Union

Street, accessed by a steep set of stairs.)

On the bridge, Miller looked at Pollard and said, 'Be good enough to tell Jock and Linda we'll be going ashore after "colours" tomorrow morning. And make sure the chest is brought up from the hold.'

'Very good, sir,' Pollard replied. 'But,' he added, raising his eyebrows, 'just what will you do if Jock can't find the grapholite?'

'Let's hope and pray it never comes to that,' Miller replied gravely, as he heaved himself off his chair and left the bridge.

CHAPTER TWENTY-NINE

Immediately after "colours" the next morning, Miller, Weir and Linda, followed by CGI Mills and the work party, left the ship. Each one wore thick, woollen gloves, thick trousers and leather boots. The hoods of their fleece-lined coats were turned up, giving them partial protection against the icy wind. Able Seaman Gale, a tall, muscular stoker named Parkinson, and Leading Seaman Knight, each held a handle of the metal chest and carried a shovel. Able Seaman Jack Wellings gripped a heavy, iron pick. Leading Seaman Waters held a hammer, with a steel chisel tucked inside his jacket.

With Miller leading, they made their way in single file down the Jacob's ladder.

Weir, who was behind Miller, glanced up at the darkening sky. 'I donay like the looks of yon clouds, sir,' he remarked to Miller.

'Neither do, Jock,' Miller replied, 'and those gusts of the wind aren't helping,' he added, making sure the heavy, iron key to the chest was safely tucked in his coat pocket.

'I don't mind the wind, Commander,' Linda said, 'but I don't think the goggles we've been given will be of any use if it snows?'

'As the snow has already fallen, we're more likely to have storms and rain,' Miller replied, regretting not to have included snowshoes with the rest of their equipment.

'Just as well I didn't wash my hair, then,' Linda added, somewhat flippantly. One of her hands grasped the rope guard rail, and the other held the shoulder strap of a small leather case containing a bottle of testing fluid and a glass pipette.

As soon as everyone was on the jetty, Miller looked at them, and in a stern voice, said, 'Now, stick close together, watch your step and follow me.'

A fierce gust of icy wind met them as they walked one behind the other down the jetty.

'Bloody hell,' Windy gasped. 'That fuckin' wind nearly knocked this bloody chest off me 'and.'

'Better hold onto it tighter,' grunted Knight, 'because if the bastard gets any stronger, it'll blow us both away.'

Ankle-deep in snow, Miller led the group along the jetty. Directly ahead of them, half hidden in the gloomy mist, a row of jagged mountains provided a picturesque backdrop to the whaling station. Miller turned right and for the next ten minutes, the group, breathing heavily, reached the summit of a steep, slippery hill overlooking the harbour.

'I know we're in a hurry,' Miller said, pointing to a six-foot memorial stone overlooking a rectangular mound of snow, 'but I thought you'd like to see where Shackleton is buried.'

Each word he spoke was accompanied by a jerky stream of breath. Battling against the howling wind, everyone, including Weir who had been here previously, trudged to the side of Shackleton's grave which was marked by a tall, snow-covered gravestone.

Linda bent down, placed her small case by her side, wiped the snow away from the front of the gravestone, then read aloud the inscription.

"Here lies Ernest Shackleton. Explorer. Born February 1874, Died January 1922". Underneath this was written, "I hold that a man should strive to the utmost for his life's prize. Robert Browning."

'A fitting epitaph, eh, Commander?' Linda said, feeling a gust of icy wind hit her as she stood up.

'Yes, it is,' Miller shouted, holding onto the hood of his jacket. 'But this damn wind is getting stronger, so we'd better get moving. Have we much further to go, Jock?' he added, looking at Weir.

'No, sir, it's doon there,' Weir replied, indicating a cluster of uneven rocks away to his right at the top of the hill. 'And that's King Edwards Point,' he went on, pointing to a tall, rocky ridge near the entrance to the harbour.

'Right, then,' Miller shouted, glancing anxiously at the others. 'Let's get cracking.'

Doing his best to avoid slipping over in the ankle-deep snow, Weir led them downhill and stopped near a group of snow-covered rocks overlooking a pebbled beach.

'This looks like the place,' said Weir, breathing heavily.

'Can you remember which rock you were working on when you found the grapholite?' Miller shouted, as a sudden blast of icy wind battered his face.

'Och, aye' Weir replied, bending down to dust snow away from the face of the largest rock. 'This is the one. You can still see the holes I made wee ma' pick.'

'Thank God for that,' Miller replied.

Wellings overheard what was said, and taking a firm grasp of his pickaxe, he began hacking at the rock. In a matter of minutes, lumps of grey stone tumbled into the snow.

'*Stop!*' cried Linda, kneeling in the snow. 'Let me do a test on a piece of the rock.'

She rested the leather case against a slab of rock, and after removing her gloves, unclipped the flap on the case and took out a small glass bottle of cloudy, grey liquid. Holding the bottle in her left hand, she used her right hand to take off the cork stopper which she handed to Miller. Everyone, including Miller, were grouped around Linda, watching her every move while providing a protective shield against the howling wind. Using a small glass dropper, she withdrew some liquid from the bottle, then carefully placed a few drops onto the rock and waited, praying it would turn bright green. But to the consternation of herself and Miller, nothing happened. The fluid simply dribbled off the rock into the snow.

'Damn and blast!' cried Linda, giving Miller a look of disappointment.

'Don't look so downhearted,' Miller said. 'Try a few more pieces of rock. You see, everyone,' he continued, noting the curious expressions on Able Seaman Knight and the other members of the work party, 'the type of rock we're looking for should turn bright green when the fluid is applied.'

For the next five minutes, Miller and the others watched anxiously as, after conducting three more tests, Linda shook her head in dismay and said, 'Are you certain this is the right place,

Jock?'

'Och, of course I am, lassie,' Weir retorted. 'Keep trying, I'm sure you'll find it.'

As he finished speaking, everyone, using their gloved hands, shielded themselves against a severe gust of wind that turned the snow around them into clouds of swirling white. By this time, Linda's fingers were so cold, she could hardly feel the bottle and glass dropper.

'It's no use,' Miller yelled. 'This is a katabatic wind, and it's getting stronger. We'd better call it a day. Stow everything behind the rocks, and we'll try again tomorrow.'

'What's a katabatic wind, Commander?' Linda shouted, carefully placing the test tube and bottle in her case. Accepting Miller's hand, she stood up.

'I'll tell you later,' Miller replied, his voice barely audible over the intensity of the wind.

Half bent against the bitterly cold wind, the work party, with Miller leading, carefully made their way down the slippery slope of the hill. Twenty minutes later, they walked down the jetty and arrived at the bottom of the Jacobs's ladder.

'Ladies first,' said Miller, stepping aside to allow Linda to climb up the ladder.

'Thank you, Commander,' Linda replied.

By this time, her hands were so numb that she could hardly feel them. Doing her best, she held her leather case in her right hand and used the other to climb up the ladder. Close behind came Miller, Jock Weir and the others. She was about to step onto the deck, when suddenly a fierce gust of wind hit her full on. For a few seconds she lost her balance. Gripping the rope, she managed to steady herself. However, her hands were so cold that she barely felt the strength of the wind whip her case from her hand.

'My God, no!' she cried, watching it flying high in the air, twirling like a bobbin, before disappearing some hundred yards away and splashing into the grey, harbour waters.

A few minutes later, Linda, Miller and the others staggered onto the ship's deck, shivering violently and streaming clouds of vaporous breath.

'*Christ Almighty, Linda!*' Miller bellowed, who, with a mixture of horror and disbelief, had seen the case soar into the air.

In an instant, he realised that all hope of finding the correct type of grapholite had vanished, as the case, along with the testing equipment, disappeared into the sea. '*What the hell happened?*'

Before she had a chance to reply, Pollard arrived.

'Everything all right, sir?' Pollard asked, noticing the look of anguish in Miller's eyes.

'No, it's bloody well not,' Miller retorted, and stormed away.

He arrived in his cabin and angrily slammed the door. For the next ten minutes he sat at his desk, fully dressed, holding his head in his hands. 'Damn and blast! he cried, thumping the desk with his fist. 'What the hell can I do now?'

Without the use of the chemicals, the chances of finding the correct mineral wallowing at the bottom of the harbour, were lost. Perhaps, he agonised, he should have made sure Linda carried them in a rucksack. No matter. As commanding officer, he was responsible, and a court of inquiry would certainly confirm this. Then he would find himself sitting behind a desk, pushing paper clips and drinking cold coffee.

CHAPTER THIRTY

Miller stood up and was about to take off his jacket when he heard a sharp knock on the door. 'Come,' he snapped.

The door opened and Linda came in. She was still wearing her hooded jacket. Her face was red with anger, and her normally emerald-green eye looked glazed. Miller glared at her and was about to say something when Linda held up a gloved hand.

'Captain or no captain,' she cried, her voice choleric with anger. 'How dare you walk away from me like that!'

'That's because I was furious at the loss of the chemicals. As you know, they're vital for the success of the mission,' Miller replied, doing his best to control his feelings. 'And now that they're at the bottom of the harbour, the reason for us being here is over, and we, or rather, I, have failed.'

'You bloody fool! I have more chemicals in my cabin!' cried Linda, glaring angrily at him. 'Surely you didn't think I'd come all this way without a good supply?'

For a few seconds Miller stood still, feeling as if a heavy weight had been lifted from him. The empty sickness that he had felt gradually drained away. 'Oh, Linda, I'm so sorry,' Miller replied, his voice filled with contrition. 'For a while, my mind was in a turmoil. Please forgive me.'

'All right, Commander,' Linda replied, noticing the relief in Miller's eyes, 'but it'll cost you a gin and tonic.'

Miller grasped hold of her by the shoulders, and staring longingly into her eyes, said, 'Of course, and it'll be a large one.'

'Commander,' Linda replied softly. They were so close she could feel the warmth of his breath on her face. 'If you come any closer,' she added, gently moistening her lips, 'you'll have to…'

At that moment, the sound of someone knocking on the door interrupted what was a moment of mutual desire.

Miller quickly released his hold on her shoulders, and stepping back, said, 'Come.'

The door opened and Pollard came in. The blush on Linda's face and the look of embarrassed guilt etched in Miller's eyes told its own story.

Pollard gave a quick, throaty cough, and averting Miller's eyes, said, 'Begging your pardon, sir. Chief Mills and Mr Weir would like to know if you'll want everyone to muster at the same time tomorrow?'

'Err... yes,' Miller replied, 'and make sure the work party have an extra tot.'

'Very good, sir,' Pollard answered. 'I'm sure they'll be glad to hear it.'

As soon as Pollard left, Linda reached up, squeezed his arm, and with a tender smile, said, 'I'd better leave and take a cold shower, but don't forget that large G and T.'

'Don't worry, I won't,' Miller replied, staring into her eyes. 'I won't forget... anything.'

During the afternoon, the ship's company were kept occupied by practicing action stations and damage control evolutions. In the engine room, LSBA Hailey and his first-aid team commandeered one of the stokers, and using a Neil Robertson stretcher, managed to transport him to the sickbay.

Under the watchful eyes of Lieutenant Young and Chief GI Mills, the metal shutter was raised, allowing the gun's crews to practise gun drill.

'Any chance of an extra tot, like those lucky buggers got who went ashore, Chief?' asked Gun Layer Jacobs, who, despite the cold wind, was stripped to the waist and sweating profusely.

'I'm afraid not, my bird,' Mills snapped. 'Now keep yer eyes on yon gun sight; you never know, yer life may depend on it.'

'Just as if we'd meet a fuckin' battleship down here,' muttered Jacobs, as he opened and closed the breech.

During dinner in the wardroom, Weir, dabbing his mouth with a linen serviette, looked at Miller who was sat at the head of the table, and said, 'Excuse me, sir. How long do yer think this wind will last?'

'It's called a katabatic wind,' Miller replied, 'and with a bit of luck, it should have blown itself out by the morning.'

'As I recall,' said Linda, who was sitting next to Pollard, and up till now, had done her best to avoid Miller's occasional glances, 'you were going to tell me exactly what a katabatic wind was.'

'Oh yes,' Miller replied, taking a sip of wine, 'so I was.' He paused momentarily, placed his wine glass on the table, and said, 'A katabatic wind is when a ferociously strong, high-density wind is forced down from the slopes of high mountains, such as those overlooking the harbour. This happens when the air becomes heavier than the atmosphere. It's not uncommon in these parts.'

'Thank you, Commander,' Linda replied, flashing Miller a beguiling smile. 'Most enlightening.'

'By the way,' said Miller, changing the subject, 'I received a signal telling us that Roosevelt has declared America's neutrality.'

'Och, just like in the last lot,' said Weir, finishing his whisky and lighting his pipe. 'But I expect Winston will have summat to say aboot that.'

'I think you're right, Jock,' Pollard remarked, as PO Feneck and his stewards arrived holding silver coffee pots. 'He and Roosevelt are as thick as thieves,' he added, as Feneck poured coffee into Linda's cup, 'and if the Germans attack American shipping, even though Roosevelt is up for election in November, the yanks might be forced into war.'

'I hope so,' said Lieutenant Morgan, 'because we're going to need all the help we can get.'

During the night, to everyone's relief, the wind dropped; it stopped raining and shortly after "colours," the early morning sky became a cloudless, eye-catching, cerulean blue.

On the quarterdeck, Miller turned to Pollard and said, 'Thank God the weather has changed. It'll make finding the grapholite easier. After we return, I want to leave as quickly as possible, so tell Lieutenant Duncan to flash up the engines.'

'Very good, sir,' Pollard replied, then frowning slightly, went on. 'But what will you do if you can't find the grapholite?'

'Don't ask,' came Miller's curt reply.

'A perfect day for a bit of hitchhiking, eh, Parky?' Leading

Seaman Knight asked Stoker Parkinson. They and the other members of the work party were fallen in on the jetty.

'Suit yeself, Parkinson grunted. 'I'd sooner be in me mick, thinking about Rita Hayworth.'

With Miller leading, the small group walked down the jetty and turned left. Linda, who was directly behind Miller, carried the small, green-fluted bottle of chemicals along with a few pipettes, wrapped in a canvas bag and safely tucked in a deep, coat pocket.

The wind had produced pockets of snowdrifts, lying deep around the rocks and between crevices, and the ground was caked in slippery ice. Progress was slow, and it took a good twenty minutes to negotiate the steep hill. After passing Shackleton's grave, they finally arrived at the group of jagged rocks they had worked on the previous day. Chief GI Mills and his work party recovered the snow-covered chest and took out the picks and shovels.

'Right, let's start at that one,' said Jock, indicating the largest snow-covered rock.

For the next fifteen minutes, Wellings wielded his pick, chipping away chunks of rock. Waters, using a hammer and iron chisel, did the same. Linda removed her gloves and took out the bottle of chemicals, and using the dropper, tested each piece. With everyone anxiously looking on, the rocks didn't, as hoped, change to bright green.

'I suggest we try one of the smaller rocks,' Weir suggested, placing his unlit pipe in his mouth. 'I'm positive the one containing the grapholite is definitely around here.'

'I hope you're right, Jock,' Miller said, feeling a trickle of nervous sweat run down his back.

Wellings and Soapy did as Weir suggested, and began hacking away at the rock. Giving Miller a hopeful glance, Linda began testing each piece. At the same time, Leading Seaman Knight, who was standing behind CGI Milles, quietly left the group and sneaked behind another row of rocks to urinate. Minutes later, Knight returned to see the look of bitter disappointment evident on everyone's faces.

'For God's sake, Jock,' Knight heard Miller cry. 'Are you

quite sure this is the right place?'

'Och, aye.' Weir replied, knocking back his hood and wiping his brow with the back of his gloved hand. 'This is where I found it. I'm positive.'

Miller was about to speak when Knight interrupted him. 'Excuse me, sir, and you, miss,' he added, giving Linda an apologetic glance, 'but I've just had a jimmy-riddle on the rocks behind us, and I noticed some of them had summat what looked like little green shrubs on them. I wondered if...'

Before he had time to finish, Miller gave Linda and those standing nearby an expectant glance and yelled, 'Come on, everyone, it's worth a try.'

A few minutes later everyone had vacated the area they were working on. Ignoring the yellow urine spots in the snow, they gathered around a large rock from which small green shrubs poked out from under the snow.

'Right, my 'andsomes,' Chief GI said to Wellings and Waters, 'brush away the snow and get weavin'.'

Miller, Linda and Weir gathered around the rock and held their breath, as Wellings raised his pickaxe and struck the rock. Seconds later, a large chunk fell away. Linda knelt down in the snow and removed her gloves. She opened a small canvas bag, took out the green-fluted bottle of chemicals and placed it by her side. Feeling everyone's eyes on her, she picked up the bottle and unscrewed the top. Holding the bottle in her right hand, she carefully filled the dropper with clear-coloured fluid.

Now came the moment of truth. The tension in the bitterly cold air was palpable. With bated breath, everyone moved closer as Linda dropped a few spots of chemicals onto the rock. The chemicals bubbled slightly, then settled own. Seconds later, the rock gradually changed colour from dirty grey to bright green. The shouting of the work party echoed around like a clarion. Miller helped Linda to her feet, and without speaking, gave her a bear hug.

Then, shaking Weir's hand, said, 'Well, Jock, you weren't far off. That's a large Scotch I owe you.'

'Och, away with yer, laddie,' Weir replied. 'I'm only too glad we found the damn stuff.'

Without any encouragement from CGI Mills, Wellings and Waters hacked away more pieces of rock. In a matter of minutes, chunks littered the snow-covered ground. Linda carefully placed the bottle and dropper into her canvas bag. Miller took out the key and unlocked the chest. With growing enthusiasm, Knight and Gale began shovelling the precious mineral into the chest. Ten minutes later the chest was over half full.

'That's more than enough,' Miller said, with an air of satisfaction. 'Let's finish and get back to the ship.'

'Great idea, sir,' said Knight, grinning as if he'd found gold. 'And if we hurry, we'll be just in time for our tot.

Despite the slippery conditions, puffing streams of colourless breath, they made their way downhill. As they walked along the jetty, Miller saw Pollard and several officers, plus most of the crew, lining the starboard side of the quarterdeck. Miller grinned, and using his right arm, sent a message of success by punching the air. This was instantly met with loud cheering and waving. WO Smith, doing his best to look and sound happy, joined in. However, the only satisfaction he could derive from finding the grapholite was the thought of seeing Katrina again when the ship returned to Rio.

Miller allowed Knight and Gale to go in front of everyone and haul the chest up the Jacob's ladder and onto the quarterdeck.

'Where do you want it stowed, sir?' Pollard asked Miller, as he stepped on board.

'In my cabin, please, Number One,' Miller replied. 'From there it'll be easier to offload when we return to Plymouth. Now,' he added, 'how soon can we get underway?'

'Two hours, according to the engineer officer,' Pollard replied, with obvious alacrity.

Miller looked at his wristwatch. 'Good. It's now eleven thirty. We'll slip at two p.m. Specials at one forty-five.'

At that moment, 'Up spirits,' was piped.

With a grin as wide as the Mersey Tunnel, Knight glanced at Gale and said, 'There, I told you we'd be back in time for our tot, didn't I?'

CHAPTER THIRTY-ONE

Endeavour slipped her moorings, and after rolling slightly, moved slowly away from the jetty. A bitterly cold wind blew from the south, and a cloudless, blue sky enabled a pale sun to cast a rippling shine on the harbour waters.

'Port five, revolutions ten,' Miller said, sitting on his chair and speaking down the wheelhouse intercom.

'Port five, wheel on. Revolutions ten,' repeated Chief Coxswain Moore.

The ship slowly turned left and gradually gathered speed.

'Increase to ten knots,' snapped Miller, bending down and peering along the compass repeater, checking the distance between King's Point and the mouth of the harbour. 'Steady as she goes.'

By four p.m., *Endeavour* had passed Mount Paget and Bird Island and continued north.

Miller decided to make the following announcement over the tannoy: 'As we are now at war with Germany, and even though censorship of private mail has not been officially introduced, no mention of the real reason for our mission or anything else that might be useful to the enemy, must be mentioned in your letters home. That is all,' and he hung up.

Shortly after five o'clock the next morning, Sonar Operator Leading Seaman Hardman reported seeing icebergs roughly five miles on the port beam. This information was piped over the tannoy. Once again, men went onto the upper deck and watched as the ship passed uncomfortably close to one of several huge icebergs.

On the bridge, Miller gave a quick glance over his shoulder and said, 'How far away are we from that damn pack ice, Pilot?'

'After we clear the ice flow and reach open sea,' Lieutenant Morgan replied, wistfully stoking his chin. 'As we're doing fifteen knots, we should sight it in about two days, sir.'

Lieutenant Morgan's calculations proved to be correct. Sunday 10th September dawned crystal clear. The temperature was well below zero, and the blueness of a cloudless sky reflected in the calm sea.

At six thirty a.m., Able Seaman Lofty Day, in the crow's nest, reported a wide expanse of ice, twenty miles ahead of the ship. OOW Lieutenant Young immediately contacted Miller, who was in his cabin. A few minutes later he arrived on the bridge and was joined by Pollard.

'Looks like we'll be faced with the same problem as last time, sir,' Pollard muttered, peering through his binoculars.

'Can't be helped,' Miller replied. 'But let's hope it won't come to that.'

By eight a.m., Endeavour was five miles away from the pack ice.

Miller unhooked the tannoy. 'Captain speaking. We are approaching an ice pack. If we can't break through it again, I shall do what I did last time. So stow all loose gear away, and as before, be prepared for a noisy few hours.' He then unhooked the engine room voice pipe.

Lieutenant Duncan answered. 'I heard you addressing the ship's company, sir,' Duncan said. 'I take it, if you can't break through the ice, you'll want me to do the same as before?'

'That's right, Jock,' Miller replied. 'So stand by,' and replaced the handset.

When the ice pack was roughly a hundred yards away, Miller ordered the ship to reduce speed to five knots. Everyone on the bridge watched and listened anxiously as the ship arrived at the edge of the ice pack. Below in the mess decks, ratings sat, hoping to hear the ear-splitting noise of the ship grinding its way through the ice pack.

'Stop engines,' snapped Miller.

Gradually, the ship came to a halt. Like a racehorse waiting impatiently for the 'off', the sharp bows pressed eagerly against the vast wall of ice. Miller unhooked the engine room voice pipe.

Miller unhooked the engine room voice pipe. 'Slow astern,

Jock,' he said.

Seconds later, the ship began to move backwards.

'Stop engines.'

'Half ahead.'

'Full ahead, Jock,' shouted Miller. 'Give it all you've got, Jock.'

Throughout the ship, everyone heard and felt the deck vibrate as the ship, doing twenty knots, surged forward.

On the bridge, all eyes focused on the ship's bows as they ground noisily against the ice pack. This was followed seconds later by an ear-splitting cacophony, as a long, deep crevice appeared in the ice. Gradually, the weight of the ship widened the gap in the ice, allowing the ship to continue moving forward.

'By Jove, sir,' cried Pollard, grinning at Miller and forcing himself not to slap his captain on the back. 'We've done it! We've broken through the stuff.'

'I think we were lucky, Number One,' Miller replied, noticing the relieved expressions on everyone's faces. 'Unfortunately, this blasted ice will slow us down. Which means we'll be late reaching Stanley.'

Miller's prediction was correct. It took nearly two days of listening to the ear-splitting noise, as the ship pulverised its way through the ice. However, it wasn't until six a.m. on Monday 11th that *Endeavour* managed to reach an open sea and floating ice.

On the bridge, Miller was sat in his chair, surveying the sparking blue waters and irregular-shaped slabs of ice, some of which resembled small islands. He looked at OOW Lieutenant Ward, and with a relived expression in his eyes, said, 'Thank God for that, John.'

'Yes, sir, I agree,' Ward replied, 'but it looks like we're disturbing some of those seals curled up on the ice.'

As he spoke, Able Seaman Thompson, the port lookout, shouted, 'Whales, sir, two of 'em, a few miles away on the port beam.'

All eyes immediately turned left, in time to see the shiny, black V-shaped tails of two Humpback whales waving in the air before splashing into the sea. Nearby, a pod of grey, snub-nosed dolphins leapt in and out of the water, their faces fixed in what appeared to be a natural smile.

'Looks like the whales have an escort, eh, sir,' PO Martin said jokingly to Miller.

'The whales know where the plankton is, so the dolphins follow them,' Miller replied.

'Crafty buggers,' Martin said, shaking his head.

The next two days passed without incident. As Jock Weir would be leaving the ship when the ship arrived in Stanley on Saturday, a farewell party was given to him on Friday evening.

After a roast beef dinner, and the port passed around, Miller gave Weir a whisky toast and thanked him for all he had done.

Early next morning, *Endeavour* sailed passed the mountainous eastern coast of the Falkland Islands. The sea was choppy; a sharp, bitterly cold wind blew from the south, and grey, cirrocumulus clouds promised rain.

Shortly after ten a.m., the rocky inlet of Berkley Sound hove into view. Two hours later, Miller ordered a five-degree turn to port as the ship entered Stanley Harbour. Half an hour later, the ship dropped anchor a hundred yards from the jetty.

Miller unhooked the engine room voice pipe.

'Engine room, engineer officer.'

'Captain here, Jock,' said Miller. 'Keep your engines flashed up, as I want to get under way as soon as Mr Weir has left.'

'Very good, sir,' Duncan replied, and hung up.

The Jacob's ladder was lowered on the port side. Standing on the jetty, a woman wearing a woollen cap and a short coat over a yellow dress, stood next to a tall, fair-headed youth in a duffle coat. Both were smiling and waving as a motorboat, manned by two local men, left the jetty and headed towards the ship. A few minutes later it arrived and was hooked onto the ladder's wooden platform.

Weir arrived onto the quarterdeck. He wore the same fleece-lined parka he had when he first came on board, and he carried the same canvas holdall.

'Good luck, Jock,' Miller said, giving Weir a warm handshake. 'And I hope you enjoy that bottle of Scotch we presented you with last night.'

'Och, I'm sure I will,' Weir replied. 'Thank you for yer hospitality, and Godspeed and a safe journey home.'

Over the past weeks, Weir had come to know many of the ship's company. Not only had he enjoyed 'sippers' in the junior ratings mess but had sampled neat rum with the chief and PO's. Many of them had gathered on the quarterdeck and port side of the ship. As Weir was about to leave, a voice began singing *For He's a Jolly Good fellow*. Everyone cheered and immediately joined in. But the biggest cheer came when Linda stepped forward, gave Weir a warm hug and a kiss on his cheek. Doing his best to hide his embarrassment, Weir gave a quick wave of acknowledgement, walked down the ladder and was helped into the motorboat. Seconds later the engine revved up, and Weir, standing in the stern sheets, gave a final wave as the motorboat turned and headed inland.

'Let's get under way, Number One,' Miller said to Pollard.

Ten minutes later, the anchor was raised. Miller ordered a five-degree turn to starboard. By this time, a crowd had gathered along the foot of the town, waving goodbye.

Miller looked at Pollard and said, 'Tell the ship's company to wave back. God only knows when, or if, they'll see a British ship again.'

CHAPTER THIRTY-TWO

Early next morning, Miller was awakened by someone knocking on his door. A glance at his watch showed six a.m.

'Come,' he said, sitting up in bed, expecting to see Feneck enter, holding his customary mug of steaming hot coffee. Instead, WO Smith came in holding a signal.

'Sorry to bother you, sir,' said Smith, 'but this signal arrived from Admiralty a few minutes ago. I think it's important.'

'I see,' Miller replied, stifling a yawn while sitting up. 'Then you'd better read it to me.'

'Right, sir,' Smith muttered. "From Admiralty: info all ships and establishments. On 17th September, HMS *Courageous* was torpedoed and sunk off the southwest coast of Ireland. 518 officers and rating were lost.'"

'Great Scott!' exclaimed Miller, snatching the signal from Smith and reading it. '*Courageous* sunk. I can hardly believe it. Thank you, Smith. Carry on, and for the moment, keep this to yourself,' Miller added, as he threw back the bedclothes and heaved himself out of his bunk.

'Very good, sir,' replied Smith.

When Smith had received the coded signal an hour ago, he had given a whoop of delight. The Fatherland had struck again! An aircraft carrier sunk, and all those men lost. *Wunderbar!*

No sooner had Smith left than Feneck arrived, holding his mug of coffee.

'Mornin', sir,' Feneck said, placing the mug on Miller's desk. 'If you don't mind me asking, sir,' he enquired, noticing the flushed expression on Miller's usually tanned face, 'are you all right?'

'Yes, thank you, Feneck,' Miller replied, making his way to the bathroom. 'Breakfast in half an hour. And ask the first lieutenant to come and see me straight away.'

Miller was stripped to the waist and about to shave when Pollard came in.

'You sent for me sir,' said Pollard.

'Yes,' replied Miller, using a small brush to lather soapy foam around his chin and face. 'There's a signal on my desk. I think you'd better read it.'

Pollard turned and picked up the signal. A few seconds later, he looked at Miller and said, 'This is terrible news, sir. But thank God, Ireland is halfway across the world.'

'Maybe so, Number One,' said Miller, pulling a face while shaving around his chin, 'but it proves the U-boats are at sea. So tell sonar to be extra vigilant.'

'Yes, sir,' Pollard replied, who, before being summoned to see his captain, was in the wardroom, halfway through his breakfast. 'Was there anything else?'

'Yes,' said Miller, swilling his shaven face with cold water. 'As we're not putting into Punta Arenas, I intend to bypass Drakes' Passage and the Straits of Magellan,' he went on, as he reached for a towel, 'and make for Rio as soon as possible. I shall announce that and the sinking of *Courageous* at "stand easy" this morning.'

'Very good, sir,' Pollard replied, placing the signal on the desk. 'I expect some of the crew will have had friends aboard the carrier.'

'Yes, sir,' Pollard sombrely replied. 'Her number one, Lieutenant Commander Phill Cardew, was best man at my wedding.'

'I'm sorry,' Miller said. 'I hope he was one of the survivors.' (Sadly, he and fifty other officers didn't survive.)

Throughout the ship, Miller's account of the carrier's sinking was met with a mixture of anger and sadness. Even the fact that they would miss Punta Arenas and sail directly to Rio failed to cheer them up.

In the seaman's mess, Waters was in the middle of dishing out the rum. 'Bloody hell, those fuckin' Jerries!' he cried, staring at O'Hanlon. 'A pal of mine, Bob Jackson, a stoker, was on board her. He was married with two kids. My missus and his played bingo together.'

'I had a mate on board *Courageous* called Harry Tate,' Bell remarked, taking a good swallow of rum. 'We went to the same school. He was a bloody good footballer and played for Doncaster Rovers before the war.'

In the senior ratings mess, Chief ERA Jones finished his tot. 'I bet those poor beggars in the engine and boiler rooms didn't stand a chance, eh, Paddy?' he asked Chief Engineer O'Malley.

'Holy Mother of God, I hope you're wrong, Jack,' O'Malley replied. 'But those places are a long way to the upper deck on an aircraft carrier. I know because I served on *Courageous* in 1937.'

The next morning, Lieutenant Morgan was staring wistfully out the window at the ugly, black, cumulonimbus clouds blotting out the early morning sun. 'Looks like we're in for some rough weather, sir,' he remarked to Miller, who had come onto the bridge. 'The barometer has dropped from ten degrees to five, and the intensity of the wind has increased.'

The time was eight a.m. "Duty watch fall in on the canteen flat," had just been piped.

'Yes, I think you're right, Number One,' Miller replied, peering through the window. 'Better rig up lifelines.'

By midday, it was almost dark. Tentacles of forks of lightning momentarily lit up the sky and the faces of everyone on the bridge. This was quickly followed by ear-splitting claps of thunder. The sea became a tumultuous mass of angry, white horses. Mountainous waves crashed over the bows, sending torrents of water swirling onto the well deck. A lifeboat broke away from its fixtures and bounced dangerously against another lifeboat. Grasping a lifeline, the buffer and a few volunteers, wearing oilskins, managed to secure it before it was washed overboard.

As during the previous rough weather, everyone off duty took to their hammocks. Once again, corned beef sandwiches and soup, delivered by unsteady hands, was the order of the day. In the engine and boiler rooms, stokers managed to stop slipping over the steel plating by clinging desperately to the stanchions and guard rails.

The storm raged for three miserable days. By nine o'clock on the morning of Thursday 21st, the wind had dropped and the black clouds had disappeared, leaving the sun blazing down from a clear, blue sky.

A little after nine o'clock the next morning, a thin line of Argentina's eastern coast could barely be seen some fifty miles away on *Endeavour*'s port beam. As the ship continued northwards, Miller put the crew through every evolution, from "Abandon Ship" to "Man Overboard". This included gunnery practice every morning and afternoon, while LSBA Hailey reminded his first-aid team how to use tourniquets, field dressings and slings.

Sunday 24th dawned warm and peaceful. Shortly after "Hands turn too" was piped at eight a.m., Miller came into the bridge, stretch his arms upward and yawned.

'What's our position, Pilot?' he asked, easing himself into his chair.

'We're roughly a hundred miles from Montevideo, sir, and we're doing fifteen knots.'

'And how far are we away from Rio?'

'Nearly three hundred miles, sir,' Morgan replied, 'and at our present speed, we should arrive there on Thursday, and as the storm season is upon us, we can expect more atrocious weather.'

Miller was about to reply when Sonar Operator Leading Seaman Harding reported seeing a black dot on his screen. 'It's about fifty miles on our port beam, and it's heading directly towards us.'

Miller suddenly remembered Admiral Backhurst telling him about the long-range XB U-boats. He gave Pollard a searching look and said, 'It can't be one of our subs, as none of them have the endurance, so it must be a German.' He paused, and with a bewildered expression on his face, looked at Pollard and said, 'But if it is, how on earth did they know where to find us?'

Pollard, who was equally perplexed as Miller, replied, 'Maybe someone on the whaling station sent a message to them.'

'Hardly,' Miller said, shaking his head. 'The Japs were on our side in the last war, and as far as I know, they haven't a treaty with Germany.'

Regaining his composure, Miller stared at Morgan and said, 'These subs can do twenty knots on the surface. At present we are well away from them, so, if we can maintain our speed, how soon will we arrive in Rio?'

Wednesday at the earliest, sir,' Morgan replied confidently.

'Signal C-in-C,' Miller said to PO Watson. "U-boat detected, fifty miles on port beam." Give our position and add: "Intend making for Rio de Janeiro at full speed. ETA Wednesday 25th. Will keep you informed."'

Miller then unhooked the engine room voice pipe. Lieutenant Duncan answered. Miller told him about the U-boat and what he intended to do.

'Twenty knots for three hundred miles is asking a lot, sir,' Duncan said. 'But with a bit of luck, I think we can make it.'

'Good man. Increase speed immediately,' Miller replied. 'And naturally, I'll take full responsibility for any damage to the engines.'

Seconds later, the vibration of the ship's engine could be felt as the ship bounded forward, sending a huge, frothy wave crashing over the fo'c'sle.

'How far away is it now?' Miller asked Sonar Operator Leading Seaman Harding.

'Still the same, sir,' Harding replied.

Miller picked up the ship's tannoy. 'This is the captain speaking. We have sighted what I think is a U-boat, fifty miles away to port.' He went on to explain what he was going to do, adding, 'If all goes well, we'll be in Rio inn three days. Meanwhile, wear lifejackets, stay below and be prepared to go to action stations at any given moment.'

'The sub's surfaced, sir, and is increasing speed,' reported Harding.

'Can't say I'm surprised,' Miller replied, who, like everyone else, was doing his best to focus his binoculars away to the right, hoping to catch sight of the U-boat.

Throughout the night and early morning, the wind remained fresh, the sea was a tranquil blue, and visibility was good.

At six a.m., Miller, who had remained on the bridge during the night, eased himself off his chair and contacted Sonar. 'How far away is the blighter, now?' he asked Leading Seaman Harding.

'The sub seems to have fallen away and is a little over sixty miles behind us, sir,' Harding replied jubilantly

'That's good news, eh, sir,' said Pollard, who had just arrived.

'Yes, indeed, Number One,' Miller replied, giving s sigh of relief. 'If we continue as we are, we'll soon leave the sod well behind.'

Petty Officer Feneck arrived carrying a mug of coffee and a plate of sandwiches.

'As you'll probably miss breakfast, I think you'll need these, sir,' he said, as he handed Miller the mug. 'The sarmies are egg — your favourite,' he added, placing the plate on the seat of Miller's chair.

Miller was about to thank Feneck when suddenly he felt the ship gradually slow down. He grabbed the engine room voice pipe and contacted Lieutenant Duncan.

'Why have we slowed down, Jock?' Miller asked.

'At the moment I'm na sure, sir,' Duncan warily replied. 'But it sounds as if there's something wrong with the piston rings.'

Duncan's words immediately sent a surge of fear through Miller like an electric shock. 'Christ almighty! How long will it take to fix them? At present, we're only doing five knots.'

'I canna say, sir,' Duncan answered, using the back of his hand to prevent sweat running into his eyes. 'I'll have ta strip the fuel system down and...'

'By then the U-boat will be upon us. Can't you speed things up?' Miller pleaded.

'I'm sorry, sir,' Duncan replied, 'but if we go any faster, we'll have ta stop completely.'

CHAPTER THIRTY-THREE

Miller looked gravely at Pollard and unhooked the tannoy. 'This is the captain speaking,' Miller said, doing his best to sound calm. 'We've developed engine trouble, and as you can see, we've had to slow down. I'm not sure how long it will take to fix the problem, but meantime we're only able to make five knots. This means the blighter will soon catch us up. Now...' He paused. 'This type of U-boat can only fire her torpedoes from aft. If she doesn't turn about, I think her captain means to board us in order to find the grapholite. Fortunately, he is unaware that we're armed. This means that when the sub is in range, we'll be able to get a shot at her. So, hands to action stations. As practiced, those ratings not required are to wear lifejackets and remain in their messes.' He paused momentarily, took a deep breath then went on, 'Would Lieutenant Young come to the bridge right away.'

No sooner had Miller replaced the handset than the gunnery officer arrived. 'I take it you heard my announcement, Guns?' said Miller.

'Yes, sir,' Young answered, 'and we've kept a shell in the breech as you ordered.'

'Good,' Miller replied. 'Now, as soon as the sub's captain sees our gun, I think he'll either order the sub to dive, or he'll open fire with his deck gun, so we won't have much time. After I give you the order, I want you to fire at will. Understand?'

'Yes, sir,' Young replied, nervously running his tongue across his lips

'Thank you, Guns, and good luck,' Miller replied, as he trained his binoculars away to starboard. 'I only hope all your gunnery practice pays off.'

'So do I, sir,' Young replied, and hurried from the bridge.

With every passing minute, the tension below decks became

palpable.

The time was eleven thirty a.m. "Up spirits. Cooks to the galley," had just been piped.

In the stoker's mess, Leading Stoker Ward gave his oppo, Nick Carter, a quick shrug of his shoulders and said, 'I suppose we'd better write a letter home, just in case…'

'What's the use of doing that, you daft bugger?' Carter quickly replied. 'When will you post it? If we get torpedoed, we'll all end up in the drink.'

'In that case, I'd better collect the rum,' said Stoker Thomas, 'as it might be our last.'

After hearing Miller's announcement, Chief GI Mills went to the seamen's mess and ordered his gunners to close up.

Able Seaman Jacobs gave Mills a hurt look and said, 'What's the hurry, Chief? The fuckin' U-boat's miles away, and it'll soon be tot time.'

'Listen, my 'andsome,' said Mills, glaring at Lofty and the rest of the gun's crew. 'If that U-boat sends a fish up our arse, you lot won't 'ave time for a tot, or anything else for that matter. Now get weaving.'

With the ship crawling along at barely five knots, QM Waters, PO Signalman Watson, PO Thompson and the lookouts concentrated their binoculars on the black dot that was slowly becoming bigger with every second.

Shortly after twelve thirty p.m., Miller contacted Sonar. 'How far is the sub?' he asked Harris.

'I'd say roughly twenty thousand yards, sir,' Harris replied. 'And closing fast.'

Miller unhooked the GDP platform intercom. 'Sonar tells me the sub is twenty thousand yards away. How soon do you think she'll be in range, Guns?'

After a slight pause, Lieutenant Young replied, 'If she's doing twenty knots, I'd say… about four p.m., sir.'

For a few seconds Miller carefully studied his wristwatch. With a grim expression etched on his face, Miller looked at Pollard and said, 'Action stations at three thirty, Number One. If the sub slows down and appears to be turning about, we'll know she's about to fire her torpedoes.'

'And if the sub doesn't turn stern on, what then, sir?' Pollard asked guardedly.

'Then, my guess is her captain will want to board us,' Miller replied. 'We'll just have to wait and see. Port ten, I want us to meet her starboard, side on.'

Everyone nervously watched and waited.

By five p.m., the bow wave of the U-boat could be seen five thousand miles away on *Endeavour*'s starboard beam.

On The GDP, Lieutenant Young felt his pulse rate increase as he peered through his binoculars. 'If she maintains her present speed,' he reported to Miller, 'she'll be within range of our gun in twenty minutes.'

'Sub's flashing, sir,' cried PO Signalman Watson. 'I think the message is in Swedish.'

Pollard picked up the Aldis lamp and replied in Swedish, 'Please repeat message.'

Seconds later the message was repeated. '"Stop engines. Do not transmit. Will board and search you," said Pollard.

'Thank you, Number One.' Miller was about to put down his binoculars when he noticed the sub had slowed down and was turning starboard beam on. Miller could hardly believe his luck, noting the sub's pennant number, XB 1, on the side of her conning tower. 'It's obvious her captain doesn't know we are armed. Hands to action stations.' Ignoring the enemy's warning, Miller looked askance at PO Watson and said, 'Signal to C-in-C, Plymouth. "U-boat, XB1, within range. Intend Attacking." And give our position.'

After writing the message on his signal pad, Watson hurried from the bridge to the wireless office. 'Better put your tin helmet and lifejacket on, Smithy,' he said, handing the message to WO Smith. 'It looks like the war's finally caught up with us.'

Smith didn't reply. As he sent the message, he wished there was some way he could contact the U-boat. Instead, he was in danger of being killed by his fellow countrymen.

On the bridge, Pollard, with his binoculars pinned to his eyes, shouted, 'They're manning their deck guns, sir.'

'Yes, they must have intercepted our signal,' Miller replied. Miller unhooked the ship's tannoy. 'Captain speaking,' he said, feeling a trickle of warm sweat running down his back. 'The U-boat will shortly be opening fire. As ordered, those ratings not required are to remain in their messes.'

As he replaced the tannoy, the U-boat's two twin 88mm gun spurted smoke. Seconds later, two tall jets of water erupted fifty yards on *Endeavour*'s port quarter.

'The bastard's seemed to have got our range pretty quickly,' Miller said to Pollard.

Miller contacted Lieutenant Young on the GDP. 'Prepare to engage.'

The drill that Young and the gunnery team had practised so often, quickly sprang into action.

A few minutes later, Chief GI Mills' voice came over Young's intercom. 'Shutter raised on starboard side, sur.'

'Range, fifteen hundred yards,' snapped Lieutenant Young, peering through his range finder. 'Stand by… *Fire!*'

As practised, the order was immediately passed to Chief Miller in the gun hangar.

'*Open fire!*' cried Chief Mills.

The ear-splitting noise of the gun firing reverberated throughout the ship. Suddenly, the air was filled with the acrid smell of cordite. In each mess, the strain of waiting for the next explosion was etched on everyone's faces. In the seaman's mess, the cacophony, together with the sudden vibrations of the firing, almost threw them out of their hammocks.

On the GDP, Lieutenant Young and everyone on the bridge watched, hoping and praying the shell would hit home. Instead, they saw a pall of water erupt some twenty yards from the sub's conning tower.

'Up ten degrees,' Young shouted. '*Fire!*'

All eyes followed the thin, black trajectory. Then came a pall of white water shooting in the air a few yards in front of the sub. Simultaneously, another salvo from the U-boat exploded a few yards from the ship's bow.

In the engine room, Lieutenant Duncan, Chief O'Malley and a

group of stokers were busy stripping down the cylinder head and piston. All were stripped to the waist and sweating profusely.

'To be sure, sir,' O'Malley yelled to Chief ERA Jones, 'if this racket continues, we'll all need hearing aids.'

'I agree, Paddy,' Jones bellowed, feeling a trickle of sweat run down his back, 'but if one of those shells hits us, we'll need more than a hearing aid. Now, pass me a spanner and wrench.'

On the GDP, the latest explosion almost drowned out Lieutenant Young's voice as he shouted, 'Up five degrees *'Fire!'*

But to everyone's dismay, the shell only exploded twenty yards away from the sub's conning tower.

The U-boat responded by sending yet another salvo that sent a fountain of water high in the air twenty yards on the ship's port bow.

'*Down ten degrees. Fire!*' bellowed Young.

Seconds later, he held his breath as the conning tower was momentarily obliterated by a cloud of water. However, when the water drained away, the U-boat remained unharmed. This was quickly followed by a tremendous *bang,* as a shell from the U-boat burst dangerously close to the lower side of the ship's starboard side. Miller hurried onto the bridge wing, peered aft and saw a large, black indentation in the ship's side. As he returned into the bridge, a rating appeared wearing a lifejacket. He was sweating and breathing heavily.

'Leading Stoker Peterson, sir,' he said. 'The seamen's mess has been damaged, and there's a few hurt.'

Quick as a flash, Miller unhooked the tannoy and shouted, '*Medical Officer to the seamen's mess!'* Turning to Pollard, he said, 'Better go down there and see what's happened.'

Like an Olympic athlete, Pollard immediately negotiated two flights of stairs onto the passageway, and met Surgeon Lieutenant Ryan, LSBA Hailey. In front of them was PO Feneck and the first-aid team.

The scene that met them when they entered the seamen's mess was chaotic. Hammocks and bedding hung loosely from their iron bars in the deck head. Bits of crockery were strewn everywhere. Metal lockers had burst open, spewing clothing and personal items on the deck. The mess table and wooden seating remained upright only because they were screwed to the deck.

LRO Bell lay against a locker. Blood was trickling down from a large gash in his forehead. Lane lay sprawled on the deck, holding his left arm alongside Brown and Lewis. Several other ratings lay on the deck. Some had nasty cuts and bruises. Others looked pale and dazed. Pollard quickly ordered those men not injured to leave and go across the passageway to the stoker's mess.

While PO Feneck, Hailey and the first-aiders attended to the injured, Ryan knelt down and dealt with Brown and Lewis, who were sprawled on the deck. The bars that held their hammocks were bent, and a large part of the bulkhead, close to where both men slept, bulged inwards. Brown lay still. His eyes were open, and he was staring vacantly in front of him. Lewis lay prone and still: one eye was open, the other was half closed. Ryan felt for a radial pulse on both men and found none. He gently opened Brown's lifejacket, palpated around his chest and heard the sickening sound of crepitus, the crackling of broken bones. Hailey examined Lewis and found similar injuries.

He looked up at Pollard and Hailey, who were standing next to him, and slowly shook his head. 'I'm afraid they're gone,' he said quietly.

Using a finger, he tenderly closed both the dead men's eyes. Before the war, Ryan had spent four years as a medical consultant at Charing Cross Hospital. During that time, he had witnessed the death of several men and women. But looking down at the ashen faces he had seen on and off during the past three months, he felt a mixture of sadness and shock.

For a few seconds Pollard stood looking down at both men, unable to believe his eyes.

'The strength of the shock wave must have killed them,' said Ryan, 'and threw them out of their hammocks.'

Pollard gave the doctor a sombre glance and said, 'Poor chaps. I suggest you don't cover them up, until the walking wounded have been taken to the sickbay and the rest moved to the stokers mess.' He turned, and after stepping over some bedding, ran a hand over the large concavity in the bulkhead and was relieved to find it was dry. With a final look at the bodies of Lewis and Brown, he turned to Ryan and said, 'I'd better report to the captain.'

As Pollard arrived on the bridge, the starboard lookout cried, 'The sub's beginning to dive, sir!'

'What!' Miller exclaimed.

He and the others instantly looked to their right and saw the German gunners disappear down a hatch as a mass of air bubbles began to flow from her ballast tanks.

My God, please help us, Miller thought to himself. *If she submerges, we'll be a sitting duck!*

Seconds later the deck and guns were awash as the sub began to slowly sink beneath the waves. At that moment, the ear-splitting sound of the *Endeavour*'s gun opening fire rent the air. This was quickly followed by a thunderous explosion as the conning tower vanished in a ball of yellow and red flames. The sub's snub-nosed bow slowly rose in the air. For a few seconds it remained still, then slowly sank, leaving behind an ever-widening whirlpool of black, oily, concentric circles. Gradually, bits of bodies, some headless, others half dressed, appeared in the water, floating among the detritus of war.

Miller looked at PO Watson, who, like the QM and lookouts, was standing white-faced and silent. 'Signal C-in-C. Give our position,' Miller said gravely. 'And say: "U-boat XB1 sunk by gunfire. No survivors."' He unhooked the tannoy. 'This is the captain speaking,' he said calmly. 'The U-boat has been sunk. We are no longer in danger. Well done to the gun's crew.' While replacing the tannoy he noticed Pollard standing next to him.

'What's the matter, Number One?' Miller remarked, noticing Pollard's ashen complexion.

Pollard took a deep breath. 'Two men have been killed and several injured, sir,' he replied.

'My God!' gasped Miller. 'Who are they, how did it happen?'

'Able Seaman Brown and Lewis. It must have been when the sub's shell exploded near the starboard side, sir,' Pollard replied. 'Apparently they were hit by the shock wave and thrown onto the deck.'

'And the damage?'

'A section of the starboard bulkhead is severely dented but is not shipping water,' Pollard replied. 'Nevertheless, I'll get the buffer to shore it up. Meanwhile, I suggest the seamen use the stoker's mess.'

The news of the death of Lewis and Brown stunned Miller and those on duty into a sickly silence. Regaining his composure, Miller took a deep breath and looked at PO Watson.

'Signal C-in-C. Further to my last signal,' he said, as Watson, who, feeling his hands shaking, took out a pad and pencil and began writing. 'Say: "Regret, two ratings killed in action, Thursday 25th September." Give their names, rates and official numbers, and add, "Please inform next of kin."'

Miller looked disconsolately at Pollard and said, 'I think we should bury them as quickly as possible, if only for the sake of morale.'

'I agree, sir,' Pollard solemnly replied. 'May I suggest tomorrow at midday, after the men have had their tot.'

'And I expect the officers will need a large one also,' Miller added with a sigh.

Like the rest of the seaman, they were sitting in the stoker's mess.

'Poor bugger,' Lofty Day said to O'Hanlon. 'If they hadn't been in their mick, they might have been all right.'

'That's right,' O'Hanlon gravely replied, taking a sip of tea from a mug given to him by a stoker. 'Their hammocks were right up against the bulkhead. That's what did it, eh, Smithy?'

For some strange reason, even though Brown and Lewis were his sworn enemies, Smith, who had been on duty when the explosion occurred, was saddened by hearing they had been killed. However, thoughts of their demise quickly vanished by thinking he would shortly be seeing Katrina. 'Yes, Scouse,' Smith quietly replied. 'I think you're right.'

That evening after rounds, Surgeon Lieutenant Ryan, Chief GI Mills, Chief Bosun's Mate Conyon and LSBA Hailey had the unenviable task of removing Lewis's and Brown's clothing and placing a six-inch shell between their legs. After securing each body in a separate hammock, they were placed into a Neil

Robinson stretcher then carried into the gun hangar. They were each placed onto a canvas wooden stretcher and covered with a white ensign. In the morning, before "Call the hands", Lieutenant Ryan and LSBA Hailey would make sure they were ready for burial.

At twelve forty-five p.m. the next day, Miller ordered the chief engineer to stop the ship. Standing on the ship's stern, QM Day lowered the white ensign to half-mast. Except for Lieutenant Duncan, the Chief Engineer and Chief ERA and staff, the rest of the ship's company mustered on the quarterdeck: officers and senior ratings close to the stern, ratings in three ranks lining the port side facing inboard. The atmosphere was unnervingly sombre. Faces were pale and drawn. Even the sea seemed to sense the sadness of the occasion and remained an undulating, calm blue, while the sun, high above in a cloudless, cerulean sky, bathed everyone in a soft, comforting warmth.

With the exception of Linda, who wore a black headscarf, white, short-sleeved blouse and black slacks, everyone else was dressed in tropical whites. At precisely one p.m., Miller, standing in front of the officers, holding a small bible, nodded to QM Day who immediately rang the ship's bell twice, sending mournful echoes around the ship.

'Ship's company, attention. Off cap,' ordered Pollard.

Seconds later the shutters slowly opened. Many were unable to watch, as the burial party, by Chief Coxswain Pony Moore, Chief GI Mills, LSBA Hailey and four ratings from the seamen's mess, emerged onto the quarterdeck. The sight of the white ensign covering the men they had come to know so well, was too much, even for three badgers who had witnessed similar scenes during the last war. Many bit their lips in an unsuccessful attempt to stifle a tear. Smith looked on, his head bowed in false mourning. The occasion was too much for Linda, who had often met Brown and Lewis and even shared a risqué joke with them. Lieutenant Morgan, standing next to her, heard her sobbing and discretely slipped a pristine, white handkerchief into her hand.

The stretchers were carefully placed on the starboard guard rail.

Miller opened the bible at a prearranged page and swallowed nervously. Then, in a quiet, reverent voice, began: 'Almighty God, who alone spreadest out the waters and rulest the ragging sea and who has encompassed the water with bounds until day and night end. Be pleased to receive the souls of our two shipmates, Able Seaman Brown and Lewis, into your most gracious protection, Amen."

He gave a quick nod to Chief GI Mills and Chief Coxswain Pony Moore, who, holding the edges of the white ensign to prevent them slipping away, looked at the two seamen who carefully tilted the stretchers. The bodies, secured in their hammocks, quickly slid from the stretchers, splashed into the sea, and in a flurry of tiny, green bubbles, disappeared.

Miller folded his bible, looked up then cried, 'Ship's company, stand at ease. On caps. Officers and senior ratings, carry on.' This was quickly followed by, 'Junior ratings, carry on.'

The QM raised the flag. The two chiefs carefully folded their white ensigns, and together with the ratings carrying the stretchers, walked into the gun hangar. In sombre silence everyone slowly dispersed. Within minutes, except for Miller and Pollard, the quarterdeck was deserted.

'Revert to cruising stations, Number One, and pipe, "Make and mend for all off duty." Now, if you'll excuse me,' he added, sighing wearily, 'I have two letters to write.'

CHAPTER THIRTY-FOUR

During the next three days *Endeavour* continued northwards, crawling along at a meagre five knots. Luckily the sea remained calm with a balmy, south-westerly breeze that enabled men to the strip to the waist while working on the upper deck. While Lieutenant Duncan and the engineers laboured around the clock, the ship's company were kept occupied by cleaning ship, inter-mess quizzes, "housey-housey", (bingo), lectures and evolutions.

Shortly after nine a.m. on Saturday 30th September, Lieutenant Duncan knocked on Miller's cabin door and was told to enter. His normally pristine, white overalls looked smeared with oil and dirt.

Miller was sat at his desk checking the signal log. He looked up as Duncan came in. 'Good morning, Jock,' Miller said. 'I hope you have good news,' he added, noticing Duncan's bloodshot eyes.

'Aye, that I have, sir,' Duncan replied, removing his oil-stained cap. 'We've managed to change the piston and partially repair the fuel injection system long enough fer you to get us to Rio.'

'That's bloody marvellous, Jock,' Miller replied, thumping his desk with his hand. 'How much speed can you give me?'

Fifteen knots, maybe sixteen maximum, sir,' Duncan replied.

'Good man!' Miller exclaimed. 'And an extra tot to your staff; you've damn well earned it.'

'Thank you, sir,' Duncan replied, 'but the injection system will require more work when we reach Rio.'

Seconds after Duncan left, Miller hurried onto the bridge.

'Duncan's performed a minor miracle, Number One,' he said to Pollard, who was standing next to OOW Lieutenant Morgan. As he spoke, the ship seemed to awake from its slumber and increase speed. 'We can now do fifteen knots.' He looked at Morgan and said, 'At that speed, how long will it take us to reach Rio?'

Morgan turned around and consulted his chart. 'Six days, sir,' he replied over his shoulder.

Miller unhooked the tannoy. 'This is the captain speaking. As you can see, we've increased speed and hope to arrive in Rio next Friday. The damage to the bulkhead is slight, but I expect we'll have to stay in Rio to have it repaired and take on fuel. After that, we'll just have to wait and see,' and hung up.

'Do you think the U-boat was able to report our position to Germany before it blew up, sir?' Pollard asked Miller.

Miller pursed his lips, then said, 'We'll have to assume that she did.'

'Do you think Hitler will send another U-boat, sir?' asked Pollard.

'He'll still be desperate to obtain the grapholite, so I think he will,' Miller replied.

'Regular gun drill, quizzes and evolutions again, sir?' Pollard asked.

'Yes, and maybe this time the wardroom will beat the senior ratings at whist,' Miller replied, grinning like a Cheshire cat.

Miller's assumption was correct. Due to *Endeavour* being five hours ahead of Wilhelmshaven, Admiral Doenitz didn't receive the signal from the U-boat until five p.m. He immediately informed Canaris.

'The signal seems unfinished,' said Doenitz. 'It reads, "Endeavour intercepted. Position forty degrees longitude, thirty degrees latitude. Firing warning shots and intend boarding but coming under fire…" Then the signal ends.'

'Thank you, Wilhem,' Canaris replied. 'That does seem odd. I'd better inform the fuhrer immediately.' Canaris replaced the telephone and picked up another containing a direct line to Hitler.

'I hope I'm not disturbing you, Mein Fuhrer, but Doenitz has just had an odd signal from the XB U-boat.'

'Yes, yes, what does it say?' Hitler answered impatiently.

Canaris immediately read out the signal.

'But that's impossible,' barked Hitler, his voice rising to hysterical pitch. 'According to the report from Buenos Aires, *Endeavour* isn't armed.'

'Perhaps an enemy warship arrived,' Canaris replied, somewhat unconvincingly.

'Highly unlikely,' retorted Hitler. 'The U-boat would have reported it earlier.' He paused, then went on. 'Nevertheless, the grapholite is still on board *Endeavour* and mustn't fall into enemy hands.'

'I strongly suspect she's making for Rio de Janeiro,' said Canaris. 'If you send another U-boat to intercept her, remember, Mein Fuhrer, our submarines don't have radar, so *Endeavour* will be difficult to find.'

'So what do you suggest?' asked Hitler, a note of agitation in his voice.

Canaris paused momentarily, then replied, 'Mein Fuhrer, at present Doenitz has forty-six operational U-boats. A dozen are already at sea in the Atlantic, the Mediterranean and North Sea. Then he has destroyers doing the same along the western littoral of Africa. As I think *Endeavour* will take the quickest route to England, I suggest Doenitz sends a flotilla of submarines to patrol the Western Approaches.'

Hitler thumped his desk with a hand, then, in his usual, high-pitched voice, cried, 'Good, good. Then inform Doenitz immediately,' and slammed the receiver down.

CHAPTER THIRTY-FIVE

The news that they would arrive in Rio sooner than expected was greeted with shouts of joyous relief. WO Smith was especially excited. At night, when he was off watch, thoughts of seeing Katrina prevented him from sleeping. He lay awake, remembering her crystal-blue eyes and how soft and smooth her skin felt. And in the morning he would awake groggy and tired, with thoughts of Katrina still circulating in his mind.

During the next three days, the weather deteriorated. A strong, westerly wind chopped up the sea, and the usually hot sun flitted in and out of the grey, cumulonimbus clouds. Nevertheless, the ship's company were once again kept busy doing evolutions, only this time they were carried out with good humour.

'Just think,' LSBA Hailey said to Able Seaman O'Hanlon, who was being carried in a Neil Robertson stretcher along the quarterdeck to the sickbay. 'In a few days you'll be pissed out of your mind, lying on the beach ogling those gorgeous, dark-skinned beauties.'

At that moment the ship rolled violently.

'Holy mother of God, for fuck's sake, don't drop me overboard,' O'Hanlon yelled. 'There's sharks around here.'

'Don't worry, Scouse,' LSBA Hailey said, laughing loudly. 'The sharks around here are very particular about who they eat.'

Friday 6th October dawned warm and clear. Overnight the wind had dropped. The sea became calm, and the sun beat down from an azure sky.

Shortly after seven a.m., Miller, followed by Pollard, arrived on the bridge and gave a cursory 'Good morning' to OOW Lieutenant Morgan and the others on duty. 'What's our position, Pilot?' he asked, while easing himself into his chair.

'One hundred and fifty miles south of Rio, sir,' Morgan

replied.

'Send the following signal,' he said to PO Watts.

Watts quickly took out a pad and pencil from a side pocket in his tropical shorts.

'To harbour master, Rio de Janeiro. "Arriving Rio p.m., Sunday 8th. Have developed engine problem. Also, sustained slight damage to starboard bulkhead. Request harbour engineer meet. Also request berthing instructions. Harbour pilot not needed."'

'Aye, aye, sir,' Watts said and left the bridge.

Ten minutes later WO Smith arrived and handed the reply to Miller.

After reading it, Miller grinned and said, 'Number 6 wharf, same as before, very close to Copacabana beach. Put it on Daily Orders, Number One,' he added.

During dinner, Miller noticed Linda occasionally smiling at him. Suddenly he felt a pang of unease. What with the burial of Brown and Lewis, and problems with the engine, he had had very little time to talk to her. After dinner, he left the wardroom and went to his cabin to write up the ship's log. No sooner had he sat down at his desk, than a knock came at his door. 'Come,' he said.

The door opened and Linda entered. She wore fawn slacks, a pale-green, long-sleeved blouse, and her hair was worn in a chignon.

'Linda,' said Miller, turning around and looking up, 'this is a pleasant surprise. I'm sorry I haven't had time to talk to you recently, but come in and sit down and don't look do so worried.'

'That's quite all right, I'm well aware of how busy you've been,' Linda replied. 'But there's something I have to ask you.'

Miller gave her a searching look, then said, 'And what might that be?'

Linda placed both hands on her lap and sat up straight. 'As you know, Bob, I am due to leave the ship at Rio and rejoin my group of mineralogists.'

'Yes,' Miller answered, frowning slightly. 'Unfortunately, I am only too aware of that.'

'Well…' She paused, then in a firm voice, said, 'I have decided to stay on board the ship.'

'But that's impossible,' Miller replied, raising his voice. 'The future is uncertain, and for all I know, another U-boat will be lying in wait for us when we leave Rio.'

'I don't care,' Linda forcibly replied. 'I'll take my chance. After all, those two sailors gave their lives…'

Miller quickly raised his hand and interrupted her. 'I'm well aware of that, but the answer is still no. And besides,' he continued, 'the journey across the Atlantic is fraught with danger, and if anything happened to you, I couldn't live with myself. You see, Linda, I've fallen in…'

Before he could go on, she reached across and pressed a finger to his lips, and in an almost reverent voice, said, 'So am I, darling, but it makes no difference. I insist on staying.'

'Sorry,' Miller replied. 'I'm the captain, and I can have you forcibly removed from the ship if necessary.'

'You wouldn't dare,' she cried, standing up and glaring angrily at him.

'Yes, I would,' Miller replied, placing both hands on his desk. 'So that's the end of it.'

'You're bloody sufferable,' Linda retorted, and stormed out of the cabin, slamming the door on her way out.

Shortly after six a.m., on Sunday 8th October, Rio de Janeiro, with its rows of luxury hotels and enticing, horseshoe-shaped beaches, hove into view. At eight a.m., hands were fallen for entering harbour. Half an hour later *Endeavour* was tied up alongside Number 6 wharf. A section of the wooden guard rail was removed from amidships and a small crane lowered onto the wharf. Two burly dockyard workers secured it, allowing a tall, dark-haired man wearing blue overalls to come aboard, where he was met by Miller, Pollard and Lieutenant Duncan

'Welcome on board,' said Miller, shaking his hand. 'This is Lieutenant Duncan, my engineer, and Lieutenant Commander Pollard, my executive officer.'

'Pleased to meet you, gentlemen. Welcome to Rio. I'm Harold Evans, the harbour engineer,' he replied, warmly shaking each officer's hands. Evan's voice, spoken with a distinct Welsh accent, was clear and concise. 'I believe you've had some damage to a bulkhead, and engine trouble.' As he spoke, the corners of his pale-blue eyes wrinkled into a warm smile.

'Aye, that we have,' Duncan replied. 'A near miss from a U-boat's gun was too close fer comfort, and we've got a wee problem with the piston. We'll go to the engine room, then I'll be grateful if yer could assess the damage to the hull.'

'After which I'd like a report,' said Miller.

'Of course, sir,' Evans replied.

Just as Duncan and Evans left, WO Smith arrived. 'Signal from the British ambassador, sir,' Smith said, handing it to Miller.

'Thank you, Smith,' Miller replied. 'Kindly read it to me.'

'"Welcome back. Request the company of you and Professor Penlowe for dinner this evening. Seven thirty p.m. Dress informal. Transport will collect seven fifteen p.m. Sir Geoffrey Knox-Johnson."'

'Reply: "Many thanks. It will be a pleasure to see you and your ladyship again."'

'He'll no doubt be wondering how long we'll be here, sir,' Pollard said to Miller.

'And so am I,' Smith muttered to himself, as he left the quarterdeck.

A few minutes later Linda came onto the quarterdeck. Her face, devoid of make-up, looked fresh and clear. Her hair was tied in a neat bun, and she wore a pair of black slacks and an open-necked, long-sleeved, pink blouse.

Doing his best to hide a smile, Miller looked at her and said, 'Ah, Professor Penlove, I hope you haven't packed your clothes.'

Linda gave him daggers then replied sharply, 'Not yet.'

'Just as well,' Miller said, doing his best not to smile. 'Because the ambassador has requested our presence for an informal dinner tonight at seven thirty p.m. Transport will collect us at seven fifteen p.m.'

'Splendid,' Linda replied, then, with an arrogant toss of her head, she turned sharply and went below.

Ten minutes later, Duncan and Evans arrived.

'Well, Mr Evans, what's the verdict?' asked Miller.

'In my opinion you were lucky to reach Rio,' Evans replied. 'But thanks to the hard work of Jock and his stokers,' Evans said, giving Duncan an appreciative glance. 'They managed to repair the fuel pipes, but the injection system and piston rings need replacing. As for the damage to the bulkhead, it'll take my engineers a couple of days to repair it, and I'll have the piston rings delivered tomorrow morning.'

'And how long do you think it'll take to install them?'

'We've already stripped down the fuel pipe, sir,' Duncan replied, using a grimy handkerchief to wipe beads of sweat from his face. 'So, I'd say a week. What do you think, Harry?'

'I'd say that's about right, Jock,' Evans replied.

Miller glanced at his wristwatch, then said, 'As it'll be "stand easy" in five minutes, I suggest we adjourn to the wardroom for coffee, or,' he added, smiling at Evans, 'something stronger.'

CHAPTER THIRTY-SIX

At ten a.m., the pipe, "Stand easy. Leave. Leave to the first and second part of starboard; from two p.m. to six a.m. Rig, number 7A. Rain expected. Money changing will be held in the ship's office in half an hour," came over the tannoy. (Number 7A being caps, tropical shirts, trousers and white shoes.)

In the stoker's mess, the air was warm and thick with tobacco smoke. Smith, along with several other seaman and stokers, were enjoying a mug of tea. Suddenly an idea flashed through his mind. If he took his Burberry with him when he went ashore, he could hide the transmitter and cyanide capsule in its lining. Furthermore, he might be able to transmit the latest information of *Endeavour*'s engine trouble and movements from Katrina's apartment. Once again, he imagined how proud his parents would be as he was showered with honours by Hitler.

'Are you all right, Smithy? You look miles away,' he heard Leading Seaman Waters say.

'Err... yes,' Smith replied, placing his mug on the table. 'Just thinking about going ashore.'

'Aye,' chimed in LWO Bell, 'keep it in your trousers and don't be adrift. Remember you relieve me at eight a.m.'

At 12.50, Smith and a dozen other ratings, including chief and petty officers, fell in on the quarterdeck. As forecast, it had started to rain, and all of them wore Burberrys. PO Thompson reminded them that leave expired at six a.m. and only two packets of cigarettes were allowed to be taken ashore.

Smith, conscious of the slight weight and bulge at the bottom of his pocket, suddenly felt a surge of panic run though him. What, he wondered, would he say if the PO asked him what it was?

After ordering them to attention, Thompson turned sharply, and saluting OOD Lieutenant Young, he reported, 'Liberty men ready for inspection, sir.'

'Thank you, PO,' Lieutenant Young replied. 'Senior ratings carry on.'

Thompson saluted, turned away then told the chiefs and PO to carry on ashore. After saluting, they turned and walked down the gangway onto the wharf. Young gave a quick glance at the junior ratings, then told them they also could proceed ashore. Smith gave an inward sigh of relief, and along with the junior ratings, filed down the gangway, laughing and joking as they made their way along the quayside onto the esplanade.

'Hey, fellas,' Leading Seaman Waters said, pointing to a small bar, 'that's where a gorgeous party gave me fifty up last time we were here. Let's go and see if she's still there.'

'Great idea,' Able Seaman Knight replied enthusiastically. 'If she is, me first.'

'Next to me,' said Able Seaman Lane, giving Knight a playful dig in the ribs.

'What about you, Smithy, do you fancy a bit of "how's yer father?" Waters said, grinning lecherously.

'Not for me,' Smith replied. 'I want to have another look around before it starts to rain.'

'Bollocks to sightseeing,' cried Lane. 'Come with us and enjoy yerself.'

'Thanks all the same,' Smith replied. 'But you lot go on ahead, and I'll see you back on board.'

'Well, whatever you do,' said Waters, shaking his head, 'try not to end up spending the night on a bench like last time.'

'Don't worry, I will,' Smith replied, conjuring up in his mind the sight of Katrina lying naked on her bed.

With a shake of his head, Waters and the others crossed the esplanade, pushed open the bamboo swing doors and went into the bar.

After they left, Smith felt tiny drops of rain on his face. He turned up the collar of his Burberry, then felt down and touched the bulky outline of his transmitter and the small box containing the cyanide. With a satisfied grin on his face, he began to walk down the wide pathway next to the beach. Despite the inclement weather, the beach was crowded. The traffic on the esplanade was thick. Smith managed to flag down a taxi and asked to be taken to the Hotel Vista do Mar, hoping Katrina was on duty.

A few minutes later, after passing a line of several hotels, bars and souvenir shops, the taxi stopped opposite the hotel. He paid the driver and hurried down the flanked pathway and up the steps. Here he was met by a tall, swarthy man dressed in an immaculate grey suit.

Noticing Smith was in uniform, he smiled affably and said, 'Good afternoon, sir, the Royal Navy is always welcome. I am *Senhor* Mendoza, the hotel manager. Can I help you?' His English, spoken with a Latin inflexion, was clear and concise.

'Yes, you can,' Smith nervously replied. 'I'm looking for Katrina, one of your receptionists.'

Mendoza raised his eyebrows, and smiling, said, 'Ah, the lovely Katrina; I'm afraid this is her day off.'

'I see,' Smith replied, turning to leave. 'Sorry to bother you.'

'That's quite all right,' said Mendoza, 'but you're more than welcome to come inside for drink.'

'Thank you, some other time perhaps,' Smith replied, then quickly left.

Hoping Katrina would be in her apartment, he made his way past the restaurant that he and Katrina had dined at. The rain had stopped. He took off his Burberry, folded it neatly then placed it over his left arm. Seconds later he paused outside a florist's then went inside. Standing behind the counter stood a pretty, dark-haired girl. He smiled and asked her for the bouquet of red flowers he had seen in the window.

'*Si, Senhor*, these are called Camelias, one of Brazil's favourite flowers,' she said in perfect English, as she wrapped them up. 'I'm sure she will like them,' she added, with a coquettish smile.

Smith thanked her, paid and left. He turned right, walked down the road and entered the yard of the hotel. Feeling his heart pounding, he arrived outside the lift's door. Clutching the bouquet, he used his free hand to draw back the gate. As he did so, a wave of panic ran through him. What, he asked himself, would he do if

Katrina wasn't in? Where would he go? He stepped inside the lift, and remembering Katrina lived on the top floor, he pressed the appropriate button. A few seconds later, the lift shuddered and slowly moved. The thought that he would soon feel Katrina's arms around him sent a thrill of excited expectancy running through him.

After what seemed like an eternity, the lift gave a series of uncomfortable jerks and came to a standstill. He drew back the exit gate, walked down the dimly lit corridor and stopped outside number twenty-one. For a few seconds he stood and listened to the faint sound of music coming from behind the door. His mouth suddenly felt like sandpaper, and he knocked on the door. At first nothing happened, so he knocked again. The door opened and the music became louder. For a few seconds, Smith couldn't believe his eyes. Standing in front of him was a tall, well-built, swarthy man with a mop of untidy, black hair. He was unshaven and wore a pair of well-worn jeans, and his bare chest was matted with tiny, dark, curly hairs.

Noticing Smith's uniform, he gave him a suspicious look and asked in Portuguese, 'What do you want?'

'Err... sorry,' Smith replied, shrugging his shoulders. 'No speak Portuguese.'

'*Quem e esse?*' (Who is it?) came a female voice from inside the apartment.

'I'm not sure, but I think he's an English sailor,' he shouted over his shoulder in Portuguese.

Seconds later Katrina arrived and stood barefooted next to the man. She looked pale, and her short, fair hair was an untidy mess. The pink dressing gown she wore was open, showing a black slip that stood out against the whiteness of her nakedness.

With a surprised look on her face, she stared at Smith. 'It's *you*!' she exclaimed angrily. 'What are you doing here?'

'I came to see you, of course,' Smith replied, then, feeling a pang of jealousy, glanced at the man and said, 'Tell me, Katrina, who is he?'

Regaining her composure, she replied, 'This is Miguel.' She placed an arm around the man's waist and gave him a hug. 'We were married a week ago.'

'Married!' Smith cried. 'But how could you? I thought...'

'Then you thought wrong, you fool! Now go away and don't come back!' she cried.

Miguel gave Katrina an angry look and said in Portuguese, 'Katrina, do you know this man?'

'Not really,' she hastily replied. 'I met him once when my friend, Anna, brought him here.'

With an angry look on his face, Miguel turned to Katrina and shouted, 'I do not believe you, you bitch! Get inside!' he yelled, giving Katrina a hefty push in the chest. 'I'll deal with you later.'

'Hey, you can't do that!' Smith cried, squaring up to Miguel.

Ignoring Smith's words, Miguel clenched a fist and struck Smith firmly on the jaw. Smith dropped his Burberry and flowers. Clutching his jaw, he staggered back and fell on the floor. For a few minutes he lay in a daze, grief-stricken at the thought of never seeing Katrina again. Finally, rubbing his aching jaw, he picked himself up and listened to the sounds of Katrina and Miguel shouting at one another coming from within the room.

Shaking his head in disbelief, he muttered, 'I told her I would come back. How could she do this to me?'

Leaving the flowers scattered on the floor, he bent down and collected his Burberry. For a moment he was tempted to knock on the door again, but remembering the angry look in her eyes when she had seen him, he quickly changed his mind.

As he slowly walked down the corridor, the thought of Katrina lying in Miguel's arms every night, made him tremble with jealousy. All thoughts of sending a message to Buenos Aires vanished from his head. Sill inwardly fulminating, he drew back the lift gate and slammed it shut. For the first time in his life, he felt like a good, stiff drink. After what seemed like an eternity, the lift reached the ground and shuddered to a stop. The time was a little after three p.m. He left the lift and made his way outside. For some reason, the promenade bustling with locals and tourists seemed unreal. He stopped outside the nearest bar. He pushed open the swing doors, and despite the rhythmic beat sound of the samba coming from a radio, all he could think of was Katrina lying in the arms of Miguel. Ignoring the stares of several customers, many of whom were tourists, he looked at the barman and ordered a large whisky.

'You are a sailor, no?' asked the barman.

'Yes, I am,' Smith grunted, placing his Burberry over a nearby stool. 'Now hurry up with that drink.'

'*Si, Senhor*,' replied the barman, somewhat annoyed by Smith's bad-tempered remark.

Three drinks later, Smith paid the bill, and feeling unsteady on his feet, left the bar and went into another one a few yards down the road. He parted the beaded curtains and went inside. Not surprisingly the place was packed with tourists drinking, smoking and laughing.

The pretty, dark-haired beauty behind the bar, flashed Smith a welcoming smile and said, 'Engleesh sailors always welcome. You want a drink, yes?'

After two large whiskies, Smith threw his Burberry over his shoulder, paid the girl and staggered through the curtains onto the pavement. The dark clouds had disappeared. The sun, high in a pale-blue sky, bathed everything in a sticky warmth.

As usual, the wide dual road surrounding the harbour was busy with traffic. For a few minutes Smith stood, wavering slightly and wondering what to do. Suddenly he felt drained of energy. He decided to go onto the beach, lie down and try to sleep. Ignoring the pedestrian crossing, he gave a tired yawn, stepped onto the road and was hit by a car.

People screamed as they watched Smith being tossed in the air like a rag doll. The car stopped, and the driver rushed out and saw Smith lying on the ground a few feet away from the bonnet. A crowd quickly gathered around and was held back by a policeman.

Smith was lying face down, his face covered in blood. His legs were bent, and his arms outstretched. A quick-thinking person telephoned an ambulance.

A few minutes later, the ambulance arrived. A doctor, wearing a short, white coat and holding a medical bag, opened a passenger door and quickly left. After pushing his way through the crowd, the doctor knelt down next to Smith's blood-stained face and checked his radial pulse, but found nothing. Smith had died instantly before he even hit the ground.

CHAPTER THIRTY-SEVEN

At precisely seven o'clock that evening, Miller arrived on the quarterdeck. Darkness had fallen. Most of the stars had disappeared behind the grey, cirrostratus clouds, partially disguising a full moon.

'Looks like we're in for a spot of rain, sir,' OOW Lieutenant Ward said, glancing ominously up at the sky.

'I think you're right,' Miller replied, returning Ward's salute while feeling a gust of wind hit his face.

Even though his bush jacket remained tight under the arms and his trousers slightly too short, Leading Steward Blake ensured they looked immaculate, having been carefully pressed. He also polished the peak of his cap, and its row of silver leaves shone like glass.

A few minutes later, Linda arrived. Her fair hair was worn in a neat chignon. She carried a small, brown shoulder bag, and the white, high-heeled shoes set off her trim ankles to perfection. Her knee-length, floral dress, open at the neck, complemented her figure.

'You look absolutely lovely,' Miller remarked, noticing that, except for a touch of red lipstick, her slightly suntanned face was devoid of make-up.

'Is that so?' Linda replied, with a surly expression. Then, turning away from him, said, 'I take it that car on the wharf is for us?'

'I expect it is,' Miller replied, hoping her demeanour would improve before they arrived at the ambassador's residence.

'Then let's go,' she snapped.

'Captain leaving the ship,' cried PO Watson.

Miller returned the salutes of Lieutenant Ward and those on duty. Noticing Linda's abrupt refusal of his assistance, she preceded him and walked rather unsteadily down the gangway. Miller followed on and immediately recognised the small, grey-haired figure of Ramon. He was wearing a dark suit and stood holding open the rear door of a shiny, black Bentley.

'Good evening, Ramon, it's good to see you again,' Miller said, as Linda climbed inside.

'And you, sir,' Ramon replied courteously, while closing the door.

As they drove off, Linda turned abruptly to Miller, and in an ill-tempered voice, said, 'I want to make one thing clear, Commander. When I meet the ambassador, I shall insist on remaining on the ship.'

Miller didn't reply. Instead, he gave a quick smile and looked out the window.

As previously, the journey to the ambassador's residence took ten minutes. They drove through the wrought iron gates and up a wide, gravel drive.

The car stopped at the bottom of three steps where Sir Geoffrey Knox-Johnson waited to greet them. His immaculate, dark-blue suit, white shirt and naval tie complemented his healthy looking, tanned face and greying hair.

Ramon quickly left his seat and opened the passenger door. Miller was the first out of the car. Once again, Linda refused his hand as she stepped outside.

'Good to see you and Linda again, Commander,' the ambassador said, as they warmly shook hands. 'My wife sends her regards. Unfortunately, she's in bed with a heavy cold.'

'Sorry to hear that, Your Excellency,' Miller replied. 'On behalf of Linda and myself, I wish her a speedy recovery.'

'Thank you, I'll pass on your good wishes to her,' the ambassador replied.

Ramon opened the oak door, allowing them to enter the hallway.

'At least it allows me to have a cigarette whenever I want one,' he added with a boyish grin. 'Cocktails in ten minutes, please, Ramon,' he said, as they walked into the lounge.

A quick look around showed Miller that nothing had changed

since his last visit. It remained elegantly furnished with Chippendale and Sheraton.

Sir Geoffrey sank himself into a comfortable-looking, black Chesterfield settee. 'Please sit down,' he said, indicating two armchairs.

As he spoke, Ramon came in carrying the drinks on a silver tray.

'Thank you, Ramon. Dinner in half an hour,' said Sir Geoffrey, as Ramon bent down slightly and placed the cocktails on a small, round coffee table, along with a brass ashtray.

Ramon muttered a terse, 'Very good, sir.' He bowed slightly and left the room, closing the door behind him.

'Now, tell me, Commander,' said Sir Geoffrey, taking out a silver cigarette case. He flicked it open and took out a cigarette. He was about to offer it to Linda and then remembered she didn't smoke. 'How long will it take to repair the problems in your engine system?'

'With the help of your harbour engineer, seven days,' Miller replied.

'Mmm, that takes us up to next Saturday,' replied Sir Geoffrey.

Using a silver lighter, he was about to light his cigarette, when Linda, after giving Miller a quick, contumelious glance, said to Sir Geoffrey, 'With respect, sir, before we go on, sir, there is something I'd like to ask you.'

'Yes, my dear,' Sir Geoffrey replied, lighting his cigarette. 'And what might that be?' As he spoke, a thin trickle of blue tobacco smoke eddied from his mouth.

With a determined look in her eyes, Linda sat forward and said, 'I have told Commander Miller that I intend remaining on board *Endeavour* when it eventually sails for England, and...' She paused and shot Miller another reproachful look, then went on, 'He has refused. Can you please help me?'

Sir Geoffrey removed his cigarette, and turning his head, exhaled another stream of smoke and said, 'To do what, exactly?'

'To stay on the ship when it sails,' Linda replied.

'Sorry, Professor, but I cannot do that,' Sir Geoffrey replied. 'As captain of his ship, Commander Miller's word is law, and I can't interfere with that. Is that not so?' he said, giving Miller a quick, enquiring glance.

'Yes, it is, sir,' Miller replied, raising his eyebrows and nodding.

With a sigh of resignation, Linda sat back in her chair and said, 'So, I take it I'll definitely be leaving the ship in Rio, sir?'

'Yes,' Sir Geoffrey flatly replied, then went on, 'And then what will you do?'

'Return to England and work for the war effort,' she said.

'And how will you get there?' asked Sir Geoffrey.

'With respect, sir,' Linda replied, 'I was hoping you could help me with that.'

'And so I might,' said Sir Geoffrey, stubbing his cigarette out. 'You see,' he added, taking out a sheet of paper from an inside pocket, 'an hour ago, I received this top-secret signal from Winston Churchill, who is now first lord of the admiralty. It says, "Vital grapholite reaches England soonest. In view of *Endeavour's* engine problems, the grapholite is to be sent under diplomatic immunity by air from Rio to Lisbon. It will then be taken by Dakota, under fighter escort, to RAF Abbots Ripon. Here it will be met by members of the Secret Service and taken to Cambridge University and given to Professor Mackenzie." After folding the signal and placing it in his pocket, Sir Geoffrey looked Linda firmly in the eyes and said, 'I would like you to volunteer to take the grapholite to England.'

Linda sat forward, a look of incredulity written on her face. 'You mean I'll be acting as a courier?'

'Yes, my dear,' Sir Geoffrey replied. 'The danger is slight but would serve to get you safely back home. However, I must stress: you don't have to do this, but if you did, you'd be doing a great service to your country. Isn't that right, Commander?'

'Yes, sir, I think it'd be very brave of her,' Miller replied, giving Linda an admiring look.

'Well, sir, I expect my minerology team have already left,' she said, nervously biting her lip, 'so why not?'

'Splendid!' exclaimed Sir Geoffrey, sitting back in his chair and lighting another cigarette. 'Due to the war, the last return flight from Rio to Lisbon leaves Rio at six p.m. on Saturday 14th. You will take this and arrive in Lisbon eleven hours later. Now, as secrecy is paramount, two days before, at say, zero one hundred on Thursday, I will send Ramon to you, Commander, with a suitcase to collect the grapholite. I will, of course, arrange transport for this.'

'With respect, sir,' Miller said, finishing his coffee, 'why can't the Americans take the grapholite to England? It would save all this cloak and dagger stuff.'

'I agree,' Sir Geoffrey replied, flicking cigarette ash in the ashtray. 'But as you know, Roosevelt is coming up for election in November, and he dare not break the neutrality pact he has recently signed with Germany.'

'So his hands are tied,' said Miller, shaking his head in disbelief.

'Now, Linda, you'll have to be on board the plane by five p.m. on the Saturday, so pack your things and stay here overnight on the Friday, when I suggest we meet at seven thirty p.m. for a farewell dinner.'

As he finished speaking, a knock came at the door and Ramon entered. 'Dinner is ready, sir,' he said, bowing slightly, then leaving.

'Right, then,' said Sir Geoffrey, slowly standing up and smiling. 'I think we'd better adjourn to the dining hall.'

CHAPTER THIRTY-EIGHT

After "colours" the next morning, Miller was in his cabin flicking through the signal log. He was about to take a sip of coffee when the telephone rang. He reached across and unhooked the phone.

'Commander Miller,' he said, placing his cup on the blotting pad.

'Good morning, Bob; Sir Geoffrey. I have some very sad news for you.' His voice, usually clipped and loud, sounded quiet and reserved. 'Yesterday evening, one of your crew, WO Smith, was run over by a car and killed.'

'Great Scott, sir!' Miller exclaimed. Stunned by the news, he sat back in his chair. 'Where did this happen?'

'On the double causeway that runs along Copacabana beach,' Sir Geoffrey quietly replied. 'About six p.m.'

'My God, the poor chap,' Miller replied, trying his best to regain his composure. 'Where is he now?'

'He was taken to Saint Saviour's Hospital,' Sir Geoffrey replied. 'His body is in the mortuary, and I'm afraid you'll have the unenviable task of identifying him. When you go there, ask for Doctor Silva. He's the head pathologist, and I suggest you bring something to collect his clothing.'

'I see,' Miller sighed. 'I'd better take Smith's boss, Lieutenant Willis, and the doctor. Perhaps you'd be good enough to arrange transport to pick us up at two p.m., sir.'

'Of course,' Sir Geoffrey replied, 'and pass on my condolences to his parents when you write to them.'

'Thank you, sir, I will. And thank you for ringing,' Miller replied. After replacing the phone, he unhooked it again, contacted the quarterdeck and ordered the QM to pipe all officers and Professor Penlowe to report to the wardroom immediately. As Miller left his cabin, the order came over the tannoy.

Every officer was waiting for Miller. Some, including Linda, looked slightly perplexed, wondering what was so important to warrant their sudden presence. Miller ordered PO Feneck and two stewards to leave and close the door.

'Good morning, gentlemen and Linda, please sit and smoke if you want.'

Everyone except Linda remained standing. She wore a white, shirt-sleeved blouse, black, tight-fitting slacks, and flat-soled shoes. Her fair hair hung loosely around her neck, and her tanned features accentuated her lovely emerald eyes. She sat down in an armchair, crossed her legs, and like the officers, looked enquiringly at Miller.

In a quiet, reverent voice, he said, 'I'm sorry to inform you that last evening Wireless Operator Smith was knocked down by a car and killed.'

For a few seconds everyone was too shocked to speak. It was left to Linda to break the silence. 'My God, how on earth did it happen?' she asked, feeling a lump in her throat.

Miller took a deep breath, then quietly explained the details of the accident to everyone. 'Smith's body is in the hospital mortuary. Transport will take me there at two p.m.' He paused momentarily, then went on, 'I'd be grateful if you, Doc, and Lieutenant Willis, would accompany me.'

Both officers, who, like the others, were still in shock and simply nodded.

'Thank you,' Miller said, glancing around. 'Please carry on.'

As soon as everyone had left, Miller went to the bridge and unhooked the ship's tannoy. He then he told the ship's company about Smith's death, ending with, 'When I know the funeral arrangements, I will tell you.'

As he replaced the handset, "Stand easy," came over the tannoy.

The news of Smith's death was met with shocked surprise.

'First Buster, then Joe. I'm beginning to think the ship is jinxed,' Able Seaman Lane said, staring blankly at Able Seaman White, who was sitting opposite him at the mess table.

'If that was true, that U-boat would 'ave sunk us,' White muttered, lighting a cigarette.

'Poor bugger,' muttered Able Seaman O'Hanlon. 'If he'd been killed in action like the other two, it would make sense, but to be knocked down by a car…' he added, shaking his head in disbelief.

'Another burial at sea, I suppose,' said Able Seaman Day, to nobody in particular.

'That's if we leave on time,' LRO Bell mumbled to himself.

At 13.40, Miller, Surgeon Lieutenant Ryan and Lieutenant Willis, carrying a canvas holdall, left the ship. The driver, a small, swarthy man in a dark suit, greeted them with a quiet, "Good afternoon", spoken in reasonably good English. He then opened the passenger door of a grey Ford, allowing them to climb inside.

Ten minutes later, after driving through the city, they arrived outside St Saviour's Hospital, a large, modern, four-storey building. They drove through an open wrought iron gate and down a wide, gavel pathway that led up to the entrance. Nearby, several ambulances were parked alongside expensive-looking cars.

The driver stopped the car near the bottom of three flights of stairs leading up to an arched, oak door. He left the car and quickly opened the passenger door, allowing Miller and the other two to leave.

'Thank you, driver,' Miller said. 'The time is a quarter to two,' he added, glancing at his wristwatch. 'Perhaps you could find a café and come back in say, an hour.'

'*Si, Senhor*,' he replied. 'I see you then.'

Followed by the doctor and Willis, Miller walked up the steps and stopped outside the door. He turned a shiny, brass handle and pushed it open. Like hospitals throughout the world, the atmosphere inside was tinged with the strong smell of antiseptic. Except for the occasional nurse and doctor on their way to a ward, the floor, tiled in pale green, was deserted. Signs over passageways in red, led down hallways to various departments.

Inside the entrance, an elderly woman with thick, wire wool hair, sat behind a reception desk, idly flicking through a magazine.

As Miller and the others came in, she looked up, somewhat startled to see three naval officers.

Miller smiled at her and said, 'Good afternoon, do you speak English?'

'*Si, Senhor*, a leetle,' she replied, placing her magazine on the desk. Next to a telephone rested a closed ledger with the word "visitantes" embossed on the front in small gold letters. 'Ow can I 'elp?'

'I am Commander Miller. These gentlemen and I are from the British warship, *Endeavour*. We'd like to see Doctor Silva,' Miller said. 'He is expecting us.'

'*Un memento, Senhor*,' she replied, picking up the telephone and dialling an internal number. 'Ah, Doctor Silva,' she said, then continued speaking in Portuguese. A few seconds later she replaced the receiver, looked up and said, 'Doctor Silva. Eee come soon. Please to sit,' she added, indicating a waiting room a few yards away.

'*Gracias, Senhora*,' Miller replied, noticing she wore a wedding ring.

They turned, and as they reached the door, a tall, deeply sunburnt man arrived. He wore a white coat with a blue fountain pen poking out of his breast pocket.

'Good afternoon, gentlemen, sorry to keep you waiting. I'm Doctor Silva, senior pathologist.' As he spoke, the corners of his dark-blue eyes creased into a warm smile. 'I take it you are *Endeavour's* captain,' he said, noticing the three silver bars on Miller's epaulets.

'Yes, I am,' Miller replied. After they shook hands, Miller introduced him to Surgeon Lieutenant Doctor Ryan and Lieutenant Willis.

'Your English is remarkably good,' Ryan said, as they shook hands.

'Although I'm Portuguese, I soon picked it up during four years at St Barts,' Silva replied, with an all-knowing smile. 'Now, gentlemen,' he continued. 'The deceased is in the viewing room next to the mortuary at the back of the hospital. So if you'd be so kind as to follow me…'

As they walked along a long, windowless corridor, their footsteps echoed on the tiled floor. As expected, the keen smell of antiseptic hung in the air. The unusual sight of three naval officers elicited more than a few admiring glances and girlish giggles from a few nurses as they passed by. They turned right, and after walking down another corridor, arrived at a stout, wooden door marked "Exit". De Silva pushed a parallel brass handle, allowing the group to leave the hospital and enter a large, concrete car park. After passing several cars, they arrived at an oblong-shaped, red-bricked building. The walls were devoid of windows, and a solitary, tall, black chimney poked up from the middle of the flat, concrete roof. De Silva opened the door, and they walked along a short, dimly lit corridor and stopped outside a door with a sign, "Sala de Visualizacao" (Viewing Room), painted in a dull green. De Silva turned a small, brass handle and opened the door.

This time they were met, not by the smell of antiseptic, but the eye-smarting effect of formaldehyde. The room, well-lit with neon lights, was cold and depressing. Two leather armchairs lay close to a stainless steel sink. Above this a glass tumbler rested on a glass shelf. Next to these was a first-aid box. However, the attention of the three officers was immediately drawn to the uneven outline of a body covered in a white sheet, lying on the table in the middle of the room. The three officers moved slowly to the table. A small, swarthy mortuary assistant wearing a white coat stood nearby. De Silva gave him a quick nod. The assistant slowly pulled back the sheet, revealing Smith's head. His eyes were closed, and a large, dark-blue bruise covered the left side of his face.

'I take it this is your man?' De Silva said, glancing at Miller, who then gave Lieutenant Willis a quick, solemn glance.

Willis, slightly shaken by seeing Smith's ashen face, nodded his head. 'Yes, that's him, poor chap,' he said, then quickly turned away.

'Were his injuries severe?' asked Surgeon Lieutenant Ryan.

'Very much so,' De Silva replied. 'The post-mortem I did this morning revealed multiple fractures of his spine and chest, as well as a broken cheekbone. He must have died instantly.'

'Thank you, Doctor,' Ryan replied. As he finished speaking, everyone watched in reverent silence as the assistant drew the sheet over Smith.

'I have Smith's belongings in my office, Commander,' De Silva said, looking at Miller, 'and there's something important you ought to see. So, if you'll come this way.'

With a look of relief etched on their faces, they followed De Silva out of the room. After walking down the corridor they arrived at a door marked "Patologista Senior" (Senior Pathologist). De Silva opened the door, allowing them to go inside. The office, lit by neon, was quite spacious. The floor was covered in dark-brown linoleum. Two armchairs faced a wide mahogany desk on which rested a telephone and two empty, wooden trays. The walls were lined with leather-bound books. A highly polished table lay close to a tall, green filing cabinet. On a table nearby rested a small, metal box next to a medium-size, black leather case.

'These are what was discovered,' De Silva said, handing them to Miller.

To his amazement, Miller saw that the lid of the box and the side of the case were embossed with a silver eagle holding a swastika.'

'Great Scott!' Miller exclaimed. 'They're both bloody German.'

'Let me see,' said Willis, unzipping the leather case. 'My God, I can't believe it, sir,' he cried, unhooking the earphones and giving Miller a look of astonishment. 'It's a bloody transmitter!'

'And what do make of this, Doc?' said Miller, opening the box and showing a tiny, cream-coloured pill to Ryan.

Ryan carefully took hold of the pill, sniffed it, then slowly replied, 'I'm not sure, but going by the swastika on the case, my guess is it's cyanide.'

'I don't believe it!' cried Miller. 'So that's how the U-boat knew where we were. Smith must have transmitted our movements to Germany.'

'But from where?' Willis said, frowning while shaking his head. 'Smith was a quiet, conscientious young lad. It's hard to believe he was a German spy. He couldn't have transmitted from the ship, as I would have seen it on the wireless record sheet.'

'So it must have been on land,' said Ryan.

'With a puzzled expression etched on his face, Miller said, 'It couldn't have been when we first went to Rio, as there was nowhere he could have hidden a transmitter when he went ashore.'

'Stanley, it could only have been Stanley!' exclaimed Willis. 'We were there for two days, and as I remember, LRO Bell was on duty and Smith went ashore. No one would have noticed the transmitter hidden under his winter clothing.'

'I wonder if he managed to use the transmitter before he was hit by that car, sir,' Ryan asked Miller.

'A good question, Doc,' Miller cautiously replied. 'I'll just have to assume he did.'

'But how did he manage to get into the navy, let alone be drafted to *Endeavour,* sir?' said Willis, giving Miller a questioning look. 'Surely his parents must have known he was a spy.'

'Or, they were one themselves,' said Ryan.

'That'll be up to the authorities to find out,' Miller replied. 'In the meantime,' he added, glancing at De Silva, 'we'd better get back to the ship.'

'Before you leave, we have to discuss the funeral arrangements,' said De Silva. 'The law here states that burials must take place within two days after death. Will you be doing this from your ship?'

'I'm afraid burial at sea is impossible, as we're not sure when we're sailing,' Miller replied.

'Mmm, I see,' De Silva said, gently stroking his chin. 'Under the circumstances, maybe I can help. We have a small cemetery used for burying — shall we say — unwanted visitors. Under the circumstances, I could arrange for your man to be buried there tomorrow. But I'm afraid it would be expensive.'

'Thank you, Doctor, that would be fine,' Miller replied. With a smug expression on his face, he went on, 'And send the bill to the German ambassador in Santos.'

'I don't think he'll be too pleased,' De Silva replied, smiling.

'Smith was responsible for the death of two of my crew, so I won't give a damn how he feels,' Miller replied grimly. 'But I think we'd better take his Burberry and uniform back, in case the police in England will want to examine them. Thank you for all your help, Doctor. Now I think we'd better get back to our ship.'

After Surgeon Lieutenant Ryan and Willis had packed Smith's clothes into the holdall, Doctor De Silva showed them to the exit.

They shook hands, climbed into the Bentley and arrived back on board *Endeavour* a little after three thirty p.m.

CHAPTER THIRTY-NINE

The first thing Miller did was go to his cabin and draft a top-secret signal to the first lord of the admiralty, info, C-in-C, Plymouth, which read: "Sir, the following information has come to light. I have discovered that Wireless Operator Smith was a German spy. Using a small, hidden transmitter, he sent information to someone, probably the German ambassador in Buenos Aires, informing him of the movements of *Endeavour* and the real reason for our mission. He will be buried locally. Suggest authorities investigate his parents."

The next thing he did was to gather all the officers in the wardroom and tell them about Smith.

'Good heavens!' Lieutenant Duncan exclaimed, wiping oil off his hands onto his white overalls. 'He always struck me as a quiet, well-mannered, young man.'

'A German spy, indeed,' said Lieutenant Morgan, shaking his head in disbelief. He then asked the same question raised earlier by Lieutenant Willis. 'How on earth did he manage to get into the navy?'

'It must have taken long-term planning,' said Midshipman Grant. 'After all, he'd been in England for years before the war. What's your opinion, Linda?'

'All I know is he's gone to his maker with blood on his hands,' Linda quietly replied.

'Thank you. Please carry on,' said Miller, and made his way to the bridge.

The time was four thirty p.m. The duty watch was fallen in on the quarterdeck, and everyone else was in their messes. At first, he had toyed with the idea of keeping Smith's treasonable activities from the crew. However, on a ship with such a small complement as *Endeavour,* it would be bound to leak out.

Miller unhooked the ship's tannoy and stood still for a few minutes, holding the handpiece and wondering what to say. How could he tell these men that the man they had lived with for the last four months was a German spy?

Finally he took a deep breath and began, 'This is the captain speaking. What I have to tell you will no doubt shock you as much as it did myself and the officers. During the last few hours, I have discovered that Wireless Operator Smith was in fact a German spy.' He paused momentarily, allowing his words to sink in, sensing the surprised expressions on the faces of everyone listening, then went on. 'Smith was secretly transmitting information about the ship's movements, including the main reason for our mission. That's how the U-boat knew where we were. How he came to be in the navy will be up to the authorities in England to find out. Under the circumstances, Smith will be buried privately shore. That is all.' He hung up.

The reaction throughout the ship was more than shock; it was a mixture of incredibility and anger, especially by everyone in Smith's mess.

'No wonder the bastard never spoke much,' said Able Seaman Williams.

Everyone in the mess either lay in their hammocks or sat at the table, smoking or playing cards.

'Come to think of it,' said O'Hanlon, 'during all the time we worked together, he never once mentioned his mum and dad or even a girlfriend. Nevertheless, it's hard to believe he was a Jerry spy.'

'Anyway, if we had to bury Smith at sea, I'd refuse to attend,' said Hardman. 'After all, the sod was responsible for Buster and Joe being killed.'

At twelve thirty a.m. on Thursday, 12th October, Miller came onto the quarterdeck. He had previously told OOW Lieutenant Ward he was expecting a visitor. He then suggested that PO Martin and QM Lane go below for a mug of tea. Both men gave each other a surprised look, wondering why the secrecy, but nevertheless welcomed the break. Five minutes later a black Bentley arrived at the foot of the gangway. Ramon climbed out of the car, and carrying a large suitcase in his left hand, hurried up the gangway.

'Good to see you again,' Miller said, shaking Ramon's free hand. 'If you come this way,' he added, indicating a hand. A few minutes later, they arrived outside Miller's cabin and were met by Pollard. 'This shouldn't take long,' Miller said, opening the door. 'My first lieutenant here has unlocked the chest, and your suitcase is more than big enough for the err… merchandise.'

The oak chest lay in the middle of the cabin floor. The wooden lid was open, showing that the chest was nearly full of grapholite. It took all three of them fifteen minutes to transfer the minerals into the suitcase and lock it. By the time they had finished, all three were sweating profusely.

'There,' said Miller, standing up. 'Thank you for all your help, Ramon.'

Miller picked up the suitcase, which was not as heavy as he had thought it would be, and said, 'Right, shall we leave?'

When they arrived on the quarterdeck, PO Martin and QM Lane had returned. Once again, they gave each other a quizzical look.

'Summat funny going on, I bet,' Lane said to Martin.

'So what? Ours is not to reason why, so shit in it,' Martin replied.

After a final handshake, everyone watched as Ramon, carrying the suitcase, walked down the gangway. He opened the driver door, lifted the suitcase onto the passenger seat, then climbed in. He switched on the engine. Seconds later, the car drove down the quayside and disappeared though a wide, arched exit.

'Thank goodness that's over,' Miller said to Pollard, as they left the quarterdeck.

'Any ideas how we're going to leave on Sunday, sir?' Pollard asked, as they ducked through an open hatchway leading into the main passageway.

'Yes, I'll tell you when I return from seeing the ambassador,' Miller replied cagily.

CHAPTER FORTY

The word soon spread around the ship that Linda would be leaving the ship on Friday the 13th. At twelve p.m. on Thursday, the officers held a farewell party for her. After a few drinks, Miller presented her with a framed photograph of *Endeavour*. She wore a yellow, short-sleeve, silk blouse and black slacks that clung to her like a second skin. For a few seconds she stood silently, too overcome with emotion to speak.

Finally, doing her best to fight back tears, she managed to say, 'I can't tell you how proud I am of the time I have spent on board your lovely ship. Everyone has made me feel welcome, and I'll never forget you.' She paused, and after looking around at the faces she had come to know so well, she glanced fondly at the picture and said, 'This will hang on my sitting room wall in Cambridge, and every time I look at it, I shall offer a silent prayer for the safe return to England for yourselves and the crew. God bless you.'

Unable to hold back her tears, she turned, and clutching the picture to her breast, hurriedly left the room. Miller was about to follow her, but Pollard put a gentle restraining hand on his arm and said tactfully, 'If I were you, sir, I'd leave her alone. Women don't like to be seen with their mascara running down their faces.'

By six forty-five p.m., all officers waited near the bow. The upper deck was full of junior and senior ratings. At 6.50 p.m., the ambassador's Bentley arrived. Ramon parked it near the bottom of the gangway. Ten minutes later Miller appeared, wearing his Number 7 uniform.

'Looks like a spot of wet weather, sir,' OOW Lieutenant Young said, saluting while glancing up at the darkening sky.

Miller returned Young's salute and was about to speak when a loud cheer greeted the arrival of Linda. In her right hand she carried her brown, leather suitcase. A dark-green headscarf covered most of her auburn hair. She was dressed in the same pale-green dress and white, high-heeled shoes she had worn at her previous meeting with the ambassador. She turned, smiled and waved.

While she was waving, Leading Seaman Waters stepped forward, and feeling his face redden, handed her a shiny, silver bosun's call attached to a silver chain. 'This ain't much, miss,' he said, 'but it's summat to remember us by.'

She placed her suitcase on the deck. 'Thank you,' she replied, and kissed him warmly on the cheek.

This was met by a chorus of cheers and wolf whistles. And even though she didn't know what it was, she held up the call, and feeling a wet haze over her eyes, blew everyone a kiss.

After shaking the officer's hands, she turned to Miller and said, 'Please Bob, let's go before I make a fool of myself.'

'I doubt if you could ever do that,' Miller replied, and picked up her suitcase.

'Captain leaving the ship. Attention on the upper deck,' shouted Lieutenant Young.

However, his order was ignored, as someone began to sing, *For* she's *a jolly good lady,* which was spontaneously joined in by everyone, including the officers.

Minutes later, with the sound of the singing ringing in their ears, they were sitting in the back seat of the car. The time was 7.20 p.m. when they arrived at the ambassador's Residence. Ramon got out of the car and helped Linda and Miller to step out. Then he opened the boot, took out Linda's suitcase and gave it to Miller. As he did so, the moon disappeared behind a low layer of black clouds. Seconds later it began to rain.

The ambassador was waiting at the top of the steps. His white shirt, dark-maroon tie and brown brogues complimented his immaculately tailored pale-grey, pin-striped suit. Lady Knox-Johnson stood next to him. She wore a white blouse, and a double row of pearls adorned her neck. The dark-blue, two-piece costume fitted her slightly overweight figure perfectly. A pair of black, high-heeled shoes served to make her look tall standing against her husband's burly, six-foot-plus frame.

'Good to see you both,' said the ambassador, as he shook their hands. 'You've met my wife,' he added.

'Welcome back. Now do come inside from this beastly weather,' she said, giving each of them a warm handshake. She took Linda's suitcase from Miller, handed it to Ramon and said, 'Take this to Professor Penlove's room.'

'Then kindly mix us one of your excellent cocktails,' said the ambassador. 'We'll take them in the lounge.'

The lounge hadn't changed. The portrait of King Joseph 1 of Portugal, hanging over a marble mantelpiece, still dominated a room tastefully furnished with Chippendale and Sheraton. The same paintings hung on the wall, and the thick, green, velvet curtains were drawn across the French windows.

'Please, do sit down,' said Lady Knox-Johnson, indicating a black Chesterfield settee lying in front of an unlit log fire set in a marble surround.

Miller removed his cap and sat down. Linda took off her headscarf, allowing her fair hair to tumble down her shoulders, then sat next to him.

'What lovely hair,' Her Ladyship remarked, casting an admiring look at Linda. 'How do you keep it looking like that on board a ship?'

'Salt water and soap,' Linda jokingly replied. 'But only when I run out of shampoo.'

Just then Ramon came in and placed a silver tray containing the cocktails in three Waterford glasses, and a round, brass ashtray, on the table.

'Thank you, Ramon,' said the ambassador. 'That'll be all. Tell cook we'll dine in half an hour.' He sat back, took out a gold cigarette case and flicked it open.

Lady Knox-Johnson gave him a caustic look and said, 'Must you, dear, you know it's bad for my chest, and our guests don't smoke, so save it for when you go to your den to do your papers.'

Linda and Miller, doing their best not to laugh, looked at one another as if to say, "There's no doubt whose boss in this house."

'Oh, very well, dear,' replied Sir Geoffrey, and shaking his head, replaced the cigarette. 'Now, tell me, Commander,' he continued, after taking a sip of his cocktail. 'Let me once again say how sorry we were to hear about the loss of your two sailors. Terrible business, terrible.' He paused, then went on. 'And we were quite shocked to hear about that chap, Smith.'

'Yes, sir. It came as a surprise to everyone,' Miller replied, before finishing his drink in one quick gulp.

'But how on earth did he manage to get into the navy, I wonder?' added Her Ladyship.

'That's something the Secret Service will have find out,' replied Sir Geoffrey.

Suddenly the loud *clash* of thunder echoed around the room. This was quickly followed by a flash of lightning that caused the lights on the chandelier to flicker. Then came the rattle of rain against the French windows.

'Sounds like one of those tropical storms we have at this time of year,' said Sir Geoffrey. 'And as it almost eight thirty, I suggest we adjourn to the dining room.'

The dining room, with its long mahogany table laid with the finest cutlery and cut-glass Waterford wine glasses, looked immaculate.

They sat down and began tucking into a crab salad, followed by roast beef and Yorkshire pudding.

'What plans have you in mind for leaving harbour?' Sir Geoffrey asked Miller, before placing a portion of roast beef in his mouth. As he spoke, the loud staccato of rain was accompanied by the crack of thunder.

'I must assume that Smith was able to inform Berlin of our run-in with the U-boat,' Miller replied. 'And that our return to England would be delayed while the problems in the engine room were resolved.' Miller paused and took a good sip of wine. After dabbing his mouth with a linen serviette, he continued. 'It's a ten-day or eleven-day journey from Wilhelmshaven to Rio. But her captain won't be able to remain underwater that long, so he'll regularly have to surface to recharge his batteries. Therefore, it'll take him longer than that. This could be to my advantage, but only if I decided to take the direct route home and risk meeting the blighter. But I don't intend doing that.'

'Then what will you do?' asked Sir Geoffrey.

'Leave Rio under darkness at one a.m. this Monday morning and...' For a few seconds he was forced to stop talking as a sudden peel of thunder almost drowned his words. 'As I was saying before nature interrupted me, I intend leaving Rio under darkness, sailing south, then, at roughly forty degrees longitude, turn due west and head for Gibraltar.'

'But won't that take you into the shipping lanes crossing from Africa to South America?' asked Sir Geoffrey.

'I expect it will,' Miller replied. 'But if we do, I doubt if they'll know who we are. And the chances of meeting a U-boat that far south are very slim.'

'Mm... that sounds plausible,' Sir Geoffrey replied. 'Because I've recently been informed that Admiral King, commander in chief of the US navy, has not agreed to America joining the convoys system, due to a shortage of warships. That'll mean Donetz will have most of his U-boats deployed in the Atlantic to attack our shipping.'

'That's good news, sir,' said Miller, 'but we'll need extra fuel, so would you kindly arrange for two barrels to be delivered on board tomorrow?'

'Consider it done, Commander,' Sir Geoffrey replied confidently.

'Sorry to sound like a defeatist,' interrupted Linda, 'but what if you meet a German warship instead of a U-boat?'

A tricky one,' Miller said, pensively stroking his chin. 'But if we do encounter an enemy ship, it's highly unlikely her captain will be aware of who we are. Fortunately, my first lieutenant speaks fluent Swedish, and as Sweden is neutral, we could pose as a Swedish merchant ship.'

'That would sound more convincing if you flew a Swedish flag,' said Lady Knox-Johnson.

'Now that's a thought,' Miller replied ponderously.

'On that optimistic note,' said Sir Geoffrey, noticing everyone had finished their port, 'now that we've finished dinner, I suggest we take coffee in the lounge before the roof falls in.'

As they entered the lounge, another jagged flash of lightning lit up the window curtains. This was accompanied by the steady clattering of rain against the French windows.

'Looks like this is on for the night,' Sir Geoffrey remarked, as they sat down on their respective chairs and settee.

'You may be right, sir,' Miller replied, as Ramon came in with the coffee.

'Perhaps it's one of those katabatic storms you told me about,' said Linda, as Ramon placed bone china cups and saucers on the coffee table.

Throughout dinner, Sir Geoffrey had been only too aware of the more than friendly glances that had passed between Linda and Miller.

'What do you think, Ramon?' Sir Geoffrey asked, before picking up a cup and taking a sip.

Ramon gave a quick, indifferent shrug of his shoulders and said, 'Eech storm ees thee same to me. Will that be all, sir?'

'No, bring up three large brandies,' Sir Geoffrey replied, 'then tell cook she can stay here overnight if she wishes.'

'Very good sir,' said Ramon, who, after giving Sir Geoffrey a slight, graceful bow, turned and left the room.

'I take it Ramon lives in, sir?' asked Miller.

'Yes, Commander, and as this storm is on for the night, I suggest you both stay overnight. I'll telephone your ship and tell the officer of the watch to expect you back about seven tomorrow morning. Ramon will leave toiletries out for you.'

Crafty old devil, thought Miller. *He must have guessed there was something between Linda and myself, and he knows darn well Ramon could easily get me back to the ship, storm or no storm.*

'Thank you, sir, that's very considerate of you,' Miller replied, doing his best not to look at Linda.

A few minutes later Ramon came into the lounge and placed the brandy on the coffee table.

'Will there be anything else, sir?' he asked.

'Yes,' Sir Geoffrey replied. 'Give everyone a coffee-call at four thirty. Breakfast at five thirty.'

'For all except me, as I need my beauty sleep' said Lady Knox-Johnson. 'So,' she added, picking up her glass and taking a sip, 'if you'll forgive me, I'll wish you all goodnight.' She stood up and was joined by Sir Geoffrey and Miller. 'Have a good night's sleep, and I'll see you before you leave tomorrow evening, dear,' she said kissing Linda on the cheek. 'And as I won't see you in the morning, Commander, Godspeed and a safe journey home, to you and your crew,' she said warmly, shaking Miller's hand.

'Thank you, Your Ladyship, and thank you for your excellent hospitality,' Miller replied.

Turning to her husband, she said, 'Goodnight, Geoffrey, and don't smoke too many cigarettes; you know your coughing will keep me awake.'

'Goodnight, dear, I'll do my best,' the ambassador replied, kissing her lightly on the cheek. No sooner had she left than he sat down on the settee, lit a cigarette and said, 'As we've an early start, and as we've finished our drinks, I suggest we call it a night. Don't you both agree?'

Feeling suddenly self-conscious, Miller looked at Linda, who simply nodded. Then, doing his best to sound normal, Miller replied, 'Err, yes sir, I expect it'll be busy day for all of us.'

Sir Geoffrey leant across and pressed a small, red button on the side of the mantelpiece. Seconds later, Ramon opened the door and came in.

'Ah, Ramon,' said Sir Geoffrey. 'Please be good enough to show our guests to their rooms, then bring me a large bandy and soda.'

'Very good, sir. This way please,' he said, glancing at Linda and Miller.

After wishing Sir Geoffrey a good night, they left the lounge and followed Ramon up a highly polished staircase and along a well-lit corridor.

'Theese are your rooms,' said Ramon, stopping outside two adjacent doors painted pale green. 'Yours is theese one, Commander,' Ramon indicated by tapping the one in front of him, 'and yours, meese, is next to it. May I wish you both *boa noite,*' then bowed gracefully, turned and walked away.

'Your room or mine, darling?' Miller asked, looking into Linda's eyes.

Standing on tiptoe, Linda reached up, kissed him on the lips, then replied, 'Mine in ten minutes.' And she opened her door and went inside.

CHAPTER FORTY-ONE

Feeling his heart rate increase, Miller opened his door, went inside and switched on the light. A lush, dark-brown carpet covered the floor. A dark-green, velvet curtain was drawn across a bay window, but the first thing that impressed Miller was the king-size bed covered with a silky, pale-cream eiderdown. He couldn't resist sitting on it, and he felt himself sink into its sensual softness. Then came two bedside lights with matching cream-coloured lampshades, two brown, leather armchairs, a highly polished, oak wardrobe, and a well-stocked dressing table complete with toilet accessories and large mirror.

He threw his cap on an armchair, stood up and walked through an open door into a bathroom tiled in white. On a glass shelf overlooking a sink, rested a toothbrush and tube of paste, a razor and a shaving stick. After washing his face and drying himself on a fluffy, pink towel, he combed his hair. He removed his shoes and socks, and like a thief in the night, quietly opened his door. After giving a quick glance up and down the corridor, he closed the door and tiptoed onto the landing. Feeling his hand shake slightly, he gave a gentle tap on her door. After what seemed to him like an eternity, the door opened, and he saw Linda. The main lights were off, and the yellow glow from a solitary bedside lamp, shining through her short, flimsy nightdress, displayed her nakedness.

'Well, darling, don't just stand there gawping,' Linda whispered. 'You'd better come inside before Ramon shows up.'

The sight of her nakedness made Miller feel dizzy with desire. He put his arms around her, and feeling the softness of her body pressing against his, they kissed and stumbled into her room. In doing so, Linda released one arm from around Miller's waist and managed to close the door.

Neither spoke. With obscene haste, Linda helped Miller to

remove his tropical blouse. Feeling his heart beating a cadence in his chest, he almost fell over, doing a poor impersonation of a pelican while taking off his shoes and trousers.

'My goodness, Bob,' said Linda, placing a hand over her mouth to stop herself laughing. 'You do look funny in those long underpants.'

'Then take 'em off,' Miller quietly replied.

She did so and couldn't help seeing his erect penis as she pulled his shorts off. In a matter of seconds, he whipped off her nightdress, and they tumbled, naked, onto the eiderdown. In an instant her legs were curled around Miller's waist.

'Oh, God, darling,' gasped Miller. 'I can't tell you how much I've wanted to feel you close.'

'I know my love, that's how I felt,' whimpered Linda.

Then, as if guided by nature, she gave a small cry as his member entered the warm wetness of her vagina. However, their throngs of ecstasy was short-lived as they climaxed together.

Miller gently rolled off her. For a while they lay close together, eyes closed, breathing heavily and bathed in perspiration.

Finally, Linda opened her eyes, looked up at Miller and said, 'Oh, Bob, darling, it's been such a long time since… That was absolutely wonderful.'

'For me, as well,' Miller quietly replied, using a hand to brush away a few strands of Linda's fair hair from the side of her sweat-stained face. 'After Dorothy died, I…'

Linda quickly pressed a finger across his lips. 'I don't think you need to explain anything,' she said, cuddling into him. 'The most important thing is we have each other.'

'And tomorrow you'll be gone,' Miller replied, kissing her gently on the forehead. 'And God knows when or if we'll see each other again.'

'After all we've been through, darling, I know we will. Now, make love to me again before I go crazy.'

They made love again before falling asleep, cocooned in one another's arms.

Miller woke up to the peaceful sound of Linda quietly snoring. He carefully removed his arms from around her. This enabled him to look at his wristwatch, which showed four a.m. The storm had abated, and the faint shadows of dawn were beginning to filter through the dark-green, velvet window curtains.

Remembering Ramon would be bringing them coffee in half an hour, he was about to turn back the bedclothes, when Linda opened her eyes, and still half asleep, murmured, 'What time is its, darling?'

'Time I wasn't here,' Miller replied, stifling a yawn. 'Ramon will be here shortly, and seeing me here won't do your reputation any good.'

'To hell with my reputation,' she muttered sleepily, while reaching up for him. 'We still have time for…'

Fifteen minutes later, he kissed her and said, 'See you at breakfast, darling.' After kissing her again, he hastily gathered his clothes, opened the door, and after making sure the coast was clear, returned to his room.

Breakfast, taken in the kitchen, was a sombre affair. Miller's slightly wrinkled tropical whites was in sharp contrast to Linda's carefully applied make-up and knee-length, floral dress. Sir Geoffrey, wearing a dark-red dressing gown, ate his usual breakfast of bacon and eggs, while Miller and Linda toyed with their food while sipping cups of coffee.

A little after five thirty a.m., Ramon knocked on the kitchen door and came in. Miller and Linda looked at him, knowing the moment they had both been dreading had arrived.

'Good morning, sir,' he said to Sir Geoffrey. 'I've parked the Bentley at the bottom of the front steps.'

After dabbing his mouth with a serviette, Sir Geoffrey replied, 'Thank you, Ramon. We'll be with you shortly.'

As soon as Ramon left, Miller stood up and said, 'I suppose I'd better be on my way, sir.'

'Yes,' Sir Geoffrey replied. 'I expect you've got a busy few days ahead of you.'

Linda forced herself to finish her coffee, and praying she wouldn't make a show of herself by crying, joined them.

During the lengthy walk from the kitchen to the terrace, Sir Geoffrey noticed Linda take hold of Miller's hand. When they reach the top of the steps, the galaxy of twinkling stars had disappeared and a full, yellow moon lay amongst beds of milk-white clouds. Sensing Miller and Linda would like to be alone, Sir Geoffrey shook Miller's hand, then walked through the doors into the mansion.

As soon as the ambassador left, Miller kissed Linda so hard he could feel her teeth against his lips.

Then, looking deep into her moist, emerald-green eyes, said, 'I'll always love you, darling.'

'And I you, Bob,' Linda replied, through a veil of tears.

'When I return, we'll met in the Savoy and drink the biggest bottle of champagne in London,' Miller replied, feeling a lump come in his throat.

'I'll hold you to that,' Linda said. 'Now kiss me again, go, and may God bring you and your lovely crew home safely.'

CHAPTER FORTY-TWO

Miller returned on board at 5.55 a.m. and was met by OOW Lieutenant Morgan. It was very rare that Miller stayed ashore all night, especially in a foreign port.

Morgan saluted, then with a slight smile, said, 'Thought you'd deserted us, sir. I take it you and Professor Penlove had an, err... enjoyable dinner?'

Ignoring Morgan's innuendos remark, Miller returned Morgan's salute and made his way to his cabin. On the way there he heard the strident voice of the duty QM calling, "Hands turn to, cooks to the galley," over the tannoy. Miller decided to tell the officers about his plans for leaving Rio, over breakfast. Noticing most of them had finished eating and were enjoying another coffee, he dismissed PO Feneck and the stewards.

'Gentlemen,' Miller said, tapping his coffee cup with a spoon. 'May I have your attention?'

Straight away coffee cups were drained, as everyone looked at Miller, wondering what he was going to say.

'I won't keep you long, as I know you're busy,' Miller said, after finishing his coffee. 'We will leave harbour at one a.m. on Monday. All leave is to be cancelled on Sunday. I intend to sail south at full speed, and at some time, turn due west and make for Gibraltar. And before you ask, Jock,' Miller said, looking at the sudden anxious expression appear on Lieutenant Duncan's face, 'two barrels of extra fuel will arrive tomorrow.'

'Thank the good Lord fer that, sir,' Duncan replied, with a sigh of relief.

'What are our chances of being spotted by another U-boat, sir?' asked Lieutenant Young.

'Thank you, Guns, I'm sure that's the question on everybody's mind,' Miller replied. 'I must assume that, before his death, Smith was able to contact Donetz and inform him of our run-in with his U-boat and the ship having to remain in Rio. I must also assume that when Donetz tried to contact the sub and got no reply, he concluded that it had developed either wireless trouble or was sunk.' Miller paused to allow his words to sink in, then continued. 'He'll know we're in Rio for five days, and it will take one of his XB U-boats twelve days to reach Rio. The sub will have at least a five-day start before her captain thinks we will leave for home. As I speak, Professor Penlove is on her way to England with the grapholite. Therefore, our mission is effectively over. So, the longer we stay here, the longer we are playing into the sub's hands. Therefore, the quicker we leave, the safer we'll be. Any more questions?'

'Yes, I have one, sir,' said Pollard. 'Supposing, just supposing, we encounter an enemy warship other than a U-boat. What then?'

Miller smiled, then said, 'How appropriate of you to ask that, Number One, because the answer could depend on you.'

'Really, sir, in what way?' Pollard asked, raising his eyebrows.

'During my dinner with the ambassador, his wife gave me an idea. She said if we met an enemy surface ship, as you speak Swedish and German, we might be able to bluff our way if we flew a Swedish flag. So I'd like you go ashore this morning to the harbour master's office, and err... borrow one. Yellow, with blue cross slightly off-centre, I believe.'

'Thank you, sir,' Pollard replied tersely. 'I'm well aware of what the Swedish flag looks like.'

'Quite so, Number One,' Miller said, giving Pollard a sarcastic smile. 'That's why you're perfect for the job. I also want you to have the ship's pennant number and name painted out. Now, I suggest everyone carries on, while I address the ship's company.'

During "stand easy", Miller informed the crew about his plans for leaving Rio. 'Mail will close at ten a.m. on Saturday. And remember, no mention of our sailing date, or Smith, in your letters, or when you go ashore. That is all.'

In the seamen's mess, Able Seaman Barnes, who, like the rest of his mess mates, had just finished his tot of rum. He looked at Able Seaman Day and said, 'I notice the old man didn't tell us when we'd get home?'

'What d'yer think he is, a fuckin' clairvoyant?' Day replied, while chewing on a piece of rubbery chicken.

'Fer all he knows, there could be a Jerry battleship waiting fer us over the horizon,' Barnes replied.

'That's why we're going south, to avoid meeting any of the buggers,' Day said.

'By the way, what does clairo what's its name mean?' asked LRO Bell, using a piece of bread to wipe up gravy from his plate.

'Someone who can predict the future,' Lofty replied.

'Then my missus must be one of them,' said Day, 'cos each time I go on leave, hoping for a bit, she tells me it's the wrong time of the month.'

The senior ratings were more sanguine.

'He's certainly taking a chance,' Chief Cook White said to Chief Coxswain Moore. Both men had finished their dinner and were sat down smoking a cigarette.

'Personally, I'd trust him anywhere,' Moore replied. 'Remember how he got us through the pack ice.'

'He's right,' said Chief Engineer O'Malley. 'Sure to goodness, the old man knows what he's doing.'

Just then, Chief Bosun's Mate Conyon came in. He angrily threw his cap onto the padded bench lining one side of the mess and said, 'Would you soddin' believe it? The Jimmy has just told me to organise work parties to paint out the ship's pennant number and name.'

'Then you'd better make sure they use the correct shade of red,' said Moore, grinning like a Cheshire cat.

The time was three p.m. Miller was on the quarterdeck talking to Surgeon Lieutenant Ryan, ensuring he had enough medical stores, when he saw Pollard coming on board carrying a Swedish flag wrapped around a bulky parcel.

'I see you were successful, Number One,' Miller said, as Pollard stepped on board. 'As a matter of interest, what's under the flag?'

'When I told the harbour master what it was for, he contacted the captain of a Swedish liner, who sent over not only one of his old uniform jackets, but also one of his old caps. Rather good of him, don't you think?'

'I only hope they fit you,' Miller jokingly replied.

'Don't speak too soon, sir,' Pollard said smugly. 'The bottles of gin I will send to the harbour master and the captain will go on your mess bill.'

At twelve p.m. the next morning, two metal barrels, each containing 500 gallons of fuel, were lowered by crane onto the port side of the upper deck passageway.

'That oughta see us through till we get home,' Lieutenant Duncan said to Pollard, as they watched a seaman chain the barrels to the guard rail opposite the fuel inlet.

'I'm sure you're right, Jock,' Pollard replied, 'or,' he added jokingly, 'we'll end up rowing home.'

CHAPTER FORTY-THREE

After "pipe down" on Monday 16th October, Miller ordered *Endeavour* to be darkened. Two hours later, with her crew closed up at action stations, the ship slipped her moorings and silently slid away from the wharf. On the bridge, the only sound that could be heard was the dull throbbing of the engines and the gentle *swish* of the water running down each side of the ship. A chilly wind blew from the west, and the incandescent glow from the bright, yellow moon shone down from an inky-black sky, turning the calm harbour waters into a mass of twinkling diamonds. Together with an array of glittering lights from the hotels and bars lining the waterfront, these gave scant cover as the ship cut through the harbour waters. Finally, with the conical shape of Corcovado Mountain slowly receding against the night sky, the ship sailed into the placid Southern Ocean.

For the next three days, doing a steady fifteen knots, *Endeavour* continued on a southerly course. Directly after breakfast on Thursday the 19th, Miller joined Pollard and OOW Lieutenant Morgan on the bridge.

'What's our position, Pilot?' asked Miller, as he eased himself onto his chair.

'Longitude thirty-five degrees south, latitude thirteen west, sir,' Morgan replied. 'That puts us about a thousand miles off Montevideo.'

'Anything on sonar, Number One?'

'Harding reports what looks like two liners approaching five miles to the north, otherwise nothing, sir,' Pollard replied.

With a sigh of relief, Miller replied, 'Good. As the range of our sonar is over fifty miles, it looks like there isn't a U-boat in the vicinity.'

'Do U-boats have radar, sir?' asked Pollard.

'No, thank goodness,' Miller replied. 'Only receivers to give them time to dive if detected. Stand down from action stations and resume cruising stations.' He then picked up the wheelhouse intercom.

'Wheelhouse, bridge,' came the gruff voice of Chief Coxswain Moore.'

'Turn east ten degrees,' said Miller, 'and increase speed to twenty knots.'

Moore repeated the order. Seconds later the vibrations of the engines could be felt by everyone, as the ship suddenly bounded forward.

'Next stop, Blighty, eh, sir, said Petty Officer Thompson.

'All being well, PO,' Miller replied, giving Thompson a hopeful look.

Shortly after "stand easy" the next morning, Miller was in his cabin checking the ship's log, when a sharp knock came at his door. 'Come,' he grunted, looking up as WO Lieutenant Willis came in.

'Sorry to interrupt you, sir, but I thought you'd like to see this,'

he said, handing Miller a signal.

That's quite all right,' Miller replied. 'Read it to me.'

'Very good, sir,' Willis replied. 'It says, "To all ships and establishments. Regret to inform you HMS *Royal Oak* torpedoed at her home anchorage in Scapa Flow on Saturday 16 October. As yet, number of killed not known. Sir Roger Backhouse, First Sea Lord."

'Great Scott!' Miller exclaimed, taking the signal from Willis and reading it. 'How on earth could this happen? Scapa's supposed to be the most heavily defended base in the navy.'

'Apparently not, sir,' Willis quietly replied.

'Thank you, Willis, please carry on,' Miller replied, standing up. 'I'd better tell the ship's company, as they're sure to know someone on board her.'

Miller left his cabin and went onto the bridge. Without returning the greetings from those on duty, he unhooked the tannoy, and after clearing his throat, began speaking. 'This is the captain speaking,' and he then informed them about the sinking of the battleship, ending with, 'This has come as a complete surprise and it means the enemy can attack us, no matter where we are or how safe we might feel. Therefore, we must be vigilant. That is all.'

Miller was right. The news of the sinking came as a shock to everyone; especially as most of the crew were old and experienced hands, and had, at some time, either served on the *Royal Oak,* or knew someone who had done so.

In the engine room, Chief Engineer O'Malley looked grimly at his oppo, CERA Jones, and wiping his oil-stained hands on his white overalls, said, 'Jerry O'Connor, the chief stoker on board her, was best man at my wedding. I pray to God he's all right, so I do.'

Jones didn't reply. Knowing the engine rooms on battleships were well below the water line, he knew the chances of O'Connor's survival, or anyone else, were less than slender.

Out of a crew of 1234 men, 835 officers and ratings lost their lives. Hitler personally awarded Gunther Prien, the commanding officer of U-34, the Iron Cross First Class.

On the morning of Sunday 22nd, the ship crossed the equator. "Stand easy" had just finished when Able Seaman O'Hanlon, high up in the crow's nest, reported seeing a dense wall of fog approaching ten miles directly ahead of the ship.

"Thank you, O'Hanlon, we've seen it,' replied Miller, who, like those on the bridge, was using his binoculars to monitor its progress. Miller glanced at Pollard and said, 'Better tell the ship's company of its imminent arrival.' He then contacted Chief Coxswain Moore in the wheelhouse. 'Reduce speed to five knots. Revolutions one zero.'

Half an hour later, the fog enveloped the ship in great wafts of cold, acrid vapour.

'Better sound the siren every two minutes, Number One,' Miller said, using a hand to wipe the condensation from the inside of the window.

'Who does he think we'll bump into, the *Marie Celeste*?' PO Thompson muttered to QM.

Knight, who was busily polishing the compass bearing, gave a quiet laugh and said, 'Or maybe one of those battleships we've heard the Jerry's have.'

'You two would be best employed keeping a sharp lookout, instead of cackling like a pair of charladies,' OOW Lieutenant Morgan snapped.

'So what, my missus is a charlady,' Knight whispered to Thompson, and carried on polishing.

In the seamen's mess, Leading Seaman Waters was sitting at the table. He was about to take a sip of his tea when the sickening sound of the ship's foghorn echoed around. 'That fuckin' noise reminds me of funerals,' he said, before taking a good gulp of his drink.

'I'd rather you didn't mention funerals, matey,' Able Seaman Wood replied. 'If we do happen to meet a U-boat, it could be our funeral.'

On the bridge, Miller was sat on his chair, watching the bows of the ship part through the clouds of ghostly greyness.

'How thick do you think this pea soup is, Pilot?' Miller asked, using a handkerchief to clean the lens of his binoculars.

'The lookout reports no end in sight, so it's hard to say, sir,' Morgan sighed.

Just then, the ever-dependable PO Feneck arrived carrying a tray full of hot drinks. 'Here you are; service with a smile,' he said, passing around the mugs of steaming, hot kye. As he did so, the sudden blast of the ship's siren almost made him drop the drinks.

At the same time, Able Seaman O'Hanlon in the crow's nest, reported, 'Ship approaching directly ahead on the port side.'

Miller felt a sudden surge of fear run through him. He grabbed the wheelhouse voice pipe and yelled, '*Hard starboard*!'

Seconds later, *Endeavour* heeled precariously to the right. Miller replaced the voice pipe and tumbled into Feneck who had dropped his tray. Pollard grabbed hold of Miller's chair, and PO Thompson and Able Seaman Wood collided with one another, along with Lieutenant Young and Morgan. As the ship slowly righted itself, Feneck helped Miller to his feet. Suddenly, looking like the edge of a dagger, a huge, white liner appeared out of the gloom. Miller froze, anticipating the worst. But all he heard was the roar of the liner's engines as it passed some forty yards off *Endeavour's* port beam.

'Christ all mighty!' yelled Lieutenant Young, vigorously rubbing the side of his head. 'How the hell couldn't they have heard our siren?'

'Too damn busy quaffing champagne, I expect,' said Pollard. 'Did you get its name, sir?'

'I'm afraid not,' Miller replied. 'She's probably bound for Rio. Now, I think you'd better go and see if there's any damage or injuries, and take Petty Officer Feneck with you and give him a brandy,' he added, looking at Feneck's ashen face.

While Pollard was helping Feneck off the bridge, Miller looked around and was relieved to see that, except for shocked expressions on everyone's face, nobody was hurt.

Miller unhooked the wheelhouse voice pipe. 'How is everything, Chief?'

'OK, sir,' Moore replied cheerfully. 'No bones broken.'

'Then port ten, speed fifteen. Steer nor, nor west.'

Seconds later, the ship turned to the left and increased speed.

Glancing at Lieutenant Morgan, who still appeared a little shaken, Miller said, 'I suggest you go below and have strong coffee, Pilot.'

'Thank you, sir,' Morgan muttered, and left the bridge.

A few minutes later, Pollard arrived. 'No structural damage, sir, but the doc and Hailey are busy patching up several cut heads and sprained ankles.'

Throughout the morning of Monday 23rd, the fog slowly cleared. A gentle wind blew from the east, and the sun beat down from a clear, blue sky onto an ocean as smooth as glass.

The time was one thirty p.m. Except for the steady throb of the engines, all was quiet. Miller was sitting on his chair. Like Pollard and the others on duty, he was watching a school of five dolphins leap out of the water, only to appear on the opposite side of the ship, their shiny, grey skins dripping wet.

PO Ward gave Able Seaman Lane a puzzled look and said, 'I

wonder why they always look as if they're smiling, Shady?'

Lane shrugged his shoulders and replied, 'Search me, PO. Maybe it's because they know summat we don't.'

No sooner had he finished speaking than all five of these endearing creatures leapt in perfect unison into the air, then plunged into the sea and didn't appear again.

As the journey from England to Rio wore on, the boredom was broken up by inter-mess quizzes, "housey housey" and tugs of war, invariably won by the seamen. On a more serious note, Miller ordered Lieutenant Young to conduct regular gunnery drills.

After the end of the first drill, Chief GI Mills, with Lieutenant Young standing near, spoke to the guns crew. 'Don't you lot think, me 'andsomes,' Mills bellowed, 'that 'cos we're well on our ways 'ome, that we're safe, cos we fuckin' ain't. That drill took almost five bloody minutes. If you'd 'ave been that fuckin' slow against that U-boat, we'd all be at the bottom of Davys.'

'But Chief,' moaned Able Seaman Jacobs, leaning against the open breech. 'If we met a Jerry warship, they'll outgun us by miles.'

'Then we'll ram the buggers,' Mills replied defiantly. 'Now shit in it, and let's do it again.'

CHAPTER FORTY-FOUR

The storm hit during the night of Wednesday the 25th. It caught everyone by surprise, including OOW Lieutenant Morgan, who immediately contacted Miller.

Miller had not long been turned in. As usual, when at sea, he was partially dressed. He switched on his bedside light and unhooked his voice pipe. 'Yes, what is it?' he asked, stifling a yawn.

'Officer of the watch, sir. I'm afraid we're heading into a storm. The wind has veered from the north, and a high sea is coming at us beam on.'

'Thank you, Pilot,' Miller replied, feeling the ship pitch and roll. 'I'll be up right away.'

A few minutes later, Miller, wearing a thick, woollen sweater, and trousers, came onto the bridge. Under the dull-blue lighting, the atmosphere seemed almost surreal.

'When do you think it'll hit us, Pilot?' asked Miller.

Before Lieutenant Morgan could reply, the ship rose as if she was going up a lift, balanced herself uneasily at its peak, then fell away and plunged into a dark trough. Seconds later it slowly arose, with walls of white water cascading over its brow like a waterfall. 'I think it already has, sir,' Morgan replied, who, like Miller and the others on duty, was clutching onto anything at hand to avoid falling over.

Over the next forty-eight hours, the barometer dropped to near zero, during which time the storm raged like a wild banshee. All loose fittings were battered down. Tons of water thudded against the bulkhead. Massive waves of water crashed over the fo'c'sle and burst over the bridge. Everyone not requited for duty remained in their messes, and cooks performed minor miracles by distributing corned beef sandwiches and soup to each mess.

'This is a damn sight worse than the last one we had. What do you think, sir?' Pollard asked Miller.

As he spoke, the ship rolled precariously. And for a while the view was obscured, as a huge goffa' of dark-green seawater cascaded over the bridge.

'I think you're right, Number One,' Miller replied tersely, 'but I've a feeling it should begin to abate pretty soon.'

The time was three a.m. on Friday 27th. Pollard was OOW. Miller had been on the bridge since ten p.m.

'I hope so, sir,' Pollard replied, shaking his head, 'because if I eat any more corned beef, I'll turn vegetarian.'

Throughout the night, *Endeavour* continued on its north-westerly course. The great orb of the moon that had cast a vivid, orange glow onto the turbulent sea, slowly sank into the eastern horizon. As if ordained by Poseidon, dawn suddenly broke. The barometer began to rise, and the wind dropped and gradually veered to the south.

'You know, Pilot,' Pollard said Lieutenant Morgan, 'the captain must have second sight. During the middle, he told me that he thought the storm would soon subside, and he was right. Look at the sea, it's like a mill pond.'

'After he got us going when we were stuck in the ice, I think he could do anything,' Morgan replied, as he finished plotting the ship's position.

"Call the Hands" had just been piped when Miller came onto the bridge. 'Morning, everyone,' he remarked, nodding at the two officers, the duty signalman and QM. 'Thank God that bloody storm is over.'

'Just as you predicted, sir,' said Pollard, grinning.

Ignoring Pollard's witty remark, Miller looked at Morgan. 'What's our position, Pilot?'

'Longitude twenty degrees north, latitude ten south. At present we are some four hundred miles off the coast of Upper Guinea.'

'Thank you; explicit as usual,' Miller replied. 'Course and speed, Number One?'

'Twenty knots, course nor by nor west, sir.'

Miller repeated the information to the duty QM in the

wheelhouse, adding, 'Steady as she goes.'

'Anything on sonar, Number One?'

'No, sir. Leading Seaman Hardman reports everything clear for over fifty miles in all directions.'

Throughout Saturday morning, the ship's company went through a series of evolutions, ranging from "fire in the galley" to "abandon ship stations".

Shortly before twelve p.m., Surgeon Lieutenant Ryan, LSBA Hailey and the first-aid team were about to leave the sickbay to go to the aid of an injured seaman. Suddenly the door opened and in came a tall, dark-haired stoker. The well-scrubbed overalls he wore were open to the waist, displaying small, black hairs curling over the top of a white vest. His ashen face was covered in sweat and contorted with pain.

'Stoker Johnson, it's me guts, sir,' he said, clutching his stomach. 'The chief stoker sent me.'

'And how long have you had this pain, Johnson?' asked the doctor, as Hailey helped the stoker into a chair.

'It started about three o'clock when I had the middle, sir,' Johnson replied, half bent with pain.

'When was the last time you had a bowel movement?'

'A what, sir?'

'The doctor means, when was the last time you had a shit,' Hailey interrupted.

'Oh, some time yesterday, I think,' Johnson replied. 'Can't you give me summat for the pain, sir? Y'see, I'm part of the damage control team.'

'We'll see about that,' the doctor replied cagily, 'after I've examined you.'

Johnson's temperature was normal, but his pulse was full and bounding. Hailey handed the doctor a sphygmomanometer, an apparatus for measuring blood pressure. Attached to the inside of the lid was a graded tube of mercury called the monitor. He then took out a length of rubber tubing with a felt cuff leading from the monitor and wrapped it around Johnson's left upper arm. Using a small rubber ball, he inflated the cuff. He then placed the resonator, a listening device attached to the end of the stethoscope, onto a vein on the crook of Johnson's arm. Carefully manipulating the valve on the bulb, the doctor watched the movement of the mercury, and at varying levels noted the pressure on the monitor. The term "systole" is used when the arteries fill and the pressure rises; conversely, "diastole" is when the pressure falls. The normal BP at rest is 120 (systole)/80 (diastole). Johnson's BP read 140/100.

The doctor removed the stethoscope earpieces, and looking gravely at Johnson, said, 'I'm afraid your blood pressure is a little high. Now lie down flat on the couch while I examine your stomach.'

'Tell me, does this hurt?' asked the doctor, gently pressing down on the lower left side of Johnson's abdomen.

'No, sir,' muttered Johnson.

The doctor continued to carefully palpate across Johnson's abdomen. It was only when the doctor pressed an area a few inches in from Johnson's right side and quickly removed his hand, that Johnson cried, 'That's the place, Doc, that's where it hurts.'

'I'm sorry,' said the doctor, 'but I'll have to examine your back passage. So take off your overalls and underpants, lie on your left side, then draw up your knees. This won't take long, but I'm afraid it'll be a bit uncomfortable.'

Johnson gave the doctor a questioning look and said, 'But it's me guts, Doc…'

Hailey quickly interrupted him, saying, 'Just do as the doctor tells you and keep quiet.'

Johnson murmured something unintelligible then turned over.

The doctor picked up a latex glove from a rectal tray that Hailey had previously prepared and slipped it onto his right hand. He then applied a coating of Vaseline onto his forefinger from a small jar. He bent down, and using his left hand, gently moved one of Johnson's buttocks to one side.

'Now take a deep breath,' said the doctor.

As Johnson did so, the doctor inserted his forefinger high into Johnson's anus. (If an appendix is inflamed or swollen, this procedure can elicit pain.) Johnson's immediate response was a painful cry as he attempted to jerk his body away from the doctor.

'Sorry, old boy,' said the doctor, removing his finger and giving Hailey an ominous look. 'But I think we'd better keep you here and see how you go.'

'But what's wrong with me?' pleaded Johnson

'I think you may have appendicitis,' the doctor cagily replied. 'It could also be a stomach upset. We'll have to wait and see.'

'Appendicitis!' Johnson exclaimed, doing he best to sit up. 'My Auntie Lottie had that, and she died!'

'Now lie back and LSBA Hailey will help you to go next door and get into bed,' replied the doctor.

'Will I have to go to hospital, Doc?' Johnson asked, as Hailey helped him off the couch.

Not knowing how far away the ship was from land and medical help, all the doctor could say was, 'Maybe, we'll see. Now do your best to relax.' He turned to Hailey. 'Sips of water only and half an hour temperature, blood pressure and pulse chart. Now get him turned in while I go and speak to the captain.'

Except for the steady vibrations of the engines and gentle roll of the ship, all was relatively quiet. Miller was relaxing in his chair, talking to Pollard. Morgan was instructing Midshipman Grant in the art of taking a midday fix. PO Thompson was leaning against the binnacle and sharing a joke with one of the lookouts, when Ryan arrived.

'Good afternoon, Doc,' said Miller, turning from Pollard. 'What brings you here? Not trouble, I hope?' he added, noticing Ryan's furrowed brow.

'I'm afraid so, sir,' replied the doctor, taking out a handkerchief and mopping sweat from his brow. 'Stoker Johnson has appendicitis.'

Upon hearing the doctor's words, everyone stopped what they were doing and looked anxiously at Miller.

'My God!' Miller exclaimed, sitting bolt upright. 'Are you sure?'

'As sure as I can be, sir,' the doctor replied.

'Just how serious is it?' Miller asked, stroking his unshaken chin.

'In my opinion, sir,' the doctor replied, 'very serious. If his appendix bursts, he could develop peritonitis, which could be fatal.'

'Then we'll have to get him to a hospital as soon as possible,' Miller replied.

'Yes, indeed, sir,' the doctor replied.

'What's our position, Pilot?' he rasped, 'and how far are we from the nearest port?'

'One moment, sir,' replied Morgan, who, like the rest of them, was stunned by what the doctor had said.

It must be remembered that this was before the use of penicillin. Appendicitis was a serious condition, and if not operated on quickly, would usually result in the patient dying.

After gathering his wits, Morgan consulted his chart. A few minutes later, he said, 'Our position, sir, is eighteen degrees north, ten south. That puts us over a thousand miles from the nearest port, which is Dakar. According to my chart, Dakar is a large port with a wide harbour, situated on the end of Cape Vert peninsula.'

'Let me see now,' Miller replied, pensively stroking his chin. 'As I recall, Dakar was occupied by France some years ago, so they must have a British consular general.' He gave a questioning look at Morgan and said, 'Tell me, Pilot: doing twenty knots, how long would it take us to get there?'

After using a slide rule, then consulting his timetable, Morgan replied, 'Including today, sometime on Monday morning, sir.'

Miller promptly unhooked the wheelhouse voice pipe.

'Wheelhouse. Chief Coxswain Moore on the wheel.'

'Turn five degrees to starboard,' snapped Miller.

Miller contacted Lieutenant Duncan in the engine room and quickly explained the problem. 'I want as much speed as you can give me, Jock. I will, of course, take full responsibility for any engine damage.'

'Aye, aye, sir,' Duncan firmly replied. 'And I hope the laddie's all right,' then hung up.

Miller looked at PO Signalman Watts and said, 'Send a wireless message to the British consular in Dakar.

Watts hurriedly picked up a pencil and signal.

'Say, "Case of appendicitis on board. Needs urgent treatment.

ETA Dakar: a.m. Monday 30th. Request berthing instructions, doctor and ambulance to meet."'

Watts gave a nod of acknowledgment and hurried away.

Miller looked sternly at the doctor and asked, 'Do you think Johnson will be all right?'

Feeling his mouth suddenly go dry, the doctor replied, 'I hope so, sir. Hailey and I will stand four-hourly watches till we reach Dakar,' and he hurriedly left the bridge.

Ten minutes later, Watts returned. 'Reply from Dakar, sir,' he said, handing a signal pad to Miller.

'Good lord,' Miller replied, 'that was quick. Read it to me.'

'"Anchor a mile outside the harbour. Pilot will come on board and take you to berth number ten. Ambulance and doctor to meet. Good luck. Sir Victor Cusden. Consultant General."'

CHAPTER FORTY-FIVE

The cabin next to the sickbay was used, not only for inpatients, but as he was on call twenty-four hours a day, as a billet for LSBA Hailey. A strip of neon from a low-slung deckhead provided adequate lighting. On one side were two cots and small, metal lockers. Next to these was a chest of drawers above which was a square-shaped porthole. Then came a sink, an electric kettle and two cups on a glass shelf. Close by was Hailey's bunk resting on top of a section of cupboards. A side door led into a small bathroom.

Surgeon Lieutenant Ryan entered the cabin and looked at Johnson, who was lying in the bottom cot, his head barely visible over the coverlet.

'How are you feeling? Is the pain any worse?' Ryan asked, peeling back the bedding and checking Johnson's pulse. He was not surprised to find that it still remained full and bounding.

'The pain's just the same, sir,' Johnson replied, still holding his stomach. 'Can't you give me summat for it?'

'Let's have a look,' said the doctor.

Once again Johnson cried out as the doctor gently pressed down on his patient's lower right abdomen.

'Sorry, old boy. For the time being, only sips of water,' Ryan replied, replacing the bedclothes.

'Fat lot of use that'll do me,' Johnson mournfully replied.

'What did the captain have to say, sir?' Hailey asked Ryan, out of earshot of Johnson.

Ryan told him, adding, 'Dakar is sure to have more than one hospital.'

As he finished speaking, he heard the click of the tannoy.

'This is the captain speaking. Stoker Johnson is in the sickbay, suffering from appendicitis. We have therefore changed course and are heading for Dakar on the west coast of Africa. We should arrive there on Monday where we will transfer Johnson ashore. Anyone with cuts and bruises are to report to the chief bosun. Emergency cases only to the sickbay. That is all.'

Johnson gave Ryan a startled look and said, 'Bloody 'ell, sir, why am I being landed in Dakar? It's a thousand miles from 'ome.'

'Relax,' the doctor replied, giving Johnson a reassuring pat on his shoulder. 'They have better facilities in a hospital to treat you than we have. That's why.'

'Does that mean I'll 'ave to 'ave an operation, sir?' Johnson asked, giving Ryan a painful look.

'Possibly,' Ryan replied. 'Now, don't worry. Either I or LSBA Hailey will be here to look after you. Now lie back and tell us if the pain gets any worse.'

'And especially if you feel like a shit,' Hailey added cautiously.

After glancing at his wristwatch, Ryan motioned Hailey to one side and said, 'This is going to be a long three days and nights. So, beginning at ten tonight, I suggest we do four-hourly watches. All right?'

'That's fine by me, sir,' Hailey replied nonchalantly, shrugging his shoulders. 'I don't sleep too well at sea, anyway. But sir,' he added, frowning slightly, 'what will you do if his condition worsens? All we have to control his pain is morphia and pethidine.'

'And if I use either, they'd mask the symptoms,' Ryan replied. 'I've read something in an old edition of the BMJ that might be helpful. I think I'll go to my cabin and see if I can find it. Remember, the main symptoms of peritonitis are high temperature, high blood pressure, rapid heartbeat, increased pain, feeling sick and swelling of the abdomen. Call me immediately if you detect
any of these, understood?'

Hailey gave the doctor an anxious look and said, 'Yes, sir, but I've a feeling this is gunna be a long three days.'

'And nights,' Ryan added warily, and left the cabin.

Like most doctors, Ryan received a monthly copy of the *British Medical Journal.* After amalgamating with two smaller journals, the first BMJ was published in 1853 and became a worldwide standard bearer for up-to-date medical information, some of which was controversial. Such was the article written by Doctors' Corry, Brewer, and Nichol, Ryan was reading. In a four-page article, the doctors wrote about the potential use of sulphanilamide in the treatment of inflammatory conditions in the abdomen.

Ryan sat back in his chair and asked himself, *Would using sulphonamide help, or make Johnson's condition worsen?* He decided to wait and only use the sulphonamide as a last resort. Until then, he would rely on palliative treatment, and trust in God.

The time was six p.m. Ryan left his cabin, went to the main galley and asked the chief cook to have his and Hailey's meals delivered to the sickbay cabin.

'But what about Johnson, sir?' asked the portly chef, using the back of his hand to wipe beads of sweat from his brow. 'Won't he be havin' anything?'

Ryan shook his head and replied, 'Not at the moment, Chief.'

He left the galley, went to the bridge and arranged with the OOW to have him shaken at 1.50 a.m., and at the appropriate times until they reached Dakar

Ryan returned to the sickbay cabin where he and Hailey continued to monitor Johnson's condition. Hailey had left the rubber cuff around Johnson's upper arm, enabling it to be attached to the sphygmomanometer without disturbing Johnson if he was asleep.

At eight p.m., "Clean up mess decks and flats for rounds," was piped. An hour later, Ryan had just finished taking Johnson's blood pressure when he heard the intermittent shrillness of the bosun's pipe as the OOW and his party passed the sickbay.

'How are you feeling?' asked Ryan, finding Johnson's BP still very high. 'Is the pain any worse?'

'No, sir, it's still the same, sir,' Johnson replied. 'Any chance of a cuppa tea?'

'Yes, but only a few sips,' Ryan replied, 'nothing more.' The doctor stood up, and lowering his voice, looked at Hailey and said, 'Incidentally, do we carry sulphanilamide?'

'Yes, sir,' Hailey replied. 'Why, did you want to…?'

'No, no,' Ryan hastily replied. 'I just wondered, that's all.'

Shortly after "pipe down", Ryan looked at Hailey and said, 'Grind up two aspirins and put them in his tea; it might ease the pain and help him to sleep. And don't hesitate to call me if you're worried about anything.'

No sooner had the doctor left than Hailey filled the electric kettle and made a pot of tea. He placed two aspirins in a mortar, and using a pestle, ground the tablets into a fine powder, emptied it into a cup of water then gave it a quick stir.

'Here, Jono,' Hailey said, supporting Johnson's head, 'get this down you. It'll do you the world of good.'

'I fuckin''ope so,' muttered Johnson. He slowly drank the tea then lay back into his pillow.

After taking away the cup, Hailey placed it in the sink then switched on Johnson's overhead bedside light. He turned off the main lights, leaving he sickbay in partial darkness. He then drew a chair next to Johnson's cot and began recording Johnson's TPR.

Unfortunately the aspirin failed to help. A little after midnight, Johnson frightened Hailey by crying out, 'Doc, please help me, it's this fuckin' pain; can't you give me summat for it?'

Suddenly Hailey had an idea. 'Heat,' he muttered to himself. 'Maybe some heat might help.'

He took out a rubber hot-water bottle from a drawer, switched on the kettle again and half-filled the bottle. After expelling the air, he screwed it tight and wrapped it in a pillowcase. He withdrew the bedclothes and said, 'Here you are mate,' and placed the bottle over Johnson's lower abdomen. 'Let's see if this helps you.'

'Cheers, Doc,' Johnson replied. 'If it does, you can 'ave my tot for a week.'

'Fair enough,' Hailey said with a rueful grin. 'Now, hold the bottle over the place where it hurts the most.'

Hailey's brainwave appeared to work. When the doctor opened the sickbay door at 1.50 a.m., he was met by the sound of Johnson's noisy snoring.

'He seems to have settled down, thank goodness,' Ryan whispered to Hailey.

How's his BP and pulse?'

'As you can see, sir,' Hailey replied, handing the doctor a TPR chart, 'his blood pressure and pulse are still high, but the pain in his side seems to be a bit better.'

'Any abdominal swelling or vomiting?'

'No, sir,' Hailey replied.

'Using a hot-water bottle was a damn good idea. Well done,' said Ryan. 'Now get turned in; you look beat.'

'Thank you, sir,' replied Hailey. 'I have half-filled the kettle, as the water will soon need replacing.'

Johnson woke up twenty minutes after Hailey fell asleep. Ryan was about to check Johnson's TPR when he heard him murmur something and open his eyes.

'How are feeling?' Ryan asked Johnson.

'The water's cooled down and the pain's returned, sir,' murmured Johnson, still holding the bottle to his abdomen.

'You'd better give it to me, and I'll warm it up,' replied Ryan, taking Johnson's radial pulse and finding it nearly ninety. 'And I'll warm it up. Now lie back and get some rest.'

At seven a.m., Miller knocked on the cabin door. Ryan was in the process of examining Johnson's abdomen. He looked up just as Miller came in. Hailey was standing near the sink holding an electric kettle, and was pouring boiling water into a small, aluminium kettle.

'Sorry to interrupt you, Doc, how is he?' Miller asked, looking anxiously at Johnson.

'Bearing up, aren't you?' the doctor replied, covering Johnson up.

Johnson didn't reply. Instead, he gave a weak smile and closed his eyes.

CHAPTER FORTY-SIX

The news of Johnson's condition soon spread around the ship. Ratings passing the sickbay glanced apprehensively at the door, wondering how Johnson was.

The time was twelve p.m. on Saturday, October 28th. In the stoker's mess everyone had downed their rum and was sitting at the table, enjoying their dinner.

'Well, you heard the old man,' Leading Stoker Webb muttered, while chewing on a tough piece of chicken. 'We won't reach Dakar for two more days, so all we can do is hope for the best.'

'Aye, but in the meantime, what can the MO do if Jonno gets worse?' said Stoker Weir, who, having finished his jam roly-poly pudding, was in the process of wiping his mouth with an off-white handkerchief.

'Well, according to what I've heard,' said Stoker Carter, 'there's nowt much anyone can do as the MO can't operate on him, and even if he did, Jonno could peg out.'

After "stand easy", Lieutenant Duncan, Johnson's divisional officer, knocked gingerly on the cabin door and was told to enter. His white overalls were stained with oil, and he was sweating profusely.

Seeing Johnson had his eyes closed, he whispered, 'How is he, Doc?'

Knowing that Johnson was feigning sleep and could hear his every word, Ryan replied, 'He's doing quite well, thank you, Jock.'

'Och, that's good news,' Duncan replied, as he wiped his brow with a piece of cotton waste. 'When he wakes up, tell him that myself and his messmates were asking after him.' Then he left.

After Duncan had gone, Johnson opened his eyes and muttered, 'Miserable bugger didn't even bring me a tot,' then closed his eyes.

It was a little after three a.m. on Sunday. Except for the dullness coming from Johnson's overhead bedside light, the cabin was bathed in eerie darkness. Hailey was sat beside Johnson's cot. Johnson lay on his back. His eyes were closed. The outline of Johnson holding the hot-water bottle to his abdomen could be seen under the bedclothes.

Hailey was about to take Johnson's blood pressure, when Johnson opened his eyes and cried, 'Doc, Doc, it's the pain! It feels worse!'

For a few seconds, Johnson's sudden cry startled Hailey. 'When did it start?' he asked, noticing the distressful expression on Johnson's ashen face.

'I'm not sure,' Johnson muttered. 'It just happened, like.'

Hailey immediately took Johnson's pulse and found it over 100. A feeling of panic suddenly engulfed him.

'Has it moved?' Hailey asked.

'No, Doc,' Johnson painfully replied. 'It just got worse, like.'

'Show me,' Hailey said, turning back the bedclothes.

Johnson let the hot-water bottle slide away off his stomach, and gently touched the right side of his abdomen.

'Thanks, Jonno,' Hailey said, taking away the hot-water bottle which was now lukewarm. 'Now lie back and try to relax.'

'For fuck's sake, Doc,' Johnson pleaded, 'aren't you gunna give me summat for the pain?'

'I'm going to call the MO,' Hailey replied, noticing beads of sweat on Johnson's brow. 'I'm sure he'll give you something.'

Five minutes later, Ryan arrived carrying a bulky, brown, leather Gladstone bag. Hailey immediately switched on the main light, as he knew the doctor would want to examine Johnson. The doctor's thick, brown hair was uncombed, and there were dark smudges under his eyes.

The doctor placed his bag by the side of Johnson's cot and took out his stethoscope. 'How are you feeling, old boy?' Ryan asked, as he checked Johnson's pulse then took his blood pressure. The flushed appearance on Johnson's face confirmed both were dangerously high. 'LSBA Hailey tells me the pain is worse.'

'Yes, sir,' Johnson muttered. His voice was almost incoherent and both hands held his abdomen. 'Much worse.'

Ryan gently removed Johnson's hands and was about to examine him, when suddenly Johnson's face became contorted in agony. He clasped his abdomen tightly and cried out, 'Can't you do summat? It's killin' me!'

Suddenly Ryan felt a feeling of helplessness ran through him. *Oh God*, he silently pleaded, desperately, *don't let it be peritonitis.*

'Shall I grind up another two aspirins, sir?' Hailey asked.

Ryan remembered the article in the BMJ about sulphanilamide. He looked up at Hailey and said, 'No. Use two tablets of sulphanilamide, stat, and then repeat them four-hourly.' He looked at Johnson whose face was bathed in perspiration. Doing his best to sound confident, he said, 'Hailey is going to give you a drink containing a different treatment. It should help you feel better. Now lie back while I warm up your bottle.'

Over the past three months Hailey had come to respect and like his boss. However, this was the first time he had seen him look and sound so desperate.

By the time Ryan had heated the bottle and placed it onto Johnson's abdomen, Hailey had ground up the sulphanilamide tablets and stirred the powder in a small glass of milk. He poured the mixture into a cup then bent down and held Johnson's head to help him drink it. 'There now,' he said, wiping Johnson's mouth with a piece of gauze, 'lie back and try to get some sleep.'

'Bugger the sleep,' Johnson murmured. 'All I want is fer this pain to go away.'

'Well, here's hoping it will,' Hailey replied, giving Ryan an anxious look.

But the pain didn't go away.

Throughout the night, Johnson's BP and pulse remained dangerously high. At four a.m., Ryan was sat near Johnson's cot.

'I'll stay here while you get your head down,' he said, sipping the cup of coffee Hailey had made.

Feeling he might be needed if the sulphanilamide didn't take effect, Hailey looked at the doctor and said, 'As it'll be "call the hands" in a few hours, sir, I might as well stay here.'

However, by twelve p.m. on Sunday, despite being given more sulphanilamide at eight a.m., the pain in Johnson's abdomen remained the same.

'At least it hasn't got any worse,' Ryan said to Hailey. He had just finished examining Johnson. 'And there isn't any abdominal distention.'

'And he hasn't been sick, sir,' Hailey added. 'Maybe the tablets are starting to work,' he added optimistically.

'Perhaps, but his BP is still too high and his pulse too rapid,' Ryan cautiously replied.

During Sunday evening, Johnson's pain gradually increased.

'Have you passed wind or felt sick?' asked Ryan.

'No, sir, it comes and goes. Sharp, like. Ain't there anythin' you can give me?' Johnson pleaded, his face contorted in agony.

Suddenly Ryan was overcome by a feeling of desperation. *My God*, he asked himself. *What can I do*? Then it came to him. 'Morphia,' he muttered to himself. It couldn't possibly disguise Johnson's symptoms any more, and hopefully it would reduce his pain. 'Yes, there is,' Ryan replied. 'I'm going to give an injection. I'm sure it'll help.'

'I 'ope it won't hurt, sir,' said Johnson.

'Relax, you won't feel a thing,' said Hailey.

After washing his hands, Ryan accepted a 10cc syringe containing 1/6 grain of morphia, from Hailey, and carefully expelled any air. Using a cotton wool swab soaked in methylated spirits, he cleaned an area on Johnson's upper left arm. This was followed by a loud "Ow", as the doctor injected the morphia.

Gradually Johnson's pain subsided and shortly after twelve p.m., he fell asleep. An hour later he suddenly opened his eyes, and in a tired voice, cried, 'Doc, Doc, the pain's worse, and I think I'm gunna be sick.'

CHAPTER FORTY-SEVEN

The time was five thirty a.m. The stars and moon had bid a fond farewell from an inky-black sky. On the eastern horizon, the sun's rays were slowly turning the calm sea into a carpet of sparkling whiteness. The darkness slowly turned to pale blue, and a new day was born.

'No matter how often you see it, sir,' PO Thompson said to Lieutenant Ward, staring out of the bridge widows, 'dawn at sea is a sight to behold.'

Ward was sitting in the captain's chair. He was about to reply, when Surgeon Lieutenant Ryan came onto the bridge. He didn't wear a cap, and his hair was an untidy mess. He was breathing heavily, and lines of perspiration ran down the sides of his face.

The doctor's sudden and unexpected arrival indicated something was wrong.

'My goodness, Doc!' exclaimed Lieutenant Ward. 'What's the problem? Is it Johnson?'

'Yes,' Ryan replied, resting a hand on the side of the chair. 'I… I'm worried about him. I must speak to the captain.'

Ward didn't reply. He slid off the chair, unhooked the captain's voice pipe and waited.

A few seconds later Miller's voice answered. 'Captain. What is it?' He sounded surprisingly alert for someone who had just been woken up from a deep sleep.

Ward quickly told him.

'Right,' Miller replied. 'I'll be up straight away.

Five minutes later Miller arrived. He wore a pair of well-worn sandals, and his hair, normally well-groomed, was a mess. His tropical shorts and blouse were slightly wrinkled, and he badly needed a shave.

'What's the problem, Doc?' he asked, noticing how tired Ryan looked.

Ryan told him, adding, 'If we don't get him to hospital soon, he could...'

'Yes, yes,' Miller replied impatiently, 'I understand. What's our ETA in Dakar, Pilot?' he asked Morgan, who had just arrived.

Morgan hastily consulted his chart, then replied, 'Roughly two p.m., sir.'

'Thank you,' Miller replied, while picking up the engine room voice pipe.

Lieutenant Duncan answered. Miller quickly explained the problem, then added, 'I know we're already doing twenty knots, Jock, but could you possibly give me a few more? It might save Johnson's life.'

'Och, I'll do ma best,' Duncan replied, 'but it could damage those piston rings and cylinder heads again.'

'Then that's the risk I'll have to take,' Miller firmly replied.

'Thank you, sir,' said Ryan, who had overheard Miller's conversation. 'Now, if you'll excuse me,' he added, and left the bridge.

As he arrived at the sickbay cabin, he opened the door and felt his heart suddenly contract. Johnson, supported by Hailey, was sitting on the edge of his cot. Both Johnson's hands held an enamel bowl into which he was vomiting a weak stream of clear fluid. With each violent retch, his face became wrinkled with pain.

'My God, Hailey!' exclaimed Ryan, closing the door. 'How long has he been like this?'

'It started a few minutes after you left, sir,' Hailey replied, taking the basin from Johnson and placing it on the deck.

'Any blood?'

'No, sir,' Hailey answered, supporting Johnson who had stopped retching.

Hailey took the basin and showed it to Ryan.

With an air of desperation in his voice, the doctor replied, 'Thank God,' then added, 'Is the pain any worse?'

'No, just the same, sir. Any chance of a drink?'

'Yes, but only a few sips of water,' Ryan replied.

'Ta, sir,' Johnson murmured weakly, as he lay back onto the

cot, completely exhausted.

During the morning, Ryan sat by Johnson's bedside, checking his BP and pulse every half hour. Johnson lay with his knees drawn up. As each spasm of pain engulfed him, he cried out, and his knees automatically flexed higher than his abdomen.

Shortly after twelve thirty p.m., the telephone rang. Ryan immediately unhooked the receiver. 'Sickbay. Surgeon Lieutenant.'

'Captain. How is Johnson?'

Blinking his eyes with tiredness, Ryan replied, 'He's in constant pain, but holding on, sir.'

Miller breathed a sigh of relief, then said, 'Thank God for that, because we've sighted the coast of Senegal. We should arrive outside Dakar harbour in about an hour and be alongside the wharf about two p.m. Do you think Johnson will be well enough to be moved?'

'Yes, sir,' Ryan replied, more in hope than good judgement.

'Good. I'll tell the buffer to pack what he'll need in a suitcase. Meanwhile, keep me informed,' Miller said, then hung up.

Ryan replaced the receiver. He was about to ask Johnson how the pain was, but the afflictive expression on Johnson's pale face told its own story. Instead, he bent down, and touching Johnson gently on the shoulder, said, 'In a little over an hour, we'll be alongside in Dakar. But we'll have to put you in a Neil Robertson stretcher in order to move you onto the upper deck. Do you think you'll be up to it?'

Johnson forced a weak but determined smile and said, 'Yes, sir. Anything's better than walking.'

'Good man. I'm going to give you an injection. It should help to ease the pain,' replied the doctor, standing up. Turning to Hailey, he added, 'Go and tell PO Feneck we'll require him and the first-aid party to report here at one p.m.'

While Hailey was away, Ryan gave Johnson the injection of morphia. 'There now,' the doctor said, rubbing the side of Johnson's left upper arm. 'Very soon you'll have some pretty nurse doing this.'

Johnson's response was a weak smile as he closed his eyes and lay back in his cot.

CHAPTER FORTY-EIGHT

A little after twelve thirty p.m., Able Seaman Day in the crow's nest, reported sighting the tops of mosques, buildings and ships masts dotting the skyline twenty miles on the port beam.

'Port ten, Number One,' said Miller, 'and stand by to lower the Jacob's ladder amidships on the starboard side.'

Twenty minutes later, Dakar's wide, horseshoe-shaped harbour hove into view. Merchant ships and civilian liners were tied up alongside several wharfs jutting out from the quayside.

'Launch approaching, starboard side, sir,' said Pollard.

Everyone looked to their right and saw its frothy bow wave curling high in the air. Senegal's green, yellow and red striped flag fluttered wildly from its stern. A small, stout man, wearing a dark uniform and peaked cap, stood in the stern sheets.

'Stop engines, Number One,' snapped Miller.

Minutes later the ship slowly came to a halt.

'Take over, Number One,' said Miller, 'and telephone the doctor to meet me on the brow.'

After making his way down three flights of stairs, Miller arrived at an open door leading onto the covered passageway on the starboard side of the ship. Here he was joined by Surgeon Lieutenant Ryan.

Meanwhile, the launch, its brass fittings glinting in the sunshine, cut its engine and came alongside the Jacob's ladder. A sailor reached out, and using a long pole, hooked onto the small, wooden platform. With the help of one of the crew, the stout man climbed out of the motor and stepped carefully onto the wooden platform. Grasping the rope guard rails, he made his way up to the ship, where he was met by Miller and Ryan. As they did so, Pollard ordered the Jacobs ladder to hoisted on board.

'Commander Miller,' he said, as they shook hands.

'And I'm Captain Le Brun, the port pilot. Welcome to Dakar. I speak English,' he replied. 'I lived in London five years. Your aircraft carrier, HMS *Hermes,* was here last week. German warships 'ave been sighted nearby, so maybe they were looking for them, yes?'

Dark rings showed below his pale-blue eyes, and his sharp-featured face was weather-beaten. A small, silver anchor adorned the space above the centre of his cap, and the bulge under his black, leather overcoat bore witness to someone with a very good appetite.

'Yes, they probably were,' Miller replied. 'Welcome on board,' he added, as he introduced him to Surgeon Lieutenant Ryan.

'I only wish it were under different circumstances,' Ryan said, as he shook Le Brun's hand. 'We have a man with appendicitis, and he needs urgent treatment.'

'This, I know,' Le Brun replied. 'An ambulance and a doctor are waiting on the wharf.'

'Excellent,' replied Ryan.

'Right, then, Monsieur Le Brun,' said Miller, stepping to one side. 'If you'll be good enough to follow me, I'll show you to the bridge then we can get underway.'

Ryan returned to the sickbay and was relieved to see Johnson lying with his arms outside the bedclothes. His eyes were closed, and for the first time in days, he appeared to be in a sound sleep.

'The morphia you gave him seems to have worked, sir,' Hailey said, giving the doctor a relieved smile.

'I hope it'll still be working when we come to move him,' Ryan replied, as he checked Johnson's pulse and found that it remained dangerously high.

A little after one p.m., Johnson suddenly woke up. His face was flushed and creased with pain. 'It's me guts, Doc,' he cried, sitting up and clutching his stomach with both hands. 'They feel as though they're on fire.'

'Steady on, old boy,' Ryan replied, bending down and placing a comforting arm around Johnson's shoulders. 'We'll soon have you in hospital.'

'Aye,' added Hailey, 'surrounded by all those gorgeous nurses.'

'Bollocks to that,' gasped Johnson. 'Can't you just give me another injection, sir?'

'Not at the moment,' the doctor reluctantly replied. 'But I'll give you another shortly before we get you ready to be taken ashore. That should ease your pain. Now lie back, and Hailey will give you a sip of water.'

As he finished speaking, Petty Officer Feneck arrived outside the sickbay. Feneck knocked on the door and was told to enter.

'First-aid party present, sir,' he said, startled at the sight of Johnson who was lying on his cot.

Both arms were tightly wrapped around his knees which were tightly drawn up against his abdomen. Lines of perspiration trickled down the sides of his face that was wrinkled with pain.

'What do you want us to do, sir?' Feneck asked the doctor.

'Tell one of your men to fetch a Neil Robertson stretcher, then wait outside.'

'Very good, sir,' Feneck replied. After giving a quick, compassionate look at Johnson, he quietly opened the door and left.

'What's 'appenening, PO?' asked Stores Assistant Jones, who was standing in the passage next to Cook Greenwood and Cook Murray.

'You'll soon find out,' rasped Feneck. 'Now go and fetch a Neil Robertson stretcher. There's one secured to the deckhead in the passageway next to the galley. And be quick about it.'

No sooner had Jones left, than Jones returned, carrying the NR stretcher. Then the ship was underway. This was followed by the pipe, "Special sea duty men, fall in on the fo'c'sle. Stand by to come alongside."

Miller sat on his chair on the bridge, surveying the busy, bustling port of Dakar. Warehouses, large and small, and tall cranes, looking like ugly, black monsters, lined the harbour's wide, cobbled road. Muscular stevedores offloaded heavy-looking boxes and sacks from cargo vessels and carried them into storing sheds In the distance, a vast area of rolling hills, shrouded by a vast area of low-lying banks of fluffy white clouds, separated Senegal from Mauritania in the north, and Mali in the south.

Meanwhile, Miller felt frustratingly helpless. Until the ship was safely alongside the wharf, his ship was under the control of the pilot, who was bent over the compass bearing, occasionally issuing instructions to the wheelhouse. After passing several merchant ships, tugs and tourists in speed boats, he gradually eased the ship alongside a wharf. In a matter of seconds, the ship was secured. A guard rail was removed, allowing a crane to lower a metal gangway. Watching some distance away, a group of tourists stopped chattering and stared inquisitively at a tall, swarthy man standing next to a blue ambulance. Part of a stethoscope hung from a pocket in his white coat.

In the sickbay cabin, Ryan had finished giving Johnson an injection of morphia. Then he sat down at his desk, quickly wrote up details of Johnson's medical history and sealed it in an envelope. Five minutes later, Johnson fell into a sound sleep.

'Thank God for that, sir,' Hailey said to the doctor.

Ryan gave a sigh of relief and replied, 'Yes, and here's hoping the effect of the morphia lasts until we get him ashore. Now, I think we'd better get him ready. Tell PO Feneck to come in.'

Hailey opened the sickbay door and motioned for Feneck to enter.

Miller turned, looked gravely at Feneck and said, 'In a little while, we'll have to move Johnson. I want you to find a canvas stretcher, place it at the bottom of the stairs leading to the deck below and open it up. Understood?'

'Yes, sir,' Feneck replied. 'How is he, sir?' he added, glancing at Johnson.

'As you can see, he's asleep, 'Miller replied. 'Now ask one of your men to bring in the NR, then tell the others to come in.'

Without replying, Feneck turned and left the sickbay.

A few minutes later, Stores Assistant Jack Jones brought in the NR. He quickly undid the leather straps, opened it up and laid it on the deck, close to Johnson's cot. Hailey undid the cot's metal guard rail. Placing their hands under Johnson's warm body, Hailey and the doctor carefully lifted Johnson up. Johnson gave a throaty cough. He shuddered slightly, and for one heart-stopping moment, Ryan thought he would wake up. However, all Johnson did was mumble something and lay still.

'Easy does it,' said Ryan, as they gently lowered Johnson onto the stretcher.

Suddenly Johnson opened his eyes. 'What's 'appening, sir?' he asked, staring wildly at the doctor.

'We're taking you ashore,' replied Ryan. How are you feeling? How's the pain?'

'Still bad, sir,' Johnson muttered. 'Any chance of a drink? Me mouth feels like a vulture's crotch.'

'Later,' said Ryan. 'Now lie back and we'll soon have you in hospital.'

Hailey bent down and tucked a blanket around Johnson, then with the help of Feneck, strapped him in. Thompson and Morgan took up a position either side of the NR. Each grasped a rope handle and looked gravely at the doctor. Ryan took a deep breath, and despite feeling his heart battering against his ribs, said, 'Slowly and carefully, now. One, two, lift.'

With Hailey holding the head rope, they carried Johnson out of the sickbay and lowered him down the stairs. Hailey and Feneck quickly undid the straps. Johnson was still awake. With the help of Hailey and Feneck, he managed to painfully push himself off the NR onto the stretcher and was covered with a blanket.

Hailey looked at Feneck and said, 'OK, PO, you take the rear, and I'll lead.'

Ryan led the way. He reached the hatchway and helped Hailey and Feneck to carefully lift the stretcher onto the quarterdeck.

CHAPTER FORTY-NINE

The tall doctor hurried up the gangway and was met by Miller. 'I, Doctore Amadou Niangn.'

'And I captain,' Miller said, as they shook hands.

'I speak English leetle. You 'ave sick man, yes?' I take to the Saint Louis hospital.'

Hailey and Feneck arrived and placed the stretcher near the brow. Behind him came Leading Stoker, Nobby Clark — the killick of Johnson's mess — carrying a green "Pussers" suitcase.

Seeing Johnson open his eyes, he knelt down and said, 'How are yer feeling, mate? The buffer and me packed your number ones and everything you'll need, including some fags, and a tot of neaters in a medicine bottle. All the lads send their best. Good luck,' he said, gently patting Johnson on the chest. 'We'll see you back in Devonport.' He stood up and joined a large group of the crew gathered close by.

While Nobby Clark was talking to Johnson, Pollard introduced Ryan to Doctor Niangn.

As they shook hands, Ryan quickly told him about Johnson and handed him the envelope. 'He was in so much pain, I gave him a sixth grain of morphia half an hour ago.'

'Thank you, I will tell anaesthetist,' Niangn replied. 'Now, we go, yes?'

They shook hands, and Doctor Niangn hurried down the gangway and climbed through the ambulance's rear doors. Hailey and Feneck gently lifted up the stretcher and made their way down the gangway. Leading Stoker Clark followed, carrying Johnson's suitcase. Two white-coated orderlies helped to slide the stretcher inside the ambulance. The orderlies climbed inside and gingerly lifted Johnson onto another stretcher. They then passed the ship's stretcher and blankets outside to Feneck and Hailey.

'All the best, Johnno,' Hailey shouted, as the doors were closed.

Carrying the stretcher and blanket, Feneck and Hailey walked up the gangway. No sooner had they reached the brow, than the crane removed the gangway, and guard rails were put back in position.

Watching the ambulance drive away, Ryan looked at Hailey, and with a tired sigh, said, 'I don't wish to sound disingenuous, but I'm glad that's over.'

Hailey yawned wearily, then replied, 'Me too, sir, and I hope he's all right.'

'Dismiss everyone,' Miller said to Chief GI Barnes, as he and Pollard turned and made their way to the bridge. Miller immediately contacted Lieutenant Duncan in the engine room. 'Both engines, Jock,' Miller said anxiously. 'I want to get underway as soon as possible.'

A minute later, everyone on the bridge felt the deck vibrate as the engines came alive.

Ten minutes later, *Endeavour* cleared the harbour and headed for the open sea.

'Starboard ten, full ahead. Steer 325,' snapped Miller. 'Fall out special sea duty men, Number One, then ask the engineer officer to come to the bridge.'

A few minutes later, Lieutenant Duncan arrived. The white overalls he wore were dotted with oil stains, as was his battered, old cap.

'You sent for me, sir,' he said, looking at Miller while using a piece of cotton waste to wipe beads of sweat from his face.

'Yes, tell me Jock,' Miller said, pursing his lips. 'Have we enough fuel to reach England?'

'Aye, that we have, sir,' Duncan replied. 'As ye know, we took on an extra two hundred gallons in Rio.'

'Thank you, Jock,' Miller replied. 'I just wanted to make sure, as I hadn't bargained for the detour to Dakar. Please carry on.'

By six p.m., darkness had fallen, and the lights of Dakar had become a faint glow twenty miles away on the port bow. A sharp but warm breeze blew from the south, and from an inky-black sky, a myriad of shining stars and a full moon turned a calm sea into a million dots of sparkling silver.

On the bridge, Miller was sat on his chair, lost in thought. He had intended to stop at Gibraltar to allow the ship's company to collect mail and enjoy a spot of shore leave. However, even if they arrived in Gibraltar during darkness, the presence of *Endeavour*, despite being without her pennant number, might still be recognised by the German spies across the harbour in Spanish Algeciras. As Hitler was still aware that the grapholite remained on board, he would move heaven and hell to either capture or sink the ship. That would inevitably mean a bloody battle and loss of life, and he wasn't prepared to risk that. So, Gibraltar must, at all costs, be bypassed.

His reverie was abruptly interrupted by the sound of someone's voice. He turned, blinked and saw Leading Steward Blake staring at him.

'Thought you'd like this, sir,' he said, handing Miller a mug of steaming, hot coffee.

'Thank you, Blake. That's just what I could do with,' Miller replied. After gently blowing across the mug then taking a sip, he stared inquisitively at Lieutenant Morgan and said, 'Let's see now, Pilot. As you probably know, England is about two thousand miles away. Doing twenty knots, how long will it take us to reach England?'

'England, sir, but I thought Gibraltar…'

Aware that Pollard and those on duty could hear them, he quickly interrupted Morgan. *'England,* I said; are you deaf?'

'Sorry, sir,' Morgan replied. Feeling his face redden, he quickly turned away. After consulting his chart and doing a few quick calculations in a notebook, he replied, 'We should reach the English Channel in nine days, sir.'

'Good,' Miller replied, slapping the arm of his chair. He leant forward and unhooked the ship's tannoy. 'This is the captain speaking. In case you are under the impression that we are heading for Gib, I'm sorry to disappoint you.' He went on to explain why, ending with, 'It'll mean yet another long haul, but with luck, we should arrive in Plymouth in about ten days. In the meantime, we must stay alert. We will, therefore, continue to practice daily drills. That is all.'

The news that the ship wouldn't be stopping at Gibraltar came as a great disappointment to the ship's company.

'There goes our last chance to get a few presents for the missus and kids,' Waters said to LRO Bell.

The time was seven thirty p.m. Waters and several other ratings were in the seamen's mess. "Duty watch fall in outside the coxswain's office. Clear up mess decks and flats for rounds," had just been piped.

'And what about all those gorgeous dancing girls in the Mexican Bar?' said Able Seaman White.

'And Lulu Bell in the American Bar,' added Bell.

'One of these days, Dinga, your dick'll drag you further than dymamite'll blow you,' Waters jokingly remarked.

'Aye, but what a way to go,' Bell replied, rolling his eyes.

In the wardroom, Surgeon Lieutenant Ryan accepted a cup of coffee from a steward, took a sip, and smiling at Lieutenant Jenkins, said, 'Now you're certain to be home in time for your baby to be born.'

'All being well, that is,' Jenkins solemnly replied. 'A lot could happen in two thousand miles,' he said.

CHAPTER FIFTY

A little after midnight on Wednesday 1st November, Miller lay in his bunk thinking about Linda. It would be about two a.m. in England. He imagined her curled up in bed, warm and cosy, sound asleep. He closed his eyes and could almost smell the intoxicating fragrance of her perfume and see her beguiling, emerald-green eyes looking deep into his. How well he remembered the night they spent together before she left Rio: the softness of her body, the strength of her legs around him, pulling him into her, and the sharp pain of her nails digging into his back each time she had an organism. When Blake woke him up at five thirty a.m., his body was soaked with sweat.

The next day dawned warm and clear. Visibility was good. A soft, southerly breeze blew from a cloudless, cerulean sky, and a piercingly hot sun shone down on a calm, deep-blue sea.

Lieutenant Ward had just taken over the watch from Lieutenant Jenkins, when Able Seaman Cronin in the crow's nest reported seeing a ship roughly twenty miles on the port beam.

'I'm not sure what it is, sir,' said Cronin, 'but by its outline, I'd say it was a warship.'

Seconds later, sonar operator, Leading Seaman Harding, confirmed the sighting.

Lieutenant Ward immediately contacted Miller in his cabin. A minute later, slightly out of breath, he arrived on the bridge.

'Can anyone make out what it is?' he barked. Like Pollard, Ward and the others, he had binoculars pinned to his eyes.

'Whatever it is,' said Pollard, 'she's making a bloody big bow wave and is steaming directly towards us.'

'Do you want to alter course, sir?' asked Ward.

Miller was sat in his chair. Suddenly he felt his heart begin to pound against his ribcage. 'No. If it is a German, altering course will only make the blighter suspicious. Steady as you go.'

All of a sudden a mixture of fear and tension pervaded the warm, stuffy atmosphere.

'But what'll we do if it's a German, sir?' Pollard asked.

Miller took a deep breath and slowly lowered his binoculars. 'I have considered this,' he replied thoughtfully. 'And our only hope is to try and bluff our way out.'

Suddenly all eyes were centred on Miller.

'Bluff our way, sir!' exclaimed Pollard. 'What exactly do you mean?'

'You'll find out,' Miller replied. 'Now, I suggest you raise that Swedish flag we brought with us.'

Miller was about to use his binoculars when Cronin cried, 'She's flyin' the Swastika, sir — she's a bloody Jerry!'

'Quickly, Number One!' snapped Miller, his voice raised and full of urgency. 'Find that Swedish captain's jacket and cap you were given in Rio and put it on. Pilot, take off your shoulder bars, then see if you can find what type of destroyer it is. The rest of you rip off any service insignia on your shirts. *Now move!*'

Lieutenant Morgan took down a copy of *Jane's Fighting Ships* from a drawer. He quickly found the section he was looking for and shouted, 'She's *Erich Koellner*, sir. Type 1934A. Heavily armed with five-inch guns, two sets of quadruple torpedoes, and she can do thirty-six knots.'

'Just our bloody luck,' Miller groaned, and unhooked the ship's tannoy. After nervously clearing his throat, he said, 'This is the captain speaking. There is a German destroyer approaching us some ten miles on our port beam. Luckily the first lieutenant speaks Swedish and German. Before we left Rio, he was given an old uniform jacket from a Swedish captain, and a company cap, for such an occasion as this, so we are going to try and fool the bastard. The first lieutenant will pose as the ship's captain and reply to any questions the destroyer captain may ask.' Miller paused momentarily, then continued. 'Now, when I give the order, I want some of you to come onto the upper deck and wear civilian clothes. As part of the bluff we'll be flying the Swedish flag, as Sweden is not at war with Germany. So act as if you're glad to see them. Our lives may depend on it. Good luck.' Feeling his hand tremble slightly, he slowly replaced the handset.

Miller's words sent a feeling of trepidation running throughout the ship.

'Bloody hell, Len, the old man's certainly taking a risk,' the chief cook said to CGI Mills.

They were in the senior ratings mess and had just listened to Miller's announcement.

'I think it's a fuckin' great idea, m'andsome,' Mills replied. 'Anyway, what else could he do?'

'To be sure, he could just tell them who we are,' said Chief Engineer Paddy O'Malley. 'That way he could be certain of saving all our lives.'

'And spend the rest of the war in a fuckin' concentration camp,' added PO Thompson. 'No, thank you.'

'Personally, I think it could work, especially as the Jimmy speaks their lingo,' remarked Chief Coxswain Moore. 'Now where the hell did I put that jazzy shirt I bought in Rio?' he added, opening his locker.

'What do you think?' Waters asked Collins, a tall, dark stoker whose pallid complexion matched those of his fellow messmates.

Waters and a few other seamen had crossed over into the stoker's mess. The conversation was heated, and at times, controversial.

'It's all right for you fish-heads,' Collins replied, taking a cigarette out of his mouth and exhaling a steady stream of blue tobacco smoke. 'If the bastard shells us, it's us what get trapped below while you lot piss off in boats.'

'Bollocks snarled at Waters. 'Us lot on the upper deck can cop it easier than you below. At least you've got a bulkhead for protection.'

'So, do you think the captain's right?' asked another stoker.

'Yes, I fuckin' well do,' Waters firmly replied. 'Like he said, if we all play our part, it could work. After all, anything's better than just giving up.'

While these discussions were going, Pollard arrived on the bridge. The jacket he wore over his tropical shirts was dark blue, with three gold buttons on either side. The cap was white with a company insignia.

'Very convincing, Number One,' Miller remarked, grinning, 'and with those four gold rings on each sleeve, you outrank me.'

'I only hope it convinces the Krauts, sir,' Pollard replied.

'We'll soon find out. The bastard's only a few miles away,' Miller replied, who, like everyone else, had his binoculars clamped tightly to his eyes.

'She's flashing, sir,' cried PO Signalman Watts, his binoculars pressed to his eyes. 'I... I think it's in German, sir.'

'Yes, it is,' said Pollard. 'The sod's asking us to stop engines and identify ourselves.'

'Better do as he asks, sir,' said Miller.

'But what the hell are you going to tell them, sir?' Pollard replied uneasily.

Miller shrugged his shoulders and replied, 'I'm sure you'll think of something, Number One., After all, you did do a communication course at *Royal Alfred.*'

Miller contacted the engine room and ordered both engines to be stopped. In the meantime, P O Watts handed Pollard the Aldis lamp. Pollard went to the port wing of the bridge, cradled it in the crook of his left arm and began signalling in German.

"This is a Swedish vessel, SS *Argo*, enroute from Dakar to Gothenburg, carrying chemical products and peanut oil."

Then he lowered the Aldis.

'That sounded convincing enough, Number One. Well done,' said Miller.

'I had to say we had a light cargo, sir, as we're too high in the water for anything heavy,' Pollard replied, with a wry smile.

Everyone waited for a reply, but none came. By this time the destroyer had increased speed.

Endeavour had stopped and was rolling gently. Three hundred yards away the destroyer slowed down, turned port beam on and came to a halt. Her pennant number, *Z26,* painted white, stood out against her open bridge, single tall funnel and superstructure that was painted a dull grey. A black swastika in the centre of a black cross fluttered wildly from the mainmast.

But what caused a cold chill to run down Miller's spine was the sight of her two sets of twin five-inch guns and light armament trained menacingly on his ship. 'My God,' he muttered to himself. 'At this range, he could blast us completely out of the water.'

Miller was about to address the ship's company but realised his voice would be heard by the destroyer's personnel. Instead, he told PO Signalman Watts to go around the ship and tell those off duty to come onto the upper deck, wave, and give the swine's a hearty welcome. No sooner had Watts left than Miller saw a dark-haired, heavily tanned officer, wearing three gold bars on the shoulders of his tropical, white blouse, come to the starboard side of the destroyer's bridge. Miller could see he was holding a loud hailer in one hand.

'I think her captain is going to speak to me, Number One,' Miller said to Pollard. 'So it's up to you, old boy, and as we're still in the tropics, I suggest you keep the jacket open. That should convince the blighter.'

'I'll do my best, sir,' Pollard replied, ensuring his cap was on straight.

By this time, many of *Endeavour*'s ships company were lining the upper deck guard rails. Some wore overalls, and others were clad in an assortment of coloured shirts, shorts and sandals. Many were waving, shouting and grinning.

'Well, they look and sound genuine enough,' Pollard said, accepting a loud hailer from Lieutenant Morgan. 'Here's hoping I can do the same.' He went onto the port wing and looked across at the tall officer standing on the destroyer's starboard wing. He took a deep breath then raised the loud hailer to his lips. Speaking fluent German, and doing his best to sound annoyed, he shouted, 'I am Captain Anders Lindstrom. My ship was on a routine trade visit to Dakar. Why have you asked me to stop?'

'I am *Kapitan* Stieger. I regret the inconvenience, but this is a routine action, and I won't keep you.'

Suddenly Pollard had an idea. 'I have a personal stock of old, Scottish whiskey. Perhaps you and your executive officer would like to come on board for a drink?'

Like the others, Miller couldn't understand what they were saying. But judging by the grin on the German's face, it seemed to be all right.

'Thank you, *Kapitan*, some other time, perhaps,' responded the German. 'I will not detain you any longer. *Heil* Hitler,' he shouted, and briskly shot out his right arm.

"Thank you, and good luck," Pollard replied, saluting. He then looked down at the crew on the fo'c'sle and shouted, 'Keep waving, the bastard's leaving.'

As Pollard finished speaking, everyone breathed a sigh of relief as they saw the destroyer's guns being trained inboard.

With a satisfied grin on his face, Pollard gave a final wave to the German and went inside the bridge.

'Well, don't look so surprised,' Pollard said, staring blankly at Miller and the others. 'It worked, didn't it?'

'Yes, and well done, old boy,' gushed Miller, slapping Pollard on the back. 'But tell me, what did you say to him?'

With a sheepish grin, Pollard told him.

'You did what?' exclaimed Miller. 'Great Scott, man. What would you have done had he accepted your offer?'

Pollard took off his cap, and using the back of his hand to wipe sweat away from his brow, replied, 'Simple, sir, we could have held them hostage. Then, after insisting the Germans didn't follow us at a later date, we could have given them a compass and set them free in a lifeboat.'

Doing his best not to burst out laughing, Miller bit his lip then replied, 'Just like Fletcher Christian did to Bligh aboard the *Bounty*, eh, Number one?'

'Something like that, sir,' Pollard replied, his face wreathed in smiles.

CHAPTER FIFTY-ONE

Miller eased himself off his chair, unhooked the tannoy and addressed the ship's company. 'This is the captain speaking. As you have seen, thanks to yourselves and the first lieutenant's excellent acting, our piece of subterfuge worked, so well done, everybody. However, we're still not out of danger. There are enemy warships in the area, so we have to be vigilant. I will keep you informed,' and replaced the handset.

Minutes later, he contacted the wheelhouse.

'Course 315, resume previous speed, please, Coxswain.' Miller looked at Pollard, and smiling, said, 'Do take off that jacket, Number One, you look far too young to be wearing First World War medal ribbons.'

Later that day, Miller received a signal from the British Consul in Dakar informing him that Johnson was, after being operated on, making good progress, and after a period of recuperation, would be well enough to be flown to England. Miller immediately informed the ship's company. The news of Johnson's well-being and the prospect of arriving in Plymouth in six days filled everyone with renewed excitement. Regular gunnery and fire drills, 'abandon ship', first-aid practice, as well as routine cleaning ship, were carried out with renewed enthusiasm.

'What's the first thing yer gunna do when you go ashore in Guz, Soapy?' Lane asked Waters.

They were in the seamen's mess. Both men were smoking a cigarette while using Brasso on cotton waste to polish metal lockers.

Waters stopped work, and with an expectant expression etched on his sunburnt face, replied, 'I'm gunna make a beeline for the Navy Arms and down a pint of Tetley's best bitter. What about you?'

Waters paused, and with his cigarette dangling from the corner of his mouth, replied, 'Me, I'm gunna go to the Long Bar in Union Street to see Big Bertha.'

'I would have thought you'd had stacks in Rio,' Lane replied. 'Is shaggin' all you can think about?'

Waters took a deep drag of his cigarette, and allowing the smoke to trickle from his nose and mouth, replied. 'I'll 'ave yer know, I once gave up sex, smokin' and beer.'

'And what 'appened?' Lane asked, a look of disbelief on his face.

Waters removed the cigarette, and with a serious expression on his face, replied, 'Let me tell you, matey. It were the worst five minutes of me life!'

Just then, Chief GI Len Mills came into the mess. He placed both hands on his hips, looked at them, and in his thick Devonian accent, grunted, 'Well, my 'andsomes. You two seem to be enjoyin' yersells, so when you've finished, you can scrub out the after seamen's 'eads.'

During the night of Monday 6th November, the weather changed dramatically. The barometer gradually dropped from a warm eighteen degrees Centigrade to a chilly ten. Rods of rain slanted down from dark clouds, peppering a high-rolling sea with tiny eruptions. A pale sun hid behind an umbrella of angry, dark clouds. Hit beam on by a bitterly cold westerly wind, the ship began to roll precariously.

Miller came onto the bridge at seven a.m. and was joined by Pollard. Both officers wore white, polo-necked sweaters under the jackets of their blue serge uniforms.

'Morning, gentlemen,' Miller said to Lieutenant Morgan and OOW Lieutenant Jenkins. 'Looks like we're into some good old British weather.'

'Yes, indeed, sir,' Jenkins replied, holding onto the binnacle. 'Shall I pipe wet weather routine, sir?'

'Yes, and hands change into winter clothing,' he replied. What's our position, Pilot?' he added, glancing at Lieutenant Morgan.

'Longitude, twenty, Latitude, thirty-five, sir,' Morgan replied.

'That puts us about five hundred miles west of Gibraltar.'

Do you want to send a signal to C-in-C, Plymouth, telling him where we are and our ETA, sir?' Pollard asked.

'Not yet, Number One,' Miller replied, as, despite a sudden roll of the ship, he managed to host himself into his chair. 'It might be picked up by some U-boat. I'll send one when we reach the English Channel, which, all being well, should be in three days.'

Unfortunately, Miller spoke too soon. During the night the weather abated. The sea became calmer, and the cold wind dropped.

Shortly after nine a.m., the strident, Yorkshire voice of Able Seaman Lane in the crow's nest came over the bridge intercom. 'Fog — roughly ten miles dead ahead.'

'Thank you, I can see it,' replied OOW Lieutenant Young. He put down his binoculars and contacted Miller, who was fully dressed, sitting in his cabin reading through the signal log.

'Bugger it, not again,' grunted Miller. 'I'll be up right away,' he added, angrily closing the log.

A minute later he arrived on the bridge, and using his binoculars, he saw a huge bank of fog rolling towards the ship like a vast, grey tide. 'Well,' he said to Lieutenant Young, 'it looks very deep, and as we can't go around the blighter, we'll just have to slow down and go through it. Unfortunately, it'll mean we'll be a day or so late arriving in Plymouth. How far away are we from the channel?''

'About two hundred miles, sir.' As he finished speaking, the voice of the duty QM, piping hands to breakfast, came over the tannoy.

'Better double the lookouts, Number One,' Miller said to Pollard, 'and when we enter the stuff, sound the foghorn off every ten minutes.'

Miller unhooked the tannoy. 'This is the captain. We are about to enter a pretty dense fog bank; consequently we'll have to slow down. This will mean we'll probably be a day late arriving in Plymouth.' He replaced the handset and contacted the wheelhouse. 'Speed fifteen knots. Revolutions one twenty.'

The fog persisted throughout the next day and night. Then, as if parted by an unknown hand, shortly after midday Thursday 9th, the ship emerged into eye-smarting daylight. A strong, bitterly cold, westerly wind gave a false impression of warmth from a sun embedded in a cloudless, blue sky. On the bridge, Miller, sitting on his chair, ordered the ship to increase speed to twenty knots.

'Even though we've lost two days, Number One,' he said to Pollard, 'we should reach the English Channel in two days.'

During the night of Saturday 11th, *Endeavour* passed the Isles of Scilly. A little after midday, roughly five miles on the port beam, the tall, circular structure of Longship's Lighthouse was sighted, perched on a small, rocky island a mile or so off the tip of Land's End. Behind, the rugged coastline of Cornwall lay shrouded in mist. Shortly afterwards, St Michael's Mount, with its medieval castle and church, hove into view, and behind, the rooftops of Penzance glistened in the early morning mist.

'A sight for sore eyes, sir,' Pollard said to Miller, who, like OW Lieutenant Young and Lieutenant Morgan, was staring nostalgically at the Cornish landscape.

With a hint of pride in his voice, Miller gave a nostalgic sigh and replied, 'It certainly is, Number One. There were times I thought we'd never see dear old England again.' He gave PO Watts an instructive look and said, 'Send the following signal to Admiral Sir Henry Townshend, C-in-C, Plymouth, repeated Sir Roger Backhouse, admiral of the fleet. Say: "Sir, I have the honour to report the arrival of HMS *Endeavour* in Plymouth on Sunday, 12th November. Request berthing instructions."'

Half an hour later, a signal from Admiral Sir Henry Townshend was received. "Good to have the Red Lady home safe and sound, after a very successful sojourn. Berth number three wharf." This was quickly followed by a signal from Sir Roger Backhouse, welcoming them home and congratulating Miller and his ship's company for a successful mission.

Shortly afterwards, Lieutenant Willis, his face wreathed in smiles, came onto the bridge. 'This just arrived, sir,' he said, handing a signal to Miller.

'Well, don't just stand there,' Miller replied impatiently. 'Read it to me.'

'With respect, sir, I think you'd better read it yourself,' Willis said.

'Very well,' Miller replied, and accepted the signal. After finishing reading it, he sat back in his chair, and with an unbelieving look on his face, looked at Pollard and the others and said, You're never going to believe this.'

He unhooked the ship's tannoy. Feeling a nervous tingle run down his spine, he began, 'This is the captain speaking. I have just received the following signal which I'm sure you'll want to hear.' He paused momentarily, then continued: '"Welcome home, and warmest congratulations to you and your ship's company on your brave and momentous odyssey. You will all be pleased to know that the material you found has been put to good use and will no doubt help us beat the Boche. "Home is the sailor, home from the sea, and the hunter home from the hill." Splice the main brace. God save the King. Winston Churchill. First lord of the admiralty."'

For a few minutes everyone on the bridge stood in silence, too nonplussed to speak.

Finally, Lieutenant Morgan broke the silence. 'Now, that's what I call a real welcome home,' he said, shaking his head in disbelief.

'But what's that bit about "home is the sailor", sir?' asked PO Watts.

'It's a phrase from Robert Louis Stevenson's poem, *Requiem*,' Lieutenant Morgan replied, 'and it's also written on his epitaph. I remember doing it for my A levels.'

'Thank you, Pilot,' Miller said, reaching for the ship's tannoy. 'That's most enlightening, but I think the ship's company will be more interested in the extra tot.' After reading the signal, he could almost hear the cheering ring around the ship. He went on to say, 'I'd like to give everyone leave when we arrive in Plymouth, but I want eight volunteers from ratings, living locally, to make a skeleton crew. Names to Chief Coxswain Moore by four p.m.,' and he replaced the handset.

'As I'm married and live in Plymouth, sir,' said Pollard, 'you can include me among the volunteers.'

'Thank you, Number One. I'm sure Delia can't wait to see

you,' Miller replied.

On the upper deck, ratings off duty lined *Endeavour*'s port side, gazing nostalgically at Penzance. All of them, including stokers, were bare-headed and wore sweaters over their number 8's and overalls.

'Nowt like it, eh, Chats?' Leading Seaman Waters said to Leading Seaman Hardman, who was standing next to him.

'That's as maybe, my 'andsome,' Hardman replied. 'But not as good a sight as dear, old Devon.'

'As you live in Guz,' Waters replied, 'I suppose you'll be volunteering to be one of the skeleton crew?'

'Too true, my bird,' Hardman replied, enthusiastically. 'A good tot every day and 'ome cookin' every night, not to mention a bit of 'ow's yer father, that's fer me.'

'Pity Joe Lewis isn't here; he was from Plymouth,' Waters sighed.

At six p.m., while most of the crew were at supper, Miller decided to address the ship's company for the final time. He cleared his throat and unhooked the tannoy. 'By the time we arrive in Plymouth, we will have travelled over twenty thousand miles. It's been a long, and at times, dangerous journey during which time we have sadly lost two of our crew. So before we arrive in Plymouth and eventually decommission, I wish to thank all of you for your bravery and excellent work. As I'm sure you know, this has been my first command, and it has been an honour to have been your commanding officer. Good luck and Godspeed to all of you.' Feeling his throat slightly constrict, he quietly replaced the handset.

CHAPTER FIFTY-TWO

A little after five a.m. on Sunday, 12th November, *Endeavour*, doing a conservative fifteen knots, cruised into Plymouth Sound. On the eastern horizon, the dawn's pale whiteness was slowly forcing the dying moon and stars to fade away. These were gradually replaced by the soothing rays from a pale sun, turning the calm sea into a mass of tiny, silver daggers. On the ship's port side, Drake's Island lay swathed in early morning mist, while away to starboard, Plymouth Hoe with Smeaton's Tower was barely visible.

'Call the hands at five thirty a.m.,' Miller said to OOW Lieutenant Young. 'And special sea duty men will be required at six thirty a.m.; winter rig.' Miller had just come onto the bridge and was comfortably ensconced in his chair. Like Young and those on duty, he wore a duffle coat and sweater. He gave a short, throaty laugh, then added, 'It'll still be quite dark when we tie up, so I wouldn't expect a welcoming committee.'

At six a.m., *Endeavour* turned to starboard and entered the River Tamar. A bitterly cold November wind blew downriver, causing the mist to slowly clear. Away to port, Cornwall's rolling hills and forests and the small town of Saltash could now be seen. In the middle of the river, a bulky aircraft carrier lay at anchor next to a heavy cruiser. Warships, from tiny minesweepers to mighty battleships, lay alongside the wharfs. Every vessel, large and small, were camouflaged in a dull-green and grey, zig-zag pattern. Thousands of feet in the air dozens of silky grey barrage balloons hovered over the city like giant predators. Downriver, Brunel's mighty Royal Albert suspension bridge, connecting Devon and Cornwall, shimmered in the morning mist. Meanwhile, the twenty-four-hour chain ferry service between Devonport and Saltash was a dark smudge as it crossed the river.

A quick nod from Miller, and the duty QM piped, 'Hands fall in for entering harbour; overcoats to be worn.'

'Number three wharf is the one where that whopping, great battle cruiser is tied alongside,' Pollard said to Miller.

'With an all-knowing smile, Lieutenant Morgan said, 'That 'whopping, great' cruiser is none other than the mighty *Hood,* and the aircraft carrier we are about to pass on our right is the *Ark Royal.*'

'Thank you, Pilot,' Miller replied. 'As we pass them, remember to dip our flag in salute.'

'Very good, sir,' Morgan replied, giving PO Signalman Watts a warning look.

'Slow ahead,' snapped Miller. 'Port five.' This was quickly followed by, 'Stop engines', as the ship squeezed against the rubber fenders on the wharf wall.

In a matter of minutes, ratings on the ship's quarterdeck and fo'c'sle threw heavy lines to burly dockyard workers, who expertly tied them around twin bollards. At the same time, a section of the port guard rail amidships was removed on the quarterdeck to allow a crane to lower the metal gangway into position.

'Not much of a welcome, eh, sir,' Pollard said to Miller, both of whom had left the bridge and were watching ratings secure the gangway.

'What did you expect, Number One? A brass band and flowers?' Miller replied. 'The admiral is probably on his second cup of coffee. Which is exactly what I need. Better pipe hands to breakfast,' and he left the bridge.

The time was ten a.m. It was "stand easy", and everyone in the messes was in a relaxed mood, laughing and eagerly looking forward to leave. Then came the pipe they were waiting for.

'Mail. Mail is ready for collection. Leave. Leave to first of starboard and both port watches from four p.m. to six a.m.'

The remainder of "stand easy" was taken up by ratings and officers reading a backlog of letters from loved ones they would soon see.

'Will you phone up your missus to let her know you're coming, Chats?' Leading Seaman Hardman asked his oppo,

Leading Seaman Harris.

'No,' Hardman replied, 'I think I'll surprise her.'

'A mate of mine on the *Prince of Wales* did that, and found 'is wife had taken the kids and buggered off with a marine,' Harris replied.

'Hmm,' muttered Hardman, stuffing the solitary, single page letter he had received from his wife, into its envelope. 'Maybe I'll give her a phone all after all.'

Miller was sat in his cabin. Lying on his desk were four letters. One was written in his mother's scrawl. Miller instinctively knew that the other three, written in small, neat handwriting, were from Linda. The first one, dated Monday, 16th October, confirmed the safe arrival of herself and 'everything else' in London, then she went on to say how much she loved and missed him. The second, sent on Wednesday, 18th, stressed her love for him, then she said that the BBC had announced that Hitler had reassured Holland and Belgium of his friendship, adding dubiously, "But I think he's lying." The third, dated Saturday, 21st, described the shop windows in London and the provinces being protected by sticky tape to prevent splintering from expected air raids. "Otherwise, darling," she wrote, "everything seems peaceful and normal," ending with, "I pray every night that you and your crew come home safely. God bless. I love and miss you so."

The letter from his mother told him that apart from several of his old college friends who were now in the forces, nothing much had changed, adding, "*The Times* is calling it a false peace and to expect air raids any time. Luckily we've had one of those Anderson shelters built in the back garden. Pity about the rose beds and Rhododendrons. Your father still takes his morning constitutional along the promenade and sends his love. God bless, and wrap up well."

A glance at the clock above the door showed eleven forty-five a.m. He put his cap on and arrived on the quarterdeck in time to hear "Up Spirits" being piped. He saw Pollard in deep conversation with officer of the day, Lieutenant Young.

'Any problems, Number One?'

'No, sir,' Pollard hastily replied. 'I was just telling Guns that a lighter will come alongside at four p.m. to take off any spare shells he has.'

'And have we any?' he asked Young.

'Only a couple, sir,' Young replied, saluting Miller. 'I'm sure you know what happened to the rest,' he added, with a satisfied smile. 'Now if you'll excuse me, sir, I have to oversee rum issue.'

Lieutenant Young was about to turn away when PO Martin appeared. 'Sorry to interrupt you, sir,' he said, nervously glancing over his shoulder, 'but the admiral's limousine is coming down the wharf, and my guess is he's gunna pay us a visit.'

'By Jove, I think you're right!' exclaimed Miller. 'Quickly, Number One. Man the side.'

Miller and Pollard watched nervously as a shiny, black limousine stopped near the foot of the gangway. A small, white pennant with a red cross flew from the bonnet. The driver, a chief petty officer, climbed out and opened the passenger door. The vice admiral, wearing an overcoat over his uniform, stepped out, then with a broad smile, turned, and to everyone's surprise, held out his hand and helped a very attractive women to step out. A smart, dark-green, Robin Hood-style hat adorned her fair hair, which was worn neatly in a chignon. A pale-brown leather bag hung from the left shoulder of her fawn, knee-length coat, under which poked the hem of a yellow dress. The colour of her high-heeled shoes matched her coat, and sheer silk stockings encased her shapely legs. She looked up, and seeing Miller, her face broke into a beaming smile.

For a few seconds Miller was too stunned to speak, then, regaining his senses, exclaimed, 'Great Scott, Linda!'

He and the others watched as the vice admiral, ignoring naval protocol, allowed Linda to precede him up the gangway. As they were piped on board, Miller, Pollard and Young sprung to attention and saluted.

'Welcome home, Commander,' said the vice admiral, as he shook Miller's hand. Then, smiling at Linda, added, 'I believe you know this young lady.'

'Yes, indeed, sir,' Miller replied, staring into those beguiling, emerald eyes he had seen so often in his dreams. 'But Linda, how on earth did you know the ship had arrived?'

Linda gave Vice Admiral Townshend a grateful smile, then said, 'When the admiral knew when you were due home, he contacted the dean at Cambridge, and here I am.'

'Thank you, sir,' Miller said to the admiral. 'That was very thoughtful of you.'

'Not at all, Commander,' replied the admiral. 'It was a pleasure.'

The word soon spread around the ship that Linda was on board. In a matter of minutes, the quarterdeck and space above the gun hanger were crowded with ratings, cheering and waving.

Linda flashed them an appreciative smile. After returning their waves, she looked longingly at Miller, with tears in her eyes, and said, 'Wouldn't it be wonderful if we could invite all of them to our wedding?'

'What a marvellous idea, darling,' Miller replied, feeling an urge to throw his arms around her.

'And I hope you'll invite me as well,' said the admiral, his weather-beaten features wreathed in smiles. 'Now, Commander,' he added, 'don't just stand there. To hell with naval protocol — kiss the woman, then let's go to the wardroom for a large gin and tonic.'

EPILOGUE

Admiral Wilhelm Franz Canaris was head of *Abwehr* from 1935 to 1944. Initially he supported Hitler, but soon became disillusioned with Hitler's plans to conquer Europe. He became involved with plots to overthrow the Nazi regime. Canaris was arrested for treason and taken to Flossenburg concentration camp, where, on 9th April 1945, he was hanged.

Gunter and Adelaide were arrested and charged with treason and were tried at the Old Baily. Gunther was found guilty and was hanged on 3rd February 1940. Adelaide was sentenced to life in Holloway Prison. A year later, she suffered a heart attack and died.

On Saturday, the 9th of March 1940, Commander Miller and Linda were married in St Bartholomew's Methodist Church, Helston. The weather was surprisingly mild, allowing women to wear colourful dresses, and men their best suits. Crowds of people, including those who had known Linda from childhood, lined the gravelled path leading from the church to the gate. Nearby, a chauffeur wearing green livery waited by a silver Bentley bedecked with white ribbons.

A little after eleven a.m., the church bells rang out, heralding the end of the ceremony. The melodic strains of the organ, playing Mendelssohn's *Wedding March*, could be heard from within the church. Suddenly, the moment everyone was waiting for, arrived. The arched, oaken door opened. Loud cheering and handclapping greeted the newly wedded couple. Linda, blushing and smiling, looked radiant. A pearl choker adorned her neck, and her fair hair was worn in a neat chignon. One hand held a small bouquet of red roses, the other grasped the arm of her husband. But it was her beautiful, ankle-length, white wedding gown with long sleeves that brought gasps of admiration from the women in the crowd.

Standing on Linda's left, Miller's handsome features were

wreathed in smiles. From the breast pocket of his immaculate doeskin uniform, hung the blue and white ribbon of the Distinguished Service Cross. One of his white-gloved hands nervously held Linda's left hand.

On either side of the newlyweds stood their parents. Then came Reverend Henry Pierce, smiling benignly while clutching his bible. Next to him stood the best man: newly promoted, Commander Pollard, DSO. Several of *Endeavour's* ship's company, including Chief GI Len Mills and LSBA Hailey, both wearing a British Empire Medal, followed on. Behind them stood some of Linda's school and university friends.

After the traditional family photographs were taken, Linda grasped Miller's hand, and slightly raising her dress, they hurried down the church steps onto the pathway. Ducking instinctively, the happy couple passed under the guard of honour. This was formed by an arc of the flashing swords of Lieutenants Young, Morgan, Ryan and Duncan, all wearing DSOs. When the happy couple reached the open gate, Linda threw her bouquet over her left shoulder into the cheering crowd.

Offering his hearty congratulations, the chauffeur helped the couple into the Bentley. With a "Just Married" sign rattling loudly from the rear fender, they drove off to the Housel Bay Hotel, where the wedding breakfast would be held.

During the war, *Endeavour* was used as a troop carrier and took part in the Sicily landings. In early 1946, she was placed in reserve. Ironically, six months later, she was sold for scrap to Marshal Shipyard Ltd in Denmark, where she was originally built.